Royally Flushed

Tech Billionaires book 2

A Novel

by:
Ainsley St Claire

Tech Billionaires: Royally Flushed/Ainsley St Claire—1st edition

Daniel for everything you do. I couldn't do this endeavor without your love and support. Always & forever, my love.

Get the Newsletter

If you like to download a free copy of *Gifted* and sign up for Ainsley's Naughty Readers to receive the latest news on my upcoming novels, sign up for my free author newsletter at **https://dl.bookfunnel.com/zi378x4ybx**

Chapter 1

Corrine

"What do you mean, he broke up with you on the news?" my best friend, Gabby Wagner, screeches.

Heads turn all along the bar to see what she's so worked up about, and I can feel my face turning red.

She's been dating her boyfriend since college, and they're very serious. He even moved to San Francisco to be with her.

I look down and feel tears forming in my eyes. "I got home late last night from work. I was watching a rerun of *NCIS* and eating popcorn for dinner. A news teaser about him came on, so I stayed up to see it. The segment was at the end of the news, so it was almost eleven-thirty when it played. The interviewer stuck a microphone in his face and said, 'I heard there's a new lady in your life. Are you allowed to date a cheerleader?' His response was that it was nobody's business but his own if he chose to date a cheerleader."

"But I thought you two were serious," she implores.

I look at her as if she's grown horns and a forked tongue. "I'm not sure he understands that concept, and now it doesn't really matter. Apparently, he's moved on without telling me."

"Have you heard from him?"

I shake my head.

"Have you tried to call him?" she pushes.

I shake my head. "He never liked that I gave so much to my job, so I knew one day this was coming. I just thought he'd have the balls to tell me—not announce it on the news to the world."

"Bartender? Tom?" Gabby waves to the man. "Another cosmo for my friend." She turns to me and reaches for my arm. "I'm sorry he was such a shit."

"I fucking hate this city. Commitment phobia must come from something in the water, and the rest of the guys don't have the social skills to date. I'm almost thirty years old, and I have two roommates. I rent a room that only fits a twin-size bed and a small storage unit for my off-season clothes. If I didn't live in this ridiculously expensive city, I'd make a decent living. I need a raise."

My drink arrives, and it goes down quickly. I'm going to be feeling this tomorrow.

"It's his loss," Gabby stresses. "Jeez, you're beautiful, smart—the whole package."

"You're my best friend. You're required to say that," I mumble through the waterworks.

She giggles. "I wouldn't say it if I didn't mean it."

I look up at the bottles surrounding the bar and push my tears away. "What am I going to do?"

"You're going to get up and not let this dickhead affect you. You can't let him take a minute more of your energy. I bet there are at least a dozen hot guys here you could take home to fuck their brains out tonight. Forget all about 'Bobby Sanders, Quarterback for the San Francisco Goldminers.'" She air-quotes and rolls her eyes.

I shake my head. "You're too much. You're right, but I'm not going home with anyone tonight." Something flashes in my periphery, and I see him staring at me. "Oh, shit."

"What?" Gabby looks around frantically.

"It's my boss and one of his Barbies," I say through clenched teeth.

"Barbie? Where?" She looks around again.

Not so subtle, that one.

"Stop! He's over there with the woman you could use as a flotation device." I point with my eyes. "Shit, do I need to go over and say something? Knowing my luck, he'll ask me to get them drinks."

"She's beautiful, in an artificial way," Gabby notes as she studies her hourglass figure, tiny waist, perfectly coiffed long blond hair, and big blue eyes.

"She definitely looks good, but the elevator doesn't go to the top on that one. It seems to get stuck at her chin."

Gabby snort-laughs.

"Try not to draw attention to us," I plead.

"He's looking over," she says under her breath.

"Fuck! Try to ignore him."

I made reservations for him elsewhere. Why is he here? I feel my grip on work-life barriers slipping. And, I've had plenty to drink. I'm probably a little *too* honest for my boss right now.

Tom, the bartender, appears with two drinks. "These are from the couple over there." He hooks his thumb toward my boss.

My heart drops to the floor. I'm a blubbering mess. I glance across the bar, paste a plastic smile on my face, and raise my glass. "Oh my goodness, it's my boss, Jackson." I mouth, "Thank you."

He smiles and nods.

"What a smug asshole," Gabby says under her breath.

Through clenched teeth, I say, "He's doing good in the world. Just be thankful for the drink and that he's not making me talk to him right now."

"Well… He's coming over with two of his friends."

"Fuck. Those aren't his friends. They're his bodyguards."

Next thing I know, his deep voice rolls through me. "Corrine, nice to see you here."

Jackson Graham is a girl's version of a wet dream. He's a Chris Hemsworth lookalike with Daniel Craig's piercing blue eyes. He's also the founder of an alternative energy company that has made him a billionaire. I'm his assistant, which I'm proud of, but in that role, I must get a dozen calls a day from women he's never met asking him out. That I'm less thrilled about.

"Nice to see you, too," I tell him. "I didn't know you'd be here tonight. I thought I made a reservation for you at Bix?"

I only make a point of asking because, with his entourage, they reserve three tables in a prime location. If he stands them up, I'll have a problem the next time he wants to go there.

"You did, but Valerie tells me she's getting bored with Bix. I called and canceled."

He can make his own calls? That's new. "Oh, I think I called her Jennifer today. Sorry about that."

He looks back at her with his brows furrowed. "She didn't mention you calling her the wrong name. Enjoy your drinks. I hope your night gets better." He smiles and walks back to his table.

Every woman's eyes in the packed bar are glued to him.

Gabby leans in with a bit of a drunken slur. "Your boss is positively hot."

I shake my head. "That might be true, but he likes the surgically enhanced, and he seems to have no interest in women with brains."

Her phone pings with a text, and she gets this funny look on her face. *Love.* I know exactly who she's talking to, her boyfriend, Damien.

I haven't had my phone on all day. While Gabby sexts with her boyfriend, I reluctantly turn mine on. I've got to do it at some point, and it might as well be while I'm partially drunk. It lights up and buzzes with multiple texts. My stomach ties in knots as I stare at the messages rolling over on the locked screen.

What happened with Bobby?

When I find out, Elly, my supposed best friend from high school, I might let you know.

I knew it would never last.

Thanks, Stepmom. In her mind, to get a man, you need to give up everything. I'd take her advice if she hadn't been married five times.

I thought you had some great summer plans with Bobby?

Angela, you're such a nice roommate. We had plans with other players and their wives to go to a lake in Wisconsin. I'm probably off that invite list. So much for any summer vacation. I can't afford to do anything.

How does any man compare after dating an NFL quarterback?

John, you broke up with me and only wanted me back when you found out I was dating him. Bobby wasn't perfect. But I liked that he made twenty million a year and was four years younger than me.

I put my phone on mute and toss it in my purse. I can respond later. It suddenly occurs to me that none of the other players' wives or girlfriends sent me texts. We were all planning for the game on Sunday. I guess in the back of my mind, I thought a few of them would stand by me, but apparently not. That might hurt more than the breakup.

Gabby is ready to go find Damien, so we say our goodbyes. As I walk out of the bar, I look over at Jackson and his date and wave. She scowls at me. Whatever.

I take a rideshare across town to my meager apartment in

Presidio Heights. It's a fancy way of saying I live behind the old Army base, the Presidio, and in the Avenues. The beautiful people look down on those of us who live in the Avenues, but it's considered affordable. I don't consider it affordable. I share a three-bedroom apartment—my bedroom used to be a closet—with two others and pay an entire half of my monthly salary toward my portion of the rent. But I do it on my own.

I let myself in and crawl into bed—still wearing my dress and without washing my face or brushing my teeth. That's very unlike me, and I cry myself to sleep. *He broke up with me on the news.*

My alarm sounds, and my eyes are crusted shut from my tears. My mouth feels like a cat strolled by while I was asleep and took a crap. I roll over and look up at the stained ceiling. Bobby Sanders is not going to get to me. Taking a big breath, I sit up. *Oh, I can't move that quickly.*

I go slowly into the bathroom and wash my face, determined to make today a better day. I can't let this keep me down. I'm better than this.

As I do each day, I stop at Starbucks and pick up Jackson's and my coffee order. He likes a double espresso with steamed milk, and I treat myself to a mocha cappuccino. No one's going to see me naked for a while anyway. Who cares about the extra calories?

Jackson typically beats me to the office, as he works nonstop, and today is no exception. Placing the cup on his desk, I remain standing and prepare for our brief morning meeting. "Here's your double espresso."

He nods without looking at me.

"Thanks again for the drinks last night."

"Glad you enjoyed them," he says, still not looking up

from the spreadsheet he's studying.

He doesn't elaborate, so I begin to walk through his calendar for the day. "You're all set for your Tuesday meeting with your team. You have lunch with Mason Sullivan at noon at Quince regarding your business plan. If you don't have any changes, I'll get that bound and ready. Your afternoon is full, and I've marked you busy from two thirty to four to return phone calls."

"Thank you, Ms. Woods."

He still hasn't looked up, so I turn to leave. He's in a bad mood today—like most days. As I open the door, I hear, "Oh, I almost forgot." I turn, and he's pointing to a box by the door. "That was delivered to you this morning."

"Okay, thanks." I pick up the lightweight box and carry it out to my desk. Before I tackle it, I take a big swig of my mocha. "Ahh."

"I saw the piece about your boyfriend," my officemate, Heather, says. "I guess he moved on."

"They always do," I say.

Heather is the executive assistant to Jackson's chief financial officer—the fourth one he's had since I've been here. We get along okay and will occasionally grab lunch together. I made the mistake of telling her about Bobby, and she shared it with the entire building. Lesson learned. If you don't want anyone to know your business, don't mention it.

Pulling the scissors from the top drawer of my desk, I cut the seal on the box, and immediately the wretched smell hits me. Before I can even discern what's inside, I slam the box shut. The overwhelming stench fills the office.

"What the hell is that?" Heather asks. Her face is scrunched up, and we're both breathing through our mouths.

"I have no idea."

I carefully pick up the box, walk it to the elevator, and ride down to the lobby. The smell is still escaping, and it's just awful. I want to vomit.

As the doors open, I see our security guard. "Tommy, can

you call maintenance? We got a package that I think is full of dog poop. Can you have them fumigate the executive level and the elevator?"

"Dog poop?" He cocks his head to the side.

"Yes, someone sent me a package. I'm going to open it outside."

"Don't! That could be a bomb! Put it down and back away."

I'm already mostly outside, so I set it on the sidewalk and look at him, confused. *Why would anyone send me a poop bomb?*

When I walk back into the lobby, Tommy is on the phone to 9-1-1. He gives them our address, and I watch him pull the fire alarm. It's barely eight, and people are still arriving. It's quickly chaos.

He stands with me as we look at the box. "The police are on their way."

He moves right into leadership mode and keeps repeating, "This is not a drill. Please leave the building."

I look at him in panic. "This may have been a threat to Mr. Graham."

As the crowd grows outside, I watch Mr. Graham exit the elevator with his bodyguard at his side.

People are piling out of the building. Some seem thrilled to have a free morning, while others are clearly perturbed.

Mr. Graham walks up to me. "What the hell?" he says. "First, our office smells like shit, and now this?"

"The box you gave me was filled with something disgusting. Tommy thinks it might be a bomb."

"Sir," Tommy interjects. "The box was filled with manure, and it can be used in bombs."

A uniformed officer pushes us away from the doors. "Please step back."

Mr. Graham looks at me. "Why would anyone want to send you a bomb?"

I shake my head as the police come racing up in a van that says *Bomb Squad.*

People give them a wide berth, and an officer approaches the three of us.

"Tell us what you know," Mr. Graham's bodyguard prods for the police.

I walk them through what happened. More of Mr. Graham's security team arrives, and they usher him away. Great. At least he'll be safe. Don't worry, I'll be fine in the superhero costume hiding under my clothes.

The bomb team pushes us farther away from the door. "Don't leave," one of them tells me.

I nod and shiver against the cold. I left my coat upstairs.

The news vans have arrived and are setting up. This is not the kind of publicity Mr. Graham is looking for. If I have a job after this is over, it'll be a miracle.

I watch the bomb team examine the box from afar. They seem to agree on something, but I'm not sure what it is until I see a robot wheeling out to the sidewalk.

The crowd begins to grow. The police have cleared out the entire city block.

An officer returns to drill me with questions. "Has Mr. Graham received any threatening letters or other mail?"

The head of Mr. Graham's security, Jim Adelson, materializes next to me. He drapes a coat over my shoulders.

"Thanks, Jim."

"We've received a few small threats in recent months, but we've passed them along to Detective Lenning," Jim informs the officer.

"Tell me more about how you got the package," the officer prods.

"It was delivered to Mr. Graham's office, addressed to me, and he pointed it out when I arrived."

"Why didn't you call the police immediately?" the officer presses.

"It never occurred to me that it could be anything other than a stinky box."

"A stinky box?"

"The stench was strong, so I just shut the box and held it as tightly as I could while I took it down in the elevator."

"How do you know the threats you've received are insignificant?" the officer asks.

I shrug. "I figured it was an extremist environmental group unhappy with the company."

They've evacuated the neighboring buildings now, and people are fleeing quickly. I can't blame them.

We watch through a camera as the robot approaches the package behind a piece of glass that I'm told will withstand a blast. I spot the television crews zooming in, and everyone can see what's going on.

An arm extends from the robot. All eyes are riveted as it carefully opens the first flap. I'm holding my breath. The robot carefully opens the second flap. I'm freezing, but sweat is running down my back. A camera extends and zooms in on the box, focusing on a note that is partially covered in what looks like feces.

Once I read what it says, I want the Earth to open up and swallow me whole. *Keep your hands off my man.*

The robot carefully removes the note, and a man or woman dressed in a Pillsbury Dough Boy suit takes it away. The robot then reaches into the box. The officer explains that the camera is looking for signs of electronics, but nothing is sending off any signals. After a moment, the bomb squad seems visibly relieved.

I watch in horror as the robot clasps an article of clothing and pulls it out. It's a Goldminers jersey— number eighteen with Sanders in block lettering across the shoulders. It's covered in feces.

This is not a threat to Mr. Graham. It's for me.

Every single one of the twenty-five hundred building occupants that have spilled onto the sidewalks are going to be pissed at me. Jackson will be beyond pissed since he's lost an entire day of productivity because someone wants me to disappear from the asshole's life. *Which I already did!*

I can feel eyes on me, and I fight back the tears. The news crews are watching every moment.

As the police pack up and people file back into the building, I take the stairs to the forty-second floor. I can't stand around and listen to the snark. If Heather hadn't spread it around the building that Bobby and I were dating, I could play dumb. Bobby didn't name me specifically when he broke up with me on the news. But thank you, Heather, for making sure everyone can fill in the gaps.

By the tenth floor, I'm asking myself why I chose to walk up. I stop to catch my breath and overhear a conversation a few levels down in the stairwell.

"I bet *she* did it for attention."

"Why would Bobby Sanders date her? She's not that pretty."

"Did you see her smile when Jackson Graham walked up to her? He was pissed."

"We should start a death pool to see how long she has her job."

"I'd bet on that..." A fire door squeaks open, and their voices grow faint. I don't hear the rest.

I keep climbing. I hear others, but I don't want to stop to listen. It only makes me feel worse.

I finally make it to the forty-second floor, and I won't have to go to the gym today—or maybe even all week.

Three women are standing with Heather when I return to my desk, and all of them look me up and down with complete disdain. I sit down hard in my chair. Jim walks out of Jackson's office with a police officer.

He smiles at me. "Come on in."

I nod. "I'll be right there." I click a few buttons on my computer, print a document, and open a few files. I'm ready to be fired. This is it.

He points me to the couch. It's just Jim and the officer in the room.

"This is Officer Parker," he tells me. "Jackson was clear

that a messenger sent over the package?"

I nod. "Mr. Graham said it arrived early this morning."

"Did you break up with your boyfriend?" Jim asks.

"I believe so," I say.

"You don't know?" Officer Parker asks.

"Well, he didn't call and tell me to my face," I explain.

"Is he ghosting you?" Jim asks.

"No." I take a big breath. "He announced it in response to a question at a press conference."

"Press conference?" Officer Parker asks.

"I was dating Bobby Sanders, from the San Francisco Goldminers."

The officer's eyebrows rise in surprise, and he scribbles in his notebook.

"Tell us about the news conference," Jim says gently.

I explain what happened, adding that I was out with a friend last night and ran into Mr. Graham.

"Have you called Bobby Sanders or gone by his home?" Officer Parker asks.

"No. Bobby made his decision abundantly clear during the press conference."

"When did you call his girlfriend?" he asks.

"Never. I don't even know who she is. I haven't reached out to either of them. The last time Bobby and I talked was Sunday after a tough practice. It was a difficult workout, and he wanted to be alone."

Jackson walks in with his team. I stand.

"I need to speak to Mr. Graham," the officer informs me.

I nod silently, wondering if this embarrassment could possibly get any worse. I guess I'm going to find out.

As I return to my desk, my cell phone begins to ring. Eight missed calls. It's Gabby.

"Hi."

"Oh my God, you made the news wire."

"What?" *This can't be happening.*

"There are at least six news agencies now talking about

whether or not you sent the package to yourself. Through his agent, Bobby's saying he and his new girlfriend, Collette, had nothing to do with it, and you're mentally unstable."

"Are you kidding?"

"I wish I was. I'll send you some links. The coverage is split. The real news stations say you called the police because it was a suspicious package."

"It was Bobby's jersey, and it was covered in shit."

"What kind of shit? Paint?"

"No. I mean actual shit."

"Why?"

"It had a note that said *Keep your hands off my man,*" I whisper into the phone. "I'm so embarrassed. The police are talking to Mr. Graham now. The whole block knows. If it's all over the news, I guess the whole world knows."

"How about drinks after work?"

"If I still have a job—we lost the morning, so I don't know how late I'll be."

"Call me if you're up for it," Gabby insists.

I hear muffled voices approaching the door. "I've got to go. I hear him coming."

"Thank you for your time," Officer Parker tells Mr. Graham.

"Anytime," Jackson says. He gives me a nod.

Officer Parker stops at my desk. "None of your fingerprints were on the inside of the box. We'll continue to investigate. What's the name of your ex-boyfriend's new girlfriend?"

"I'm not sure. Someone called her Collette, but I don't know anything for certain—other than evidently she's a cheerleader for the Goldminers."

I watch him leave. Heather is ignoring me, so at least that's a positive.

Finally, Jim steps out of Mr. Graham's office. "Corrine, can you please come in here a moment?"

I nod. This is it.

Chapter 2

Jackson

"Please have a seat," Jim says to Corrine.

She's twisting the ring on her finger, clearly nervous. "I'm really sorry."

I smile to reassure her. "No need to apologize. We know you didn't send the package to yourself."

She shakes her head. "I promise you I didn't, and I didn't call the police about a bomb."

"We know," Jim assures her. "Tell us about the wives and girlfriends of the Goldminers."

Corrine's brow creases. "What do you mean?"

Jim sits back in his chair and gives a one-shoulder shrug. "Are they friendly and welcoming?"

"Not to new blood," Corrine says quietly.

"New blood?" I ask.

She nods. "To new girlfriends. They usually want to be

sure you're going to stick around before they'll commit to even talking to you."

That makes sense. I'm sure most professional athletes have a string of girlfriends. "How long did you stick around?" That came out of my mouth before I realized it. I'm not sure why I asked or why I want to know, but I do.

Corrine looks out of my office window at the spectacular view of the Bay Bridge and Treasure Island. "For most of the season. I made a few friends." She looks down at her hands and picks at her nails. "But after the news conference, none of them reached out to me."

"Who were you dating?" I ask.

"I was seeing Bobby Sanders, the quarterback," she says shyly.

I'm surprised—not because I don't think she's attractive, but because not once did her work product suffer. She never asked for time off, and she never mixed her social life with her work life. It's just like her not to tell everyone she knows. She's always kept things low-key and professional at the office.

"He's number eighteen?" I ask.

She nods.

"Why did you break up?" I prod.

"I'm not sure. Bobby didn't tell me."

"What did he say?" Jim nudges.

"He didn't." She sits up straight and looks him in the eye. "I found out the night before last when he announced he had a new girlfriend during a television news conference."

I've been accused of being an asshole, but at least I end things in person. Jeez. "Is that why you were at Of All Places last night?"

"Yes." She looks at me and squares her shoulders. "If you don't mind telling the staff after I leave, I'd appreciate it." She slides me a piece of paper across the desk. "These are my passwords to all the software and company electronics I use and control. The docs open on my computer are my open tasks. I appreciate the opportunity…" Her voice cracks. "…you provided. I've learned a tremendous amount working for you."

I'm dumbfounded. "You're quitting?"

My heart begins to race. She's the best support I've ever had. The thought of replacing her is insurmountable. It took me working through more than a dozen admins to find her. She can't leave me.

Corrine's brow creases and her lips purse. "No… Aren't you firing me?"

"Not at all," Jim quickly asserts. "We're trying to figure out if you need protection. The person who did this has gone to some pretty extreme measures. We're concerned about your safety."

"My safety?"

"Yes, your safety. This threat brought out two full fire stations, half of the San Francisco Police Department, and ended up clearing two city blocks. And not to mention, probably twenty-five thousand employees got the morning off. We're not taking this lightly."

I can tell Corrine is overwhelmed and confused by the idea that this is a significant threat. But even Officer Parker made it clear that this was a big deal.

"The police will find out her name. Bobby announced that he was dating a Goldminer cheerleader. I bet she didn't intend for this to be this big. Once they talk to her, I'm sure she'll calm down," Corrine says.

"I still think a team stationed outside your home twenty-four/seven is appropriate, and you'll need someone to pick you up each morning and drop you at home after work," I tell her.

She looks alarmed. "No. That's not necessary."

"I insist that you be picked up each morning and taken home at night." To placate her, I add, "At least for the next few days."

Jim is nodding.

"This can't go away fast enough." She puts her hands to her forehead and flushes a beautiful shade of pink.

Disturbingly, my cock stiffens. I'm a bit surprised by this.

Most women I know would love to have a car pick them up at their front door and drop them off, and they'd be fighting to keep it for months. But not Corrine. She's different.

My dick's straining against my zipper now, and I should pay attention.

She stands. "If you're not firing me, I need to return to work. You have a meeting with Mason Sullivan in—" She looks at her Apple Watch. "—less than an hour, and I need to get the proposal printed and bound." She looks at each of us. "May I be excused?"

She asked for permission. Now my dick is standing at attention. My lips feel parched, and all I can do is nod and watch her walk out the door. For the first time, I wonder how her tits feel—what it would be like to bend her over my desk and have her beg me to fuck her. This is *so* not good. She's forbidden fruit. I need to clear my mind.

Jim turns to me. "I'm not sure she's taking this seriously. I'll reach out to SFPD and see who's assigned to the case."

"Is the FBI involved?"

"No, I don't think so. I'll make sure." He shakes his head. "She's really embarrassed."

"Do you blame her? First her asshole boyfriend breaks up with her on the news, and then his new girlfriend sends her the mammoth load—literally. The person who did this is completely unhinged."

"I agree." Jim looks at me. "Are you going to Cecelia Lancaster's funeral?"

I nod. "What a mess for Nate. How's he doing?"

Jim shakes his head. He may be the head of a private security firm, but he's in this business because Nate is his best friend. Nate's wife went missing while we were in Vegas a few months ago and was just found murdered.

"Do they know anything?" I ask.

"The FBI is working with the Las Vegas and San Francisco police, but nothing much yet."

I scrub my hands over my face. "I really liked Cecelia. She was smart and funny and had a great way of getting people to be generous. I gave a quarter of my earnings last year to the Lancaster Foundation. Corrine was working a lot with Cecelia; I was going to ask her to come with me."

"Nate would like that. It's a small group, relatively speaking."

"Relative to what?"

"They're expecting maybe two hundred guests. If we opened it to the public, we might see two hundred thousand trying to pay their respects. She was beloved by so many. Nate's getting mail and condolence cards by the sack, and the letters are overwhelming. It's taking both his and Cecelia's assistant to go through each note and catalog them. He's heard from two presidents, the British royal family, and tons of strangers. He's also had a few threats and multiple marriage proposals."

"That's just gross," I say.

"Her parents are distraught," Jim adds. "This is the second child they've buried in the last three years."

"That's awful. Please let me know if there's anything I can do."

Jim leaves, and I finalize my prep for my meeting with the investors. Mason is a dynamo when it comes to numbers, and I will need to be ready with my A-game.

As I look everything over one last time, Corrine appears with the proposals in hand, my overcoat, and a cup of coffee.

"You need to leave if you're going to be on time," she says. "Your car is waiting downstairs. Ben is driving. Would you like Brian to come up and walk out with you?"

I shake my head. "Are you going to be okay alone?"

Corrine seems startled by my comment. "I'm not alone. I'm surrounded by people working. I'll be just fine. You're scheduled to return calls when you're back, and I have the foundation work and a project with marketing. I'll be working all afternoon and most likely into the evening."

"I should be back at two thirty. If you leave, make sure someone from Jim's team drives and escorts you wherever you go."

"It's not necessary," Corrine says again.

"But it is. Promise me you won't go anywhere alone."

Corrine holds up her hands. "Okay, fine."

"Before I forget, Cecelia Lancaster's service is next week."

"Yes. I have it on your calendar. I figured you'd attend."

"Would you like to join me?"

I feel like I'm asking her on a date. What is it with me? Jeez.

"It's invite only," she reminds me.

"Yes, but you knew her well, and we can go together."

It's absolutely reasonable for her to attend with me. It wouldn't raise any suspicions. She worked with Cecelia.

"I'd love that." She puts her hand on my back and pushes me softly to the door. "Now go knock Mason Sullivan on his ass with your proposal. Go get us some money for your phenomenal idea."

I walk out of my office feeling like a million bucks. Corrine's incredibly dedicated to my company. That Sanders ass may be a hero to many in this town, but I'm glad Corrine's rid of him. She can do much better than some dumb jock who can't see how great she is.

After a short drive, we arrive across town at Quince. They rarely do a lunch seating, but Mason knows the chef, and this gives us the chance to eat alone. When I walk in, he's waiting with Cynthia Hathaway, a salesperson from his office. This is my time to shine.

Unfortunately, I'm not even halfway through my presentation when Cynthia gets a call.

"I'm sorry," she says. "I need to take this." She steps aside and mostly listens for a moment before she returns. "I have a mini emergency I need to attend to. Jackson, Mason has gone through your numbers, and we think you're too conservative in some of your startup costs. We're seeing much higher numbers from some of your competitors. We like your approach—translucent solar film panels that attach to windows are a brilliant idea. This is a no-brainer for us. We'll offer you twenty-five million and bring up our stake to twenty percent in the new venture."

I'm stunned. It's ten million dollars more than what I was asking, for only two more percent.

"We'll send over the contract." She stands and kisses me on the cheek. "Now that I'm leaving, you and Mason can gossip without me about your poker club."

"Club?" Mason acts offended.

Cynthia waves as she rushes off.

"Her sister-in-law is having a baby, but she's right; we think you're not evaluating your needs with enough inflation to cover the rising staffing costs," Mason explains. "Franklin Technologies is struggling right now because they thought their name alone would get them great candidates. Unfortunately, living here in the Bay Area is prohibitively expensive. We don't want you to have the same challenges, so as Cynthia said, we're upping our bid. And we'll reserve the option for a second round with an additional twenty-five million for an additional ten percent of the company. How does that sound?"

"I think we have a deal. Send over the contracts, and we'll make this work."

"Great. Let's enjoy our lunch."

Like magic, our plates arrive and are placed in front of us.

"I heard you had an exciting morning," Mason says.

"Not my favorite way to lose productivity, but it does make the highlight reel."

"What happened?"

"A messenger delivered a box for my admin—"

"Corrine?"

"Yes, I brought it upstairs and thought nothing of it. When

she opened it, it smelled of shit. She took it downstairs to open it without offending our senses. And, trust me, it was pretty bad. Our security guard is a former Army explosive expert—trained by Jim and Clear Security, of course—"

"Absolutely."

"He recognized that because it was fertilizer, it could be a bomb."

"Corrine is lucky it wasn't."

"No kidding. She was halfway out the door when the security guard insisted that she put it down. He called the police department, and the bomb squad came. It was complete chaos. They cleared the building and the rest of the block."

"What a mess."

I shrug. "We lost the morning."

"Who sent it?"

"There was a message in the box that told her to keep her hands off her ex-boyfriend."

Mason sits back, looking shocked. "Was she messing with her ex?"

I shake my head. "I know I'm not known to be the most sensitive guy out there, but this asshole broke up with her on the news."

"The news?"

"Yeah, he's the quarterback of the Goldminers."

"Corrine's a cheerleader?"

Mason obviously saw the segment where he talked about that.

"No, he dumped Corrine for the cheerleader."

He takes a drink of his water. "That *is* insensitive."

"I can't believe it. It pisses me off. Talk about not having any class. How do people even like a guy who breaks up with his girlfriend during a news conference? It's no wonder his new girlfriend feels so threatened."

Chapter 3

Corrine

While Jackson's gone, I ponder his invitation to Cecelia Lancaster's funeral. I'm honored to get to pay my respects, but I'm also completely surprised that he thought of me long enough to make the offer. I guess maybe he's more aware of me than I think. Or he was today. That stink bomb made my presence hard to miss.

I sigh. Cecelia's death is such a loss. She was terrific to work with and fantastic at getting technology billionaires—Jackson included—to contribute to her foundation. Her goal was to make sure every child has access to a computer. Her foundation leveled the playing field for those unable to afford them, and hopefully lessened the poverty divide.

Jackson has been very generous, but then again, he's worth billions, so why wouldn't he be? He seems to make smart decisions and doesn't flaunt his money all over the place with too many flashy toys. He doesn't buy a ton of expensive gifts for his girlfriends, either. He seems to dump them as soon as the timing would warrant it.

When Jackson returns from his lunch meeting with Mason Sullivan, he has a spring in his step. He asks me to follow him into his office.

"I see it went well," I tell him as I do.

"Even better than we'd hoped," he says proudly. "We should celebrate."

I smile at him. I know he doesn't mean *we* as in him and me, but him and the current Barbie.

"I'll see where I can get you and Valerie a dinner reservation," I tell him. "Would you want to try French Laundry up in Napa and a night at the Meritage?"

"No! I meant you and me." He points at me. "We should celebrate over dinner. I owe you for all our success. You completed the patent application and put the funding proposal together so well, they didn't even need me to pitch to them."

"Me?" I'm completely taken aback. This is the strangest day ever.

The closest thing to a personal interaction we've had before today was when he interviewed me and asked me to tell him something about myself. And all I shared was that I went to college at the University of Texas in Austin, and how working for him would be perfect because I want to save the environment. I arrange his dates, but he and I don't get personal.

He's still smiling at me. "Sure. Why not? Without you, I'd have nothing to celebrate. They gave us an extra ten million for a minor percentage increase and a commitment for round two."

"That's fantastic." His enthusiasm is contagious. "But I only make the package look pretty. It's all your ideas and numbers. Don't worry about me." I change the subject. "You received a package, by messenger, from Viviana Prentis. She's selling you an estate in Maui for a dollar? Must be nice."

"I think it's just a beach house I won playing poker. I'll need to fly out and see it before the next tournament. I may want to keep it or maybe let her win it back."

When you trade multimillion-dollar pieces of property in a poker tournament, you are in a completely different stratosphere than the rest of the world.

I school my features so I don't look astounded. "I'll look for a few days you can work from Maui in the next few weeks. I have the next tournament on the calendar, tentatively set for next month. However, with Cecelia's death, that will likely change."

He nods. "I'm in the mood for a good steak. How about you make us a reservation at Morton's or Ruth's Chris? Whichever one can seat us at eight."

"I'll make sure Valerie is there," I say as I walk out.

"No. You and me. No Valerie. *Definitely* not Valerie."

I've learned that if he's determined, there's no stopping him. So, I'm better off just letting him have his way. "If this is your way of making sure someone drives me home, I get it. You don't have to buy me dinner."

"You know my net worth better than I do. It's not a financial hardship for me to make sure you're safe. In fact, look at it as my own self-preservation. If this psycho scares you off, I'll have to find someone half as good as you are, and that would be near impossible. I'll let Brian know when we'll be leaving."

I hold up my hands in mock surrender. "Okay, I'm not fighting it. It's not worth the argument."

That evening, when we arrive at Morton's, they seat us in a prime location. It's the spot to be seen, which also means we're interrupted a dozen times.

A creepy man approaches the table. "Jackson, I heard you

met with Mason Sullivan today."

"Ronny, this is Corrine, my assistant. She's the one you harass each time you call my office."

He doesn't do much more than glance at me and give me a half-smile. "I hope you'll give me the chance to bid on your new venture."

"I think anything Golden Gate Capital can bring won't be enough to beat SHN. We've worked together before, and they've made a significant commitment to maintaining that relationship."

"I'll call and set up a time on your schedule next week." He winks at me and walks away, seeming satisfied.

I shudder with dread. "In your dreams," I mutter.

"I agree," Jackson says.

I hope I'm not blushing. "I'm sorry I said that out loud. Give me one drink, and there goes my filter. I'm happy to make the appointment, if you'd like. I just don't trust that man."

"No, it's not necessary. Plus, the dickhead didn't even acknowledge you."

I shrug. "That's not abnormal. I don't usually put those guys on your calendar unless you specifically ask."

"I'm good with that. I would think anyone who wants to meet me would know they have to get through you, so they'd spoil you."

I shake my head. "I don't need gifts or anything, just respect. If they don't treat me well, I figure they'll be a problem later."

A man with his hair slicked back and looking a little too smooth for my liking approaches the table. "Jackson, I heard about what happened today at your office."

"What did you hear?" Jackson plays dumb.

"Your secretary couldn't let her ex, Bobby Sanders, go." He clicks his tongue like he's riding a horse.

It's very odd and incredibly off-putting. I feel myself turn a horrific shade of red.

"Actually..." Jackson looks at me and smiles. "The cheerleader was marking her territory over a man who's a bigger asshole than you are. If you'll excuse us, we're trying to eat our dinner before it gets cold."

We're interrupted several more times as we eat our steaks. Some visitors inquire about Jackson looking for funding, but mostly they gossip about what happened today.

"Is it always like this?" I ask.

"Depends on where they seat me."

No wonder the women he dates never last long. They aren't able to say a sentence without interruption. "I'm sorry. I didn't know. I'll make better reservations from now on.

"My dates usually love the attention."

That's surprising. "Why? They don't get to talk to you."

"I'm not sure talking is why they date me."

He's a beautiful man, but he does like his women to look like Barbie. He likes their looks, and they want his money. No surprise there.

"Well, from my limited conversations, they don't strike me as conversational types." My attempt to recover is terrible at best.

"No, I suppose not." He seems uncomfortable, so I shouldn't give him too hard of a time, but sometimes a girl can't resist. "You have a type you like to date."

"Apparently so do you."

"Yes, I seem to like assholes."

He laughs a deep belly laugh. "And what would you call the women I date?"

"Barbies."

He nods.

"Floatation devices," I add.

"What?" He was drinking his water, and I think it came out his nose.

Not a smart move with your boss.

"What's a floatation device?" he asks, giving me the side eye.

I shrug, a little embarrassed about my honesty with the man who signs my paycheck. "She doesn't have any original parts—a plastic surgeon's masterpiece."

He looks at me and takes another drink. "What kind of girl *should* I date?"

"I'm not sure this is something I should have to explain," I tell him. "But what about someone you can talk to and enjoy as a human being, and who isn't interested in your checkbook? Looks can fade, and the way you're betting when you play poker, so could your luck."

He looks down, and I can see him fighting a laugh. "Where is your family?"

"In Texas."

"Ah. That explains so much. Dallas or Houston?"

"You can't insult me about Texas. I've heard it all. My folks live much farther south in the Rio Grande Valley. My mom is, uh, in Corpus Christi, and my dad lives in McAllen."

"What do they do?"

I typically hate these conversations, but this one is just strange. Jackson and I have worked together for over a year, and he's never shown any interest in me personally before today.

"My dad has a farm—cattle mostly these days."

"He used to farm other things?"

"Yes. He stopped growing cotton when I was in elementary school because the market wasn't there, and he stopped growing sugarcane because of the drought and the effect it had on the Rio Grande when I was in high school."

Jackson looks at me, surprised. "I never pictured you a cowgirl."

I sit up straight and put on my best cowgirl act. "When I was six, I won the mutton busting at the Texas State Fair for staying on a sheep's back for two minutes and twenty-seven seconds. And I can rope a calf. In high school, I even had a bull win the stock show. That's how I paid for college."

He looks at me dumbfounded. "How did that work?"

"Are you sure you want to know?" Most men want to run away when I tell them this.

He nods.

"Don't say I didn't warn you."

He looks at me, concerned.

"I sold my prize-winning bull's sperm."

Jackson chokes on his rare cut of beef. "What?"

I nod. "A prize-winning bull catches twenty-five thousand dollars per sample."

He looks at me carefully. "Did you have to stroke off the steer yourself to get his sample?"

I'm laughing so hard people are turning to look at us. "I'm sorry. I'm just kidding. I grew up in Houston, and my dad is an executive for a large oil and gas company. His brother runs the farm in McAllen. I did win the mutton busting when I was six, and I can sort of rope a calf. But I've never had a bull win the stock show or sold sperm—although that is what prize-winning sperm costs."

Jackson is laughing just as hard as I am. "I totally believed you. I can't believe you had me. You're very funny. Why did you tell me that story?"

"Besides the fact that you're a city boy, I told you because we work to combat what my dad produces."

"I'm going to get you back for that," he assures me. He's still chuckling.

I'm on fire tonight. "Don't make promises you can't keep," I warn with a giant grin.

He shakes his head.

"Everything I've done since I left home is to fight climate change," I explain. "I may not be able to design solar panel film or wind turbines, but by supporting you, I do my part."

Jackson looks at me with a twinkle in his eye. "Our new project would be dead in the water without your help." He lifts his glass. "To a strong partnership."

I lift my glass in return, and we enjoy the rest of our dinner with a few more interruptions before Jackson has Brian drop me home on the way to his place.

"See you in the morning." I wave as I get out of the car.

I'm still laughing to myself about pulling the wool over Jackson's eyes. I hate saying that my dad works in oil and gas. People are so derogatory about that. I get it, but it's not like they're willing to give up driving their cars.

I'm still smiling when I walk into my apartment. It's dark, which means both my roommates are staying with their boyfriends. I pull my cell phone out to play some games while I mindlessly watch television to unwind. I missed a call. The caller ID says it's from Bobby. He'd better be apologizing for his skank girlfriend.

I push play and listen.

"You attention-seeking whore. How fucking dare you call the police over some bullshit! Collette didn't have anything to do with that shit, and you know it. Do you want to know why I broke up with your fat ass? Because you sucked in bed. I was being nice by not telling you, but since you made up some fake reason to try to get me back, now you know why. Leave Collette and me alone or I'll pull a restraining order." And he hangs up.

I'm numb. As if this could get any worse. With a trembling hand, I do the only thing I know how to do and call Gabby.

"Hey, babe, what's up?"

"Can you come over?" I fight through the tears and sniff.

"I'm on my way."

When she arrives ten minutes later, I'm a complete mess.

"What happened?"

I can't talk through the tears, so I hand her my phone. She listens to Bobby's message.

"What the fuck? What a complete asshole! Bad in bed—that man wouldn't know a clitoris if it jumped out in a well-lit room. So, I know that's not true. And fat? Maybe your big toe is fat, but the rest of you is all curves that the guys go crazy for."

"Maybe I am bad in bed. And compared to the

cheerleader, I am fat, but really—"

"Stop it. That's not true. Don't let him demean you in any way. He's a first-class asshole. Where are your roommates?"

"At their boyfriends'." I sniff.

"Well, you can't stay here, and we don't both fit in your twin bed. Come back to my place."

"Thank you, but I can't."

"Why not?"

"I feel silly being so upset over some meathead being mean to me."

"Which is why you're coming to my apartment. Plus, I have a pint of Chunky Monkey and a pint of Chocolate Fudge Brownie at my place."

"Are you sure? It seems like I'm being a baby."

"I'm positive. Pack an overnight bag and let's go. I'm in the mood for ice cream."

I adore Gabby for making me feel better. By the time we arrive at her apartment and eat all of her ice cream, we've solved the world's problems, picked out engagement rings, and even made a voodoo doll of Bobby. Of course, breaking his playing hand makes me feel much better. We fall asleep just after two, and I feel loved.

When the alarm sounds at five thirty, it's way too early.

"Why do you get up so early?" Gabby mutters.

"Big day today and every day," I answer, more chipper than I actually feel.

Gabby rolls over and pulls the covers over her head. Through the sheets, I can barely hear, "I'll check in with you later today."

"Thanks for last night." I pat her through the blanket and run out of her apartment. The sun is just peeking through the clouds when I catch the bus down to the financial district and march into Starbucks. I keep telling myself today is going to be a better day. I mean, Jackson did acknowledge me as a full-fledged human yesterday. That has to be a positive step forward.

Since I order our drinks from the mobile app on the drive in each morning, I whiz in and pick them up and prepare to walk across the street. I'm just leaving when Jackson calls.

Before I can speak, he yells, "Where are you?"

"I'm leaving Starbucks. I should be at the office in three minutes. Is everything okay?"

"Brian's been ringing the buzzer at your apartment for the last thirty minutes."

I look up to the sky and move even faster toward our building. "Crap. I'm sorry. I ended up staying with a friend last night. I forgot I agreed to have a ride in."

"This is for your safety. We'll talk when you get here." He hangs up.

He's grumpy this morning. So much for the fun we had last night. But I'm not going to let his mood affect me.

"I'm just downstairs. I'll be right up," I say to a dead phone line.

The elevator door is inches from shutting when I poke my hand through the door. It's surprisingly full for this time of the morning.

"Sorry," I mutter to the groans.

"Do you still have a job?" Dan, from our IT group, asks.

It takes me a moment to realize he's talking to me. "Yes. Of course, I do."

"You must really be good at giving blowjobs." The people in the elevator snicker.

"Excuse me?" I'm sure I misheard him. No way someone would talk to me or anyone else like that.

"Anyone else who pulled a stunt like you did would've been fired," he snottily explains.

My blood pressure is climbing. "What exactly did I do?"

"Everyone knows you sent that box to yourself. What? You

didn't feel like working that hard yesterday and thought emptying two city blocks over a fake bomb would give you the morning off? I had to come in early today because of you."

"I don't know who told you I sent that box to myself, but it isn't true, and Mr. Graham and the police know that."

"Right." He gets off the elevator, along with most of the other employees.

I'm left standing with our CFO, Jeremy Knowles. "Can you believe that guy?"

He looks at me and seems to want to say something, but when the elevators open on the forty-second floor, he walks right by me, jostling me so I spill my mocha.

Great. What an asshole.

I walk to my desk and call maintenance to ask them to help me clean up the mess. Now even they are put out with me.

Jackson's on the phone when I walk his coffee in, so I leave his drink on his desk and return to my office. I'm behind, too, and I continue to argue with Dan from IT in my mind. I'm never fast enough in the moment to say the right thing. Now I can think of a dozen things to say.

I know if I were to mention this to Mr. Graham, Dan would get in trouble, which gives me great satisfaction. But I will never say anything. Jackson's not here to solve my problems. He's busy solving the world's problems.

Chapter 4

Corrine

Throughout the day I hear whispers, but I ignore them. It's not worth it. After I had to listen to Mr. Graham explain to me *again* about the importance of getting a ride to and from the office this morning, I've stayed at my desk. I ordered lunch in for him and me, and we ate in our offices and pushed through.

It's after seven now, and people have come and gone, and Jackson's been on the phone all day. In my desk phone log, I look back through the day's calls. He's had over two hundred and fifty—it's a record. At the moment, he's finally off the phone.

I grab the phone log, take a deep breath, and knock on the door.

"Come in, Corrine," he announces. He smiles up at me when I enter.

"You had several calls today."

He nods. "No kidding. I'm impressed you were able to order lunch. Thank you for getting me my favorite."

"You're easy to please." I smile. Ever since dinner, I feel more comfortable with our relationship. "The big calls that merit your attention include Ronny Huddleston, who called nine times, insisting you wanted him on your calendar. I explained that he misread you, and that was not the case, but he kept calling."

"I'll call his boss, Tim Lucas, over at Golden Gate Capital and let him know." Jackson writes himself a note.

"Your mother called and wanted to know your plans for her birthday. You have four days late next week, including the weekend. Would you like to take her to Maui with you?"

"We can plan Maui for me on those days, but not with my mother. Too much pressure. Let me think about what she might like. What did I do for her last year?"

I smile because it's going to be hard to beat. I had just started, and that was one of my first projects. He gave me no limit. "You booked a river cruise for your mom and her friends, but she was disappointed that you didn't make an appearance. She warned me that I'm to make sure you do so this year. I think she wants to introduce you to one of her friend's daughters."

Jackson rolls his eyes. "No, thanks. I may need help coming up with something—although it doesn't need to be as extravagant. She turned seventy last year. Seventy-one doesn't have to be quite so over the top. If you think of something, let me know."

I take a deep breath. Now for the problematic message. "Also, Dawn Decker from HR called. They have over two hundred applicants for my job. They'll screen them down to the five best for you to meet with here in your office. She has access to your calendar and will be doing some scheduling."

"Okay, great. Wait. For *your* job?"

"That's what Dawn said," I say, trying not to cry.

"I'm not looking to replace you. Jesus! I'm sorry. I'll call her. She's gone for the day, but what is her cell phone number?"

I have the number on my phone, and I rattle it off to him.

He dials and won't look at me while we wait. I'm not sure if he's pissed that I found out or if he's distraught over this situation. "Dawn, who told you to open a search for a new admin?"

He listens a moment.

"I want you both in my office tomorrow morning at seven. Make sure he's here, too. All work on this project needs to stop immediately. Your number-one priority is staffing for the manufacturing of these new solar films. I'll see you both tomorrow morning."

He hangs up the phone and smiles.

"That's handled for now. What else?"

"Here are the other messages." I hand him a sheet of more than a dozen calls. "I'm happy to dial these for you."

He takes a deep breath and nods.

I return to my desk and for the next two hours, I dial and find the person looking for him. Once I do, I pass them over.

"This is the final call, and it's Linda Hilgers, your IP attorney."

"Thank you, Corrine. It's after nine. Call Brian, and you can head home."

"Thank you, Mr. Graham. He's sitting here. Ben is here waiting for you, too. See you in the morning."

Brian escorts me outside to a waiting Suburban.

"I'm really sorry you have to do this," I tell him.

"Oh, I don't mind. You're far prettier than Mr. Graham anyway."

I chuckle. "I'm not sure your wife would appreciate you saying that."

"I already told her. She knows. Mr. Graham is good to us, and she thinks he's much more handsome than me." He grins as he opens the door. He's teasing.

"Let your wife know Mr. Graham got a marriage proposal today from a woman he's never met."

"That's crazy. Mr. Graham's a good guy, but that's totally whacked."

"Any recent pictures of the twins?"

He hands me his phone. "Check them out."

"They're getting so big." The two boys are mini versions of Brian with giant grins and look like they're up to no good.

A few minutes later, we pull up to my apartment building. "I'm really sorry about this morning," I tell him. "I forgot. I won't forget tomorrow morning. Promise. I'd like to leave at six-thirty, if that works for you?"

"Not a problem. Mr. Graham wants you escorted. I do as I'm asked. I'll meet you here at six-thirty."

"Thank you for making me feel better." I begin to get out of the car, and suddenly Brian is standing before me.

"I'm sorry. Mr. Graham insists that I walk you to your door and make sure everything is okay in your apartment."

"Brian, that's really not necessary."

"I'll lose my job if I don't."

I let out an irritated sigh. "Fine, come with me."

I stomp up the stairs and put my key in the lock. As I open the door, my two roommates turn to look at us. They're watching the latest episode of *The Bachelor.*

I turn to Brian. "All is safe."

"I'll be here tomorrow morning at six-thirty."

"Thanks." I shut the door behind him.

"Who is that?" Stacy asks.

"Did you hear about the debacle downtown yesterday?" I ask.

She nods.

"The box was sent to me, so now my boss has assigned me a bodyguard."

"You work with the hottest guy in tech, and he requires a hot bodyguard? Your life is amazing."

"If this is amazing, I'm giving up and going home. I'm

exhausted. See you tomorrow."

"Just a reminder, Sean and I are going to Mexico for a week."

"That's right. Have a fantastic time. Angela? Will you be around?"

"I have a trade show in Orlando, and I'm extending a few days for some sunshine."

"You both have incredible lives. Have a good time. I'll be slaving away here."

I wash my face and stare at my reflection in the mirror. I think I see a gray hair, and my crow's feet are getting deeper. Ugh. Maybe I should go find a quiet, peaceful job at home in Houston. The cost of living is somewhat affordable, and there'd be no one sending me poop bombs, so I wouldn't have to deal with bodyguards. But then again, there's no Jackson Graham there either.

I crawl into bed. I'm a little jealous that the girls are getting out of town to warm places, but I like the idea of having the apartment to myself. I'm behind on my sleep, and the stress has made for too many short nights. At least I'm halfway to the weekend. Then I can sleep. I fall asleep dreaming about Jackson.

When the alarm goes off, I wake up a little off-kilter. It takes a few moments for my brain to engage.

At six-thirty, I'm ready and waiting in my apartment lobby. Brian is right on time.

"You should wait for me in your apartment," he says as he jumps out of the car and opens the backseat door.

"I didn't want you to wake my roommates. Plus, I'm locked in the lobby, so no one can nab me."

"You don't lose many arguments, do you?" he asks sardonically.

"I wish that were true. People have confronted me about what happened on Wednesday, and I haven't done so well there."

Brian becomes hyper-alert. "Has anyone confronted you

with a weapon or touched you?"

Crap. "Brian, I'm exaggerating. I hear whispers. One person told me he was sure I sent the box to myself and got on my knees for Mr. Graham to keep my job. The others are contributing to a death pool."

"Death pool?"

He's looking very serious. I need to tone it down and be factual.

"Meaning the death of my employment at Soleil Energy, not death of my person."

"Have you spoken to Mr. Graham about this?"

"Absolutely not, and you won't either. I also get slaps on the back and praise from the lazier people in our office, but many are angry with me because they think I was behind the mess. If Mr. Graham gets involved, it'll only get worse."

"I think you need to speak to him," Brian insists.

"No. He's not going to fight my battles, and that will only make it worse."

When we arrive at the office, Brian parks in front of Starbucks. As we cross the busy street, he's close behind, making sure I'm safe. At the counter, our coffee is waiting. I hand a cup to Brian. "Doctor this as you need, and I'll order you a proper drink tomorrow."

"Thank you. Black is perfect, but you didn't need to get me coffee."

"Don't worry about it. It's the least I can do if you're getting less sleep than I am."

"It's part of the job," he assures me.

We walk across the street and into the building. It's just before seven, and we get into the crowded elevator. I see looks of disdain on several people's faces. I cringe when I see Dan from IT.

He makes a big deal of looking down at my knees. "As often as you must be getting on your knees, I'd think they'd be all bruised."

The people in the elevator snicker, and I'm pissed.

Through clenched teeth, I say, "Dan, I suggest you apologize immediately."

"Or what? Are you going to tell your precious Mr. Graham? When will you do that with his cock slammed down your throat?"

It takes all my willpower not to slap the stupid grin off his face. He's staring me down, and I'm not going to give him the satisfaction of reacting. There are too many people in the elevator.

When he gets off on the twenty-fifth floor, Brian looks at me. "Is that the kind of crap they're dishing out?"

"Just ignore it," I warn.

We exit the elevator on our floor, and I spot Dawn from HR sitting outside Jackson's office. I smile at her, but she won't look at me.

"Does he know you're here?" I ask.

She shakes her head.

I take off my coat, put my things away, and pick up the calendar I printed before I left last night. Jackson's not on the phone, so I walk in with his coffee and a copy of the schedule. "Dawn Decker is outside waiting for you."

"And Jeremy?"

Jeremy? He was the one who asked Dawn to start a search for my replacement? I blame Heather and her big mouth for that one. "I didn't see him."

He runs his hand over his face. "What's on my schedule today?"

"You have senior staff at nine. At noon, lunch with Dave Wilkinson of Blue Energy at Waterfront Café. A marketing call at three. Project development at four-thirty. Review of the training curriculums at five. And drinks with Devin Abbot at six-thirty.

"Thank you. Have Dawn come in, ask Jeremy to come in when he arrives, and please join us."

"Yes, Mr. Graham." I step out of his office. "Dawn, you can go in."

She looks frightened. I don't blame her. Neither Jeremy nor Heather are in the office to join her for the potential verbal lashing, which is not fun.

I knock and stick my head in Jeremy's office, but he's not there. I call his cell phone, and it goes directly to voice mail.

Returning to Mr. Graham's office, I stand in the back.

"Where's Jeremy?" he asks.

"He's not in his office, and his cell phone goes directly to voice mail."

Jackson takes a deep breath. "I see." He looks at Dawn. "I want to be abundantly clear that I'm not looking to replace Ms. Woods. You were misinformed."

"Yes, Mr. Graham. My apologies to you and Ms. Woods."

Jackson nods. "You can leave."

She gets up, and I follow her out the door.

"Ms. Woods?" Jackson calls.

I stop and turn around.

"Please let me know when Jeremy arrives. And, can you get me Emerson Healy at SHN on the phone?"

"Of course."

Chapter 5

Jackson

I'm so angry right now. Jeremy's up to something. This crap of calling HR to replace Corrine is the last straw.

Jeremy worked for me at my last company. He was a good accountant and was looking for a growth opportunity, so I didn't have any problems bringing him along when I sold my last venture off. But recently, he's been really negative. He was sure we wouldn't get funding for the new solar film product, and he really put Corrine through the ringer when she needed financials. She covered for him at times, and I knew it. But when I talked to him about it, he consistently blamed her. For some reason he doesn't like her, and it's affecting me. If I have to choose, he's going to be very disappointed, because it won't be him.

What does hiring someone new do but set us back?

"Emerson Healy is on line one," Corrine informs me over

the intercom.

"Thank you, Corrine."

I pick up the phone. "Hi, Emerson. Thanks for taking my call so early."

"Hello!" she singsongs. "Please forgive me if you hear my son in the background. The nanny will be here anytime, and Dillon is watching him, but there's no telling how well that will go, and I didn't want you to wait."

I grin at the idea of Dillon Healy, Emerson's six-foot-five husband, bending to the will of a toddler. I have a feeling the toddler will win every time. "I don't mind the noise. I need some help from your team. It's looking like Jeremy will be leaving us, so I'm going to need a new financial officer. You guys are in the process of greenlighting my project, so that should give you some guidance on our needs. Of course, we prefer someone with alternative energy experience."

"I may have some people in mind," she says. "We just had one of our investments bought by a wind turbine company that may be a good solution. Their CFO is Cheryl Wedgwood. Do you know her?"

"I do, and if she's on the market and willing, I'd love to talk to her."

"She might be a good fit for you. Before I commit, I'll sit down with Dillon and Cynthia."

"Perfect. You also have Jeremy's contract. Can you have Sara in your legal group look it over? It looks like he may be in breach, and I'll be looking for what needs to be done to violate without any golden parachute."

"Of course. Are messages through Corrine okay?"

"Yes, she has access to my email, and that works, too."

"I'll be in touch soon."

I hang up, and I'm preparing to buzz Corrine when she steps in.

"I don't know what's going on, but neither Heather nor Jeremy is in."

"Does that strike you as odd?" I ask.

"Yes, it does."

What could they be up to? This doesn't make any sense. I look through my emails for something from Jeremy, and it's been several weeks since he's sent me anything. Another troubling event.

"Have someone come up from IT," I tell her.

"Right away, Mr. Graham."

Fifteen minutes later, Dan from IT is in my office.

The door is hardly closed behind him when he starts in. "Mr. Graham, please let me explain."

I nod. I'm not sure what he needs to explain, but I'm going to let him talk.

"I was furious at Ms. Woods over the box incident on Wednesday."

What the hell is this guy talking about?

"I had a big project, and it was almost completed, but because she sent herself the box and we were out of the office all Wednesday morning, I had to start over. I was upset and said some inappropriate things. But I apologize, and it won't happen again."

What kind of madness is going on at my company? "That's not why I asked you up here but be assured I will have HR fully investigate your actions and determine if you should remain employed here."

He shuts his eyes, and I almost laugh. Corrine set him up. She'd never tell on anyone because she knows I'd string them up and fire their asses.

"Please give Ms. Woods access to Mr. Knowles' and his assistant Heather's emails immediately."

"Yes, Mr. Graham. I'll give her the admin password. It will give her access to any computer in the company, including yours."

"She already has access to mine. I'm not worried, but please keep this information I've asked of you confidential."

"Yes, Mr. Graham."

"You can go." As Dan reaches the door, I add, "Please

know that the police have confirmed that the package on Wednesday wasn't sent by Ms. Woods, so not only were your comments inappropriate, they were also misinformed. You'd do well to correct anyone you hear say otherwise."

"Yes, Mr. Graham." He almost runs out of the office.

I push the intercom. "Ms. Woods, can you come in here, please?"

"Right away, Mr. Graham."

She steps in, and for the first time, I notice her pencil skirt and blouse with kitten-heel boots. Her breasts strain behind the buttons. The flare of her hips and her mouthwatering ass cheeks are enhanced by the way the skirt accents every curve. For a brief moment, I dream about kneeling before her and tasting her, but then I remember why I asked her into my office. My balls ascend into my abdomen because I'm being an ass and ogling my assistant.

"You didn't tell Dan why I wanted to see him," I prompt.

"No, Mr. Graham. I thought it best for confidentiality's sake that he just come up to your office." She smiles.

"I take it he's been a little inappropriate?"

She nods. "Yes, he has."

"I'm opening an HR investigation regarding his behavior. Why didn't you report this?"

"A lot of people blame me for what happened on Wednesday. I thought reporting it would only make their anger worse. Plus, the only person who needed to know I wasn't guilty was you. The rest I could care less about."

"Regardless, we're opening an investigation. I don't tolerate that kind of harassment."

"I never believed you did. I did hope Dan would tell you for me, and it seems that's exactly what he did. Thank you for addressing this."

I nod at her. Corrine never ceases to amaze me.

"Mr. Knowles and Heather have arrived," she adds after a moment.

"Please send Jeremy in. Dan should be getting you both

Jeremy and Heather's passwords. I want a thorough look at their email accounts, along with their sent boxes, and a comparison to the backup files."

"Yes, Mr. Graham."

She turns and leaves, and I watch her go. I'd love to see her face when she comes. I wonder if she's loud or quiet. My dick twitches.

I quickly phone HR and ask for an investigation regarding Dan in IT and his comments to Corrine since Wednesday. Boy, do I feel like a hypocrite.

As I hang up, Jeremy walks in.

"Where were you this morning?" I ask.

"Heather and I had the solar gala breakfast kick-off, remember?"

"I asked you to be here at seven to meet with Dawn from HR and me. I was surprised to learn you'd asked them to start a search to replace Corrine."

"I did. After all the mistakes she's been making and the box incident, I thought it was most prudent."

"First, I'm not aware of any mistakes—"

"Heather has been catching them before they get to your desk."

I don't believe that even for a moment. "And second, Corrine's my admin, so I make that decision. You took valuable resources away from a big recruiting effort for production of our new solar film, just to waste two days of work."

"I was doing my job."

Jeremy's up to something, and he's full of shit. "Apologize to Corrine on your way out."

"Sure."

He turns to go, and I pop the speaker on to listen for his apology. He doesn't stop to talk to Corrine. Yes, he's definitely up to something.

Chapter 6

Corrine

At the end of the day on Friday, I grab the phone log and walk into Mr. Graham's office. It's been a long week, and it's after seven. I'm ready to go home.

"You had a few phone calls today."

He glances at the clock. "Where did my day go?"

I tick off his meetings and conference calls.

He smiles. "I'm sorry you're stuck working so late these days. Any calls that can't wait until Monday?"

"No, you've managed all the emergencies. Jeremy and Heather both left about an hour ago, but I didn't get a chance to go through their computers. It was too easy to get caught with them here."

Mr. Graham tends to work from home on Saturday and come in on Sundays, so before he can offer to go through the computers himself, I share my plan with him. "I'll come in tomorrow and go through them and let you know on Monday if anything shows up."

"I appreciate all the work you're putting in on this."

I'm embarrassed by the accolades. "I just want them gone if they're doing something that could hurt the company."

"Agreed. Brian's going to take you home this evening. Any weekend plans besides work?"

"I have plans for drinks with my best friend, Gabby, tonight."

"And Brian's going with you?"

"No man will talk to me if he's hanging around," I tell him.

"I don't find a problem with that. You keep forgetting that this week someone sent you a box that cleared an entire city block for half a day. You shouldn't be wandering alone right now."

"That's over," I retort.

He huffs. "Let's let more than three days go by before we declare it's over. I'm more interested in your personal safety."

Going down this rabbit hole isn't working, so I need to try something else. "Brian has a family. They want to spend time with him on the weekend."

"He's well compensated. I also expect you to contact him when you move around this weekend."

Jackson is my boss; he's not the king of my life. I feel like I'm a teenager dealing with my father. I roll my eyes.

"Did you just roll your eyes at me?"

Shit. "I did, but only because you're overreacting."

Jackson takes a deep breath. "Do you know what it cost to have two divisions of the San Francisco Police Department, the bomb squad, and two fire stations roll out for the box you were sent?"

I shake my head not sure I want to know the answer.

"At least one hundred thousand dollars, if not more. This woman is not just a little crazy, she's a lot crazy."

"I haven't reached out to Bobby, and I know the police have talked to his girlfriend," I say.

Jackson sits up straight and alert. "How do you know?"

Crap. "Because Bobby called and was pissed I'd told them about our breakup." I watch his face contort in anger.

"He told you that?"

"Well…he left me a voice mail." *Please don't want to listen to it.*

"I want to hear it. Do you still have it?"

I do, but I'm not going to let my boss know my ex thinks I'm fat and bad at sex. I shake my head.

"Did he call the office or your cell?"

I really don't want the embarrassment of him listening to the message. I cross my arms and look down at the ground. "My cell."

"Hand it to me. I might be able to recover the message."

"Don't worry about it. I'll use Brian this weekend, and Gabby and I will just have drinks at my apartment."

"I'm glad to hear that." He holds his hand out. "Phone, please."

"You can't make me give you my cell phone," I say like a petulant child.

He cocks his head to the side. "Now, Corrine."

I slowly reach into my pocket. I wish I could erase the message without it being obvious. I place it in Jackson's hand.

I shut my eyes, hoping this is a dream. "He says some things I'd rather you not hear," I quietly explain.

Jackson pushes some buttons, and Bobby's voice mail plays on the phone's speaker.

As soon as it starts, I can feel his eyes boring into me. "Why didn't you send this to the police?"

"They wouldn't have done anything. Everyone reveres Bobby in this town." The idea that Bobby thinks I'm fat and suck at sex is not a humiliation I could handle if it got out.

Jackson listens to the message several times before pushing some buttons and handing me back my phone. "He's an asshole. I hope you know that."

I fight back the tears. "Thank you."

I return to my desk and gather my things. Brian follows me out to the Suburban. In the car, I send a text to Gabby.

Me: I'm just finishing work. I'm stuck with the bodyguard so if you still want to get together for drinks, we can meet at my place. The girls are gone, and it's just me this weekend.

Gabby: Great idea. I'll pick something up at the bodega at the corner.

Me: Perfect. Thanks.

Things will get better. "Brian, what do you have going on this weekend?"

"I'm working for you," he says.

"You're not doing anything with the twins?"

"Not this weekend. I'll be parked in front of your building by seven tomorrow morning, unless you need me earlier."

"I hope to still be sleeping. How about nine instead? I'm going into the office for some work."

He's watching me in the rearview mirror. "I'll meet you at nine."

When we arrive, Brian walks me to my door and hands me a card with his cell phone number on it. "I can be back in less than twenty minutes with the car. Please don't sneak out. That's a good way to get me fired."

"You know my soft spot."

He does a quick walkthrough of my apartment and waves goodbye.

This is not what I ever expected my week would look like. I get out of my skirt and pull off my bra. *Ahh.* The bra was definitely invented by a man. I put on a ratty UT sweatshirt and a pair of yoga pants. So much better.

I turn my tunes on loud and pop a giant bowl of popcorn—not air-popped, but with coconut oil in a pan. I then melt an entire stick of butter, and as I pour it on and salt it well, the buzzer rings. Gabby's here!

You can tell Gabby is excited. Her eyes are big, and her smile is enormous. "You'll never guess what I found."

I shake my head.

Out of the paper bag, she pulls two four-packs of berry wine coolers. Her grin is infectious.

"I haven't seen wine coolers since college. They're perfect." I giggle.

Gabby begins to sniff the air. "I smell popcorn."

"You do. I put an entire stick of butter in." I show her the giant bowl and pop a few kernels in my mouth. *Delicious.*

"Love it." She takes a big handful of popcorn and stuffs it in her mouth.

I can sort of make out her saying, "What's on Netflix?"

"You pick, and I'll tell you about my day—starting with the worst part where Jackson listened to Bobby's voice mail."

She stops, and her head swings away from the television and focuses on me. "What?"

I nod. "He listened to it a few times and also forwarded it to someone."

"Who?" She studies me carefully.

"I don't know. He did call Bobby an asshole."

"Good. He can be an honorary member of the I Hate Bobby Sanders Club."

She stops at a romantic comedy we've watched a few dozen times. It's perfect for catching up and if we can't finish watching. "What else did he say?"

"Not much. I'm working tomorrow."

"You're always working on weekends."

"We're busy, and now we think our CFO and his admin are up to something, but we're not sure what. I'm going to do some snooping."

"Are you going in by yourself?"

I stuff a big handful of popcorn in my mouth. "No, Brian is picking me up at nine."

"That's good. After the week you've had, it's good you're not alone at work. Damien is out to drinks with his boys, and I'm going to meet up with him later. Is that okay?"

"Of course." I shovel more popcorn in my mouth. We watch the movie for a little over an hour before she has to go.

"Enjoy those wine coolers."

I laugh. "I'll save the leftovers for your next visit."

I lock the door behind her, and suddenly I'm nervous about being alone. I'm so rarely alone. I share an office space with Heather outside Jackson's office. And I live in a literal old-time closet between two women, and usually one of them is home. I like the idea of being alone in theory, but with so much going on, I miss my roommates. There's safety in numbers.

The baseboard electric furnace snaps, crackles, and pops, and it sends my heart racing. It takes me a long time to fall asleep. I keep thinking of Jackson's face as he listened to Bobby's message. He was shocked at first and then seemed to understand why I was embarrassed. He wouldn't look at me while Bobby told me why he broke up with me. It's not like I have anything to offer Jackson that he'd want, but still—no one wants to know their admin is terrible in bed.

At some point, I fall asleep and wake naturally when the sun comes up. Saturday is the one day I can sleep in, but my body has other ideas. When my mind starts circling around Bobby and his new girlfriend, the package, and Heather's strange behavior, I can't take it anymore. I throw off the covers to brave the cold air of my apartment.

I make myself a plate of eggs and piddle around. I pick up our mess from last night and read the *San Francisco Chronicle* for the local update and *Cosmo* from my phone. It has tips on how to satisfy your man. I look at a few diets, but none of them has enough chocolate in it.

When the buzzer to my apartment rings at nine, I realize I never got dressed. I buzz Brian up and quickly slip on a pair of jeans and a cute sweater with my Ked sneakers.

"Sorry, Brian. I got up early and have done nothing this morning."

"You don't have to hurry on my account. I'm also fine if you want me to wait in the car."

I flip some mascara over my lashes, smooth on some lip gloss, and walk out. "No, I'm ready. Do you mind if we stop at Starbucks?"

"I go where you want, not the other way around."

After our Starbucks run, we walk to the office. Brian alerts the weekend security guard of where we'll be and asks him to inform us of anyone coming upstairs. "I wouldn't want to shoot anyone," he explains.

Up on our floor, we get settled in. Brian has a book, and I start poking around on Jeremy's computer. I notice he's been talking to someone at our competitor, and they set up lunch plans. It's a conversation that goes back and forth—they're catching up to watch a football game and meeting at trade shows.

Each of their plans has a few errors. The football game was on my birthday, and they mention watching a Goldminers-Giants game. The Goldminers' season was long over, and the Giants play baseball. I do a quick search and find the Giants haven't even started yet.

I also don't remember Jeremy going to any trade shows or processing any of his expense reports for a trade show.

I place a copy of some of the strange emails on a cloud server and keep going.

Heather's email also has a few messages that seem out of place. I store them all in the cloud drive. Nothing points to anything in particular, and there's no smoking gun. I'm a little disappointed but not really surprised. If they're up to no good, they wouldn't be doing it on their company email.

My office phone rings, and it's the security guard. "Mr. Knowles is on his way up."

"Thank you."

I alert Brian and quickly move to a new file and pretend

I'm working on something else. The elevator pings, and I look up as the doors open. Jeremy and I lock eyes.

He stops short, seeming surprised to see me. "What the hell are you doing here?" he grumbles.

Brian stands up, and when Jeremy spots him, his demeanor changes from aggression to ignoring my existence.

"Thank you," I mouth to Brian, and he nods.

Jeremy goes into his office and shuts the door. He's never been in the office over the weekend even once in the year I've worked here. He works long days, but I can't remember a weekend.

Opening a mirror image of his computer, I watch Jeremy open the presentation, patent application, and research file from our recent solar film venture and begin copying them to a private cloud drive. They're big files, so it takes some time. It's so quiet that I can hear him on the phone. I can't make out who he's talking to or exactly what he's saying, but I hear him murmur.

I pick up my phone and text Jackson.

Me: I'm at the office. Jeremy just walked in and is copying the presentation, patent ap, and research file from your new venture to a private cloud drive.

I send the text and take a picture of my screen that shows the download.

Jackson: Is Brian with you?

Me: Yes.

Jackson: Make sure Jeremy doesn't leave. I'm on my way.

Me: OK

I look at Brian. "Mr. Graham doesn't want Jeremy to

leave."

He nods and takes his cell phone from his pocket. It must have vibrated because he looks at it.

I continue to watch what Jeremy is doing. He opens up File Explorer and begins deleting files from his computer and the server.

I frantically start writing the file names down. They'll be in the backup on the server, but this will at least let us know what Jeremy's erased. When I can't keep up, I do the only thing I can think of and begin recording a video from my cell phone, watching as the files disappear.

A few minutes later, the elevator pings its arrival, and Jim walks in with two big, burly men and Jackson behind them.

Silently I point out what Jeremy is doing and continue to write the file names down.

Jeremy's office door opens suddenly, and he seems stunned to see so many people standing with me.

"What's going on?" He tries to play it cool and puts his hand in his pocket, but then pulls it out.

The elevator pings again and four policemen step out with a man with disheveled dark hair dressed in rust-colored corduroy pants and a green plaid shirt under a khaki overcoat.

"Detective," Jim says.

Jeremy's eyes grow big.

"Do you want to tell us why you copied all the research, the patent application, and the presentation for funding for the solar film?" Jackson asks.

Jeremy pushes his shoulders back. "What are you talking about? I didn't do anything like that." He gives me a look that would make most people wither.

I smile because not only did I watch him do it and report it, but I took pictures and video. I hand my cell phone to Jackson.

Jackson's eyebrows rise. "Why were you deleting files from the server?"

"What do you mean?"

"Here's a list of most of what he deleted." I hand a piece of paper to Jackson.

He looks at the list and shows it to the detective. "The files you deleted are all the research on the new venture that was just funded this week."

"I clean up my files all the time," Jeremy rants. "There's nothing wrong going on here."

"Why don't we go down to the station to clear this up," the detective offers.

"I'm not going with you," Jeremy says.

The detective shrugs. "I can take you in handcuffs, if you prefer." Jeremy's shoulders fall. "Don't worry. You can call your attorney after we get there and you've been processed."

Jeremy is escorted out by the four policemen, and the detective remains behind.

"What else did you find?" Jackson asks me.

"I'm not sure of anything."

I open the cloud drive and begin to look at my notes. I explain the football-baseball issue. "Some things seem off. Here's an email that says, 'Benchmark will meet with us on Thursday morning.' Didn't he say he had a breakfast that morning?"

Jackson looks at Jim. "Would Benchmark Capital fund something like this?"

Jim shrugs. "I know Stephanie, the founder. Let me do some checking." He turns to me. "Can I get the link for the cloud drive?"

I look at Jackson, and he nods. "Of course."

"I'm going to have Gage in my office check this out," Jim says. "He'll need to look through his computer."

Jackson seems distracted by all his hard work running out the door. "That's fine," he says absently.

"What about Heather?" I ask. "She may have more incriminating things on her computer."

"We can have Gage go through that too," Jim suggests.

"I also found that when they were late and supposed to be at a meeting with the accountants, it looks like they had a meeting with Hydro Energy Partners."

Jackson turns white, then beet red. I've seen him upset, but never this angry.

"I'll nail the son of a bitch."

"Do you want me to continue looking?" I ask quietly.

"I'll have Gage work with you." Jim turns and looks at Jackson. "I have a contact at FBI Cybercrimes if we need her and her team. She's solid."

Suddenly there's an enormous amount of activity going on. I sit back and watch, and when someone asks for my help, I respond.

Jackson goes in and sits alone in his office. He's been working for months on this invention, and if it's out there now, that's all toast.

"Brian, I know you're not an errand boy, but if I order coffee for everyone, would you be willing to help me pick it up?" I ask.

He nods. I ask everyone what they want and go on my mission. It's almost lunchtime, so I also order an assortment of sandwiches. I need to do what I can to help.

Chapter 7

Jackson

After Saturday morning's discovery, my weekend was completely absorbed by what Jeremy has been doing. I've made statements to the police and worked with Jim's team to root out what I both feared and expected: Jeremy has pitched the plan for our new solar film panels to a variety of competitors.

Now it's Monday morning, and even as we come up with a plan, I can hardly believe this is happening.

Morning traffic is dense everywhere in San Francisco. I miss the days of working from my apartment. Thankfully, Ben drives me into the office, giving me the chance to talk to Jim on the phone.

"I'm meeting with Stephanie Pierce at Benchmark," Jim tells me. "And I think you and Mason Sullivan should join me."

"When and where?" I ask.

"Let's meet on neutral ground. How about the private room at the Waterfront Café? Noon?"

"That works," I tell him, stifling a yawn.

I haven't been sleeping worth shit. I can't believe Jeremy Knowles tried to steal from Soleil Energy and from me. When I spoke with Mason, he was sure the repercussions were significant enough that we could fire Jeremy without paying any severance or even compensating him for the stock options, which we will claw back.

We'll meet with Benchmark and try Hydro Energy Partners. I have my lawyers preparing letters explaining that any material they've seen is stolen and we'll go after any like materials, if they choose to produce them, vigorously. I'm confident Benchmark will walk away, but Hydro is Chinese owned, and we're in a race with them for this technology. It's difficult for non-Chinese officials to prosecute theft in China, and they don't recognize US patents.

My mind wanders to Corrine. She's definitely not fat. She has some curves, but she's a natural beauty, very sexy in a girl-next-door kind of way. And, I'm not sure Bobby Sanders knows how to enjoy a woman. It's much more satisfying to give a woman so much pleasure that getting your own becomes unnecessary. What a full-blown ass. I can tell Corrine believes what he said, but it isn't my place to tell her she's beautiful and probably great in bed. That has lawsuit written all over it.

The elevator from the garage stops at the lobby. When the doors open, Corrine appears, looking stunning in her dark dress. Her blond hair is piled on top of her head, and she's holding our coffee order.

"You're earlier than usual," I say.

"I figured after my mess on Wednesday, and then all the activity on Saturday, it would be a long day."

"Good thinking. The FBI will be by this morning to deal with Heather. They'll call you when they arrive."

"Do you think she knows?" she asks.

I shrug. "I have a lunch at noon today with one of the firms Jeremy solicited. I'll meet with SHN before that at eleven."

She nods. We arrive at our floor, and she takes off her coat and hangs it up. I watch her pick up my calendar and follow me into my office with my coffee.

"I'll move your twelve-thirty appointment to next week. Would you like me to cancel going to Cecelia's service tomorrow? With so much going on, it's hard to fit everything in."

Corrine is always so good at supplying me with the rationale to politely excuse myself, but I like Nate. This must be terribly hard. I saw them together, and they were almost one person. I need to go to the service for him. "No, let's still go. "

She nods. "Do you want a copy of your presentation to go with you to your afternoon meetings?"

"No, I think we'll be fine without it."

I watch her turn and leave. God, she has a great ass. It would sit well in my hands. How pink would it become if I spanked it?

Why is it that we worked together for months and I never had a less-than-pure thought, but now when she leaves it's imprinted on my brain?

Her luscious tits. Are the areolas light pink? What sounds does she make when they're sucked? What if I were to pinch, pull, bite, and play with them?

What about those long legs wrapped around me, pushing me deeper inside her—or holding them open as my tongue dives for her honey.

I shake myself out of this utterly inappropriate daze. I try to concentrate on my work, not what my cock wants.

My phone rings, and it's Corrine. "Why are you calling me?"

"I'm in the lobby. The FBI has arrived for Heather, and she just walked into the building. They're arresting her here. Do you want to come down?"

"I'm on my way."

I can hear her screeches before the elevator doors open.

"You can't detain me! I know my rights! Let me go!"

She's struggling with the two FBI agents holding her back as she lunges at Corrine. "You bitch! I'll make sure your beloved Jackson knows all about you!"

I step into her line of sight.

"Mr. Graham, Corrine is behind this mess to get me arrested. She sent the box to herself. I saw her do it."

Corrine stiffens, but before she can deny it, I speak. "Heather, Jeremy was arrested on Saturday for theft and corporate espionage. Your emails indicate you were helping him. I suggest that rather than lobbing lies about Ms. Woods, you use this time to consider who you're going to hire to represent you. Because if the solar films are produced by anyone other than Soleil, I promise I'll do my best to take every penny you earn for the rest of your life."

Her eyes grow wide. "I have no idea what you're talking about. You can't arrest me. I only did what my boss told me to do."

She's still kicking and screaming as they lead her out of the lobby and place her in the back of a black government vehicle.

I turn around, and a large crowd has accumulated behind me. "Okay, everyone, show's over. Get back to work."

The crowd disperses, and I walk over to Corrine and the agent in charge.

"I'll go as soon as she lets me," Corrine says, motioning to the blond woman next to her.

"I'm not worried," I assure her.

The female agent extends her hand. "I'm Agent in Charge Cora Perry."

I nod. "Jackson Graham."

"There are some things we're investigating. Heather won't be back today."

"Keep her as long as you need. I'll work with my HR team

to make sure she never comes back."

I don't notice Corrine leave, but after a moment she returns with my coat. "You need to be at SHN in twenty minutes."

"Thank you."

Ben walks me to my car at the curb. When I spoke with Mason about the theft over the weekend, he wasn't happy. But he knows we're pursuing this through all possible avenues. That still doesn't mean my meeting this morning is going to be enjoyable. I'm thinking it's more akin to a root canal.

When I arrive at SHN's offices, I'm shown to a conference room. The office is open and all glass, so I watch the receptionist go to Mason's office, and he must send her to Sara's office. She's SHN's attorney. Sara stands, and I see a noticeable baby bump. Good for her and her husband.

Mason arrives and brings me a cup of coffee. "We have whiskey, Bailey's, or Kahlúa if you need it."

"Today I'll be fine. Saturday I nearly lost my shit," I tell him.

"I don't blame you. What a fucking mess. But I think Sara has some good news for us."

"That would be outstanding."

Almost as if on cue, Sara steps into the conference room. I stand and give her a hug. "You're glowing."

"Thank you. I am six months along, and the paparazzi is just figuring it out." Sara's husband is an Arnault. They're old money, and Mason is engaged to her husband's twin sister, Caroline.

"Well, I have good news." She slides a piece of paper across the table. "This is Jeremy's employment agreement. It includes an inventions clause that covers theft, and he can't compete in the alternative energy sector if he leaves Soleil

Energy for five years."

"Great. What about the payout and his options?"

"I believe you're in the clear. Even if he can make a case that he didn't steal the information, his behavior is a violation of the ethics clause."

"Now, let's talk about an exit strategy," Mason says.

"He isn't allowed in the building," I inform him. As far as I'm concerned Jeremy's dead to me.

"That's good, but we don't know what he's stolen at this point," Mason reminds me.

"We think it's just our proposal and the patent application, which unfortunately has a lot of research—significant data and design work—but it could be more. Jim's tech team is looking into it."

"I hate to say it, but this isn't the first time we've seen this happen," Sara says. "It's our investment, too, so we want to be sure we do what we can to protect it."

She leaves with our thanks, and Mason and I prepare for our lunch.

"How well do you know Stephanie?" I ask him.

"We went to grad school at Stanford together."

"Okay, so more than just simple knowledge of her."

He nods.

When we arrive at the Waterfront Café, we're shown to a private room. Rumor has it a wealthy patron wanted a place to meet his mistress, but I'm not sure that's the case. Private rooms like this are perfect for this kind of lunch, and they make good money. We don't have to worry about being overheard or interrupted.

Jim is waiting for us, and we order drinks just as Stephanie arrives with a flourish.

"Jim…" She leans in and gives him an air kiss on his cheek.

Turning to me, she extends her hand. "I'm Stephanie Pierce."

She looks Mason up and down. "Good to see you, Mase."

"Stephanie." He gives her a curt nod.

Based on the tension between them, I realize they're former lovers. This is going to be interesting.

"Marriage agrees with you," Stephanie assesses.

"Caroline and I will marry next spring," he corrects her.

"How lucky for you," she snarks. "So, what's going on that's so urgent?"

Jim gives me a nod to go ahead.

"It's my understanding that you met with Jeremy Knowles regarding the funding of a solar film for windows last week."

She looks at me. "Maybe."

I pull Jeremy's employment agreement from a file in front of me. "Jeremy has been an employee of Soleil Energy for over five years as our CFO. Not only has he stolen the information he presented to you, but he was arrested on Saturday for that theft."

"Now that's unfortunate. It's a brilliant idea," she murmurs.

"Thank you," I say. That's quite a compliment coming from a venture capitalist.

She eyes me carefully. "I don't suppose you're looking for funding?"

"No, we've already funded it," Mason jumps in.

"No need to get bitchy," she snaps. Turning to me she asks, "Are you willing to hear our offer?"

"Only in the context of understanding what he was peddling."

"We offered twenty million for a forty-percent share of a solar film startup."

That's a shitty deal compared to what I got from Mason, but he knows I can deliver.

"There's a good chance FBI will be reaching out to you regarding this," Jim informs her.

"We have contact sheets. We've been down this road before with someone shopping technology that wasn't theirs," Stephanie says.

"Do you mind telling me who he was partnered with?" Jim

asks.

"Two gentlemen from China." Stephanie shrugs.

"I see."

My gut clenches. I'll need to act quickly with this, or I may lose my idea to some thief.

Lunch is served, and our conversation becomes more congenial.

"Will you all be attending Cecilia Lancaster's funeral tomorrow?" Stephanie asks.

"Absolutely," Mason says. "So tragic."

I nod. "We were in Las Vegas when she disappeared."

"I've heard about this mysterious card game," Stephanie says. "Who gets to play?"

"Nate actually organized it," Mason tells her. "We met in Vegas at the Shangri-la. One of the partners at my firm grew up with Jonathan Best, the owner."

Looking at Jim she asks, "Do any women play?"

I snort. "Mia Couture and Viviana Prentis are regulars. I recently won a beach house on Maui from Viviana. I'm going to check it out next week."

"Wow. You guys play for some serious dollars." She looks at Jim. "Are you playing, too?"

He shakes his head. "I go with clients. We also help with security at the Shangri-la."

"Well, if Mason can hang, I'm sure I can, so if you end up needing another player, I hope you'll call."

We finish our lunch, and as we walk out of the Waterfront Café, Stephanie pulls me aside. "I'll beat whatever Mason has offered you."

"That's very generous of you, but we've already committed to the first round, with an option for round two."

She shakes her head. "Damn. You've got a good idea. I was really excited about it."

"I'm sorry. I worked with Mason to start Soleil, and we've stayed in touch."

"Mason told you we have a history?"

"Just that you went to grad school together." I don't have the heart to tell her *she* gave away that they were former lovers. It doesn't matter in business anyway.

She nods. "Before you go back to them with your next venture, please call me."

I nod.

As she walks to her waiting car, she adds, "And make sure Nate knows I want to play poker. What's the buy-in?"

"It's steep at five million," I warn.

"I can make that happen," she says, but she's visibly disappointed. "I'll see you tomorrow."

"Thanks, Stephanie. See you tomorrow."

Chapter 8

Corrine

Cecelia's service is at ten in Sausalito, across the Golden Gate Bridge from San Francisco. On the ride over with Jackson, I look down at my black sheath dress. Gabby insisted I buy it a few years ago, and I wear it often. The hem is looking a bit ragged. I need to go shopping, but who has the time—much less the funds. I hope the dress is appropriate.

Jackson's on the phone the entire drive, bouncing from call to call. He's moved from his office in our building to his mobile office here in the car. I watch the emails come in on my cell phone and forward them to the appropriate people, but they're slowing because most of Silicon Valley is going the same place we are.

Jackson has been trying to get a meeting with Hydro, and they've been less than responsive. I know that worries him. Jim and his team have been working on it, too. I've seen our financial statements, and I know we won't close, but if Hydro hijacks his idea, I'm not sure anyone will be able to be around Jackson, he'll be so angry and miserable to work for.

As we approach the Catholic church, I'm amazed at the people lining up along the streets. They have bouquets of flowers and signs.

Cecelia Lancaster You're Missed

Find her killer

Nate, will you marry me?

People are crying. She was a beacon of light. A shroud of darkness covers us as we get closer.

"She'll be missed by so many," I murmur.

"That she will. She was such a force of nature." Jackson stares out the window.

We patiently wait in the car as it inches toward the church in the heavy traffic. People are lined up four and five deep on the sidewalks, and most of them probably didn't even know Cecelia. When our car finally pulls up to the front of the church, I'm shocked to see an actual red carpet laid out and photographers huddled behind a red velvet rope barrier. They're yelling Jackson's name, and their bulbs are flashing. He looks so striking in his black suit, crisp white shirt with French cuffs and diamond cufflinks, and a light blue silk tie.

"This isn't a movie premiere. What are these tabloid journalists thinking?" Jackson pulls me in close.

I'm sure he can tell I'm terrified. His touch is electric. His chest is hard, and a fleeting thought of what it must look like underneath his shirt crosses my mind.

We walk in, and they don't even ask my name. Inside the church is packed full of a who's who of Silicon Valley—not only every tech millionaire and billionaire, but politicians. The governor of California is talking to Nate, and I spot Jim with a beautiful dark-haired woman holding his hand. Her eyes are red-rimmed and swollen from crying. There is no joy in this room. It's low murmurs and sniffling in the solemn church.

The service is beautiful. Nate Lancaster speaks, and it's

difficult for him to get through without choking up. "Cecelia was my soulmate. You all knew how persistent she could be…" There is a chuckle in the room. "She talked almost all of you out of money for our foundation. Her passions included helping those who'd lost limbs in wars, landmines, and accidents, but also educating our future by making sure everyone has a computer."

He shares with everyone how they met and how much she meant to him and his girls. By the end, he is full-on weeping.

I'm ugly crying, as are most of the others in the church.

Cecelia's sister, Alicia, stands and gives a beautiful eulogy, which is followed by a full Catholic mass. It's absolutely lovely. After the mass, Nate follows the casket out with his girls on either side of him, and he breaks down all over again. There isn't a dry eye in the house. The girls are wailing as they roll their mother's casket into the back of the hearse. Jim holds Nate up to keep him from collapsing in despair, and the woman with him is holding one of the girls and their aunt is holding the other. It's heartbreaking.

Following the ceremony, there's a very nice reception. I like that Jackson is by my side almost the entire time.

Mason Sullivan and his fiancée, Caroline Arnault, approach us. He extends his hand and Jackson clasps it. "Hey, man." There's a sadness in his voice.

Caroline turns to me. "That certainly sucked."

I nod.

"Caroline, this is Corrine from my office. She worked with Cecelia."

"She was so lovely." Tears begin to pool in her eyes. "We worked with her foundation, too. I don't know anyone who met her who didn't want to work with her. She was kind and real. You know what I mean?"

I smile as Mason and Jackson step away.

"I'm not usually this weepy." Caroline wipes the tears from her eyes. "It's a good thing I went with waterproof mascara today." She smiles at me, and I understand. I'm sure I look like a giant raccoon with all the crying I've done.

Still, I'm a bit awestruck to be talking to *the* Caroline Arnault. She's American royalty. I'm ready for something a little more positive.

"I've seen in the supermarket tabloids…" I begin, realizing as I speak that this is a crappy thing to admit. "Will your wedding be in Italy?"

She smiles and links her arm with mine. "Cecelia would not want us crying. You're so smart. Yes, it'll be in Italy. One of my best friend's in-laws own the Bellisima vineyards, and we're getting married in Tuscany."

"How romantic. Will it be big? Or small and private?"

"A bit of both. I hope you'll come with Jackson."

I shake my head. "Oh, I'm his assistant. He'll take one of his regular girlfriends. I'm only here because I managed the relationship between the foundation and Jackson."

She cocks her head to the side. "You look good together, and he hasn't let you out of his sight all day."

I snort-laugh. "Trust me, I'm not his type. He likes Barbie dolls."

"Oh, I've met a few of them. They're not right for him. But you…" She shrugs and nods.

"What trouble are you two finding?" Mason asks as he and Jackson return. Jackson hands me a drink, and I see Mason kiss Caroline on the temple.

I'm impressed by their obvious love for one another. That's what I want.

We mingle for another hour. Each time Jackson and I get separated, I search until I find him talking to someone, and he spots me and smiles. My heart beats a bit faster. I'm not sure why I'm feeling this way about my boss.

Jim approaches me and introduces me to the pretty woman he's with. "This is Kate Monroe, my fiancée."

I grin. "So wonderful to meet you. What a crappy day."

"I know. Cecelia had sent out invites to my bridal shower, and I had to cancel."

I shake my head. "Oh no. That's not very fun."

She shrugs. "I had a friend do it for me. I'm actually fine without one." She looks over at Jim and smiles. "All I care about is getting married to that handsome hunk over there."

I blush, not because Jim isn't a good-looking guy, but because it's great to see her lust after him so clearly.

Kate sighs. "Can you believe Alicia's eulogy? I loved when she said Cecelia knew the money she and Nate had was more than enough for many generations, and she wanted to be sure it was shared."

"I agree. She met Nate long before he had a penny to his name. It's amazing what they were able to accomplish together. I was shocked when she said they lost their brother last year to violence. How terrible for their parents that they've buried two children."

She nods. "Heartbreaking for sure. But I was glad to hear her say they've just hit a bump in the road, and the work will continue."

"Is she going to take over the foundation?" I ask.

"I don't think so. She's the main caregiver for her parents, and she wants to be a strong influence on Cecelia's kids."

After we chat a little more Caroline excuses herself, and Jackson reappears by my side. The crowds slowly dissipate, and people return to the City. It was a sad event, but also full of joy—definitely all Cecelia Lancaster.

As we drive back over the Golden Gate Bridge and head into town, I watch the sailboats tack and cross one another while the barges line up to enter port below.

"Would you like to join me for dinner tonight?" Jackson asks.

I can feel heat emanating from him across the backseat. I want to. I want to learn more about Jackson. What drives him? Why does he push himself so hard? Where did he grow up? What's his favorite color? What does he like to do when he isn't working?

"Thanks, but I should get home. We have an early

morning tomorrow."

He nods. "You're right."

The drive back to my apartment seems endless after that. The crackle in the air is palpable, but I'm exhausted from the flood of emotions today. Still, it's taking all my willpower not to jump my boss. I can't explain why I feel like this, but I think it must be my psyche searching for comfort after such a crappy day.

We arrive at my apartment. "Thanks for the ride." I open the door and begin to exit, but Jackson gets out behind me.

"Where are you going? Isn't someone from Jim's team always walking you to your apartment?"

"Yes, but it's not necessary."

"It *is* necessary." He steps back and opens his arms. "Lead the way."

It's not worth the argument, so I trot up the stairs.

He follows me up, and when we reach the landing below my apartment, my front door looks off—as if it's cracked open. I stop and study it. That's strange. Could Stacy or Angela have returned home early?

Jackson follows my gaze. "Did you leave your door open when you left?"

Brian stood with me as I locked the door this morning. "No, but maybe one of my roommates came home early."

Everything in Jackson's body tenses, and he stomps up the last few steps. He pushes the door open and blocks my view.

I scurry up after him, and despite his broad shoulders, I can see the mayhem in my apartment. My hand goes to my mouth. Everything has been ransacked, and I catch a glimpse of blue spray paint on the walls.

"Who... Who...would do this?" I begin to sob.

I try to pass him and get a better look. There's so much to clean up. What am I going to tell my roommates?

"Come on. Don't touch anything," he says. "Let's go downstairs and call the police."

We return to the waiting car, and Jackson gets on the

phone. "Jim, there's been a break-in at Corrine's. Call Detective Lenning and please meet them at her apartment. Then when you're ready, we'll be at my apartment. I'm taking Corrine there."

I'm numb. They were in my apartment. They touched our things. I feel absolutely violated.

Jackson takes me in his arms and holds me tight as the car zips up the hill to his apartment. As we drive, he jumps from call to call, and they're all concerning me and my apartment. I try to listen, but I can't follow what he says.

When we arrive, I stagger to the elevator and follow Jackson into his penthouse apartment. He sits me down on the couch and returns with a small glass of amber liquid.

"Here, drink this. It shouldn't do anything more than calm your nerves. Jim is on his way over. The police are headed to your apartment."

I nod. "Who could've done this?"

"When you left your apartment this morning, Brian escorted you down, and he saw you lock up."

I'm unclear if he's asking for confirmation or stating fact. "Were my roommates home? Stacy is supposed to be in Mexico with her boyfriend, Sean. And Angela has been at a trade show in Orlando. Were they there? Are they okay?"

Jackson shakes his head. "No one was in the apartment. But all the bedrooms and the kitchen look the same as the main room. When are they due to return from their trips?"

"Both on Sunday night." I cover my face, but I'm all cried out from the afternoon.

"I think everyone will need new beds, and your couch is destroyed. Whoever came in was very angry."

"Why me?" I lament.

"I have a guest room, and you'll stay here," Jackson informs me.

My head whips up. "I can't stay with you! You're my boss."

"Why not?"

Is he off his rocker? There are so many reasons staying with him is a bad idea.

He cocks his head to the side and in a low voice asks again, "Why not?"

"We spent all day together," I respond. I don't add that I'm also thinking he's a god, and I have dirty dreams about him.

A glorious grin crosses his face, and my heart melts. "You'll have your own room with an en suite bath."

I'm not about to tell him I think he's sex on a stick. And since when do I think that anyway? I have lost my mind.

"Corrine, where do your parents live? Texas, right?"

I nod.

"Hotel rooms in the city start at four hundred dollars a night. Do you have that kind of money for the next few weeks?"

I shake my head and realize my life just took a monumental shift. "I'm going to have to move home to Houston," I murmur. It feels difficult to breathe.

"No. You can't do that to me," he counters.

I look at him, confused. Do what to him? What does he mean?

I stand. "I need to call my father. I'll get a hotel room for two weeks so I can train my replacement."

"No, you won't." Jackson runs his hands through his hair. "I can't… I won't let you. I have plenty of room here." He's almost pleading with me.

But I have to keep work and the rest of my life separate. There's no fucking way I can see him with disheveled hair or without his shirt. Nor could I stand to see him and any Barbies kanoodling. It would be beyond torture.

There's a knock at the door, and Jim walks in. He gives me a sad smile. "How are you doing?"

I'm lost, and I don't know what to do. "It was nice to meet Kate today."

"She really liked you, too." He opens a folder and hands me some photos.

I sit down hard. They're pictures of my apartment. The first is a picture of the living room. The couch is a wreck. It's as if someone took a knife and cut every pillow and cushion, then pulled out all the stuffing, which now covers every inch of the floor. The books from the bookshelf are dumped in a disheveled pile. Every picture and frame had been shattered. The walls have blue spray paint that says, "You were warned!"

I look up at Jim. I'm confused. I'm totally finished with Bobby. "I haven't talked to Bobby Sanders."

The next picture shows our tiny kitchen. The normally overstuffed cabinets are all open and empty. It looks like broken glass everywhere, along with a fine covering of white powder, which I assume is the flour from the canister on the countertop.

"Why is she doing this to me? I don't want him."

"Could it be someone else who perceives you were in her way to Bobby Sanders?"

"He has thousands, literally thousands, of women who chase him. He has a stack of nude and partially nude selfies women have emailed him. He's printed them out."

Jim looks surprised. "We'll check it out." Then he turns to Jackson. "Where is she staying?"

"She wants to go home to Houston," he replies, sounding disgusted. "I've offered her my guest room. It even has a private bathroom."

Jim turns to me. "There's an investigation. You can't leave, Corrine."

"I need to call my dad. I'll see if he can lend me some money, and I'll find a hotel room." I despise the idea of giving my dad any way to control me, but I don't see any option.

"You don't need to do that," Jackson insists.

"Corrine, why can't you stay here?" Jim says. "He has a guestroom, and my team can provide plenty of coverage—much easier than you being in a seedy hotel."

I look at Jim. I'll be fired once I say this, so maybe this is my chance. "I wait on Mr. Graham all day. It's my job, and I love it. I'm good at it, but I can't come home and do that all night, too. We work long hours, and I can't come back after a long day in the office and fetch things for him and whatever girlfriend shows up at his apartment."

She pauses to look at me. "And I hate that he dates airheads and not women with a brain," I conclude, crossing my arms.

Chapter 9

Jackson

Corrine is analyzing the women I date again. She seems to have given this some thought. Interesting.

Jim smirks like he totally understands. He must think the same thing. Also, interesting. I never thought of a relationship as something I had time for, so I guess I haven't been too strict with my female quality standards. But whatever. Now is not the time to ponder that.

I turn to my assistant, who still stands defiantly with her arms crossed. "Look, Corrine, none of the women I date has ever been to my house," I assure her. "And here, *I* do the taking care of. It would make me very happy to take care of you. I promise you don't need to cater to me here. And no Barbies. Promise."

I can see she wants to refuse.

"Just try it for a few days," Jim suggests. "Let the police

work through the case before you move home."

She starts to weep. "What am I going to tell my roommates?"

"I'll call them," I assure her as I gather her in my arms. "Once the police release the scene, I'll have a crew come in and clean it up, and I'll replace any of the furniture, clothes, and items that were damaged."

She pulls away from me. "No. You can't do that. I'll get it picked up and see what I can get repaired."

"Really, let me take care of this. You work hard for me, and it isn't a hardship." I take out the photos and show them to her again. "I'm sorry, but I don't think this is salvageable. Please let me do this for you."

With a big sigh and a cringe, she nods as she pores over the images. "Why didn't one of my neighbors call the police? Someone had to have heard something."

Jim shakes his head. "It seems Mrs. Collins from downstairs was at a doctor's appointment, and the rest of your neighbors were at work."

Corrine sighs. "Figures. She owns the building and is always home. I still should call my dad."

She needs to be doing something—she's struggling right now. "Let's do that together, so your dad can feel assured someone is looking out for you." I pull out my phone and hand it to her.

She dials and places the phone between us on speaker.

"Woods residence."

"Hey, Monica, it's me. Is my father available?"

"Just a moment. Let me check."

Wow. So formal. I may need to go back and review Corrine's background check. What's going on there?

"Sunshine," booms through the speaker on the phone.

That's more of what I was expecting.

"Daddy!" Corrine's shoulders tense. "Sorry to bother you. There's been a problem here." She slips into the most delicious southern drawl.

"Worse than what happened earlier this week?" he asks.

I can hear the stress rising in his voice and the fluster in Corrine's.

"Mr. Woods?" I interject. "This is Jackson Graham. I'm standing with Corrine and Jim Adelson, the head of my security team and owner of Clear Security. Today, while Corrine and I were at Cecelia Lancaster's funeral, someone broke into Corrine's apartment. The home was ransacked. Anything that could be broken was. The police are investigating, so we need Corrine to remain here in San Francisco. I wanted to let you know, I've offered her a guest suite in my apartment. Jim's team has been on duty with her since Wednesday. She's safe with us."

"I see." There's a small moment of silence, and I know he must be trying to determine the best way to protect his daughter. "Corrine? Can you pick up the phone?"

"Yes, Daddy?"

I can still hear his question. "What do you want to do?"

She looks at me and gives me a half-smile. "I don't know. Jim can probably watch me here better than if I'm in a hotel."

I hear him say, "I'd like to talk to Jackson again."

"Yes, Daddy." She hands me my phone.

I take a deep breath, ready for the wrath of a protective father.

"Mr. Graham," he says in a deep baritone. "Look, I checked you out when my little girl went to work for you. If this is a player move to get her into your bed, you'll regret this."

I chuckle. Corrine has heard every word. She blushes and covers her eyes.

"No, sir, it's not. As you know, your daughter is very proud, but we believe this is a real threat, and it's easier on Jim and his team for her to be here."

He sighs. "I never liked that apartment. She literally lived in a closet. All that fit in her damn room was a silly twin bed. There certainly isn't room for anyone else at her current place."

Twin bed? Closet? I've got to get her out of there.

"I promise to look out for her," I assure him.

"Thank you. May I speak with Corrine again?"

"Of course." I hand her my phone, and she walks away. I don't know what to do without my phone.

"He's my boss," I hear her say. "Yes, I know that's how you and Monica met. Trust me, Daddy. I'm not his type."

That stings worse than anything she could've said. She's exactly my type—beautiful, smart, a wicked sense of humor, and most importantly, she doesn't care about my money. Then I remember she refers to my dates as Barbies—all beautiful women when naked, but that's it. Nothing more. I have no doubt Corrine would look delectable naked, and she's everything I want in a woman.

But I can't go there. She works for me. That's a horrible idea, especially right now. Someone needs to tell my dick that.

"I'm going to check on Detective Lenning. This is taking too long. I'll be back," Jim tells me.

I really am lost without my phone. It occurs to me that Corrine needs to eat. I go over to the stack of takeout menus I have and order Chinese from my landline. It's getting late, and I'm sure she must be hungry. Plus, this could show her I'm not entirely inept at taking care of things myself.

As I wait for my phone and Corrine, I watch the game on TV. After a few minutes she walks out in her bare feet, and she's pulled her hair up. The curls that have fallen from her updo look sexy. She really doesn't know what she does to men.

She's in my apartment, and she looks stunning. She's my assistant. I need to stop thinking like this.

"I ordered dinner," I tell her.

"Oh, right. Thank you. I forgot it was late."

She looks out the window. It's dark outside.

"Jim went back to your apartment to find out what's keeping the detective."

"I can wait in my room and be out of your way."

That's not what I want. "No, that's silly. Please, I want you to feel at home here."

Her brow knits.

I'm trying too hard, and it's glaringly obvious.

"Let me give you a tour." It's all I can think of to pass the time and fill the awkward silence. I walk her around the apartment. It's enormous, even by non-San Francisco standards.

"What made you buy such a palatial space?" she asks, her eyes wide as we walk from room to room.

"My mom used to work in real estate, and she talked me into it. It was the first thing I bought when my first company went public."

"She has excellent taste."

"She'd love that you think that. It's so much more house than I need, but I think she hopes I'll grow into it."

"Not likely," she mutters.

"I have nothing against marriage. Look at what Nate and Cecelia had. If I can find that kind of love, I'd go for it and have as big a family as she wants."

"I guess you need to look for it."

That comment has a ring of truth. Her honesty stops me cold. "I suppose I do."

The bell rings, and our dinner has arrived. I'm saved.

As we sit down to eat, I'm very proud that I knew Corrine's favorite Chinese dish—kung pao chicken. She always chooses it when she orders Chinese for lunch at the office.

Corrine clears her throat. "I'm sorry. I have a terrible habit of being too honest. Who you date is none of my business. You're my boss, and I do what I'm told. I apologize for what I said."

I shake my head. "Your honesty is always appreciated and is important for me to hear. Don't ever change."

I'm almost ready to ask her some personal questions, to get

to know her a little better when I hear Jim arrive—and he's talking to someone. As they round the corner, I see it's Detective Lenning.

"I hope we're not interrupting," Detective Lenning says.

"No, I'm just making sure Corrine eats something today," I tell him.

He nods and opens a folder. He places several crime-scene photos on the table in front of her.

She looks at them mid-bite. I see tears in her eyes. "Everything is destroyed," she whispers.

There's blue spray paint on the walls.

I warned you. Next time will be worse.

Whore

Bitch

Keep your hands off my man

She can't look any of us in the eyes. "I haven't contacted Bobby, nor have I contacted his girlfriend. You can check my cell phone records, the landline phone records, and the office phone numbers. I'm telling the truth."

Detective Lenning sighs. "We've already checked, and you're correct. We've also reached out to Mr. Sanders and spoken to his current girlfriend, Collette. They both have good, strong alibis for today. We're looking at some of the women who've sent him pictures and other women from his past. He shared with us the name of a woman he was seeing while you were dating, but he doesn't think any of the women who send him fan mail would go this far. We have collected the letters and photos, and we'll go through those."

I can tell by the pained look on Corrine's face that she didn't know he was seeing anyone else while they were together. *Jackass.*

I look down at the pictures of her bedroom. Every article of clothing she owns has been cut and sliced, and they're all in a pile on her trashed bed. I can see the coils of the bed springs. There is a picture of her with a man and a woman, probably her parents. It's destroyed. The glass is shattered. The frame is no longer square. In another picture, the plants in the living room have been dumped and the dirt spread across the carpet. There is nothing here that's salvageable.

Detective Lenning asks Corrine more questions about possible women who may be upset over Bobby Sanders. He then asks about women who may be upset about me.

"Jackson?" she asks, alarmed.

My head whips up. "Detective, I... I don't really have any...any real girlfriends."

"So, you're a love-them-and-leave-them kind of guy?" he presses.

He doesn't like me much.

I'm feeling a little attacked, but I know they're just trying to find out who's behind this.

I clear my throat. "No, I date women, and I may date them for a while, but it's never serious, and I'm very clear about that upfront. I run a multinational company, and I'm in the process of starting a new venture. I don't have any time for a serious relationship."

"And what about women who contact you that you've never met?"

"I have a phone log in the office," Corrine offers. "Jackson gets about two dozen or so dinner invites a day and probably a marriage proposal once a week."

I do?

The detective nods. "I'd like that phone log and a list of the women you've dated so we can make sure to cross them off our list."

"Of course."

Detective Lenning asks Corrine a few more questions about where she was today and what we were doing.

"I'm sorry for the loss of your friend," he says.

She nods and looks weepy again.

Detective Lenning excuses himself, and we agree to have the items he's asking for sent over. Jim remains for a few moments.

"Corrine, are you okay to stay here tonight?" he asks.

She nods, and I feel a great sense of relief. "It's not like I have any other choice."

"We can cover you wherever you want to go," Jim assures her. "If you don't want to stay here, you let me know."

She shakes her head. "I'm fine. I'm already inconveniencing everyone."

"You're not inconveniencing me. In fact, quite the opposite," I tell her. "You're just fine."

I walk Jim to the elevator. "Is she going to be okay?" I ask.

He looks over at her. "I imagine at this point she feels highly violated. Anything she had in that apartment of any value to her personally is absolutely destroyed. Detective Lenning and I both agree that someone is incredibly angry with her, and she is not safe by herself."

"Her roommates return in the next few days. Do I need to put them up in hotel rooms away from the apartment?"

"I think that's not a bad idea. Maybe if you frame it as you're fixing the apartment after the break-in, it'll feel less intrusive to them."

I nod. "I'll call them tonight."

There's a sudden scream in the darkness. I sit straight up, and I'm out of bed before I know what's going on.

"Corrine?" I run down the hall to her bedroom. Usually I sleep naked, so I'm grateful I thought to sleep in boxers tonight.

I swing her bedroom door open. She's thrashing back and forth in the bed and whimpering. Her exposed thigh distracts me.

I realize she's having a nightmare. I walk over and shake her shoulder lightly. "Corrine?"

She wakes up, startled. She looks around and recognizes

me after a moment, but she pulls the covers up tight.

"It's okay," I say in a soothing voice. "You were having a nightmare."

"I forgot where I was." She begins to whimper.

"Please don't cry. You're just fine. I'm here for you."

She sniffs. "I'm sorry. I didn't mean to wake you."

"Don't worry about me. I don't sleep well anyway."

I sit down at the edge of her bed and the neck of the T-shirt I lent her slips over her shoulder. My cock pays attention. I try to concentrate on her nightmare and not her beautiful alabaster skin.

"It's nothing. Really."

The light from the hall casts this beautiful glow on her, and despite her disheveled hair, I've never seen her look so lovely. I reach for her and pull her close. She collapses into me. Her arms snake around my waist, and I take in her smell. She wears a perfume I can't quite name, but I recognize the scent. You have to be close to smell it, and she smells so good.

"I'm sorry. I don't know why I'm reacting like this," she says through tears.

Usually, tears have me running to the hills, but I want her to feel better. I want her to feel safe.

"You can stay here as long as you need."

I start to stand, but she doesn't let go. "Please don't leave me." Her tears begin to fall. "He's hurt me so badly. Not only did he say those awful things, but he was cheating on me, too. What did I ever see in that guy? Why is my picker so bad?"

We lean back against the headboard, and I hold her tight. Her arms remain around me, and I feel content as we sit in silence.

After some time, I hear the rhythmic sound of her breathing. She's fallen asleep curled up against me. I almost never want to spend the night with women, but I'm shocked at how right this feels.

Sometime later, when I wake to the sunlight, I can tell instantly that it's much later than I usually wake. We're spooning, and my cock is nestled against Corrine's backside, pulsing and begging for entry. My hand is holding her soft breast. I should let it go, but I don't want to. I smell her floral-scented shampoo. I want her.

She rolls over. My hand falls away, but my cock is still obviously as hard as a steel rod.

"We should probably get into the office," she says.

"I know." I enjoy a few more moments lying next to her. I don't want this to end. Then it occurs to me. "My flight to Maui is tomorrow after work, right?"

"Yes. I should be able to move back into my place by then. I have a lot of cleaning up to do before my roommates get home."

"I don't think that's a good idea. I already told you I'll have somebody come in and clean up the apartment, but I think you should come with me to Maui."

I say that last part quickly, so I can't change my mind.

She sits up and turns to me. "What? Why on Earth would I do that?"

I try not to notice her pebbled nipples beneath the T-shirt, but I've never been so sure of anything. "I don't want you staying alone, and you could use some time away. When was the last time you took any vacation?"

"It's been a while, but we already discussed that Detective Lenning needs me to be close by."

That was really just my excuse to get her to stay at my place. "You'll have the jet at your disposal, so if he needs you back, you can come back." I look into her caramel-colored eyes, noticing their gold flecks. I could get lost in there forever. "Please come with me to Maui."

"What will people at the office think?" she asks as she begins to bite her thumbnail.

"Who cares?"

She takes a big breath. "I truly appreciate your offer. Maui sounds amazing, but people already think I've gotten on my knees to keep my job. If I go with you to Maui, that will only reinforce that rumor."

"All that matters is that we know the truth," I tell her.

Her shoulders fall, and I know I've said the wrong thing.

I try again. "Look, you're my assistant. The house has multiple bedrooms with their own bathrooms. Just because I take my admin doesn't mean you get on your knees for me. It means I work a lot, and together, we are assessing whether the house should remain in my portfolio."

A smile crosses her face that finally reaches her eyes. "If my boss requires my assistance for a work-related trip, then I must go."

I can't wait. What is this ridiculous giddiness I feel?

She sighs. "I should warn you, though, my bathing suit was in my apartment, and I'll need to do some shopping."

"You have access to my personal card. Buy whatever you need."

"I can afford a bathing suit," she informs me.

"I know you can, but I want to do this for you."

The idea of four days away with Corrine with her in a bathing suit does something to me. But for now, I need to get to work. I still need to get a meeting with Hydro before they start producing my solar film with stolen plans.

Chapter 10

Corrine

Maui. I'm so excited. Time away from this place has never, ever sounded better than it does right now. I have nothing to pack, and I'm not even sure where to start.

I'll worry about that later. Right now, I need to make it through my day. I look around my desk for the next task I need to tackle.

Waking up with Jackson was way too comfortable. It took all of my willpower not to jump him this morning. His not-so-little friend wanted to play, but things are already awkward enough.

My cell phone pings.

Gabby: Hey. Where are you?

Me: At work. Where are you?

Gabby: I'm at work. Are you OK? Where have you been? I went by your place last night, and the police were there. I called and texted, but I didn't hear back.

Me: I'm sorry. I started to text you and got pulled away.

Gabby: What happened?

Me: Someone broke into my apartment and completely trashed it.

Gabby: OMG!!! Are you OK?

Me: Yes. But everything was destroyed. Every dish broken, glass shattered, and clothes, beds, couches all slashed.

Gabby: Are you fucking with me?

Me: I wish I were. The asswipe spray-painted the walls with crap, much like the note from the box last Wednesday.

Gabby: Do the police think it's related?

Me: Yes, and Jackson and the security team won't let me go home.

Gabby: Where are you staying? Are you going to be OK?

I'm not going to tell her I'm staying at Jackson's. She'll have a fit at first, then talk me into sleeping with him, and I don't need any nudges in that direction. My body is already on board with that idea.

Me: Yes, I'll be fine. I'm just disappointed about the damage. Jackson has some business in Maui, and he's

insisting I join him, so we're leaving for Maui tomorrow.

Gabby: What? Is his business naked twister with his latest?

I laugh out loud. Thankfully Jackson's latest isn't coming, but it is a good reminder that while he's flirty, he has a long line of women.

Me: He's surprisingly protective. He even called my dad to give him an update and assure him he's looking out for me.

Gabby: Can you meet for drinks tonight?

Me: Sorry, I can't. Late night here, and we're leaving tomorrow. Gotta run. Phone ringing.

I quickly answer the office phone. "Jackson Graham's office."

"Hello, my name is Tiffany Newton, and I'm calling with Nordstrom. I'm looking for Corrine Woods."

"Speaking. How may I help you?"

"Mr. Graham has asked that I put together some clothes for you. He mentioned you were heading out on a business trip. He suggested you come to the store today. Are you available at three?"

"Ohhhh… I appreciate your help, but as much as I'm sure everything you pick would be amazing, in all honesty, I'm his admin, and I couldn't afford it." I have three hundred and forty-seven dollars in my checking account, and a ten-thousand-dollar Visa bill doesn't sound appealing at all.

"He warned me you'd try to refuse," she says, and I can hear her smile. "He's paying for everything. He's outlined what you need for your upcoming business trip. I can send a car for you, or do you already have one?"

"Let me get back to you." We hang up, and I look up and stare at the white, square ceiling tiles. How will I ever pay him back? When I left my father's house, I was determined I'd never let any man control me with money again.

I need to talk to Jackson and explain. I see the red light on my phone, which indicates he's on the phone. I watch, waiting for it to go black as I formulate my plan.

Twenty minutes later, I have notes on what I want to say, and I'm ready to confront him now that he's off the phone.

I knock and enter. "Mr. Graham?"

As I approach his desk, he smiles and sits back. "I'm guessing you spoke with Tiffany and you're refusing the offer of a wardrobe."

I stop short. "How did you—"

He holds up his hands to stop me. "Look, I get it. You'd rather buy it all yourself."

I nod, a bit dumbfounded.

"We're going to Maui for possibly a week. It depends on when Hydro will meet with me and if the police need you back sooner. Every piece of clothing you own was destroyed. To replace that will cost you thousands of dollars."

"I understand, but—"

"Hold on. I'm not done." He takes a breath. "You don't even borrow from your father, who I gather is somewhat wealthy."

I nod.

"You know how much money is in my personal accounts. You've seen my investment portfolio. You know I can afford for you to buy anything at Nordstrom without issue. We have things to do while we're in Maui, and you need some business clothes, a bathing suit, and other things to wear. I'm certainly fine if you choose to go naked, but I get the impression that isn't your style. Please accept the wardrobe as a gift. Not a loan."

I know he's right, but this is a lot. And even gifts can come with strings attached. He and I have entered The Twilight

Zone these past few days, and I still have no idea what to make of it.

"What if you consider it your bonus this year?" He crosses his heart and holds up three fingers.

I take a deep breath and channel my grandmother. "Okay. Thank you for your generosity." Lord knows I do deserve a bonus.

"That was really hard to say, wasn't it?" He's grinning because he knows he's won.

"You have no idea. I guess I'm going to Nordstrom at three. You have an interview at two that I suspect won't be over by then, unless it's a dud."

"I know her. Her name is Cheryl Wedgwood. If she commits to working for us, we'll be in great shape."

"My fingers are crossed, and I'll do a secret dance for your success." His eyes gravitate to my hips, and his eyes turn dark with lust. *Why did I just say that?*

"Enjoy shopping. Promise me you won't look at price tags. I'll see you at the apartment tonight."

"Thank you." *The apartment.* He says that so casually. Working for him and living in his house is complicated—not to mention flying three thousand miles away. It's not the work, and it's not him specifically; it's me and the fact that my body wants him and is talking a lot louder than my mind.

Two and a half hours of shopping is absolutely exhausting. I'm out of practice. I used to be able to do that all day. And, shopping with a personal shopper is a little different. Once Tiffany had my sizes, she figured out my style and came up with everything, finding dozens of outfits for me to try on. And because Jackson had warned her that I would be price-conscious, she removed every price tag, so I knew nothing other than these were beautifully made clothes that looked incredibly nice on me.

In the end, she set me up with ten business outfits, several changes of casual clothes for Maui, and a tankini. She also insisted on some very racy lingerie. When I explained I had no one to wear it for, she said, *"Never wear something for a man, and certainly never for another woman. Always wear your clothes for you."* I also left the store with jewelry, shoes, more handbags than I could count, and cosmetics.

It's more than I need, but I can return what I don't wear and credit his credit card. I don't want him to think I'm taking advantage.

Tiffany said she would wrap things up and send the packages to me. She sent me home with just a small bag.

When I finally get back to Jackson's apartment, I immediately lie down and put my feet up. I can't believe how tired I am.

My phone pings.

Jackson: How did it go at Nordstrom?

Me: I bought one of everything. I hope you're happy.

Jackson: Can't wait to see it. Any interest in dinner tonight?

Me: I was just thinking about some takeout. Any preference?

Jackson: There's a great Thai place that delivers.

Me: Sounds perfect. I can order. What would you like?

Jackson: I got it. I promised to take care of you, remember? Do you want the pad Thai noodles with shrimp, tofu, and chicken?

That's what I always order. I'm stunned he's paid

attention. Stunned.

Me: Yes, please.

The doorbell rings, and Brian begins to bring all the shopping bags back to my room. There are so many, it's embarrassing.

I follow him and begin to open the packages of clothes. Tiffany even included a suitcase and an overnight bag. As I unwrap, I feel like it's Christmas morning.

It also feels like a big project. This is a lot of clothing. I've never bought this much at once *ever*. This might actually be a bigger wardrobe than I owned before my apartment was destroyed. I set about hanging things up, making piles, and filling the drawers in the room. That feels a little too much like I'm moving in—which I'm not—but I don't know what else to do.

Finally, I come up for air and am pleased with the order I've imposed on the chaos. I open the small bag Tiffany sent home with me and hold up a bikini I didn't pick out. There isn't much to it.

Jackson sticks his head in. His eyes immediately go to the thin fabric. "Can't wait to see you in that."

I drop it and immediately feel my blush. "I didn't pick it out. She included it with a note." I stuff it back in the shopping bag.

"What did she say?"

I reluctantly pick it up. Why did I tell him she sent a note?

> *Corrine,*
> *Thank you for spending the afternoon with me. I hope to see you again soon. A small token from me. This will look fantastic on you. Take a chance and wear it.*
> *Tiffany*

Jackson smiles. "Tiffany knows what she's talking about.

Dinner's here. Come on out." He disappears down the hallway.

Oh my God, I can't wear this with Jackson. I might as well walk around naked. I take a few breaths and attempt to collect myself.

"Are you coming?" he yells.

I take one more deep breath. "Yes, I'm coming."

Jackson has set the table and actually plated our food. I'm impressed.

"I have a nice bottle of pinot gris. Would you care for a glass with your dinner?"

"Sure."

He places a glass of golden wine in front of me and sits down.

I take my first bite, and it's outstanding. "How did the interview with Cheryl go?" I sip my wine and wait for him to tell me.

"I think she's going to take the CFO position. Emerson Healy at SHN was clear with her about why the position was open, and she shared some thoughts about completing an audit if she's hired. She's worked in alternative energy before. But she's asking for some serious options in the new venture."

"How many options and what percentage of ownership would she hold? Can you give her what you got back from Jeremy?"

"That's my hope. I need the lawyer at SHN to officially verify. That would make it easier. She's looking at twenty percent, which is more than Jeremy had, so I'd have to give her some of mine. If he keeps his shares because of the contract, together they would own thirty percent, and I can't let that happen."

"Makes sense. What are your concerns about her?"

He sits back in his chair and studies me a moment. "That's a great question. Without a doubt, she knows her stuff. I guess she reminds me of my mom a little bit, and I worry I'll subconsciously treat her like I do my mom."

This is a surprising statement. He dotes on his mom. "I've never seen you treat your mom poorly."

"When she gets too bossy, I tend to tune her out, and I ignore her even if I know she's right."

I sit back and laugh. "You do that to me sometimes, too."

"I do not." His hand goes to his hip, and the noodles from his dish dangle from his chopsticks.

"Sure, you do. Remember when I told you Marilyn in the user interface group needed help? You ignored me, and she went out on stress leave."

"I did that once, and not because I was ignoring you. I just didn't want to hire anyone that might threaten Marilyn."

I have many examples, mostly because it's something that drives me crazy. "Okay, then what about when engineering wanted Mr. Pibb in the employee fridge?"

"What's wrong with Dr. Pepper?"

"It's not the same. You ignored me, and it cost us two days of work over some silly drinks."

"Fine. I do it to all the women in my life."

"No, you don't. You don't do it to the women you date," I remind him.

"Of course I do."

"What about the one who talked you into taking her to Vegas with you? It was evident to me you didn't want her to go."

He holds up his hand to stop me. "Okay, you're right. I took her, and while she was there, she hit on the owner of the casino, so I dumped her."

I'm giggling. "She must be pissed to know you won a beautiful place in Maui, and she'll never see it."

He smiles back at me. "No, she won't. She's never even seen this place."

He mentioned before that none of his girlfriends ever come to his apartment. I need to explore that further, but not tonight.

"All I ask is that you try to listen. If you don't like what a strong woman tells you, politely tell her you'll think about it. Then you don't look like an ass when you realize she's right."

"Great advice. Are you always right?"

I snort. "God, no. One small reminder: Bobby Sanders?"

Jackson rolls his eyes. "He's an ass. But it's his loss, certainly not yours."

We have a lovely dinner. Jackson is fun and self-deprecating. He underplays his intelligence, and I love the twinkle in his eyes. When we're finished, I look at the clock and realize we drank an entire bottle of wine.

"I need to pack for tomorrow," I tell him. "Hawaii is typically casual. What should I be prepared for?"

"Pack a dress, as we may meet the guys from Hydro, so I want us to be ready. But otherwise you're right. Shorts and bathing suits are all you need."

"Shirts are optional?" I tease.

"I'm good with that if you are." He grins wide and looks down at my chest.

He wouldn't know what to do with my natural breasts. Ha!

Holy cow. My panties are soaking wet.

The next morning my office line rings before I can even take my coat off and put our coffee orders down. "Hi, this is Matt Bird, your pilot. The airport in Maui is having some runway work done. It'll be closed from 8:00 p.m. until six o'clock the next morning. So, if you want to arrive today, we need to take off by 4:00 p.m. Otherwise we can't leave until after 3:00 a.m."

I thank the pilot and promise to get back to him shortly. When I go in to alert Jackson, he just looks at me.

"We can sleep on the plane," I offer. The idea of sleeping on the flight doesn't exactly sound restful, but it is Maui. "It's up to you. We can work or sleep."

He looks down at his desk and taps his pen.

"What does my schedule look like this afternoon?" He studies me carefully.

"Phone calls."

"What's on your calendar?" he asks.

"Fielding date and marriage proposals for you," I quip.

"That's so weird, isn't it?" He quirks his face in confusion and disgust.

"No comment." I think it's psychotic, but he doesn't need to know that.

"You know, if we leave before four, we can work on the flight and land in time for dinner. Can you alert the house staff we'll be in for dinner?"

"Sounds good to me." I feel like skipping out of the room.

Chapter 11

Corrine

No surprise here, but we've finished lunch, and instead of getting ready to go, Jackson's on the phone. Brian and Ben patiently wait in the chairs outside his office, across from me. We're running twenty minutes late.

I call the pilot. "We haven't left yet. What's the window?"

"We've got some time. The headwinds aren't too bad," he assures me.

I hang up with my stomach in knots. I know we can go later, but when I spoke to the majordomo, Jason Crier, and the cook, Leilani Palakiko, they were excited we were coming, and Leilani was planning a big feast. I'm already hungry.

I have about two dozen projects I could work on, but I know if I start on any of them, Jackson will walk out, and all of that work will be for nothing. Maybe if we need to go, I should do just that.

I open a file on my computer and begin balancing some account receipts for his expenses and try to ignore the passing time.

The light indicating he's on the phone is still bright red. And we're coming up on an hour past the time we needed to leave. I call the pilot again.

"We're still good," he stresses.

"We still have thirty minutes in clear traffic," I explain. "We aren't just across the street. And the longer we wait, the worse the traffic's going to be."

"Let me know when you leave, and I'll file the flight plan."

I sigh as I hang up. If he's not stressed, I'm going to follow his lead.

Finally, Jackson's light goes off, and relief floods me. I begin to save the file and gather up the receipts when *dammit* if the light doesn't go on again.

This man is going to kill me. How does he get here at the same time every day, yet once he gets here, I have to herd him around with his schedule.

We're getting close to an hour and a half delay. I scribble a note to hand Jackson.

> *We're nearing the close of our window to arrive before they shut down the runway. You're so busy, why don't we wait and go in the morning?*

I knock softly and enter his office. He looks up at me. "Emerson, that's fantastic news. Great. I'll give her a call."

I hand him the note. He glances at it, holds up a finger, and shakes his head.

I'm not sure what he means.

"Thanks so much for all your help." He hangs up and looks at me. "Did you know I have a private plane license?"

"Yes, Mr. Graham. I did know that."

"Did you know my Learjet 75 can fly almost Mach One? That's really fast."

"I can't say that I've studied your plane's capabilities." I put my hands on my hips, ready to sass him.

"Well, what takes a commercial flight six hours will take us under five. I know Matt, and I know how he padded the time because he thinks I'm always late." He stands, throws a few things into his bag, and picks up his dark cashmere coat. "He also knows I know he likes to fly fast."

"He didn't give me a drop-dead time to leave. I just felt I was putting pressure on him."

Jackson swings the coat over his shoulders and looks more delicious than usual. A part of me can't believe I'm going to Hawaii with him, but the little voice in my head reminds me I'm not going as his date but his assistant.

"How many times did you call him?"

I shake my head and smile. I'm caught. "Twice."

"You've been a naughty girl." He winks at me, and my insides melt. Maybe all the flirting we're doing will lead to something. *Would that be a good thing?*

I can't help myself. "I suppose I must be punished then."

Jackson stumbles a bit and grins as he looks at me. "Ten spanks it is," he says.

My heart beats fast. "Ten?"

"Yes. Five for each call."

I don't know why, but the idea of being spanked by him is very appealing. I bite my lip and try to control my breathing. I gather up my things under his watchful eye. The guys stand to escort us out.

I reach for my coat, which he holds for me, and as he slips it over my shoulders, he leans in and whispers, "If you continue to bite your lip, I might have to add five more spanks."

In the elevator, our reflection shows he's watching me. I chew on my lower lip, and I wish he'd step in and kiss me. I really do. I'm staring at his beautiful, plump lips, and I want to taste them. I want to feel them pressed against my lips while our tongues explore.

He stares back at me, and I think he wants the same thing.

As we near the ground floor, we continue watching one another, waiting for the other to make the first move.

When his phone rings, I close my eyes. I can't let him see me disappointed.

"Mason." He looks at me and shrugs.

Divine intervention, I suppose.

He's watching me and ignoring Ben and Brian. I pull out my phone and scroll through my PeopleMover page. This is for the best. Maybe I can take care of myself in the bathroom while he works and get him out of my system.

Not likely.

Downstairs, we get in the back of the car and Brian heads for the private plane terminal at San Francisco International Airport. I pull out my Kindle and start reading a steamy romance, but it only makes things worse. I turn it off. I can't believe how sexually frustrated I am.

Jackson jumps to another call. "Cheryl? I've spoken to the attorney, and I can offer you the two-hundred-and-fifty-thousand-dollar base pay with stock options that will vest over the next ten years."

As he listens, he looks at me and winks.

Two-hundred-and-fifty-thousand-dollar base salary? Being an admin sucks wind. I make forty-six-thousand dollars a year. No wonder I can't make ends meet. Fuck. It doesn't surprise me. I know Jeremy made less money than what Jackson just offered Cheryl, but he joined the company back when we didn't have all the funding secured.

"I can't do twenty percent, but I can do fifteen in stock options—the same amount Jeremy had."

I know I'd see all this eventually in the paperwork that crosses my desk, but hearing it is different. My sour feelings about all I do for the company and how little I get for it ruin my mood. Does Jackson think I'm a Barbie too?

We arrive, and Matt is waiting for us with a co-pilot that isn't introduced to me. I'm invisible. It's a stark reminder that

I'm just the admin.

Jackson continues his call as I find a seat on the plane. It's smaller than I thought, with only eight captain's chairs, but it's much more luxurious—pale leather seats that recline flat, plush gray carpeting, and shiny wood accents, each seat with its own screen.

I sit next to the window, and I'm shocked when Jackson sits next to me and winks as he takes his seat. Out the window, I catch Brian loading my giant suitcase into the back of the plane. I know I brought too much. I brought more than half of everything I currently own.

The plane taxis out onto the runway. The flight attendant gives me a quick rundown on safety, and I sit back and try to relax.

"Cheryl, I've got to run," Jackson says into his phone. "My plane is taking off. Let's talk on Friday. I should have your agreement at that time."

He hangs up and turns to me. "Are you nervous?"

I shake my head. "Not really."

"We have access to tons of movies we can watch on the big screen. I'll let you pick the first one. Or if you're tired, you can put your seat back."

I look at him, and I'm not sure if that was an invitation or not, but I go with the movie option. "What sounds good—comedy or action?"

"Action, I suppose," he says. "No romance?"

"I have books for that." I shrug. I'm still miffed. I don't even have any stock options. Every other employee who joins us will become a millionaire, and maybe I'll make fifty thousand dollars with a small bonus—oh wait, I've already gotten that in wardrobe form. And I should be grateful, but at the moment I'm not. I'm regretting agreeing to go to Hawaii. I don't know where I wish I could go, but I suppose I should take this opportunity to rethink my future with Soleil Energy. I'm not exactly in a position to ask for a raise at the moment.

"What kind of books?" Jackson wiggles his eyebrows at

me.

"If you're asking if they're steamy, the answer is yes." I search through the movie selections and spot a good one. "How about *The Bourne Identity*?" I push a few buttons, and the movie starts.

"Is your book in here?" He holds up my Kindle.

I nod.

"May I?"

Shrugging, I try to concentrate on Matt Damon. Damn, he's hot in this movie.

"Holy shit! This is what you call steamy? This is explicit," Jackson exclaims after a moment.

"So?" I'm not going to explain to him that women are more cerebral, while men are visual.

He grins wide. "I like it."

I look over, and he's skipped a bunch of pages to get to the sex scenes. "You missed a bunch of the story."

His brow creases. "I've never been able to do what this guy is doing."

I'm not sure I want to know what he's referring to. "What?" I ask anyway.

"He's gone three rounds in one session."

I smile. "Oh. Well, it's fiction."

"But I'd love to see a girl do that to me."

I glance over, and the girl is deepthroating the guy. "Your girlfriends don't give you blowjobs?" I'm stunned at this thought. I get the swallowing thing, but if the girl's not going to go down on him, why would he go down on her?

"Of course they do, but I'm more into their pleasure. They don't… Well, never mind."

I'm a little stunned by his admission. He goes back to my book, and I shift uncomfortably, trying to take the pressure off of my clit. It's begging for some serious attention.

I lay my chair back, and he grabs a blanket from somewhere and covers me while I watch the movie. I doze off to sleep.

Sometime later we hit turbulence, and I immediately sit up. I shake the sleep from my head. "I'm sorry."

"What do you have to be sorry for?"

"I didn't mean to fall asleep."

"Don't apologize for that. The last few weeks have been stressful. I'm sure you're not sleeping well."

I shake my head. *You know what?* Screw it. What do I have to lose? "The only night I slept halfway decent was when you slept with me."

I threw it out there. It's the truth. His eyes become hooded. I know if I'm not careful, I'm going to sleep with Jackson and end this portion of my career. But after what I was reminded of about my salary compared to other employees, I'm not sure I care so much about this job anymore. Jackson's company is doing important work for the environment, but it's not the only place I can make a difference. So maybe I should just sleep with him and not regret it. Then I can move on—and he certainly will. San Francisco and I may be about done with each other anyway. My decision made, I feel more relaxed. I give Jackson a sassy grin and turn over to resume my snooze.

Sometime later, he rubs my arm. "Hey, we're beginning our final descent."

I sit up. "That was fast." There's a different movie playing, and I'm a little disoriented.

He hands me back my Kindle. "I actually quite enjoyed that."

"Don't sound so shocked."

"You're certainly a woman of many surprises."

"You have no idea," I warn.

When the plane lands, Brian and Ben step out of the back section, bring a Suburban around, and load our bags.

I look at my watch and see we just made it before the airport closes. Phew. Also, I'm starved.

I stand up and stretch. Jackson's eyes go to my obviously pebbled nipples. He forces a smile and walks out the door to our waiting car.

The warm air seeps into the cool cabin and removes the chill of the airplane, and I can smell the salt from the ocean. I pick up my things and make my way to the door and down the steps. Jackson disappears ahead, leaving me to walk out on my own. So much for chivalry.

I'm shocked to find him standing at the base of the stairs with a beautiful yellow and pink plumeria lei. *Ooohhh…* He steps into my space and places the lei over my shoulders. "Welcome to Hawaii." He kisses me on both cheeks.

"Thank you. I can now say I've been laid in Hawaii." I laugh at my own joke as his eyes darken, and I decide I'm throwing all caution to the wind.

I'm going to have fun with Jackson in Hawaii. I have no apartment, my best friend is probably getting married soon, I'm underpaid, and I can use the fuck-up of sleeping with my boss and ending my job as my excuse to leave San Francisco.

I lean in and kiss Jackson softly on the lips. He kisses me back, furtive and sweet. Suddenly he breaks the kiss and steps back. I try to hide my disappointment. Boy, did I read that wrong.

He only wants to flirt. So much for throwing caution to the wind. I'm embarrassed. Now I have an awkward weekend with him ahead—and I've likely trashed my ability to work at Soleil Energy for no reward at all. *Great work, Corrine.* At least I'll have my own room here.

"Thank you for bringing me." My voice cracks, and I bite back tears as I follow him to the car.

Chapter 12

Jackson

I step away from Corrine, and my cock is pounding.

While she slept, I read her deliciously naughty book and determined she is a little minx. She sighed while sleeping, and I knew right then that I wanted to hear her moan my name and have her come all over my tongue.

I was surprised when she leaned in and kissed me. It was soft and delicious. I had the urge to take her here, but with Ben, Brian, and the flight crew close by, I wanted to be respectful. However, later? I'm going to make her scream my name and beg me to let her come.

It's almost dark. "Let's go check this place out."

We settle into the car and begin the drive, but it's difficult to see much. The houseman who greets us when we arrive shows us to a table on the cliffs above the ocean, where there's a beautiful torchlight dinner set for two.

"I'd say this is more than a beach house," she says, taking in the view of the ocean.

She's not kidding. I thought it was a large home on the water, not an estate with a large house and several buildings.

We're served an excellent whitefish, with seasoned white rice and a mix of vegetables. It's perfect for the day we've had. Corrine moans her appreciation, and again my cock strains against the buttons on my jeans. I look at her across the table and I realize she's more than beautiful in the torchlight. She's perfect.

She sits back in her chair with her glass of wine and looks out into the darkness. "I don't know about your other properties, but I might hold on to this one for the view alone."

Right now, I'll do anything she asks. "I may not allow Viviana to win this back. It would be a great place to get away to."

She nods, and I notice her eyelids are heavy with exhaustion.

"Let's check out the inside. You look tired."

Her eyes blink slowly. "It's hit me all of a sudden."

We walk inside, and the houseman shows us to our rooms. I was secretly hoping they'd assume we were together and put us in the same room, but I'm glad she's at least next door.

"Goodnight." She yawns.

I'm a little disappointed. I don't usually have to ask a woman to come to bed with me. Often, they offer. "Goodnight," I tell her. "Sleep well."

My large bedroom opens to the ocean and overlooks the pool, which is beautifully lit at night. The sounds of the ocean will put me to sleep, no problem. Someone has unpacked my clothes, and it takes me a few moments to find my pajama bottoms. When I travel, I wear pants to sleep. It only takes one time for a fire alarm to go off in the middle of the night…

I pull on my pajamas and walk shirtless toward what I believe is the bathroom. I open the door and jump as I spot Corrine brushing her teeth. She jumps, too.

"Oh my God, you startled me."

"I'm sorry. I thought this was my bathroom, not a shared bathroom." I stop to take in what she's wearing—a black, baby-doll negligée—and feel my cock rise.

She bends over to rinse her mouth, and I have all sorts of dangerous thoughts, but she says, "I'm done. I'll get out of your way."

As she rushes past me, I reach for her. "You're never in my way."

She smiles and steps aside. I can see she's upset about something. I could ignore it and go to bed, but instead, I quickly brush my teeth and knock on the door she exited through.

"Corrine? Is everything okay?"

She sits up in her bed as I open the door and strains to smile. "Yes, I'm fine."

I know women well enough to know that's not what *fine* looks like.

"Are you sure?" I ask.

She nods. "Sorry if I was too forward earlier. It won't happen again."

"Wait. What?" My heart beats triple time. "You were not being too forward earlier. It was perfect. I only stepped back because if I didn't, I would have bent you over the hood of the car and fucked you until you screamed my name. I have too much respect for you to do that with an audience."

She turns scarlet, including her chest, and I wonder what her breasts would feel like if I played with them.

"Oh."

I walk over, open the covers, and crawl in to lie next to her. "You can tell me to leave at any time."

Her breathing hitches, and I kiss her. It's soft and delicate, but I can only hold myself back for so long. Our kiss becomes sensuous. I want her to know the depth of my desire for her. Our tongues do an aggressive dance. I pull her on top of me, and she straddles me with her wetness rubbing against my hard cock. *God, she feels so good.*

I reach for her breast beneath the lace, and it's soft and pliable—so much better than the hard rocks of so many of the women I date. I roll her nipple between my finger and thumb and pull.

Corrine breaks our kiss, throws her head back, and moans as her hips move back and forth.

I don't think I can get any harder. I want Corrine Woods. I want her on me, under me, and in front of me.

When she rubs her slit against my cock, I'm in heaven. The straps of her negligee fall from her shoulders and expose her breasts. They are incredible. A little more than a handful with dark pink, pebbled nipples. I circle her chest with one hand while my fingers dip deep into her slick channel.

"Jack…son," she moans, short of breath. "That…feels…soooo…good."

God, I want this woman.

She kisses me. Her delicate hand reaches into the opening of my pajama bottoms, and she begins to stroke me.

"I want to taste you," she moans.

I'm euphoric. Corrine slips my pants over my hips, and my cock springs to attention, waving its desire.

She bites her lip as she looks at me. Then she bends down and licks the head of my cock while she cradles my balls, watching my reaction with a lusty smile.

Her mouth envelops the head and then the length. This feels so good. I can feel her relax her jaw, and my cock slides down her throat while her other hand rolls my balls.

"Holy shit!" I say between clenched teeth. It's taking all my willpower not to come down her throat.

The suction pulls as she takes me to the crown, and her tongue flicks the tip. She goes down again, and her moans send vibrations around my cock, which nearly causes me to lose my load.

My dick is wet, and when she comes up, she licks the tip. "You taste amazing," she breathes.

She releases my balls, and I watch her hand disappear down her panties as she strokes herself. She's enjoying this as much as I am, and that only makes it better.

"If you don't stop, I'm going to come," I warn her through clenched teeth, concentrating hard.

She moves up and down on my cock, her big doe eyes watching me lose control. When she releases me, I'm almost there.

She rolls my balls again in her hands. "I think we might be able to get you off at least three times tonight."

"Holy hell," I groan as I feel my cock hit the back of her throat and slide farther down. I try to hold back, but between the moaning, the playing with my balls, and her sucking a steady rhythm on my cock, I can't hold it any longer. I send rope after rope of cum down her throat with a loud grunt.

I'm breathing so hard, you'd think I'd just run a marathon.

She sits up and wipes her mouth. My cock is still hard. She smiles at me. "Have I been naughty again?"

"Oh, woman, you have no idea." I kiss her and can taste myself on her tongue, but I don't care. "Allow me to show you what it's like to be multi-orgasmic." I roll her on her back and kiss her again. My tongue continues dancing with hers while I tear her panties off and press two fingers deep inside her. She's so wet. The only sounds are the slickness and her moans. I kiss her lips, running my tongue along them, pulling her lower lip inside of my mouth. She stiffens, but it's a small orgasm. I won't settle for that. I want to hear her moan my name.

Grabbing both globes of her ass, I settle between her legs and lift her up just a bit. I take her swollen clit in my mouth and begin feasting on her, my tongue swirling around her throbbing clit—pressure, swirl, pressure, swirl, suck. My fingers find that spongy spot inside her, and I rub her furiously. Her hips move as she fucks my hand and face.

She keeps going and going, and I move to meet her. My heart is racing, and I can see stars. I nip the flesh inside her thighs and dive back in. She tastes so good.

After a moment, her body goes rigid, and she moans. I drink her orgasm.

With her chest heaving, she grabs my fingers and puts them in her mouth. As I lick every last drop of her orgasm, she sucks my fingers clean.

This was incredible, and we haven't even gotten to the main course yet.

She sighs and lies on her back, closing her eyes. I fit myself into her arms.

"God, this was better than I ever imagined," she says.

"We've only just begun." I hold her tight and rub small circles on her back. There's no way I'm letting her fall asleep already.

"We need a condom," she urges.

I kiss her nose and run to my room to grab one from my shaving kit.

When I return, I place it on the side table and get back into bed with her. I kiss her, and she moans quietly, wrapping her hands around me, holding me tight to her.

I love the way her stomach tightens each time she's climaxing. As I travel down to kiss her navel and her hips, I can smell how aroused she is again. I peek up at her face. Her eyes are still closed, but her lips are pursed ever so slightly. I know she's wide awake and waiting for me.

She's beautiful. I lie between her legs with my cock resting on her entrance. I rip the foil package open and sheath my cock. She looks into my eyes, and with a cute little smile, she centers the shaft at the entrance to her channel.

"Please," she whispers in my ear, "I need your big, fat cock inside me."

I love when women talk dirty to me, and I'm more than happy to oblige. I begin to push into her. She's so tight, I can tell it's a strain.

"Relax, baby," I tell her.

"I can do this," she pants.

I rock in and out until I'm balls deep.

"You feel so good," she moans. "Give it to me hard."

She doesn't have to ask me twice. I pull out and slam my cock in. In and out. I love the jiggle in her tits, and I pinch a nipple. She groans her appreciation, and her muscles tighten around my cock.

She's biting her lip and closes her eyes.

"Look at me, baby," I grunt.

She opens her eyes, and my hand goes to her clit, stroking it hard and fast. Her mouth forms an O and again, she becomes rigid. This time she screams my name. I feel ten feet tall, and I follow her down the rabbit hole to complete bliss.

When we're both spent, I collapse next to her. My cock slowly slips out, and I take the condom off, knotting the end and dropping it on my pajamas on the floor. I turn back to her and hold her tight. There's no way I'm getting out of this bed—an impulse that definitely surprises me.

Chapter 13

Corrine

The heat emanating from Jackson rolls over me before I open my eyes. The stickiness between my legs isn't left over from the fantastic sex we had last night. No, it comes from waking up next to him, and I want to go again.

Jackson seemed to enjoy himself last night. Does he think I'm bad at sex? Am I a cold fish in bed? Technically we only got him up twice, but he seems far more interested in my satisfaction than his own.

Jackson rolls over and snakes his arms around me to spoon me in tight. Kissing my temple, it's as if he's read my mind. "Don't go there."

I roll onto my back so I can look into his glorious eyes. "How did you know?"

"I can say this now, and it will be the only time someone else will be in our bed, but Bobby Sanders is a complete idiot.

Not only are you positively stunning, with perfect curves whether you're naked or dressed, but you're absolutely fantastic in bed. He's an idiot for letting you go, but I'm glad he did, because now you're mine."

My heart soars. To protect it, I remind myself that this will be short-lived. He means *mine* right now, for the moment. We'll return to San Francisco, and he'll find another Barbie, and I'll find a new job somewhere else. But damn if I'm not going to have fun right now.

I smell coffee and fresh baked goods. I sit up. "Let's see what's for breakfast."

"In a little bit." He pulls me back down and begins suckling my breast as his hands wander. "I've had a taste, and I want more."

We can't seem to get enough. I roll over on all fours and present myself to him. "I think I was promised ten spankings." I wiggle my ass and slap the cheek so he knows what I want.

His grin is like a boy on Christmas morning. His lips immediately attach themselves to my clit, and his magical hands bring me quickly to climax. I groan into the pillow.

I hear the rip of the foil package, and I play with myself to tease him. He shoves my hand away and pushes into me from behind. I groan as I stretch to accommodate him. I swear he's bigger than he was last night.

He pumps in and out of me, hard and fast, and smacks my ass.

"Yes," I moan.

"You like that, don't you?" He slaps my ass again.

"Yes," I moan, taking in the pleasure and the pain.

He grabs a handful of my hair and pulls me up. His fingers roll my nipples, pulling hard.

"We're made for each other," he says through gritted teeth.

I get the rest of my ten spankings, which send me over the edge with another orgasm. In no time, he joins me with his own.

I collapse in bed, out of breath. "I told you we'd get three times out of you."

He laughs hard. I love to make him laugh. "Apparently I've been doing this all wrong."

I throw my legs over the side of the bed and take in the room in the daylight. It's beautifully decorated with teak furniture and pale greens and blues. I stand and look out the window, listening to the waves pound the rocks below the backyard, which is peppered with coconut palms and green grass.

"The view is stunning."

I feel Jackson come up behind me and wrap his arms around me. "It's beautiful, but you're all I see."

A voice in my head is continually chirping, *Enjoy this while you can.*

"What do you want to do today?" I say this over my shoulder as I walk into the bathroom.

"I thought we'd check out the house this morning with the majordomo, and I made arrangements for a helicopter tour of the property and the island this afternoon."

I feel like I should be taking notes. I'm technically here on business.

"I'm starved. I need some nourishment so I can continue ravishing you." He approaches and kisses me softly. "You've woken a voracious sex monster in me."

I laugh. "I need a quick shower, so I don't smell like sex when we walk downstairs."

"It's still early." He picks up his phone, and I've almost immediately lost him to the problems in his email.

I shower and dress in a cotton sundress and a pair of pretty flat sandals, ready to walk everywhere today. I can hear him talking in his room, and I wander over. He's in an in-depth discussion with one of his developers, so I kiss him on the head and go in search of the kitchen. I find a Hawaiian woman with long, dark hair wearing a pink plumeria flower tucked behind her ear and a pink floral muumuu humming a beautiful song.

"Good morning," I say, announcing myself.

She turns to me with a smile. "Aloha. Welcome to the Halona Moana Estate."

"Thank you. Are you Leilani Palakiko—the one who made our dinner last night?"

"Yes. Was it satisfactory?" She tucks her hair behind her ear, and I see a slight tremble.

"Dinner was outstanding. I just wanted to make sure you knew that." I smile at her warmly, and she visibly relaxes. "We thought it was perfect for our first night here on the island."

"I'm so glad to hear that. It was a simple meal, but I'm happy you enjoyed it." She turns to her oven a moment. "I have some breakfast?" She points to a platter of delicate pastries on the table, and my mouth waters. "And I can make you a traditional Hawaiian egg scramble."

"Both sound amazing. Thank you." I spot the coffee pot and pour myself a cup. "Have you seen Ben and Brian, the security guards that flew in with us?"

She nods. "They're walking around the property with the majordomo and the security staff we have on site."

"You need security?" I ask.

"We have a small team. We're the largest privately-owned estate on the island. People often try to camp on the property since we're next to the national park. And we have to be aware of theft, but their biggest job is to protect the curlew. They're an endangered bird that nests on our property, and we want to be sure they don't feel threatened."

"I had no idea." I take a sip of my coffee. "Ahh… This is delicious."

"It's Kona coffee, freshly grown and roasted on the Big Island."

"It's outstanding. I'll need to take some home." I take another big sip, and it's the perfect amount of flavor without any bitterness. With sweetener, it almost tastes like dark chocolate. Amazing.

"It's roasted just for the estate. We'll make sure you have as much as you'd like when you go home."

Jackson walks in. "Did I hear something was outstanding?"

"Good morning. You must be Mr. Graham. Welcome to the Halona Moana Estate. My name is Leilani, and I am your cook. I was told there were no food allergies. If there's anything you don't care to eat, please let me know."

She seems very nervous as she speaks with Jackson. I get it—he can be intimidating.

"Of course. But your bread and coffee smells made me come running."

Leilani smiles. "I was just telling Ms. Woods that my homemade pastries and a traditional egg scramble are options for this morning. Of course, if there is something else you'd like, I'm happy to make that, too."

"The egg scramble and pastries sound perfect. Ms. Woods and I are taking the helicopter tour of the property and the island today. We'll have lunch out but will return for dinner."

"Thank you, Mr. Graham. Is there anything in particular you'd like for dinner?"

Jackson looks at me and raises his eyebrow, and I shake my head.

"I think you can surprise us, but I have to say I am not a fan of poi."

Leilani chuckles. "I think unless you grow up eating it, it doesn't appeal to you."

"I think it tastes like paste," he says with a twinkle in his eye.

"You've eaten a lot of paste?" Leilani teases.

Jackson laughs. "I did when I was a kid and didn't like it."

"Dinner tonight without poi. Got it. I think I have a few other options." She fusses around the kitchen. "It'll be a few minutes before I have your breakfast. There is a table set for you on the lanai." And she points to an open, covered porch area. The entire house has glass windows from floor to ceiling that the staff has opened up to catch the cool breeze coming off the ocean.

We sit down and take in the expansive view. "This is even more beautiful than I pictured in the dark."

He nods and leans in. "How are you feeling this morning?"

I'm embarrassed that he's asking—not because he's my boss or my lover, but because our relationship has changed. We're really in The Twilight Zone now. "I'm good. A bit sore, but in a good way."

He grins. "Good to know. We'll have to work on stretching out those muscles more often." He winks at me.

I'm ready to respond when Leilani arrives with our breakfast. "Here's the egg scramble. We serve it with steamed rice." She places a tall glass of yellow juice in front of each of us. "And some fresh pineapple juice."

"Looks fantastic," I gush.

We both take heaping forkfuls of our egg scramble, which is stuffed with meat, peppers, cheese, and green onions—all sprinkled with sesame seeds and a big dollop of steamed white rice.

I don't know if it's the Hawaiian air or what's inside the egg scramble, but I eat everything and hold myself back from asking for seconds.

"That was outstanding," Jackson says as he sits back in his chair and rubs his belly.

Leilani preens, and I know we've won her over.

"Mr. Graham?" An older gentleman approaches.

"Yes?"

"So wonderful to have you here. Welcome to the Halona Moana Estate. I am Jason Crier."

Jackson is not familiar with the staff of the estate, but I am, and I realize this is the majordomo.

I jump in to save him. "Mr. Crier, I'm Corrine Woods. It's so lovely to put a face with the voice. You and the staff have done an outstanding job making us feel welcome."

"Yes, positively exceptional." Jackson smiles and extends his hand to Jason.

"Please forgive your room accommodations. Ms. Prentis had begun a major renovation of the central part of the house, and while your current rooms are a bit small, they have an impeccable view."

That explains so much. I wish he would have told me before we arrived so I could have set Jackson's expectations.

"We managed." He looks at me, sharing the inside joke. "The views were outstanding. Is it possible that after we finish our breakfast, we get to work?"

"Of course, sir."

Jackson gestures to a chair at the table. "Please sit. How long have you been with the estate?"

"Coming up on ten years. When I started, we were owned by a large pharmaceutical company. Ms. Prentis bought us last year, and then she sold to you. We didn't know of the sale until just a few days ago."

"I don't think it was planned," Jackson says, but he doesn't expand.

After we finish our breakfast, Mr. Crier leads us around the palatial property.

When we arrive at the estate's master bedroom, I'm amazed by its size and location. It has a 360-degree view, and 270 degrees is all ocean.

"Don't get me wrong, the rooms where you put us are beautiful, but this is what I was expecting," Jackson says.

"My apologies, Mr. Graham," he says. "We should be through with the renovations in a few weeks."

We hear the helicopter approaching before we see it. And Mr. Crier ends the tour just as a helicopter touches down.

The pilot extends his hand. "Mitchell Matthews. Welcome to Hawaii."

Jackson nods. "Thank you. You ready to show us around?"

"Yes, sir. The Halona Moana is the largest independently

owned estate on the island, and the second largest in the state. We'll take an aerial tour of the grounds, and then I'll give you a tour of the island. The property runs adjacent to the Haleakala National Park, so we'll see the island's famous volcano. You'll also enjoy the Hana rainforest, the North Shore, and I promise a view of Jurassic Rock. That should take two hours. My understanding is that I'm to drop you at the Kahului Heliport, where your team is picking you up."

"Yes, that's the plan," Jackson confirms.

I didn't arrange this tour, and I'm honestly a bit surprised he did. But I'm okay with it. I do like a surprise now and again.

We're set up with safety gear, and we both get into the backseat of the helicopter.

"Have you ever been in a helicopter?" Mitchell asks.

"I haven't, but I'm super excited," I say.

"I have a few times," Jackson says.

We lift off, and we communicate with headphones and microphones as Mitchell points out the property from the air. The estate sits atop a point, with cliffs that lead to a sandy beach. He identifies several curlew nesting sites, and I'm proud to know we're helping bird species that are close to going extinct. We pass over the adjacent Haleakala volcano and then continue on to see the rest of Maui.

When we set down two hours later, it seems like we just left.

Chapter 14

Jackson

Kahului is the largest town on the island, and the shopping district is lush with greens and flower bushes and full of tourists and locals wandering in and out of the stores and open-air markets. Corrine and I hold hands and walk in and out of several stores. I chuckle when she stops at a tourist stop and picks up macadamia nuts, a carved wood plumeria key chain, and a sticker that says Hawaii.

She looks at me and shrugs. "I'm not sure when I'll have the chance to come back."

She's welcome to come to the house anytime she wants. "I'm hoping we can do this more," I tell her. "You know, escape from San Francisco and hide here atop the cliffs, enjoying the beautiful breeze of the ocean and making love all night."

She smiles, but I can see her mind working overtime.

I spot a beautiful floral dress in a small shop window that would look spectacular on Corrine. It takes some work, but she finally agrees to try it on. I explain to the saleswoman while she's in the dressing room, "If the dress fits, I'd like to buy it. She'll be reluctant about this, so here's my credit card and please deliver it to the Halona Moana Estate."

"Of course. It would be my pleasure," she says.

When Corrine steps out of the dressing room, my heart skips a beat. The dress in the light blue sets off the beautiful golden tones in her skin, and the red hibiscus flower print sets off the golden highlights in her hair. The tight bodice accents her luscious breasts, and the full skirt gives me just a teasing peek at her glorious long legs.

My cock is absolutely alert. I knew it would look great on her. "What do you think?"

She leans in and just above a whisper says, "It's over a thousand dollars."

"It's worth it. You look stunning," I assure her.

She turns and looks at herself in the mirror, studying it carefully. She sighs in frustration. "I can't. I can't afford it."

I don't understand at first. "I'm happy to buy it for you."

She shakes her head. "I don't want you to buy it for me. I can buy my own clothes. It's a beautiful dress, and it does look good on me, but it's not practical outside of Hawaii. For that price, it should be something I'll be able to wear a lot."

Once she's dressed, she hands the saleswoman the dress and thanks her.

I give the saleswoman a nod, and I know she'll have it delivered later today.

As we walk out, I grasp Corrine's hand. "I don't want you to think about money on this trip."

She smiles at me. "I understand your position, but for most of my life, I didn't have to stand on my own. Now I don't want to be dependent on others."

"I hear you, but I want to spoil you." I want to own her at work, home, and in bed. But for now, I'll settle for owning her in bed.

"How about you buy me some lunch?" Corrine offers.

She's changed the subject. There's more to why she wants to be so independent, but I'm not sure how to ask her.

"I'll happily buy you any lunch you'd like. What sounds good?"

"How about a burger?"

"That's easy. There's a spot around the corner." We walk in, order at the cash register, and take a number. When it's ready, they'll deliver our meals to our table.

"What did you order?" I ask.

"I ordered a cheeseburger Hawaiian style—it has a ring of pineapple, a slice of SPAM, and teriyaki sauce."

"You know that sounds disgusting." I grimace.

She shrugs. "It may be. I'll try anything once. What did you get?"

I grin. "Same as usual."

"You're in Hawaii, and you ordered a cheeseburger with onion rings, bacon, and barbecue sauce?"

"You forgot the extra-large fries." I wiggle my eyebrows.

"I'm counting on you sharing those." She bites her lip, and it drives me crazy. I lean down and kiss her.

"For you, anything." I realize I genuinely mean that. I want to give Corrine everything she could ever want, everything I have. *Wow.* That's huge.

It scares me that I'm thinking like this, but I realize I want more from her than a casual weekend in Hawaii. That's more than I've wanted from anyone in a long time.

"I have some work to get done this afternoon," I tell her. "You up for some pool time?"

"I have some work I should be doing, too."

"It's Friday," I remind her, just in case she forgot.

"And I'll bet the emails haven't stopped coming. Plus, tomorrow I may have to squeeze a few things in."

I cringe. I don't pay her enough to work weekends. She lives in a fucking closet. How could I have been so blind to this?

Our meals arrive. A thick, juicy burger with all the trimmings is placed before me, and I jump in without paying attention. The mixture of barbecue sauce and all the fixings is perfect. It's one of the better burgers I've had.

After about three bites, I'm finally satiated enough that I can look at her. I watch her take small bites. I know her well enough to see she doesn't like what she ordered.

"Not good?"

She shrugs. "Mayo and teriyaki sauce is interesting. The SPAM and pineapple are different." Her brows crease and her lips purse. "It's…just…a lot of flavors."

I sit back in my chair and laugh so hard people turn to stare. "Please go order a regular cheeseburger. It's great that you wanted to try something new, but if you don't like it, you shouldn't struggle with it."

"Maybe if I take it apart," she offers.

I love that she's willing to stick with it, but I can't make her do it. I get up and go to the counter to order her a basic cheeseburger.

"You didn't have to do that." She smiles as she reaches for my plate. "I can survive on fries."

"Not with what I have planned for you," I warn.

She looks away as her new burger is delivered, and a blush crosses her chest.

"I hope I didn't embarrass you," I say in a low voice.

"No, not at all." She paints a smile on her face. Something's bothering her. I don't think I did anything, but there's always a possibility.

When we return to the estate, she grabs her Kindle and puts on the bikini Tiffany gave her. *Damn, she looks sexy.* The little triangles just cover the front of her breasts, and the bottoms are so low that they barely cover anything. I know I said I needed to work, but my cock has other ideas. I wonder if she's reading something super naughty? The thought makes my imagination go wild.

I need to focus, but watching her walk in that tiny bit of fabric is distracting. I mean, the top is essentially just eyepatches.

Focus.

I need to make a few calls.

As she strides across the pool deck, her grace reminds me of a dancer. She sits under the open gazebo, and I watch her put sunscreen on. When she massages it into her chest, it's like watching her play with her breasts, and my boner struggles to remain contained.

This woman has no idea what she does to me.

I check in with my developers and watch Corrine sunbathe. Then I look around and there are two groundskeepers and a houseman standing by watching. What. The. Fuck?

"Sounds like you're making progress, Lou. I'll continue to check in. Enjoy your weekend." I hang up and walk over to Corrine, giving all three men a do-not-fuck-with-me look. They immediately disappear.

She looks up from her book and smiles. "Are you getting everything done that you need to?"

"You're a bit distracting."

She picks up her cover and puts it on. "Sorry."

"I don't want you to feel bad, and you don't need to cover up. But, because I'm watching you and not getting enough done, you can make it up to me tonight."

"I'm sure you can think of an adequate punishment for me." She bites her lip and grins.

"Woman, you're going to kill me yet," I growl.

"Not until I get a casting of your dick." She grins, teasing.

"What would you do with a casting exactly?"

"I'd never need another man *ever* if I had that."

My phone rings. "We'll continue this when I tie you up later for your disobedience."

She licks her lips. "I can't wait."

God, this woman is turning me into a horny teenager. I

can't remember the last time I behaved like this.

I reluctantly answer the phone and walk inside. "Jackson Graham."

"Jackson, this is Kala Simpson. I've been able to set an appointment for you tomorrow with Governor Alex Chow for dinner at seven on Oahu."

"Thank you. I'll be there."

I hang up and notify Brian and Ben of my plans. I let them know what to expect for tomorrow and that we'll return to Maui after dinner.

When I finish, I wander back out to Corrine. She's lying on her stomach, and her heart-shaped ass is incredibly enticing. I look around, but it isn't private enough for me to take her here.

"Did you get everything finished up?" she asks.

"I did. I have an unexpected surprise." Her brows crease with worry. "We're having dinner with the governor of Hawaii tomorrow in Honolulu. How would you like to come with me to Oahu?"

She stands, puts her cover on, and grabs her Kindle. "Okay, you're the boss."

I think I like that she refers to me as the boss, although it reminds me that I'm in complicated territory here with her. I step in close. "I'm going to show you I'm more than just the boss later tonight—unless you change your mind. You're in charge." I reach for her hand and rub it over my cock. "Or shall we retire to our room now so I can show you?"

She kisses me softly on the lips, and I want her even more. "I'm meeting with Jason in…" She checks her phone for the time. "…twenty minutes. You can give me the abridged version." She massages my cock through my shorts.

I'm disappointed, but I do want her to oversee the operations here at the estate. "I have no abridged version. We'll have to wait, and I'll show you after dinner."

She kisses the side of my jaw and whispers, "I can't wait."

We walk into the house. "I do have a treat for you."

"Other than a long night of fun?"

"It will be a long night, too. But yes. Come with me." I lead her back to her bedroom and show her the dress.

As she looks at it, hurt crosses her face.

I immediately know I've made a mistake. "I know you like standing on your own, but you looked amazing in this dress. You know I can afford this. Please let me spoil you—like you spoil me."

"I don't buy your clothes." Her voice is choked, and I'm worried she's going to cry.

"No, but you take care of me in other ways. Every day you pick up coffee on your way into work. You make sure I eat lunch. You move me from meeting to meeting, and you constantly save me like you did with Jason Crier this morning. You take care of me all the time." I stand behind her and hold her tight. "I will return this if you don't want it, but I want to do this for you. No strings attached."

She stands on her tiptoes and turns to put her arms around me, giving me a deep kiss. I like how she feels in my arms. I know I'll need to figure out how to make this work once we return to reality, but for now, I'm going to enjoy every minute I can.

"Thank you for the dress," she finally says.

Chapter 15

Jackson

Corrine was already gone when I woke up this morning. It's Saturday. Doesn't she know we're supposed to sleep in? We don't have to be on Oahu until tonight. I stretch and feel some muscles that haven't seen a lot of action in a while. They're a little sore this morning. I smile. At least she isn't the only one sore.

Last night we retired to bed shortly after dinner. Corrine has a voracious appetite for sex, and I can't seem to get enough of her.

There's rustling at the door, and Corrine pokes her head into the room. "Ah, you're awake."

I stretch. She's dressed in cute capri pants and a floral print blouse, and I'm naked. "I brought your coffee, and Leilani made her special pineapple pancakes with her own pineapple syrup."

"That sounds decadent." I stretch, allowing the sheet to expose my erection.

Corrine stares and licks her lips. I know she's thinking about what she'd like to do with it.

"Trust me, they are." She places a tray in front of me. "I need to pack. Do you want me to wear the dress you bought me to dinner tonight?"

"Sure. You're beautiful no matter what, so whatever you feel the most comfortable in. This is Hawaii, and men will be in dress pants and Hawaiian shirts. Most women will be in dresses similar to the one I bought you. Whatever you want to wear."

"Even my bikini?"

I internally groan. "Absolutely not." I shake my head. "I won't allow anyone to ogle you except me."

She laughs. "So, my birthday suit is out, too."

I raise my brows at her, and she knows it's a warning.

"The pilot called and said we need to leave on time," she continues. "Honolulu doesn't have a lot of flexibility for late arrivals."

"Okay, and actually, the governor has asked us to join him and his wife at their private club. We're hoping the US partner of Hydro, Jeff Wong, will be there."

"Whoa. Okay. I'm happy to go, but don't feel like you have to take me if this has morphed into something different. I get it—business first."

"No, no," I assure her. "You're essential to tonight. I have a feeling the only way he's going to be there is if you come. I got the impression that his wife won't go without you, and he can't go without his wife."

She nods. "I know tonight you'll kindly remind Jeff Wong that the plans were stolen, and if he sells anything he's produced from them, you have the weight of the law and the governor of Hawaii behind you."

I love that she feels so strongly about this. She has no profit sharing or interest in the company beyond her paycheck, and she's talented enough to get another job—God forbid—in minutes, but she believes in my company and me, and that means everything. However, I need to make sure her value to me is clear. I'll send off some reminder emails this afternoon, so they fast-track the updates to her compensation package I asked for after we got funding for the solar film.

I smile at her. "And I have you, too. Right?"

"I'm sure I can take him out with my wicked organizational powers if he gets out of line." She puts up her hands like the claws of a cat, makes her best mean face, and growls.

I throw my head back and laugh. "Let's get ready. At a minimum, we can have drinks at a beautiful restaurant on the beach in Honolulu before we meet them. Governor Chow made me promise I'd bring you back for dinner at one of the high-end restaurants."

"You failed to tell him we leave on Monday."

"I still own the estate. We can come back whenever we'd like."

"You have a long list of people to bring here. And once we go through the estate's payroll, you may want to lose it in the next poker tournament."

"It's that high?" Viviana may have lost it to me on purpose if it's that expensive.

"The staff is needed, but there's no income. There could be some, but it'll never cover the costs."

With that, her pants drop to the floor and she unbuttons her blouse. I'm consumed by her white lace panties and her gorgeous tits. I pull her into my arms and suckle her nipple through the lace.

"But maybe you need the tax deduction," she breathes.

God, I want this woman. "We can go over what you learned on the flight."

"I transferred…five hundred thousand…dollars…to their operating account…" She moans. "…this morning. That way they can…complete the—don't stop…" She breathes heavily as my hand dips inside her panties. "…renovation, pay…some bills, and…make payroll."

She's so wet and responsive. Her hips buck as she pushes herself into my hands. She bites her lip as I suckle her nipples, and she moans her climax. She's drunk from pleasure and breathing hard.

I suck my fingers clean. "Wow. Okay. I'll definitely walk through that."

"I should go take a shower, "she announces.

"Can I watch?"

She blushes. "You're the boss."

"You keep saying that. I hope you know that we're *partners* at work, and you can kick me out of your bed whenever you want to."

She smiles. "Mostly I like you being bossy."

I step in close, and she strokes my cock through my pants. I kiss her hard. She gets down on her knees before me.

"You're quite the beautiful sex kitten. I'm secretly glad you're stuck at my place when we return. I have so many plans for us."

She looks surprised. I hope she understands this is the beginning of something. After a moment, she takes me into her mouth, and I lose all sense of time and place.

A little while later, once we've recovered, I notice she's gathering things together.

"Remember, we'll be back here tonight," I tell her. "We're coming home after dinner."

"Yes, and we fly home on Monday." She continues working around the room, putting things aside and preparing to pack.

"Tonight will be fun, and we'll see the sun set over Diamond Head—a little different view than here at the estate."

She nods.

I get out of bed and walk naked to the bathroom. Corrine stops what she's doing and stares. I take great pride in having the same effect on her as she has on me.

Chapter 16

Corrine

That evening, as we wait to be seated at the restaurant, I adjust my dress for the third time.

Jackson leans down and whispers in my ear. "You look beautiful. No need to be nervous."

I have a just-fucked flush on my face, and I'm worried everyone will know. We're shown to our table, and an older Asian couple stand.

"Aloha. Welcome to Hawaii, Mr. Graham," the man says.

"Governor, this is my girlfriend, Corrine Woods."

My mind spins. *Girlfriend?* I suppose with my current look, it wouldn't go well to say, "This is my assistant."

"So nice to meet you," the governor says. "Please let me introduce you to my better half, Courtney."

I extend my hand. "So nice to meet you both."

I begin to sit, and there is someone behind me pushing my

chair in. The club exudes wealth and prestige. There are definitely no tourists here.

I hear the governor order bourbon for Jackson, and he looks at me. I eye Courtney's fruity-looking drink. "I'll take one of those."

"Mai tais are my favorite." She smiles. "I understand you're visiting from the mainland."

"We are. We're staying on Maui for a long weekend." The waiter places my napkin in my lap. "Are you originally from here?"

She shakes her head. "No, Alex and I met at the University of Washington during law school, and I followed him here."

"You're a lawyer?"

"Not anymore. Too many long hours, and we wanted to start a family." She looks at her husband and smiles.

It's good to see two people in love.

"What about you? What do you do?" she asks as she sips her drink.

I hate this question. If I tell her I'm an admin, she'll think I'm not up to her legal standards. If I tell her I'm *Jackson's* admin, she'll think I'm sleeping my way to the top. I paint a smile on my face and go with my standard answer. "I work in operations and project management." No one really pushes hard with that kind of response.

"How did you and Jackson meet?" she asks.

I'm about to answer when he interjects. "We met at work. She's one of the most valuable employees at Soleil Energy."

The governor and Jackson begin to talk, and Courtney and I listen politely.

"Thank you for the donation to my reelection campaign," the governor says.

"I appreciate your agreeing to meet with me." Jackson bows his head courteously.

"Of course. I'm happy to help, but I'm not sure there's much I can do," he says.

Jackson takes him through the invention of the solar panel

window film. "We have a patent pending, but recently my CFO was arrested for theft of our plans and schematics and was seeking funding. He approached Hydro Energy Partners without authorization. Are you familiar with them?"

"I'm familiar with the owner, Jeff Wong."

"I was told that, which is why I'm asking." Jackson picks up his glass of bourbon. "Would you be willing to make an introduction?"

"Is this why you're here in Hawaii?"

"No, I have a place on Maui, but when I thought you could help, I begged for this dinner."

The governor nods. "Tell me more about your invention." The two of them talk about Soleil Energy, and I talk to Courtney about adjusting to living on an island so far away from her family.

An older Chinese gentleman approaches the table, and the governor greets him. "Jeff, I was hoping to see you tonight. Please let me introduce you to my dinner guests. I understand you may run in the same circles."

A look of smugness crosses Jeff Wong's face.

"This is Jackson Graham, CEO and founder of Soleil Energy."

Suddenly, he looks horrified. I'm sure he wasn't expecting to see Jackson in Hawaii, and the fact that he ran into him in his private club visibly unsettles him.

"Mr. Wong, nice to meet you," Jackson says. "I've been trying to reach you."

"Sorry. I haven't received any messages," Jeff Wong says. "I'll have to speak to my girl about that."

"That's fine. I'll just tell you in person what I tried to tell you over the phone. My attorney has sent you a notice. The technology for the solar film you're preparing to sell was stolen from me. Its application has been submitted for a patent, and it's been financed in the US."

"I'm sure it's different from my technology." Jeff turns a gold signet ring on his right pinky finger.

"Well, I would certainly hope so since you were digitally recorded meeting with Jeremy Knowles, the former CFO of my company. I'm not sure if you're aware, but he was arrested for stealing the plans and patent information."

"I assure you, I've never met a Jeremy Knowles."

The men nod, sizing each other up. Jackson is significantly taller than Jeff Wong, and in much better shape. My bet is on Jackson.

"That's great news for you. Because should you choose to move ahead and find yourself unable to prove ownership of your technology and development, I have more than enough money to pursue this." Jackson leans in so he's not overheard by the neighboring tables. "Both in the US and in China."

"I have no idea what you're talking about." Jeff Wong paints a fake smile on his face.

"That's fine, but I have my eye on you." Jackson sits back in his chair, seeming confident. "I've spoken with Electrical Alternatives, and they've told me you mysteriously launched technology they created in the past, and while they didn't have the funds to pursue this, I not only have more than enough money but also the connections. You can check."

Wong turns to the governor. "I can't believe you brought this *haole* mainlander, who has no interest in Hawaii and our culture, to our private club."

"Actually," I interrupt. "This *haole* mainlander owns the largest private estate on Maui and the second-largest private estate outside of the Robinson family in all of Hawaii. He employs over fifty people." I should've just kept my mouth shut, but I couldn't help myself.

"You own the Halona Moana Estate?" he asks.

"I do," Jackson says.

"How did you buy it? It wasn't listed for sale," he challenges.

The waiter arrives with our drinks, and Jackson takes his time, knowing Jeff Wong must have been watching the estate if he knew it hadn't been up for sale.

"I bought it from Viviana Prentis," he finally says. "I just put five hundred thousand dollars into the operational budget this morning. I now have a big footprint in Hawaii."

Jeff Wong begins to turn red, and he balls his hands at his side.

"I have no beef with you today, Mr. Wong, but if you continue to try to sell my technology, you *will* be sorry."

Wong turns and walks away. He says something to his probably paid-for date, and they leave the club.

That was tense. I didn't realize I'd been holding my breath until he walked away. Jackson grasps my hand under the table and rubs his fingers over my knuckles. I steal a look at him, and he has a smug smile. He's won round two, but this might not be over. We'll wait to find out if there's going to be a round three.

The governor motions to the waiter. "A bottle of champagne for the table."

"Yes, Governor."

The champagne flows, and the food is outstanding. Dinner runs long, and by the time we fly back to Maui and get to the estate, it's well after midnight.

Jackson and I curl up in bed together. A part of me wants to talk about how we're going to manage when we return to San Francisco, but before I can figure out how to talk about it, he's softly snoring in my ear.

I'm going to miss this. Can I get a casting of his dick? Sadly, I know it wouldn't be enough.

The sun cutting through the blinds wakes me in the morning, but Jackson is up and gone. That's too bad. I would have loved to start the day with sex. We gave Leilani the morning off, but she's going to make us a huge dinner tonight.

I reach for my Kindle, and immediately it starts with a

very naughty scene. The hero has tied up the heroine and is withholding her orgasms. Sounds like pure torture. I'm grateful Jackson gets pleasure from giving pleasure.

Just then he walks in wearing his pajama bottoms with a tray of coffee and fruit.

"You're awake." He kisses me on the forehead.

"I was lonely here without you."

"What can I do to curb your loneliness?"

"Kiss me, please." I point to my lips.

He sets the tray down, and his mouth softly touches mine. He bites at my bottom lip.

"And here." I point to my shoulder, and he nibbles. My pussy is aching for his touch, and I know he can't be too far behind me in his desire.

"Here, too." I lift my heavy breast to him, and he suckles it, taking it deep in his mouth. I lean back and moan.

"Was that okay?" he growls.

I nod. "But I think I need another kiss." I point to my pussy.

He pulls the sheets back, and my knees fall together. He opens them and lightly kisses my clit. "Does this work for you?"

I shake my head.

He does a single lick through my slit, just brushing my clit, and I almost explode.

My hands go to my breasts, and I begin to knead the nipples. "More," I plead.

He gives a deep chuckle. "You want more?"

"Please." I'm panting.

He goes to work, and his magic tongue and fingers send me over the edge. When I beg to satisfy him, he shakes his head and begins again. He sends me to my climax three times before I collapse in exhaustion.

"What about you?"

"I got off just getting you off."

It takes some time, but I gather the energy to wander into

the bathroom and shower. I'm both exhilarated and exhausted.

Jackson is gone when I return. Putting my bikini on, I grab the cold coffee and some pineapple from the tray and walk out to the pool deck. I find myself a place with indirect sun and enjoy the warm weather until I'm ready for lunch.

When I go back inside, I find Leilani busy in the kitchen with bags of groceries. "Is all of this for dinner tonight?" I ask while I pull together a sandwich to eat by the pool.

She nods. "I spoke with Mr. Graham, and he wants a quiet dinner for the two of you on the cliffs again tonight."

"Can I help?"

She smiles. "No. This will be a special treat, and I want you to enjoy it." She takes several things out of her bags that I don't recognize.

"I'm excited."

"I'm looking forward to it too."

I explore the house, but I can't find Jackson. I wonder where he got off to.

Chapter 17

Corrine

"You ready?" Jackson asks as he hands his bag off to Ben on Monday morning.

"Leilani, thank you for the fantastic food all weekend. I will have dreams of the egg scramble and the ono you made last night," I tell her.

"When you come back, I'll make it for you again."

"Jackson will be back in a few weeks, but I'm not sure when I'll return."

She winks at me. She knows. "You two are good together. I think we'll see you again."

I smile. I don't have the heart to tell her Jackson doesn't keep women around long, and I've determined I'll need to begin looking for a new job when we return.

Jackson and I sit in seats next to one another with our laptops open and work our way across the Pacific. He jumps from call to call on the satellite phone, talking to his team. I sort through my email and his. As I go through, there are several requests for his time, and I begin a list. There's even an email from a journalist at the *San Francisco Chronicle,* who I know he's slept with, asking for dinner.

I don't know how I'm going to be able to do this—even for a little while. I add that to my list of questions for him.

I see an email from my roommate Angela. My stomach tightens. She and Stacy have been living in the Fairmont while the apartment was repaired, and I haven't heard much. I've been assuming they were okay with being displaced—mostly because Jackson has done more than right by them. I hope this email doesn't indicate otherwise.

I smile when I open it to find a picture of Angela and Stacy with wide grins and glasses of champagne. The walls behind them are white, and the furniture is all white and robin's egg blue. It's beautiful. Then it hits me—they're in our apartment, toasting to being back with new furniture. "Please thank Jackson," Angela's message reads. "See you soon."

If my apartment is done, I should go home tonight. It's going to be hard when the Band-Aid comes off, but I might as well do it sooner rather than later. I will miss Jackson at night, but for now, we'll have our days together. I won't have to go cold turkey, but I'm determined to keep my heart safe and step away before he does.

When I get to the end of the inboxes, I've done all I can do without my phone. I pull out my Kindle for the last two hours of our flight. I've given up on romance, and now I'm reading a mystery. But I've already figured out who did it, and I'm bored. Nothing else looks good.

I stare out into the ocean. It's just a solid blue form below us, with ripples and puffs of clouds. The day I've been dreading is here, and I can't avoid the momentous wall I need to climb. It's right in front of me. Everything hinges on the next few days. I can already tell I'm not thinking straight—I put my wallet in the wrong pocket of my bag and then panicked when I couldn't find it. My hands spread like pale starfish around the ivory coffee cup in front of me. They're cold and not absorbing the heat from my drink. The closer we get to San Francisco and our normal life, the fork in the road weighs more heavily on me, like a San Francisco fog.

By the time we arrive, it's after five. I'm tired, but we have work to do.

"You look exhausted," Jackson tells me. "I'm going to go into the office for a few hours, but why don't I meet you back at the apartment? Go get some rest and we can have a late dinner." He kisses me on the temple.

His phone rings, and he answers. "Jackson Graham."

I grab his arm and whisper, "I'm probably going back to my apartment tonight."

He nods and gets out of the car, talking on the phone. I turn to Brian. "My apartment on Lake Street, please."

He turns and looks at me. "Are you sure?"

"Yes, I have to return at some point." I can't look at him, and I watch Jackson disappear into the building.

"Does Mr. Graham know?"

I look at his eyes in the mirror. "I told him, and he didn't seem to have a problem with it."

Brian stares back at me. If he calls Jackson or Jim, they'll probably veto it, but I pay rent for that apartment, and I should go home if it's ready for me.

"Look, Brian, the long weekend was fantastic, but you know as well as I do, it's impolite to stay too long at the party."

"I don't believe that for a minute," he responds.

"I'm only trying to recognize this for what it is. We'll still see each other at the office. You can't get rid of me that easily." I wink and smile to assure him I will be okay.

I'm trying to protect my heart, but I've already fallen for Jackson. And I don't believe a zebra changes its stripes. Growing up with an alcoholic teaches you that—no matter how many promises they make.

Brian drives me to my apartment. Everything looks the same, but I don't feel the same.

"Should I walk you in?"

I already have my hand on the door handle. "Nope. My roommates should be at home. Enjoy your night and give that beautiful family some love. I'm sure they've missed you."

I carry my suitcase up the stairs. Why is it that suitcases seem so light until you have to lug them up three flights?

I put my key in the door and drag my bag over the threshold. "Hello?"

"Oh my God, you're here." Angela walks out of the kitchen and gives me a big hug. "This place looks amazing!"

"Give me a tour."

She walks me around. The furniture is high end in beautiful shades of robin's egg blue and lots of white.

"Did you pick the stuff out?" she asks. "Stacy and I love it."

"No, Jackson had a designer do it." I look around, and I'm impressed with all the detail and what he did for my roommates. "I'm really sorry about the apartment."

"It wasn't your fault. They were able to save a few things that were important to me. It's all good."

I open the door to my room and see it's been converted back to a closet. The girls have hung all their clothes up and placed their shoes on the shelves.

"Oh…" *What do I do? Where do I go?* "I guess I'm not living here anymore."

Angela turns red. "Sorry. When the decorator didn't do your room, we thought it was because you were moving in with your boyfriend."

My heart drops. I'm not particularly close to my roommates, and last they knew I was still dating Bobby—though they never knew *which* Bobby. I have no place to live. "No, I don't have a boyfriend," I whisper. "I'm not dating anyone anymore," I add more forcefully.

"Oh…" Angela doesn't seem to know what to do. "I don't

think Stacy will be home tonight. You can stay in her room."

I'm lost. I have no idea how to manage all this. It's time I face the facts and move home.

"That's okay." I manage a smile. "I can stay with my friend Gabby. I'll figure it out."

I pick up my suitcase and begin to descend the stairs. "Be sure to thank your boss for fixing our place," Angela yells after me.

"I will." I want to scream out my frustration as I walk to the curb. I never saw San Francisco as my permanent home, but I thought I'd have the chance to leave on my own terms—not in debt and homeless.

I call Gabby.

"Hey!" I say when she answers.

"Oh my God! You're back."

"I was only gone for four days." I laugh. Already Gabby's voice makes me feel better.

"It seems longer," she counters. "Can you meet me for drinks?"

"As good as a nice glass of something crisp and white sounds, I don't want to lug this stupid suitcase around. I may need a place to stay tonight."

"Even better. Come on over. I have margarita mix and tequila."

Margaritas sound perfect. I call a rideshare and make my way to her apartment. During the drive, I mull over why Jackson didn't replace my things, too. What sort of message is he trying to send? Does this mean I don't have a job? Or I have no choice but to stay with him? Maybe he gave me a trip and clothes, so I can replace my own bed? I should be grateful for what he's done. I don't know what I'd be wearing right now, otherwise. But I'm done being told where I have to live.

When I'm dropped at the curb, I look up at Gabby's apartment, and she's there in the window, waving at me. She's my best friend, and I'd be lost without her.

"Girlfriend! Welcome back." She brings me into a tight

embrace, and I immediately break out in tears. Things are such a mess.

"Oh, honey, you're going to be okay. Did that bastard fuck you over?"

"We just got back. I went to my apartment, and the designer he hired refurnished the apartment, but they didn't do my bedroom, so the girls have made it their closet. It's stuffed with their clothes and shoes."

"Are you shitting me?" Leave it to Gabby to say precisely how I feel. "You paid rent, didn't you?"

I nod.

"I don't have any place to go."

"You can stay here." Gabby gets up, and I hear her in the kitchen.

"I fucked my life up so bad," I lament.

"That's crap, and you know it," she yells from the kitchen. I hear the blender, and I'm grateful for the drink coming my way.

Though I can't drink too much or I'll be sorry tomorrow, and I'll need all my wits about me.

I reach for the drink she offers me and take a big gulp. *Perfect.*

"What do you mean?" Gabby asks. "How did you fuck up your life?"

I take another big sip and call on the liquid courage. "I slept with Jackson."

"Shit, girl! How was that a fuck up? Was it amazing? I bet he's incredible in bed. Don't get me wrong, Damien doesn't leave me wanting more, but I've seen those hips of his, and I bet those abs are mouthwatering." She takes a big gulp of her own drink and shuts her eyes, fanning herself with her hand.

I want to save some of what we had because it was special to me. But I can't help smiling. "Jackson's not a selfish lover."

"Let me get some popcorn popped. I want to know all of it." She jumps up and runs into the kitchen.

"There isn't much to tell," I yell after her.

"Tell me everything. Did he go down on you? I hate guys who want you to go down on them but refuse to reciprocate."

I cover my face with my hands. I can't have this conversation. I need to talk about something else.

"I'll be right back." I walk to her bathroom and take a few moments to gather myself. I don't want to hash this all out and dissect it.

When I walk out, Gabby's waiting for me. "Let's curl up in my bed and talk about it."

I realize all I have to wear is sexy lingerie, and I don't want to wear that with her. She wouldn't care, but I'd be embarrassed.

"I left one of my bags at the apartment. Can I borrow something to sleep in?"

"Of course."

She gets up, and when she returns, she tosses me a T-shirt and a pair of boxers.

"What are you going to do?" she asks.

"I think San Francisco has run its course, and it's time for me to move home. I don't have an apartment anymore, and I don't think I can work for Jackson now that we've been together. He moves on quickly, and I don't want to wait around for that. I want to make my own decision, not let him control me."

Tears spring to Gabby's eyes. She reaches for my hand, and we talk most of the night. I don't give her the bedroom details, but I do tell her the highlights of our trip. It was a great time, after all. She thinks I'm giving up too easily with Jackson. She has a boyfriend who gave up an incredible job for her. But Jackson changes women like people change underwear—often.

We both cry and laugh. Eventually, we fall asleep, but for me it's not restful. I keep trying to figure out a plan. Finally, I get up a little before six. I search for some business-appropriate clothes. I'll need to pick up the rest of my stuff from Jackson's place sometime—preferably when he's not around.

After a quick shower, I head into the office. My cell is dead, as I forgot to charge it last night. Shit. Rather than order online and pick it up, today I have to go into Starbucks and stand in line with all the stockbrokers. Oh well. It's a gentle reminder of what it's like to be normal again.

I manage Starbucks and walk across the street into the office. Todd, the security guard, greets me in the quiet lobby. "Welcome back, Ms. Woods."

"Thank you, Todd. It's good to be back."

"You look rested."

"Thank you." I wish I felt relaxed and rested, but I know what lies ahead of me.

When I step off the elevator, the office is chaotic—a stark contrast to the lobby. There are police, and I see Jim, Brian, and Ben. Everyone looks upset.

My heart stops. *What happened this time?*

Then I spot Jackson, and he's a mess.

Immediately my radar comes alive. Something's happened, and it isn't good. If it's Bobby Sanders' girlfriend, I'm going to lose it. A person can only take so much. This is over the top for some slimy guy who can't even break up with a girl like a decent human being. He's not worth this much passion. I may have to hit her over the head a few times to get her to understand. She can have him. Good riddance. He's a narcissist and only cares about his own satisfaction.

"Oh my God, there you are." Jackson comes rushing over. "Where have you been?"

Everyone has stopped what they're doing. I look around, and there are easily ten people waiting for my answer.

"I went home to my apartment yesterday."

"But when we went by, you weren't there, and your roommate said you'd left," Jim says.

"Well, my room had been converted back to a closet. I didn't have a place there to sleep, so I went to my friend Gabby's," I explain.

"Why weren't you answering your phone?" Jackson demands.

"I didn't realize the battery was dead until this morning."

He pulls me into a tight hug. "I was so worried."

I step back. "I told you where I was going."

"When?"

"As you were getting out of the car, I told you."

He shakes his head. "I didn't hear that. When I went back to my apartment after working a little, you weren't there. I kept calling. Brian said he dropped you off at your place, so we went there, but you were gone."

"I'm really sorry. I didn't mean to panic everyone. I told Angela I was going to my friend's place."

After everyone settles down, the office begins to empty out.

"We need to talk," Jackson grouses. "Just give me a minute."

I hand off his coffee and go to my desk. I throw the mail we got on Friday and yesterday into a basket on my desk and boot up my computer to print today's schedule. Jackson's door is still shut, with Jim and the police behind it with him.

I've really fucked up now. If the writing on the wall doesn't scream it's time for a new job, then I'm blind. I send a note to HR via our internal instant messaging system.

Me: I'm giving my two weeks' notice to Mr. Graham today. Can you start the search for a replacement?

Dawn Decker: No problem. We'll miss you.

Jim walks out and smiles. "We're glad you're okay."

Brian is behind him, and he doesn't look too happy with me.

I didn't intend to trick anyone; it just was an unfortunate set of events. "I really am sorry," I tell them. "I didn't mean to cause so much commotion."

"We still don't have a bead on your stalker, so just be careful," Jim says.

"Hopefully she's moved on," I say with more confidence than I feel.

"You can go on in." Jim waves me into Jackson's office.

I pick up a copy of his schedule and walk in. I feel like I'm facing a firing squad.

Jackson is pacing behind his desk. "I didn't sleep last night. I was so worried about you."

He isn't looking at me.

"I'm really sorry." I look down at his schedule. "You have a meeting with Cheryl this morning, which includes lunch with the management team. At two o'clock you have a call with the development team. At two thirty a call with the patent lawyer. At three, you have to return calls. Four thirty is your meeting with Dash Gates at Stargate Energy, and you have drinks with Mason Sullivan and Dillon Healy at seven at The Press Club in the Four Seasons."

He looks me over carefully, definitely evaluating me. "That's a full day."

It is, but it's a typical day for him. "I'll try to keep the riffraff at bay."

"I'd rather spend time with you," he says quietly, despite the door being shut.

I sit down across from him, and I will myself not to cry. "I sent a note to HR and asked for applicants to replace me."

"No." He shakes his head. "No. That's not what I want. We're a partnership. You can't leave."

It's nice that he feels that way—or says he does. But I can't let him control me. I know what's going to happen eventually, and I need to protect myself.

"I'll review resumes and narrow down candidates for you to interview," I continue. "I know I'll find someone even better than me."

"No. I'm not interested in making any changes." He stands up and rubs his hands through his hair. "I can't do this right now."

"I'm sorry, but you know that after the ways our relationship has changed, we can't go back to being just boss and employee. And when I returned to my apartment and no longer had a bedroom, I felt like that was a neon sign telling me it's time to leave San Francisco."

"I don't know what happened with your room, but we can fix it. And in the meantime, you have a place to stay with me. Given all that we've shared, we'll collaborate even better. And I've been working on stock options and a raise for you," he says with desperation.

I take a deep breath. "It's not just the money."

His phone rings, and I start to reach for it.

"Don't," he begs.

"Jackson Graham's office." I can't look at him, but I listen to the caller.

"Of course. Just a moment." I look up at him. "It's your lawyer."

I get up to leave.

"We're not done," he tells me as I walk toward the door. "We need to finish this conversation."

I close the door behind me. Despite what he says, I can't stay. I can't work with him after all the glorious ways he's made my body feel and know that soon enough he'll be doing those same things to other women.

I work through my day and move Jackson around as I've always done, making sure he's somewhat close to his schedule. He receives several calls from women in his life looking for time to see him. I write them down in the daily call log as usual, and I'll let him know. These only validate my feelings that it's time to protect myself and move on.

At six thirty, I give up. It's been a long day, and I'm ready to watch some mindless television and relax. Gabby is staying with Damien tonight, so I'll get her bedroom to myself.

I walk into Jackson's office and talk him through the phone calls he needs to return. "I'm heading out. You need to leave in ten to meet Mason and Dillon. I'll see you in the morning." I turn to leave.

"Before you leave, can you shut the door?" he asks.

I don't want to have this conversation, but I look at him.

"I heard what you said this morning." He genuinely looks upset. "You're the most valuable person at this company. What will it take for you to stay?"

I look down at my hands. "I'm nowhere near the most valuable person at this company."

"You are because you're valuable to me."

Arguing with him is futile. New tact. "I had an incredible time with you in Maui. It's something I'll never forget. But I can't go back to the way it was."

"I don't want to go back to that either." He sighs. "I'm not very good at this, but I want you in my life. I want you here in the office, keeping me on task and taking care of me at work. And I want you at home, in my apartment and in my bed where I can take care of you."

I look down. "I love my job, and I love the time we spent together, but I can't do this." I can't tell him it took fourteen calls today from women who are pursuing him, and my self-esteem can't manage to watch him move on to date someone else after I've had a taste.

He looks down at his lap. "I can't lose you. You're too important to the company, and to me."

"I can't stay." I look at the pattern on the carpet while I make the decision. "I'll remain long enough to train someone, but that's all I can give you."

Jackson sits back in his chair and turns to look out the window. "That's not enough."

"That's all I can give you." I need to hold firm. I need to make the choice that's right for me.

"Where will you stay?"

"I'll be at Gabby's for as long as she'll allow it."

"You're always welcome in my guest room."

That's a terrible idea. *Why doesn't he see that?* "Thank you."

Chapter 18

Jackson

I'm late for drinks with Mason and Dillon. I need to get my head in the game, but I honestly didn't sleep last night. Why didn't Corrine's roommate tell us where she went? Selfish bitch. She was too busy coming on to me.

I don't want anyone but Corrine.

I'm grateful she's agreed to stay—at least for the time being. She can try to find someone else as efficient as she is, and I'll get to approve or veto. I guarantee there will be nothing more than vetoes in our future. And I won't let her leave until she fully trains someone to replace her. I will use as much time as it takes for her to realize she belongs here at our company and with me.

I don't understand what happened. We had a great time in Hawaii. I depend on her for so much, and I'd love to see where we can go personally. It's been a long time since I've been in a relationship—since I've even been interested in a real relationship. I won't be perfect, but Jesus, at least I'm willing to try.

Ben drops me at the Four Seasons, and I head into the Press Club. It's an excellent place for a discreet meeting, and it's not too loud. I spot the guys immediately and walk over.

"Nice tan," Dillon mocks.

"What tan?" I'm confused because I don't have a tan.

Dillon has a glint in his eye. "My point exactly." He sizes me up. "No tan means you were inside the entire time, either working or doing some*one* else."

I shake my head. I have no desire to share.

"Tell us about the estate on Maui," Mason urges.

"It's beautiful. It has several bedrooms in the main house, and there are a few guesthouses. It sits on a peninsula of sorts, surrounded by two-hundred-and-seventy degrees of water, which means every room has a spectacular view. Viviana was in the middle of a renovation, so I had to give them some serious cash to keep it going so they could make payroll. It has almost fifty employees."

"What do they all do?" Dillon asks.

"Corrine went through it with the majordomo, but it's security, groundskeepers, and an amazing cook—stuff like that."

"Maybe you should host the next poker event at your place," Mason suggests.

"I never thought about the game moving around. Great idea." It might be fun to have everybody at the house.

We get down to business, and I walk them through my conversation with Jeff Wong.

"Do you think he heard you?" Mason asks.

"He was angry, but I think mostly because he'd been ducking me, and I managed to get to him in the one place he felt absolutely secure, thinking I would never have access."

Dillon drains his beer. "We've lined up an incredible IP attorney who has experience in managing these kinds of trade-secret thefts. She's drafting documents for the Chinese government."

"We may also have a small reprieve," I offer.

"What do you mean?" Mason asks.

"We discovered a flaw. We've fixed it, but if Hydro Energy's in a rush to get it out, they won't have tested it long enough to see the flaw, which prevents the film from working past thirty days. In a month, their buyers will find they have a panel on their window that doesn't work and is difficult to remove."

"There is a God." Mason looks up to the skies with his arms open.

As we're finishing our meeting, it's late, and I realize I'm starved. I don't want to go home to an empty apartment. I debate all of half a second, and I call Corrine.

"Hello?"

"Hi. It's me."

"How was your meeting with the investors?"

"I would've rather been with you."

She doesn't respond.

"Have you eaten?" I close my eyes and say a silent prayer that she hasn't.

"No."

Relief floods through me. "Will you join me for dinner tonight?"

"It's not a good idea."

I can talk her into this. I need her, and I need to prove that to her. "I promise I won't bug you about leaving. I just want to spend as much time with you as I can before you go."

She sighs loudly. "Where can I meet you?"

"My place?" I tease.

"That will only end with us naked."

"What's wrong with that?"

"We're back from Hawaii. We can't do that anymore."

"What are you in the mood for? Thai? Indian? Pizza?" I may not talk to her about leaving specifically, but I have every intention of discussing why being home means we can't continue our relationship as coworkers during the day and lovers at night.

"How about Thai?" she offers.

"Great. Let's go to Bangkok Alley. I can pick you up, if you'll let me."

"Gabby doesn't live too far from there. I can walk."

"Corrine, I understand your desire to distance yourself from me. I may not like it, but I understand. But you still have someone trying to do you harm. Please, at least let me pick you up. Brian will walk you to the door, so you won't have to worry about being alone with me." I don't understand *why* she wants to distance herself from me, but I will do what I need to so she's safe.

After a few moments, she relents. "Fine." She rattles off Gabby's address.

"We're on our way. Brian will walk up when we arrive."

"You're welcome to walk up. You just can't stay."

I'm elated. Two victories tonight—dinner *and* I can walk to her door. I can win her over. I know I can.

When we arrive, I ring the apartment, and she buzzes me into the building. I bound up the stairs. When she swings the door open, she looks stunning in an understated way—jeans, an Irish wool sweater, and her hair up. I want to nibble that luscious neck.

"You look beautiful."

She smiles. "What would HR say if they heard that?" There's a twinkle in her eye.

"You're worried about HR, now?"

She blushes. "No. I don't care about them because I'm not going to complain."

She locks the door, and we walk downstairs. It's awkward. There's so much I want to say.

On the drive to dinner, I tell her about the development with the flaw in the solar film and our workaround.

She puts her arms around me. "That's incredible news!

Take that, Jeff Wong."

It feels good to have her in my arms. I don't want to let go when she breaks away. "I know. It's great news, but we need to make sure the fix works, too."

"I believe in you."

I know she means that. She's made her dedication clear every day she's worked for me. With her, I feel like I can do anything. Why does she want to leave?

Over dinner, we continue our conversation but move on from work to favorite things.

"I love live music," she tells me.

"I do, too. Who's your favorite band to see live?"

"My favorite was probably Iggy Pop."

I put my chopsticks down. "How old are you?"

"I know! He was an icon before I was born. But that man does a fantastic show—four sets, high-voltage action, and great music. My favorite song he performs is "Candy." I only hope when I'm his age, I have half the energy he does. What about you?"

"There have been so many great shows. U2 did a private party I was at, and it was incredible."

She shakes her head.

"I know, it sounds a bit pretentious."

"A bit?"

"I didn't grow up with a silver spoon in my mouth, you know. My mom was an awesome single mother. She worked hard, and I learned a lot from her."

"You're still close, from what I can tell."

I nod. "She drives me absolutely crazy. She's my number-one fan and also my number-one critic. She likes you, though. And she doesn't typically like my girlfriends."

"She likes me because I'm *not* your girlfriend. I'm your assistant, and I put you through to her."

"Why do you insist on not being my girlfriend?" I ask.

"I don't want to fight," she says, just above a whisper.

I stare into her beautiful, caramel-colored eyes. "I don't

want to fight either. Please tell me."

"Because I'm not staying."

I reach for her hand. "Come home with me tonight."

"That's not a good idea."

"Why not? I miss you." I know she wants to be strong, but she must feel the same pull I do. I know I can convince her.

"I want to, but I think it's better to tear the Band-Aid off now, rather than later."

I don't know quite what she means by that—other than she doesn't seem to trust me. But I'm not going to debate her. I'm doing all I can to keep her at work, but I also need to convince her to stay with me personally. It has to be her idea. I don't want to force it on her.

We finish our dinner, and I pay. I don't want tonight to end. "Do you want to take a walk?" I ask.

"If it's okay with Brian," she jokes.

"He'll be close by," I assure her. "So, make sure you keep your hands to yourself."

She smiles and though she hesitates when I offer her my hand, eventually she takes it. We walk in the cold night air.

"Where do you see yourself in five years?" I ask. I want to know everything about her—her favorite colors, the places she wants to travel, her passions outside of work...

"I suppose I'll be home in Houston, married, and possibly with my first child."

"Your first?"

She nods. "I was an only child. I want at least two, if not three or four kids."

The idea of kids always makes my pulse race and my stomach flip-flop, but usually it's because I'm worried that the girl I'm with doesn't want to use a condom. But I don't feel like Corrine would trap me with a child.

I look at her in the moonlight. She's so beautiful. I stop and draw her close. My first kiss is soft, but our pull is electric, and it becomes more aggressive.

She makes a frustrated sound, but then she says, "Please

take me home with you."

She doesn't have to ask me twice. We walk back to the car with my cock at half-mast. Once we're seated, I look over to find her brow creased.

I caress her arm. "Are you sure? I can drop you back at Gabby's. I want to be with you, but I don't want you to feel any pressure."

"My brain and my body are at war with one another." She smiles. "My body is winning."

"I'm pleased your body is winning. I think we should reward her. Do you need to pick anything up from Gabby's?"

"Unless you returned all the clothes from Nordstrom, I think I'll be okay."

"Your clothes and everything you had at my place are exactly where you left them." I pick up her hand and softly kiss the back. "You've made me very happy."

"I haven't even gotten started yet." She reaches over and caresses my cock through my pants.

I kiss her, and we make out like teenagers in the backseat as the car whisks us across town.

When we arrive at my apartment building, we leave Brian behind.

We ride the elevator up to my apartment, my hands exploring while I taste, nibble, and suckle my way across her neck.

Chapter 19

Corrine

Jackson makes me feel so beautiful with the way he worships my body. I feel like I'm the only woman in the world. In this moment, I struggle to remember it won't be like this forever.

I take in a sudden breath, hold it, and let it out. My head tilts back to be next to his. My arms come up so I can put my hands in his hair. His hands cover my breasts as he rubs the nipples into hard points. I arch my back and lean in.

"Your breasts are so soft." He pulls on my nipples and lavishes them with his tongue.

He runs his palms down my stomach and between my legs where he parts the lips and begins to stroke my hard nub.

My hands fall from his head, my back straightens, and my legs tremble. Jackson nuzzles my neck through my hair.

I sink into his arms as my quivering legs sag.

Jackson moves his hands back to my hips and turns me to face him.

I see so much pleasure in his blue eyes. He wraps his arms around me and clasps my ass as he kisses me.

As we taste each other's mouths, I slide my hands between us and under the waistband of his boxers. My fingers wrap around the tip of his cock, trying to encircle his girth. He's hard and ready for me.

He gasps in my mouth. I break the kiss and look up to find him gazing at me.

I move my hands down his thick shaft and bite my lower lip. Reaching the base, I whisper, "I want you inside me."

I release him and remove his boxers. I kneel as I slide them to the floor. His hands slide off my butt and up my back.

I catch his arm, his hand still on the light switch, and my breasts brush across him. He takes the cue and turns the light back on. He reaches into the side table next to his bed and places three condoms on top.

"You're learning." I smile.

"You're the only one who excites me enough."

He settles next to me, and I relish his warmth in contrast to the cold air. He watches me watch him and runs his hand down my sides, my hips, and almost to my knees.

I respond with fluid motions of arching, shifting, and raising my legs to allow him to explore farther. He traces with his hands and soft kisses—moving from my feet, up and across my stomach, and across my breasts. He avoids my center, teasing me.

I quiver at his touch and sink into his kisses. He drops down to kiss my breast and lap his tongue around it.

My back arches to push it deeper into his mouth. Every new touch is answered by wiggles, quivers, twitches, or sighs of pleasure.

He gives the other breast equal attention, stopping to trace lines through the freckles in between.

I want to taste him and give him the pleasure he gives me.

But each time I try to move to my knees, I lose focus as the pleasures he gives takes away my control.

He takes his time, kissing my neck, using his tongue to trace around my earlobe, across some freckles, and even kissing my eyes when they languidly close.

Jackson props himself up on one arm and locks eyes with me. Then he slides his hand down my stomach.

My body arches, moving to follow him downward. I relax into the bed and into what he's doing, spreading my legs to welcome him.

He slips in and draws a finger across my wetness, dragging my slickness up across my clit. My mouth falls open. "Oh, that feels so good," I moan.

His fingers dance around erratically, and I feel the pressure building. When he puts his mouth over my nipple and sucks hard, my whole body jolts sharply and shudders—more than once. I moan my appreciation.

I finally open my eyes. I look around, not able to focus until I find Jackson's face.

"Did you enjoy that?" He nuzzles my neck as his fingers continue to strum my clit, building me to yet another orgasm.

Words elude me, and I can only nod as I concentrate on the pleasure he's providing.

His smile grows more prominent. I know this night's goal: he wants to see how many times he can make me come.

He coaxes me to roll onto my stomach. His fingers move from the top of my neck down my spine to my tailbone. My forehead presses into the pillow, my fingers curl to grip the duvet, and my hips roll upward as his finger runs down.

He rubs at my back door. "I'm going to take this one day."

It feels glorious as he rubs his fingers back and forth. Right now, he could do anything, as long as he continues to touch me.

My legs spread slightly, my shoulders tense, and my hips roll. Jackson runs his hands up the inside of my legs, just teasing me again.

"Please," I beg.

"Ask me again." My nipples pebble at his warm breath as he whispers in my ear.

"Please, fuck me." My fingers clench and unclench. My hips roll high and my thighs spread, clearly presenting my glistening pussy.

His hands stroke over my ass and slide smoothly up my back.

I melt onto the bed, my hips shifting side to side.

He keeps his hands traveling around my body for at least another five minutes. Sometimes he kneads my muscles, other times he runs his palms over my body. I'm on high alert, and my pussy clenches. I need him inside me to fill me up.

He coaxes me to return to my back, and it takes me a moment for me to recognize his request. I'm caught up in all the sensations.

His lips touch mine, and he runs his tongue along my bottom lip. Our kiss is deep. Rising up, he lets his hands slide from my face, down my neck, over my breasts and stomach, and then brush by my core before traveling to my feet.

Jackson starts to kiss the soles of my feet while massaging my toes. My knees twitch and bend, pulling him slightly forward, and my legs spread. His hands slide up to my inner thighs, and he opens my glistening pussy. He begins to massage, coating his fingers with my wetness.

My stomach muscles roll, my breathing halts and restarts, and my fingers clench the duvet and release. Jackson's fingers drag through my moisture, and he massages my clit gently between his thumbs. He watches my face, waiting for a jolt.

I purse my lips tightly, and my eyes go wide as my body freezes for a moment. My legs start quivering. Several sharp jolts shoot through me as my mouth falls open, and I scream Jackson's name. Finally, my body sinks back to the bed, and I breathe rapidly.

He kisses my heaving breasts and trails his kisses down my stomach, its muscles still tight and rolling at his touch. He runs his tongue around my slit and slides it into my center.

I grasp his cock firmly. Looking into his ice blue eyes, I rasp, "Please..."

He kneels between my legs. I put both hands around his shaft and roll my hips up so I can coat his crown with my wetness. I reach for a condom from the bedside table, and he watches as I rip open the package. Despite my shaking hands, I roll it onto him, position him at my opening, and pull him down into me.

He fills me completely. I roll my hips, pushing him in another inch. My eyes close briefly, and I feel him hit my cervix.

He pulls out completely, and my body immediately misses him.

"Tell me if it becomes too much."

I nod, and he watches my face as he sinks into me. His hands grip my sides as he pushes with long, slow strokes. I try to keep my eyes on his, but my gaze keeps wandering off as the sensations he's creating flow through me.

He's only a dozen or so strokes in, with the head of his cock pushing hard against my g-spot, when my orgasm begins to build.

He slows his strokes further. "You're so fucking tight."

I try to hold it back, but I can't, and for a third time, my bliss hits like a tsunami. This time I clamp around his shaft so firmly that he almost can't move.

He stills as the walls inside me hold and release him until all my shaking and twitches slowly subside.

I'm entirely wrecked, with three orgasms to his none. I want him to find his pleasure. "Come inside me."

He smiles wickedly. He begins to pivot in and out of me, cautiously at first. I grasp his arms at my sides to brace myself. His breath becomes short huffs, and he drives me deep into the bed. My back arches off of the mattress as the sensations surge through me each time he plunges into my depths.

He ramps up the speed, slamming against me again and

again.

His breathing ceases, and his eyes freeze open, wild and unfocused; he loudly grunts my name as he collapses on top of me. I can feel his cock pulsing inside my body.

After a moment, his soft shaft oozes out of me.

"Wow!" He sighs, holding me tight. "You do things for me I've never experienced."

"Is that a good thing?" I ask.

He chuckles as his fingers circle my arm. "Definitely."

We lie in each other's arms and drift to sleep.

Morning comes quickly. I wake, and Jackson is propped on his elbow, watching me. "I like you here." He leans down and kisses me. "Please stay here until you leave. I won't lie; I want the chance to change your mind. But if I can't, I still want to spend as much time with you as I can."

"It just makes work hard."

"Tell me how, so I can fix it."

"You've dated a lot of different women in the time I've worked for you—none of them for very long—and you get tons of calls from so many different women. They all want this." I motion between the two of us.

"We'll hire someone else to answer the phones."

He doesn't understand. It's not the calls, but the fact that they're out there. Even if he were to tell the world he's serious with someone, I don't think it would prevent women from pursuing him. That's how it was with Bobby, and evidently it was too much to resist. I don't want to be a part of that competition again, because eventually I'll lose. I lean my head on his shoulder and kiss his chest.

He sighs. "It doesn't have to be difficult. We keep things normal at the office, and at night we enjoy each other."

I don't want this to end, but I can't manage another

devastation like Bobby. I just don't see how there's a way. "I need to think about it."

He nods and gets out of bed.

I watch his perfect ass walk away. On the other hand, he seems focused on me for now, and I do have an exit strategy… *What am I thinking?* Sex with him is probably the best I'll ever have. Why not enjoy it a little longer?

He turns and looks at me. "Like what you see?"

"Absolutely."

He smiles and pulls on some workout shorts, likely heading to the gym in his apartment.

I shower, and as I step out into the fog-filled bathroom and begin to towel away the water, Jackson walks in.

He stares at my breasts and growls, "Do you need help with that?"

I shake my head, because I know if I permit him, he'll take me here in the bathroom.

He leans down and circles my nipple with his tongue, and I shut my eyes. He parts the towel, causing it to fall at my feet.

"You're going to make me late for work, and I work for an ogre," I protest. "He'll probably fire me before I can quit." *He is so distracting.*

"I promise, if he knew why you were late, he wouldn't mind. He'd probably want to bend you over his desk and take you from behind."

He makes it really hard to walk away, but despite my few remaining days, I can't be the center of gossip. "I should go. You have a big day."

He sighs. "Okay. Dinner tonight?"

"Sure. I can cook," I offer.

"That sounds perfect." He gets in and out of the shower while I dress, and I still need to dry my hair and hide the whisker burn on my face beneath some makeup.

He kisses me on the cheek. "I'm going in. I'll have Brian come back for you."

It's not quite seven o'clock, and I don't usually get to the office until about seven-thirty anyway.

"I'll get coffee and see you shortly."

He kisses me and heads out the door. My mouth waters, but my brain reminds me he doesn't do real relationships. That's why he dates Barbies. I need to protect myself before I fall head-over-heels in love with him and decide to stay in San Francisco—where I have no apartment or anything to protect myself when the bottom falls out.

My hair is done and my makeup is as good as it's going to get when Brian alerts me that he's downstairs. I grab my coat, slip on a pair of come-hither pumps, and as I ride the elevator down to the lobby, I put in our coffee order for a mobile pick up at Starbucks.

Fifteen minutes later, I'm at my desk, pulling up Jackson's calendar and walking into his office with his coffee.

"Good morning, Mr. Graham." I leave the door open, just as I do every morning.

"Good morning, Ms. Woods."

He licks his lips, and his eyes are on my breasts as I approach.

"Nice shoes," he says. "You'll have to wear those later."

"Maybe," I whisper with a smile. I walk him through his schedule, and before I finish, his phone's ringing. When the calls start at seven thirty, that means it's going to be a busy day.

Our work is nonstop all morning, and before I know it, I'm ushering Jackson out for his lunch. I need a break, and Gabby has been bugging me to meet her. I call her, and we agree on a spot halfway between our offices.

When I walk in, Gabby is already waiting for me. Before my coat is off, she starts her inquisition. "So, you weren't at my place last night."

"Jackson invited me to a late dinner."

"Which ended when you got to work this morning?"

"Shush! People I work with eat here, too."

"You're fucking your boss and you're moving. Why do

you care? Can he talk you out of running home?"

"No, and I'm not running home."

"Then what are you doing?" She reaches across the table and grasps my hand. "I want you to stay. Quit your job, find something that uses your degree, and sleep with Jackson as often as you want."

"I have a degree in political science with an emphasis on environmental policy. I'm using my degree. I could find something else, but it's not likely to pay any better than what I have now, and I'm done living in a closet. Also, there's no one who wants to send me poop bombs or destroy my apartment back in Houston."

I try not to sound too emotional. I enjoy my job. I make shit money, but Soleil Energy is doing something, and while I can't do the math required for any development, I work as the assistant to the CEO. It's my way of contributing to the cause I studied in school. Unfortunately, it's too hard to live in this town and be successful.

Gabby rolls her eyes. "You could find something here if you really wanted to, and you shouldn't let a crazy lady run you out of town. They'll find her eventually. Promise me you won't give up just yet." She raises an eyebrow, and when I don't respond, she forges ahead. "How about tonight we get together before I meet Damien for dinner? Evidently my ability to see you when ever I want is going away."

"I can't. I have dinner plans tonight with Jackson. I'm going to cook."

"He's in for a treat. What are you going to make?"

"Something easy. Probably my fajitas."

"That man will propose by the end of the night if you make your mom's margaritas."

I laugh because when we turned twenty-one, she shared her recipe. It's equal parts tequila and Everclear, which is pure grain alcohol and one-hundred-ninety proof. You don't taste it, but it definitely has a kick, and it softens the bite of the tequila. They were very popular with family friends, and she was always asked to bring them to parties, but she'd never shared the recipe.

"No, they can't sell Everclear in California, so he'll be stuck with just tequila. It tastes the same anyway."

"Why are you really moving home to your father? You know that will be a mess."

"The job I do pays the same in Houston as it does here, and the cost of living is a fraction of what it is in San Francisco."

"Use the experience you've gained the last year to find another job that pays better."

"I love my job at Soleil. Nothing will ever compare."

"Then demand a raise. He knows he's paying you shit money. Tell him if he wants to keep you, he needs to pay you more."

"Do you know how many phone calls he got this morning from strange women? He got eighteen. Yes! Eighteen. He can't stop those calls. They will come regardless, and even if he makes a commitment to me, what if one day the temptation gets to be too much? My dad cheated on my mom, and every single boyfriend I've ever had cheated on me."

"Not all men are pigs."

I fight the tears. "I know, but every relationship has its challenges, and when that happens, sometimes they forget their promises."

"I think you're wrong. And if he isn't willing to change his world for you, then fuck him. You don't want him."

I need to change the subject. "Like what Damien did for you?"

She smiles. She's so in love with Damien, and they really are right for one another. "He's great isn't he?"

I nod. "What cute thing has he done for you lately?"

"He's taking sailing lessons so we can go on a sunset sail, just the two of us."

"Awww, I love that."

We transition to lighter topics, and after we giggle our way through the rest of our lunch, we part ways, and I head back to the office. It's a busy afternoon, and the phone seems to ring continually. I'm able to answer some questions, but I keep a running list of those I can't and will need to call back after I have the answers. I also take sixteen calls from women chasing Jackson. I just add them to his list. I don't keep them from him, but they seem to think I do. If he wants to talk to them, he has their numbers.

While I wait for Jackson to return from his last meeting, I start looking at the job boards in Houston. There isn't much if you don't want to work in oil and gas. I find a job for a political and environmental affairs position at my dad's company. I apply. I know if I were to ask him to walk my resume in, they'd interview me and probably hire me, but I want to do this on my own.

Based on the lack of tech jobs open in Houston, I move over to the Austin job boards and apply for a project manager position at an environmental startup. That has promise. I need a real plan if I'm going to move back to Texas. If I return to Houston without a job, I'll have to move home. I'll be at my dad's mercy, and he'll have me doing whatever he says.

My cell phone pings to notify me of a text.

Jackson: Sorry, but I've been pulled into a dinner meeting. Please still meet me at my place. I'll try not to be too late.

I take a deep breath. I ordered groceries this afternoon and had them delivered. I try to push back the bitterness of disappointment. I wanted to impress Jackson with my cooking skills. I text Gabby.

Me: Dinner plans canceled. Still open to meet for drinks?

Gabby: Absolutely. Same bat time, same bat channel?

Me: Yes. See you in 20.

I alert Brian that I'm heading out to meet a friend for drinks. I text Jackson.

Me: We'll try dinner another night. I'm meeting Gabby. Talk later.

As I walk in, Gabby is walking out. "Let's go somewhere else tonight," she says, grabbing my arm.

"What? What do you mean? I'm in the mood for one of Tom's mojitos."

"I think the Cuban place up on Cole has the best mojito."

"Okay, but I need to go to the bathroom." I dart around her to the ladies room.

As I exit, I look over the crowd of happy hour drinkers and spot Jackson, who is with Jennifer or Valerie—whatever the fuck her name is.

Now I understand. I'm not leaving. I want Jackson to see that I know he's lied to me.

I sit down at the bar, and Gabby sits next to me. "I'm sorry."

I put my arm around her shoulder. "You're a terrific friend. I knew this would happen. I should have listened to my gut. I'm going to have a drink here, and then I'm going back to your place tonight."

"Sounds like a great plan." She looks over at the bartender "Tommy, please bring my friend here a mojito and for me… Well, I think I'll have the same."

"Sure thing."

Jackson spots me and comes over. "I know this looks bad, but I swear it isn't what it looks like."

I take a big, deep breath and try to paint a smile on my face. I will not cry in front of him. I cannot give him my power. "Don't worry about it. I'm leaving soon. I get it."

"She called and needed my help—"

I hold up my hand to stop his lies. "Really, you don't need

to explain. I'll see you at work in the morning."

"Please..." he begs.

Tom puts my drink down in front of me. In one gulp, I drink half the glass, and my hand is shaking. Jackson just stands and watches me. I pull a twenty-dollar bill from my wallet and place it on the bar. "Thanks, Tom. Keep the change." I turn to Jackson and take a deep breath. "Mr. Graham, I'll see you tomorrow morning. Gabby, I'll be at your place."

"Nothing is going on with Valerie. She had an emergency."

"I believe her name is Jennifer." I turn and walk out, and Brian follows me to the car. I ask him to take me to Gabby's, and my cell phone pings.

Jackson: Please, let me explain. I'm begging you. I'm sorry.

I turn my phone off and hold back the tears until I'm securely in Gabby's apartment and in a hot bath. Of the hundreds of bars in the city, he picks the one I go to the most? My tears flow. Sleeping with him was such a colossal mistake. And on top of that, I fall for him? From the moment I started almost a year ago, he's had a string of women. I ended up being one of them. I'm so angry with myself.

When the water turns cold and my fingers are pruned, I finally get out.

I smell Gabby's popcorn—her ultimate comfort food—before I see her. I put on some yoga pants and a T-shirt and head out to the living room for some BFF love.

"Hey." She hands me a large glass of white wine. "I'm not excusing him not telling you what he was doing, but I think she lied to him about why she wanted to meet him. She ran out after you left and made a huge scene."

I do find some comfort in what she says. But this will always happen with Jackson. I should have let my mind win.

Instead, my body did. But I've let myself get burned for the last time.

"Thanks for coming home," I tell Gabby. "I know you had other plans."

Gabby brings me into a hug. "Tomorrow will be a better day."

Chapter 20

Jackson

I've managed to fuck up huge. When Valerie called, she said her boss had asked her brother to do something, and he'd landed in jail. She implied that she had information from him about my company, and she said she needed my help. I didn't even want to see her, and of course, she picked the bar Corrine would come to with her friend. *Fuck!*

Boy, was Valerie mad when I told her I couldn't help her. Her story had started to sound fishy, and I realized it was all a ploy to get me to take her home with me. We've been out a few times, and I slept with her once in a hotel room at a trade show. It wasn't that memorable. I'd never take her to my place. Corrine is the only woman I'd allow in my home.

Fuck.

I keep thinking about what Corrine's friend said after she left. *"You were the one I needed to convince her to stay. You were my way to keep her from going home to that miserable house. You saved her from Bobby's shit, took her on a whirlwind trip to Maui, and promised her everything. But now instead of showing her she can stay, you've done everything every man has done to her her entire life. You're a first-class jackass."*

I tried to explain, but her friend wasn't interested.

"Why?" I scream at myself. There is no excuse for meeting Valerie without telling Corrine.

I call Brian. "Did she get back to her friend's okay?"

"Yes."

I can hear the anger in his clipped answer. "Did she agree to have you pick her up in the morning?"

"Yes."

That's a good sign. At least I know she's coming in to work. I can talk to her then and apologize.

"What time?"

"I'm picking her up at seven ten."

"Do you want to pick me up first?"

"She warned me that if you were in the car, she'd wait and go in later."

"I really fucked up." I rub my hand through my hair, trying to figure out how to fix this when she won't talk to me.

"Yes, you did. I'll pick you up at six forty."

"Goodnight, Brian."

Brian doesn't respond and hangs up.

Even he hates me. If he's not going to be respectful, maybe I should call Jim and have him replaced. No, I'm an ass. That's one of the greatest things about Corrine. Everyone likes her.

I look out across the darkness and watch the lights of the cars crossing the Golden Gate Bridge. Corrine is special, and I don't know how I can fix this. We were already on thin ice. The timing of this mistake couldn't have been worse.

I don't sleep well despite being exhausted. I keep thinking of ways I can get Corrine to stay—a big salary? Lots of stock options? An apartment? Clothes? Another long weekend in Maui? Everything I come up with, I can think of twenty reasons why she'd reject them. She wants to stand on her own two feet. A significant salary increase or stock options are too little too late now. But Soleil Energy will suffer without her, because I will struggle without her.

Sleep eventually comes in small spurts. When I watch the clock turn five, I give up. I throw back the sheets and walk into Corrine's room. I smell a trace of her perfume, and it makes me miss her more. While I work out and run five miles on my treadmill, I work on a plan to convince Corrine that while I made a huge mistake, she can't walk away from something that could be amazing.

Brian arrives as promised. A week ago, I was enjoying Corrine by my side in the beautiful sun in Maui. Now I'm here in San Francisco, Corrine isn't talking to me, and despite the sun not being up yet, the rain indicates it's going to be a gray day.

When I get to work, I can't concentrate. But I know what I need to say, and I know how I'm going to say it.

I watch for her, and when she arrives, I'm flooded with relief. There was always the chance she'd never come back to the office. She comes in as usual with my schedule and phone log, along with my coffee.

"Please shut the door and sit down," I ask.

She takes a deep breath. Her eyes are red-rimmed, and she looks exhausted. It pains me to know I did that to her. She shuts the door and takes a seat across from me. Without any chance for me to talk, she begins walking through the phone log.

"You need to return phone calls to Mason Sullivan, your IP attorney at Dunn Gibson, and Jeff Wong."

My head whips up. "What does Jeff Wong want? Did he say?"

Corrine shakes her head. "No, his admin called and asked for you, and when you weren't available, they asked that you return the call."

"Corrine, please? Can we talk about what happened last

night?"

"No. We're two professionals, and our relationship will remain that way." She looks down at my schedule and tells me where I need to be and when.

"Corrine, this isn't acceptable to me. I'm so sorry. When she called, she told me she needed my help."

Corrine stands to leave. "We have no commitment to one another. I think we should keep the relationship professional. I have four interviews today for my replacement, and I'm hoping two will make it to you for final approval."

"I don't want you to leave," I say much more forcibly than I mean to.

Her shoulders fall. "I guess I shouldn't have had sex with you in Maui." And with that, she turns and leaves.

She's infuriating. Why won't she listen to me? And what is she even talking about? I really fucked up yesterday, but I wouldn't change our weekend in Maui for anything. I don't regret our personal relationship.

She can't leave me.

"I left a message with Jeff Wong's admin to call you back," I hear over the speaker. I feel completely gutted. She's not giving me any room to fix this.

My phone rings, and it's Cheryl Wedgewood, my new CFO. "Good morning. How are you today?" I ask.

"I'm doing okay," she says. "I was here somewhat late last night, and I will be here this weekend. Can I come in and show you a few things this morning?"

"Of course."

I sit with Cheryl for the next two hours, going through some puzzling things Jeremy did.

"You're privately held, so we won't have any stockholders upset, but these three 'vendors' have a monthly payment of just under ten thousand dollars," she says. "And I can't find them registered with the Secretary of State as real businesses. I need to go back, but it looks like these were set up a while ago."

I take a deep breath. "That means our investors' money is at risk."

"I have some forensic auditing experience, but I think we'll want to get ahead of this with Dillon Healy at SHN."

A sharp pain in my head starts at the base of my skull and works its way to between my eyes. *How is everything falling apart at the same time?* "This is not good. Let me know what you find. Do you think you'll have answers by Monday? I'd like to get on Dillon's calendar."

Cheryl nods. "I'll work all weekend."

I call Corrine.

"Yes, sir?" she answers.

"We need to finish our conversation. Are you free for dinner tonight?"

"I'm sorry, I'm not. Is that all you need?"

"I need *you*. But I'm also asking if you could please call Dillon Healy and see if he can meet with Cheryl and me on Monday. Move anything I have scheduled around to meet him at his convenience."

"Would you prefer a meal?"

"No, I think this will be better in his office or ours."

"What should I tell him it's regarding?"

"Cheryl would like to go over the P&Ls with him."

"Okay, I'll get it on your calendar. Your ten thirty is here."

"Send him in."

Chapter 21

Corrine

I'm holding to my resolve to keep my relationship with Jackson professional. It's hard, because I can see he wants to explain, and I can tell he didn't sleep well last night, but in the back of my mind, I wonder if his panic about my leaving is more about the strong work relationship we've developed.

I don't know what Cheryl's found, but setting up a meeting with Dillon is not a good sign.

My phone rings.

"Corrine, Lisa Dixson is here for your ten-thirty interview."

"Send her up to the executive floor. We'll meet in the conference room."

When Lisa steps off the elevator, I like her immediately. She's a bit older than I am, if I had to guess. Her resume told me she has strong admin skills, and while she's never worked for a CEO, she has worked for other senior executives.

After we make some polite conversation, I launch into it. "Tell me about how you've managed your hours in the past when working with a busy senior executive."

"In my previous positions, they didn't necessarily need me the minute they walked in, but I like to be early enough that we can map out their day and make sure there isn't anything they've added to their calendar that I'm not aware of. And, I will stay until they leave or if they're going to pull an all-nighter, I'll take off around seven. By then it's calm and quiet, and they don't need my assistance."

I really like that answer. The hours can suck, but the rewards are usually worth it. "Mr. Graham is quite popular with the ladies and receives many phone calls a day from women trying to get on his calendar. How would you manage that?"

She chuckles. "I think I'd handle it like I would anyone else. I'd take their name and number and the reason they want to meet with him, and I would leave it up to him. If he wants to see them, I'll set the appointment, or if he prefers, he can do that himself."

She's right on track. "Things are pretty crazy around here," I tell her. "This position requires flexibility and the ability to juggle a lot of balls at the same time. Tell me about some of the other things you've had to do in your previous jobs."

"Well, I understand crazy. That can come with working for a startup—"

The fire alarm begins to blare, and Todd comes over the loudspeaker, "This is not a drill. Please move quickly down the stairs and vacate the building."

Lisa looks at me, alarmed.

I shake my head. "I don't know what's going on, but let's do as we're told."

Brian comes rushing in. "We need to get you downstairs quickly."

"What is it?" I ask, trying not to alarm Lisa.

"Someone set off the alarm on the eighth floor. We need to get down the stairs immediately."

I nod and do the only thing I know to do—grab my bag and cell phone. If the building is closed for the rest of the day, I'll need to be able to get into Gabby's house.

"Where's Jackson?" I ask.

"He's with Ben."

As we descend the stairs, I smell smoke, and Lisa stops.

"We need to keep going," I urge.

Lisa shakes her head. "There's a fire."

"Yes, but right now, there's only smoke, and we need to keep going."

Lisa shakes her head.

I reach for her hand. "We can do this together." I take my sweater off and offer it to her. "Here, put this over your nose and mouth."

The three of us walk down the stairs. The smoke seems to be thinner by the fourth floor, so it seems the fire is contained around the eighth floor.

When we get down to the lobby, Jackson rushes over and joins us as we move outside. "Are you okay?"

I nod. "Mr. Graham, this is Lisa Dixson. We were in an interview."

He looks over at Lisa. "We're not usually this exciting."

Lisa has a strained smile. "My husband told me to cancel since you got a bomb threat three weeks ago. I think I'm going to pass." She turns and walks away. Just before she disappears, I realize she still has my sweater.

"That worked out better than expected," Jackson quips and smiles at me, leading me across the street.

My blood pressure rises. "Did you pull the fire alarm?"

He holds his hands up. "Absolutely not, but I didn't like her."

"How could you know how you felt about her without even talking to her?" I demand.

"She had your sweater, which tells me she needed it to get

down the stairs. I need someone who is not only good at their job but not paralyzed in an emergency."

I'm freezing now, and it's beginning to rain again. I see Jim approach.

"Someone lit a trash can on fire and pulled the alarm," he says. "It looks like they wanted their Friday afternoon off."

I watch the color rise in Jackson's face. "When can we go back into the building?"

"Shortly," Jim assures him. "Maybe twenty minutes or so."

I feel a blanket around my shoulders, and I turn to see Brian. "Thank you."

He nods and steps away.

"Do you have any room under that blanket for me?" Jackson asks.

I want to tell him to dream on. If I was smart, I'd just hand it to him and walk away, but he's only wearing a dress shirt and jeans, and it is raining. I open up, and he steps inside. The body heat is an added bonus, and we huddle under the building's awning across the street.

"Thank you for sharing. I did notice that Brian brought *you* the blanket and not me."

I cock my head to the side and look at him skeptically. "He likes me better."

"*I* like you better than I like me," he moans.

I'm surprised by this, but he's only trying to be charming.

We stand in silence. I look at my watch. "You have lunch in twenty minutes at the Waterfront Café."

He picks up his phone, takes a picture of the crowd, and sends it off. "All set. He'll understand why I need to reschedule."

When we're permitted into the building, Brian and Ben take us back to Jackson's floor in a private elevator, and we are in our offices in no time. But as soon as we enter the executive space, we're overcome by the smell of shit—again.

My stomach tightens. Ben and Brian stop us from going any farther. The smell is overpowering, and I'm trying not to gag. The elevator has returned to pick up the other executives from our floor. I walk to the stairwell, but Brian stops me and shakes his head. I pull the blanket up to my nose to stop the scent.

I glance at my desk. Everything is on the floor and overturned, and someone has written on the walls with the shit.

Whore

You were warned

You'll be sorry

Ben and Brian back us into the elevator when Cheryl and our VP of sales and marketing arrive.

"What the hell?" Cheryl asks.

"I guess we now know why the fire alarm was pulled on the eighth floor. Someone ransacked my office." Jackson looks at me. "Are you okay?"

Tears sting my eyes. I try to nod, but I'm not sure what I'm doing. My phone rings, but I ignore it. I don't understand why anyone would do this.

I'm moved to a Suburban and sandwiched between Jackson and Brian as we drive quickly away. I'm in a complete daze. When we arrive at Jackson's building, I'm moved into the elevator and up to his apartment.

I'm in shock. I sit down on the couch, and someone hands me a warm drink. I hold it and sit while there is a flurry of activity around me. *Who is so pissed at me? What could I have done? I'm not even seeing anyone.* I watch the rainfall as it hits the windows. Gabby, at some point, arrives and sits next to me.

"It's going to be okay," she says.

Before I know it, the sun has set, and Jim and Detective Lenning have arrived.

"How are you feeling?" Jim asks.

"I've had better days," I say.

Detective Lenning steps forward. "I'm really sorry about this."

I nod.

"Who did this?" Jackson demands.

"That's what we want to know from you," Detective Lenning says, looking at me.

"I haven't called Bobby or heard from him since the bomb threat," I say.

"Jim, I sent you the message he left her," Jackson reminds him.

"Have you been seeing anyone else?" Detective Lenning asks.

I snort. "Not really."

Detective Lenning writes something down on his pad of paper. "Did you go to Hawaii with Jackson Graham?"

I look down at the dark hardwood floors. "I did." I take a deep breath. "We were romantically involved while in Hawaii, but not before and not really since."

"What does that mean?" the detective probes.

Why not spill all my ugly, dirty laundry out in front of everyone? I'm leaving San Francisco and never coming back. "I'm Mr. Graham's assistant. I cover his phones; I attended a funeral with him; we eat out occasionally together, just the two of us. Because this crap started, I lived here for a short time in his guest room and went to Hawaii with him for a weekend to look over his property. When we returned, my apartment had been redecorated, but because my room was so small, it got missed, so I've been staying with my best friend."

"Are you sleeping with your boss?" Detective Lenning asks.

I'm positively humiliated to have this conversation, and when I glance at Jackson, he's not looking at me. "We slept together in Hawaii and once after we returned, but I've given my two weeks' notice, and I'm moving home to Texas," I say just above a whisper.

Gabby, still sitting next to me, begins to cry.

"I see," Detective Lenning says. He turns to Jackson. "Have you spurned anyone recently?"

"No! I've not been involved with anyone for months. I go out for dinner and drinks on occasion, but that's it. They're only friends. No benefits. Corrine is the only woman in my life."

I'm shocked at Jackson's declaration. Under different circumstances, I might have liked to hear that, but it doesn't matter anymore.

Gabby suddenly stands. "You can't let her go back to Texas."

I close my eyes and silently pray that Gabby doesn't tell everyone why.

"I understand her desire to return to Houston and be far away from this fiasco, but you're right, she'll be unprotected there." Jim gives me a sympathetic smile. "We have some other ideas."

"I'll be fine. This crazy will leave me alone, and I won't need any security if I'm not here," I say. "Houston is my last choice, but right now, I don't have a lot of savings, so I may not have a lot of options."

"No, I can't allow you to go back." Gabby turns to Jackson. "This is all your fault. You owe her money so she can rebuild her life far away from Houston and far away from you!"

"Anything," he says.

"I have a solution, but let's get through Detective Lenning's questions, and then we can discuss options," Jim offers.

Jackson won't look at me and is avoiding the glare from Gabby.

Detective Lenning asks a few more questions. I tell him where the call logs for Jackson are. "I do pass along every call he gets, and while these women may feel like I'm the gatekeeper, he ultimately makes the decision on returning their calls."

Detective Lenning takes the seat next to me and looks me in the eyes. "Whoever this is, she perceives she's been slighted by you. We know this isn't you, and it isn't Jackson or Bobby.

For all we know, it may be someone who has never made any contact directly with you, Jackson, or Bobby."

"Okay." But I'm not sure that makes me feel any better.

Detective Lenning shifts his attention to take care of a few more details with Jackson and Jim.

Gabby holds my hand fiercely. "Promise me you won't go back to Houston?"

"I'm not sure what else there is to do," I whisper as I bite back tears.

The weight on my shoulders is immense, and I know Gabby is right, but I'm not sure I have any other choice. All my options leave me with less control than I'd like.

After Detective Lenning leaves, Jim and Jackson sit down with Gabby and me.

"Do you feel comfortable talking about what's in Houston?" Jim asks.

"My father," I answer.

"Why does Gabby feel going home to Houston is so bad?" Jim presses.

I look out the window, away from everyone. "My relationship with my father is not healthy."

I look over at Gabby, and she nods her support.

"My mother was an alcoholic," I continue. "The pressure of my father's job as he climbed the ladder at his company was incredible. I don't ever remember her being drunk, but I think her tolerance was so high you could never tell, and alcohol was part of an executive's lifestyle, so it was always around. Anyway, my father was not always kind or tolerant of my mother. I was a kid, so I didn't understand what was going on behind closed doors. He pushed her into rehab, and she'd go to meetings. I didn't understand it, but she'd be dry, and then something would happen, and she wasn't. She was never a stumbling drunk, but she'd make plans with me and then not show up. And every now and again, I'd walk home from school because she forgot to come get me. When I was in high school, my dad orchestrated an intervention and put her in a treatment program for ninety days. I didn't know at the time that he also served her with divorce papers while she was in rehab."

I stop and take a drink of my water. My hand trembles, and I'm not sure I can continue. Everyone waits patiently for me.

"When she was released, my father had an apartment for her, and I wasn't allowed to see her. He told me she didn't want to see me. He made it sound like my mother thought she couldn't be sober and be around me—like it was my fault she was an alcoholic. I didn't understand, and I missed her so much. Then one day, she showed up outside my school my senior year, and I spent the afternoon with her. It was so much fun. We went out for burgers and ice cream and hung out. I didn't think it was a big deal, but when my dad found out, he cut her off financially and took away my car. We only wanted to spend the day together, and I needed my mom in my life. I didn't care about the car, but I began to see how my father used his money to make people do what he wanted. Mom never said a bad thing about my dad, but some of the things she said and he said didn't add up. My father remarried a very formal and cold woman named Alicia, who didn't have a maternal bone in her body. She pretty much counted the days until I left for college. Unfortunately, my mom didn't have any skills beyond being a hostess to get a job."

I look around the room, and everyone is listening intently.

"My mom did the best she could for a few years without my father's financial help. She lost her apartment and would live on a friend's couch or in her car. I went to college in Austin, and she would come down and sometimes stay with Gabby and me. She was drinking, and when my dad learned she was in Austin, he got ahold of her and promised her money and an apartment if she'd leave me alone, but she refused. She didn't want to be manipulated by his money. I guess they got into a big argument about my graduation, and the week before the ceremony, she took a handful of pills and left me a long letter, and that was it. She was gone. She was buried where she grew up on Corpus Christi. I almost didn't take my finals. I was devastated, but Gabby was with me the whole time and was my only support. She got me up off the floor, into counseling, and worked with my professors to make sure I graduated. I owe everything to her."

I hold Gabby's hand and smile as the tears rim my eyes.

"My mother hadn't had any money since the divorce. Alicia took all her jewelry, and they gave her clothes away. That was upsetting, but there was one thing my mother did leave me when she died, and it was that letter. The police told me about it, but my father kept it from me. I pressed for it, but he still refused. Gabby's father is an attorney, and with his help, we finally went to court. My father argued that it would only hurt me, but I won. The judge admonished my father for being controlling and manipulative."

I'm full-on ugly crying now. "I realized then how my father had used his wealth and power during his marriage to my mother, and after the divorce. He'd agreed to give my mother money if she'd sever all ties with me. He would have happily paid her off with a fancy apartment and a huge allowance, but only if she wouldn't see me again. She didn't agree, so he left her homeless and penniless. Her alcoholism wasn't my fault. It was a disease. He means well, but his vision is so warped. He uses his money to get what he wants. In my mom's final letter to me, she apologized and said without funds or a means to work, and her inability to quit her addiction, she couldn't go on. She told me I was the best thing in her life, and she'd love me forever."

I'm physically drained. My head drops into my hands.

"Thank you for sharing your story," Jim says after a moment. "It's important to have all the information as we plan our next steps. You need to be a part of choosing these steps, but let's discuss them in the morning. You must be exhausted, and nothing needs to be determined tonight."

Jackson leads me to the guest room, and Gabby stays with

me. As we lie in bed, she tells me, "You're the strongest woman I know, and whether it feels like it or not, you have a lot of options. We just have to find the right one. You will get through this."

Chapter 22

Jackson

When I walk back into my living room, Jim hands me a glass of bourbon.

"Thanks."

"It looks like you need it," he says.

I nod. "I fucked up with Corrine—big time." I take a deep pull on my drink. "I won't lie, until all this started a few weeks ago, I was very strict about our employer/employee relationship. I thought she was pretty, but that's where I stopped. She's an incredible assistant. Because of her, I was able to get our patent application in place and get funding for a new product we're working on. She's positively invaluable."

I drain what's left of my glass and look out across the bay. Jim sits back and listens.

"You know she's nothing like any of the women I date. She's naturally beautiful. Did you know she calls the women

I've been out with Barbies and flotation devices?"

He smirks.

"I didn't *see* Corrine until all this mess with someone tormenting her started. But now I can't unsee her. She's amazing. I need her in my life."

Jim nods. "I understand. I've been there. I thought I'd die a bachelor. Now I'm getting married to an amazing woman."

"But I fucked up. Valerie, a woman I was involved with briefly, and mostly for work purposes, asked to see me. She wanted to meet for dinner, and I pushed back because I already had plans with Corrine. But she insisted—said her boss had put her brother up to something that led to him being arrested and jailed. So, I agreed to meet her for drinks. And I didn't tell Corrine why I had to change my plans with her. Once I got to the bar, I quickly realized this woman had not been honest when she set up our meeting, but of course, as I'm trying to escape, Corrine walks in."

"Did she follow you?"

"No, she was truly shocked to see me. Did you know there are over eight hundred establishments that sell liquor in the City? I looked it up. How could we possibly have ended up at the same one? I immediately went to her. She was upset, but I only knew because her hand trembled. We were already struggling to sort out our relationship after the trip, and in that moment, everything that had happened between us was gone. A wall went up. Then this shit happened."

"Tell me more about Valerie," Jim said. "We checked her out, but maybe we missed something."

"She works for an environmental startup called Organic Energy. She's in marketing, and we met at a trade show in Las Vegas. We've been out a few times, but it was more professional than personal."

"What did she want to talk to you about?" Jim probes.

"She said her boss had information on Soleil from her brother, so I was going to meet her to find out what she had. He would have met with me, but he was in jail, and she thought I needed to know as soon as possible, hinting that maybe I could use the information to get him out of jail. The bar we went to was close to her office. I forgot I'd run into Corrine there before."

"With Valerie?"

I nod. "I don't deny I was a total shit for not telling Corrine why I was breaking our dinner plans, but fuck! It was supposed to be business. Only it looked like a date, mostly because Valerie wanted a date and used that story as a ploy to meet me."

"Send me her contact information. We'll run a background check on her again and maybe do a face-to-face interview."

I nod.

Jim stands. "We need to figure out our next steps. I don't think Corrine should go back to Houston, but that may not be our call. For now, though, she can't be in San Francisco."

That's not what I wanted to hear. I wanted to hear that Corrine should remain under my roof—even if it was my guest room. But who am I kidding? I can't force my way into working this out with Corrine.

"When do you want to meet tomorrow?" I ask Jim.

"Since it's Saturday, I've promised to take a quick trip to the farmers market with my fiancée." He thinks a moment. "Let's meet at my place for lunch. Corrine can hang out with Kate, and we can make it a little less formal. If we have to put her into deep hiding, we can do that, but I don't think it's necessary."

"I agree." After I show him out, I send him Valerie's information, return to the living room, and pour myself another glass of bourbon. I have several ideas that may work for Corrine, but nothing I come up with has her working in the office, and she refuses to stay here—except when she has to. That leaves a gaping hole both at work and in my heart.

At some point, I went to bed last night. I didn't sleep well. I'm worried about Corrine, and that doesn't seem to work for me.

When I wake, though, I smell bacon and coffee. I walk out in pajama bottoms, a T-shirt in my hands, and find Gabby and Corrine in the kitchen, talking in hushed tones.

They stop talking when I come in. Gabby's jaw drops, and Corrine stares. I admit that my desire to lure Corrine back into my bed has crossed my mind this morning, so I'm reminding her of my physical prowess, which she seems to like. I see her nipples pebble beneath her shirt, so my cheap shot worked. I put my shirt on, so things aren't obscene.

"We were just talking about what Corrine wants to do," Gabby informs me. I can tell by her tone she isn't crazy about the plan.

"There's a great energy company in Austin I might be able to work for as a project manager," Corrine says.

I know exactly where she's talking about, and over my dead body will she go there. Not only do I know the founder, but he ran off to Austin after stealing information from another one of our competitors. He shopped their proprietary information to me, and I refused it.

"I thought if you made the introduction, he might make room for me on their team," she adds.

I turn to Gabby. "Why don't you like the idea?"

"To start with, we went to school in Austin. It's only two and a half hours from Houston and still within her father's reach." I can tell she's making her case more for Corrine than me.

"Even if I'm close, I won't be living in his house. If I have a job, I can be free of him and his influence."

Gabby offers her a give-me-a-break look. Then she turns to me. "What do you think?"

I take a deep breath because I don't want this to sound like I'll hate every idea she has—but anything away from me, I'm going to try my hardest to prevent from happening. "I know the founder. He used to work for Blue Energy, and he took some information with him when he was fired and offered it to several companies in the energy sector. I have no doubt he'd hire you without my recommendation—"

"See? I told you. A good job will keep my dad away," Corrine proudly tells Gabby.

"But given that he took some information from Blue, I'd have to consider the noncompete you've signed for the energy sector."

Corrine's shoulders fall.

"I have an idea, and Jim has some ideas. He's invited us over for lunch today." I turn to Gabby. "You're welcome to join us."

"Thanks, but Damien needs some of my love and attention." She stands. "Let me know what you come up with."

"Are you leaving?" Corrine's eyes grow large, and panic distorts her face.

"Yup." Gabby gathers her purse and heads for the door.

Corrine follows her, and I can hear them whispering on the way to the elevator. I smile. It's about me and my shirtless chest. I suddenly feel hot, so I take my shirt back off. I have no shame. I'm going to do whatever I need to do to get her back. I help myself to a plate of eggs and bacon and a cup of coffee.

Corrine comes back into my kitchen and stops short. "Where'd your shirt go?'

"I was hot."

"You don't play fair." She makes herself a plate of food and sits down at the bar, one stool away from me. "You could put your shirt on."

I look at her and know I've made my point, so I pull my shirt over my head. I want to hold her and assure her we're going to get through this, but I know she needs to figure this out on her own. The harder I push, the harder she'll resist.

"I'll check with Jim about what time they want to see us." I type a text and send it off.

She nods, and we eat in silence.

Jim: How about 12:30? Can you both eat clams? Kate's signature dish is linguine and clams. If that doesn't sound appealing, we have lots of other options.

I let Corrine know what he said.

"Linguine and clams sounds great. Ask Kate what we can bring."

I text Jim, and he quickly replies. "Jim says we don't need to bring anything, just be at his place at twelve thirty."

She begins to clean up after breakfast. "We can't show up empty-handed. We can stop for flowers and wine."

I'm not about to argue with her. "Okay, I'll alert Ben to pick us up at eleven thirty."

"I'll be ready." She finishes cleaning up and leaves me in the living room. This shouldn't be so hard. I swear that woman is going to break me.

My phone rings and brings me out of my haze of lust. It's my mother. There goes my erection.

"Hi, Mom."

"You don't call or write..."

I love mom guilt. "Sorry, it's been beyond hectic. I was in Hawaii last week dealing with a new property."

"Ohhhh. Maybe that's where I should do my birthday party. We can all fly in on your jet and spend a week enjoying Kauai."

I'm sure I told her about it. "The property is on Maui."

"Well, that works, too."

"Probably not this year—it's in the middle of renovations."

"Oh, that's too bad. What are we going to do for my birthday?"

My mom is great, and as an only child, I don't spend nearly enough time with her. "What do you want to do?"

"Actually, I'd like to spend time with you."

That makes me smile. My mom gave me the best years of her life and never complained. "Well, that's a given. What about with your girlfriends?"

"Let them come up with something. I'm fine with that."

"Well, have them send me the bill."

"We'll see. I did want to find out if I could set you up with my friend Susan's daughter. She's probably a bit young and most likely too brunette for you, but she went to Yale, and I understand she's a total delight."

Mom's so not subtle when it comes to her desire to have grandbabies.

"I'm seeing someone, Mom. I think she may be the one." I smile, knowing I've just made Mom's day, week, month, and year. Now to get Corrine on this same train.

"What? When do I get to meet this woman?"

"Soon. Right now, we're dealing with some crazy stuff at work. But I promise soon."

"Okay, sweetheart. I'll call the office on Monday and let Corrine know to schedule dinner with you for my birthday."

"Sounds good. And Mom, I know I don't say it enough, but I love you. Thank you for all you do."

"Oh, baby, I love you, too. You just made me so happy. I can't wait to see you."

"Me too."

Chapter 23

Corrine

Leaving Jackson in the kitchen took more will power than I thought I had. When I walked Gabby out, she suggested I fuck him to get him out of my system. But that will never happen. I think my addiction to him could only get worse.

I spend the morning getting ready. I have to convince Jim to go along with my idea of moving to Austin. I'm not strong enough to remain under Jackson's roof, particularly if he's going to walk around without a shirt.

Nope. I've got to make a change, and Austin may be the right place.

Just before eleven thirty, I'm dressed in white jeans, cute flats, and a blouse that Tiffany insisted on, which shows a little more cleavage than I usually would. But I love the classic lines, soft colors, and abstract pattern. It exudes money, but at least it's comfortable.

I walk out to the living room to wait for Jackson, and he and Ben are there waiting for me. "I'm sorry. Am I late?"

Jackson's eyes immediately go to my cleavage. He breaks a smile, and I know he likes what I'm wearing.

"Not at all. Ben just arrived early. We're mapping where you want to stop."

I put my purse down and walk over. "What's the plan?"

He points to his phone. "The best flowers on a Saturday are at the farmer's market. Ben can drop us at this entrance. They're in the middle, so we'll have to do some walking. Is that okay?"

"Sure. No problem. No stilettos today."

Jackson nods. "And there's a liquor store not too far from Jim's office."

"Are we meeting at his office for lunch?"

"No, but he lives on the top floor of the same building. It makes it easier for him to be accessible."

"Okay. That works."

I follow Ben out the door, and Jackson follows. We get in the car and drive to our first stop at the farmer's market. Once we exit the car, Ben walks slightly behind us. Jackson has his hand on the small of my back. His touch is electric, and it is wearing down my walls.

"Jackson?" I hear a woman say.

My radar is instantly on high alert.

"Mia! Hey, great to see you."

Mia's a petite woman with beautiful, shiny dark hair and big brown eyes. She's stunning, and I fight the green monster of jealousy.

Jackson turns to me. "Corrine, this is Mia Couture. She's the CEO of Reconnaissance. She's also a big winner when we play poker."

I extend my hand. "So nice to meet you. I'm Corrine Woods. He won the Halona Moana Estate from someone else, right?"

She chuckles. "Yes, that was Viviana Prentis. That was a

fun hand to watch. She was sure she had him, so she went all in. When he beat her, the room lit up."

"I'm sorry I missed it." I look at him and smile. "Sounds like a fun night."

"Have him bring you next time," Mia says. "We're due for a get-together soon."

Jackson nods. "We *are* due for a get-together. I was thinking about hosting out at the estate. Do you think people would travel to Hawaii to play?"

"I'm up for a few days in Hawaii. Plus, I think we're more likely to get Nate to join us there. I'm sure he's in no hurry to return to Las Vegas."

They talk for a few minutes more, and I really like Mia. The green monsters of jealousy quickly evaporate.

When we walk away, Jackson chuckles. "Don't be fooled. That woman is a pure card shark. She's won a ranch up in Montana and interest in a web company."

"You guys have too much money if you're throwing businesses and property around like that."

"Probably, but Mia, along with several others, has gifted a big chunk of her fortune to the Lancaster Foundation."

"That's pretty amazing." We arrive at the flower seller in the market, and it's enormous.

A woman in overalls approaches us. "Can I help you find something?"

"Do you have any premade bouquets? We're heading to a friend's for lunch, and I thought we could bring some flowers."

"I don't, but we can easily put one together for you. Do you have a color preference?"

"Just bright colors." I turn to Jackson. "Right? Or should we go subtle?"

He shakes his head. "You're in charge of flowers."

Our florist smiles. "Let's see what I have. How about a mix of lavender, pink buttercups, daisies, and yellow forget-me-nots?" I look at what she's pulled together, and it's stunning.

"It's beautiful. That's perfect."

"Do you deliver?" Jackson asks.

"We do."

Jackson writes down an address. "This is my mother. Any chance I can have a similar bouquet sent to her today?"

She looks down and nods. "We can make that happen."

"What's the occasion?" I ask.

"I realized how lucky I am."

That makes me smile. Jackson's mother, while often a pain in the ass, is really a sweet woman. I like that he's thinking about her.

When we get back to the car, Ben heads toward the SOMA neighborhood.

"I didn't realize Clear Security was so close to the Giants' stadium," I say to Ben as I stare out the window.

"In the summer, when the windows are open, we hear the crowds and the crack of the bat," he says proudly.

"I'm impressed."

We pull up in front of a corner liquor store, and a man pops out and hands Ben a bottle through the window.

"How did he know we were coming?" I ask.

Jackson smiles. "I know Paul. I called him while you were looking at flowers and ordered a bottle of a nice pinot gris. I thought that would go well with the clams."

"I guess we're ready to determine my future."

Jackson watches me. "It's not your forever future. It's just for your safety until things get figured out."

Ben pulls into an underground garage and stops at a door. We get out and take the elevator to the PH level.

We step out of the elevator just off the kitchen of a substantial loft-like space with floor-to-ceiling windows. Despite the gray outside, it's quite bright. The apartment is nothing like I expected. It's full of warm colors and doesn't seem like it's above what I suspect are high-tech offices on the building's other floors.

Kate is standing next to the stove, stirring a pot. "Welcome to Casa Adelson."

Jim steps forward. "Welcome."

Kate walks over and opens her arms. "Hi. It's great to see you again, and under much better circumstances than Cecelia Lancaster's funeral. Welcome to our apartment." Her smile is warm."

I hand her the bouquet. "Thank you for inviting us and going to so much trouble."

Jackson hands her the bottle of wine. "We thought you might like this. You're welcome to open it now or save it for another time."

Jim looks at the bottle. "I think this is perfect with lunch."

"Lunch will be a few minutes," Kate says. "Jackson, I think Jim wants to show you the new spy toys he got for his collection."

"Thanks." Jackson disappears.

"Jim collects spy toys?" I ask, trying to discern what a spy toy might be.

Kate laughs. "He kept it from me when we were dating, but he collects old-time spy gadgets. Stuff like you would have seen on *Get Smart* or James Bond—cool toys that do hidden spy things."

"That's kind of cool," I say, picturing lipstick microphones and rings that release poison.

"Some of it is pretty lame, but some of it is neat. You can check it out, if you'd like."

"That's okay. I can help you."

"I'm good. I'm not necessarily a good cook, but I can make a decent clam linguine. I want to take a cooking class and learn how to make other things."

"That sounds fun. I wouldn't mind doing that. I can make fajitas and a few other Tex-Mex things, but mostly I order well."

"Me, too." She checks her pasta. "So, I understand you have a stalker."

I shrug. "Apparently they don't like that I dated my

previous boyfriend."

"Why do you think that?"

"The first threat included his football jersey."

"He played football?"

I nod. "For the Goldminers."

She pours the noodles into a colander in the sink. "Wow, that's a serious football player."

"He dumped me for a cheerleader on the news," I say, trying not to sound bitter.

"Some men have no class."

I knew I liked Kate.

"They don't. But I haven't seen Bobby in a while, so they worry it's a crazy stalker I don't know—maybe someone even Bobby has never met."

"Are you seeing Jackson?"

"Not really. He's my boss."

Her brows crease. "Jackson's not your current boyfriend?"

"No," I say, because he's not. But Kate's so easy to talk to, after a moment I'm telling her everything. "We went on a trip to one of his properties in Hawaii last weekend, and we fell into bed together. But I've seen the way his love life works. So, I've decided I can't work for him anymore and watch him eventually move on to other women."

"I can't even imagine. Needless to say, the women who work for Jim could kick my ass, but they are all married to other guys who could probably kick Jim's ass."

"That's not true," Jim says. He puts his arm around Kate's waist and kisses her forehead.

This is a side of him I've never seen before. He's always so firm and professional. Nothing ruffles his feathers, and God knows he knows all about Jackson and me and doesn't flinch. But with Kate, he's all smiles and flirty. It's the exact opposite of his professional kick-ass disposition.

Jackson stands next to me a little possessively, and I'm secretly grateful. With all this abundant love, it feels a tiny bit awkward.

I watch Kate mix the pasta and sauce, and I'm in awe. As she plates our lunch, she says to Jim. "Oh, I forgot the bread. Can you grab it from the oven?"

Jim jumps up and when he opens the oven, smoke escapes. "I don't know if this is going to work."

"Shit! I burned the bread again."

We laugh as we watch the blackened loaf smoke.

"It's perfect. Bring it over to the table," Jackson says.

We have a pleasant lunch, even without bread. I enjoy the way the guys take off on a conversation, and Kate and I do the same with a completely different topic. When we've finished eating, Jim moves Jackson and me to the living room while Kate cleans up. I offer to help, but she refuses. I wouldn't mind putting off this conversation.

"Thank you for lunch," I say as I take a seat on the couch.

"I'm glad you came. Kate likes to meet the people I spend so much time with. I am getting a bit round in the middle, though." Jim smiles, and while I haven't seen him without a shirt, I don't think he has an ounce of fat on him.

"I presented Jackson with an idea this morning for a job in Austin," I tell him.

"I have a counterproposal." Jackson sits next to me on the couch and takes my hand. "I would be lost without you. I never would have made it through the patent application or getting funding for the solar film without your help and expertise."

I shake my head. "I can't stay," I whisper.

"How about a compromise?" Jim offers. I look at him and feel Jackson's grip on my hand become tighter. "The estate in Hawaii needs some overseeing."

"What about the majordomo?"

"Jason Crier was wooed away by the City of Honolulu," Jackson says. "He hasn't left yet, but he called me yesterday and gave me his two weeks' notice. What if you were to go over and help keep the staff working? You can oversee some of the renovations, do some of the project-management work your position requires, and we'll hire someone to answer my calls and manage my calendar."

I sit back. *Move to Hawaii?* "How long do you expect me to be in Maui?"

"Well, you'll need to interview for a new majordomo and make sure everything is taken care of, and that should also give us a chance to do some more in-depth searching to solve your situation here." Jim brushes at an imaginary spot on his thigh. "We still think the person behind this is someone in Bobby Sanders' world."

"I've seen the stack of Polaroids and emails Bobby had printed, so I imagine there are a lot of possibilities."

"We have a behavioral specialist who used to work on tracking people with the FBI, and she's amazing," Jim says. "She's on it."

"When would I leave?" I stare down at the carpet, not sure it's a good idea. No friends and all by myself in Hawaii sounds lonely.

"We can go tomorrow night," Jackson offers. "I'll work from Maui next week and help you get set up."

"You don't need to do that. I'll be fine. Would it be okay if I go on Monday or maybe Tuesday?"

Jim nods. "I'll send Brian and his family. That way he's with you for the next few weeks."

"And Gabby and her boyfriend are welcome, too," Jackson adds. "I'll fly them out for a long weekend, if you'd like."

I nod. "So, this is what you've decided?"

"Corrine, I know this isn't what you envisioned, but do you really want to go back to Texas?" Jim asks.

"I don't know. I think this is totally overblown. Once I leave, whoever is doing this will move her fixation to Collette or back to Bobby."

"While that may be true, we certainly can't be sure. We'd rather be safe than sorry," Jim says.

The two of them continue to talk logistics. I excuse myself and go to the restroom. On the way back, I see Kate working in a home office.

"Is this where you get to work every day?" I ask.

She laughs. "No. If it were, I'd never leave my job, and I'd work for days nonstop. There just isn't enough time in the day. But these days my office rents space downstairs from Clear Security."

"At least you don't have to deal with traffic."

"Not now, but we're growing. We may have to branch out, which gives Jim heartburn. He likes me close."

I chuckle. "Jackson is surprisingly the same way all of a sudden."

"He likes you," she says.

"He likes anyone with a set of tits—sorry to be so rude."

"I think he likes more than just your tits. He's worried whoever is stalking you is serious."

I shrug. "I think we're heading out, and I was just told I'm going to Hawaii with Brian and his family."

"I'm jealous. I hate the gray this time of year. I'm ready for spring and sunshine."

I nod. There are certainly worse places to be, but I don't like feeling that I'm not in control of my life. At least it's just temporary. "I sometimes miss the Texas sun," I tell Kate. "Not in the summer with humidity, but certainly in the winter."

After I return to the living room, Jackson and I say our goodbyes and meet Ben downstairs.

As we drive back to Jackson's apartment, he reaches for my hand. "I'm really sorry about Valerie. She told me she had information for me and needed my help. Given that Jeremy had shopped my plans around town, I thought that might be why she was calling—not for a date. I promise."

I nod. "I'm not happy that Valerie called and that you went running, but I was upset because you *lied* to me. You said you had a business dinner. And even if it wasn't that, you could have said, 'I got a call from someone who's telling me a startup may have gotten our solar film plans. Can we meet later or have dinner another time?'"

He leans his head back but doesn't let go of my hand. "I haven't been in a relationship in a very long time. I'm going to make mistakes. It isn't because I'm trying to be a shit; it's because I'm out of practice. I haven't had to explain myself to anyone for a while."

"That's fair. And now you know why I'm weird about money—and about being controlled. But you're putting me on a plane to Hawaii for the foreseeable future, which I am trying to accept. But once that project is over, I will look for work elsewhere."

We arrive at Jackson's building.

"Thanks, Ben," he says as we exit the car. "See you in the morning."

He doesn't let go of my hand as we go up to his apartment and into his home office. "Don't worry. I want to fuck you in every room and on every surface of this apartment, but until you're ready, I won't touch you." He lets go of my hand and offers me a file.

I open it up. It's a notice of stock options. Jackson's offering me twenty percent of the company.

I look up at him, confused.

"Jeremy had fifteen percent, which we moved over to Cheryl. I now have thirty-four percent, and SHN owns eighteen percent, leaving thirteen percent to employees. I'm giving you twenty percent—five from the employee portion and fifteen from me. I will still remain the majority holder, but the shares are yours. You can have them even if you leave Soleil Energy, and there's no vesting. But without you, we'll be lost. You'll also see in those documents that you're getting a raise. Emerson Healy did a salary survey of senior-level admin, and your position often pays twice what you make. But you also do a lot of project management, so I'm almost tripling your salary. You don't need me or my money. I know that. This isn't a handout or something to make you feel obligated to stay. As you can see from the paperwork, I requested this the day we received funding for the solar film.

I'm just correcting a mistake. You have not been compensated appropriately. You're valuable to Soleil and to me. Please don't give up on us yet. We need you."

Chapter 24

Corrine

I stare back at him. My salary just tripled, and I now own twenty percent of Soleil Energy? How is that possible? Why would he do that? I sit down and look through the pages. There is no vesting period for the options, nor are there any requirements for me to stay. Just like he said. It's all done.

"Why?" I search his eyes. "This is not the way to apologize."

"I get that." He comes over and sits next to me. "I'm not trying to manipulate you with money. The options remain yours whether you stay or go. You've earned them."

"I've only worked for the company for a little over a year." My mind is reeling. This is worth at least a million dollars, and if the solar film is successful, it will be worth a hundred times that. This is too much. My breathing starts to quicken, and I'm paralyzed.

"Corrine, you're the secret to my success with the solar film. You may not have developed the product, but you moved us significantly ahead with our patent application. And the biggest part is that *you* put together the entire proposal for SHN, and they approved our request for more than what I expected. Plus, you did all this without complaining to me about extra work or how little you were paid. You were underpaid compared to others in your position, and that was my mistake. You're well-liked and respected. This was not a decision I made lightly, and this was put into motion long before we went to Maui."

"I'm overwhelmed. I don't know what to say, other than thank you."

"You're welcome. I know I shattered your trust. I will earn it back, but I won't sleep well knowing you're in danger here in San Francisco. Please help me with the estate in Maui for a few weeks—six weeks tops. You have internet and cell phone coverage there, and you can work by the pool."

I nod.

"Just don't work in your bikini. That attracts too much attention."

I look at him, confused. But he isn't expanding.

"I'll notify the flight crew that you'll be flying back to Maui on Monday morning. Does that work for you?"

"As long as that works for Brian and his family."

"They went this morning on a commercial flight. They'll meet you there. Brian's getting a few security upgrades started that Jim is suggesting."

"Okay. I'll be ready to go whenever the plane's ready."

I get up and move with Jackson toward my bedroom, still not sure what to make of the news. Three weeks ago, I never would have thought this was possible. Now I'm moving to Hawaii, and I'm flush, with no strings attached, for the first time in my life. I've scoured the paperwork. Jackson put this in motion because of my work as his assistant. Not anything else. I'm feeling pretty good. I still don't know what this means for us or our future, but I feel like I can breathe, and maybe trust myself a little.

He's still holding my hand as we walk down the hall, and when we approach, he pulls me into his room. It looks the same as it did the last time I was here. As soon as we enter, I'm on him. His lips press firmly against mine for a moment before our tongues begin to dance. We stumble back, closer to the bed, and start undressing each other. The lust and desire building over the last two days is all about to come to a head; it's carnal.

Eventually, while his T-shirt and jeans remain, I stand in front of him in a white, lacy bra and matching thong.

"You're so beautiful." He grasps my breasts, which relieves the ache of my need. I struggle with the buttons on his jeans, and it isn't long before I push them and his boxers to the floor. Then he's standing naked, his cock ready for me.

I reach for his bare chest, and I feel his muscles tense. I need him like a woman crossing the desert needs water.

He pulls me in close, his hands squeezing my ass roughly. He hoists me up, and I wrap my legs around his waist. He pushes me against the wall, and our kiss is electric as it becomes more intense. More passionate. More urgent.

He carries me to the bed, and I kneel before him. His cock is big, beautiful, veined, and achingly hard. I need to taste it, to feel it deep inside my mouth.

"You don't need to do this," he groans.

I stroke his cock. "I want to."

He stands, facing me on the bed, where I sit on my knees. I lean down and lick the head of his cock, and I can taste the pre-cum. Salty and musky. Holding his balls in my hand, I take him into my mouth until he hits the back of my throat.

I look up at him, and his eyes are hooded with lust.

I relax my jaw and push him farther down my throat. His jaw tenses, and his hands run through my hair and caress my back. I begin to slowly bob and suck. His hips undulate with the rhythm he needs as he fucks my mouth and moans.

"I'm going to come," he announces.

I don't stop, so he pulls away. "I've missed you, and I want us to go all night." He places his finger under my chin and guides me back to my knees.

Kissing down my neck, he plays with my breasts. He unhooks my bra and reaches for my nipple, squeezing and pulling before he takes it into his mouth and sucks.

I shudder with pleasure.

Slipping my thong over my hips, he leans me back to pull them off. Opening me wide, Jackson's fingers caress my legs and explore.

"You're so wet." He circles my clit, and I moan his name. He sucks my clit deep into his mouth while his fingers pivot in and out of me, urgently. He's watching me watch him, and I play with my own nipples, pulling and twisting. The overwhelming sensation brings me to my pinnacle quickly.

He continues to lap up my juices, and it sets me on a path to come again. "I need you inside me, baby, right now," I moan as he continues his work on my clit.

He smiles and kisses me as he snakes himself up to my mouth. I can taste my own musk on his lips.

He lavishes my breasts. "You're beautiful in every way, but these are my favorite part of your body." I enjoy the sensation as he plays with my nipples. "It's easy to get lost in them."

"Do you have a condom?" I ask. I need him to fill me. I'm so close again to my second climax.

He gets up on his knees, opens the side table drawer, and pulls out two. "These are my last two. I'll need to go get some when I pick up dinner later…much later."

I watch him rip open the package and roll it over his cock. I marvel at his size and beauty. I know men aren't supposed to be beautiful, but his hair is tousled, and there's a slight sheen of sweat on his chest, which is perfectly sprinkled with hair.

Gripping my hips, he spreads me wide and rubs his cock

up and down my slit. He pushes in slow, and I flinch as he stretches me. He stops. "Is that okay, baby?"

I've lost my ability to speak, so I nod as I try to adjust.

"We don't have to do this."

I shake my head and take a few deep breaths. "Keep going." He rocks his hips slowly, moving in and out, each time diving deeper until he hits my cervix.

"Faster," I groan.

He moves faster and harder, pushing me deep into the bed. My orgasm builds. "Fuck me, Jackson! Deeper! Make me come!" My breathing is deep as the head of his cock hits the right spot. "Oh, that feels so good."

"Come for me, baby."

As he ruts in and out, his finger diddles my clit, and it sends me over the edge. "Ohhhhhhh…Jaaaaaaaacksssssoooooon."

My entire body shudders as my orgasm overtakes me in waves. My toes curl as he finishes, and all the tension leaves my body.

His hips stop rocking, and he moans. "Arghhhhhhh." He collapses next to me out of breath. "God, you're amazing. You clamp down on my cock like a vice when you come, and it's such a rush."

His chest is still heaving, and I see his cock is still hard.

He smiles. "You'll have to give me a minute. Don't forget, we only have two condoms."

I smile at him, but I'm sure I'll be hungry soon.

Sometime later we break for dinner, and eventually we end the night just cuddled naked in bed together, dozing off.

Jackson's grip on me is tight. "You've surprised me in so many ways."

"I hope that's a good thing."

"I'm going to miss you while you're gone."

Reality hits. I'm leaving for several weeks. Jackson's staying here. I'll talk to him, but who knows what will happen. "You can always call or text me."

"I want to come to visit you, too."

"It's your house. I'd never stop you."

He lets go and rolls up on his arm to look at me. "I'll only come to Maui if you ask me to, but please know I will be here waiting for your return. My hope is that when you come back to San Francisco, you'll move into my apartment and be with me. If that means you need to find a different job, we'll make it work. If you want to marry and have kids, I'm there. If you want to go slow, I'll try to go slow. If you want to walk away, I will try to let you go. But please know you've affected me in a way I never thought possible. I want to know everything about you. I love spending time with you, and I want to be with you, always."

I look at him, searching his eyes, and I believe he's serious. It's a lot to take in. He didn't use the L-word, but the way he's talking, it seems he wants to. I'm not sure where I am with my feelings. We've known each other for over a year, but he barely saw me as a human until three weeks ago, and I still can't quite sort that out. I worry that those who fall in love quickly fall out just as fast.

All I can be is honest. "This is the second time today that you've left me speechless with a lot to think about." I take a deep breath. "I have mixed feelings about the raise and stock options. It seems too much for what I did—which was my job, by the way. And, we've been out maybe four times and not really dated. We seemed to skip over that. Let's get the renovations done and this crazy person who is after me gone, and then we can figure out if we should move forward or part ways."

I see clouds in his eyes. He isn't overjoyed by my answer, but it's so much so quickly. I have to give myself time to be smart about this.

He nods. "I won't push—at least not yet. But I want to spend the day with you tomorrow before you go. What do you want to do? We can go wine tasting. We can become tourists in our own city. Go for a boat ride. It's a little cold to go to the beach, but we can do that. Or we can just be naked in bed. You tell me. What do you want to do?"

He just makes it impossible to fight him. "I'm kind of liking that last option for at least part of the day."

"Then we'll need another box of condoms."

Chapter 25

On Monday morning, the plane takes off as planned, and I settle back in my seat. I'm still happy, confused, scared, and concerned. So much is happening so fast. In some ways, this is what it felt like when my mom went away. It was crazy around the house, and then it changed forever.

Yesterday with Jackson was nice. It wasn't forced. We went out to breakfast, with Ben close by. Then we walked down the hill to Pier 39 and wandered in and out of all the stalls on the wharf. It was mostly full of tourists, and it's easy to forget it's there, but it was quite fun. The office was still closed for cleanup, so we both did some work from the apartment in the afternoon. He gave me a list of things I'll probably need once I get to Maui. I packed, and then we made love all evening until we collapsed. Then what seemed about ten minutes later, my alarm went off.

Matt, the pilot, could only get a landing time for just before nine, so that meant an early departure for me, but at least I'll be online on the plane and working as everyone comes into the office back in San Francisco. Jackson will work with HR to get the temp up and running today, and maybe with her handling the phones and keeping him on his schedule, he might be okay.

The flight attendant puts a small glass of orange juice in front of me. "Would you like some breakfast?"

"Just some fruit and yogurt, if you have it."

She nods. "We have both."

My email is quiet, but my cell phone pings.

Jackson: I miss you already.

I miss him, too. I debate telling him and decide, why not?

Me: Miss you, too.

He probably won't be able to visit as often as he thinks, but I'm hopeful—we have to spend time together if we're going to see if we actually have a future—and we did agree to talk every day. Gabby and Damien are talking about coming next weekend, which would be a blast.

I lean back in my chair as the morning news plays, and before I realize it, the flight attendant is telling me we've landed.

Just after we touch down at the Kahalui airport, Brian pulls up with a Range Rover. He's relaxed, in khaki shorts and a Hawaiian shirt.

"Welcome to Hawaii," he says.

"Thank you." I smile. "You look like you're enjoying the Hawaiian life."

"We are. Thank you for allowing my wife and sons to join us."

"Of course. I suspect you'll be bored with just me

overseeing the renovations."

"I have plenty to keep me busy. I have a long list of things Jim and Jackson want done at the house."

"I'm meeting with Jason Crier…" I look at my watch and subtract the three-hour time difference with San Francisco. "In about an hour and a half."

He nods. "We're doing some background checks on some of the candidates for the majordomo position. We have a few that look interesting."

"Good. I look forward to those. How are the renovations coming from your perspective? I know it's only been two weeks, but they seemed a little slow."

"You know how Hawaiians like to take it easy," he says. "I tell you, they've got it figured out."

I laugh. "I'm not sure I disagree."

We arrive at the estate, and Jason and Leilani come out to greet me. "Aloha! Welcome back!"

"And you thought you wouldn't be coming back," Leilani teases.

"If Jason hadn't received such a spectacular job offer from the city, I probably wouldn't be here."

"Well, I, for one, am delighted you're here. It's much more fun having you around." Leilani pulls me into a light embrace.

"You're very sweet." I turn to Brian. "Can you have the houseman put my bags in the same room as I was in before?"

He looks at me, startled. "Of course. But you are welcome to stay in the master."

"Well, I suspect Mr. Graham will be staying there when he comes."

He exchanges a look with Leilani. "Of course. Good thinking."

"I need to check in with the office. They have a temp taking over my position today, but I'd also love your scramble, if you have time."

"I'll make that right up." Leilani immediately begins to move around the kitchen, pulling things out. "The chickens have been generous lately, so we have lots of eggs."

I head to the library, which I will use as my office while I'm here, and call San Francisco.

The phone rings three times. I've always tried to answer in one ring, but there are times the phone is just crazy busy. "Hello? Jackson Graham's office."

"Hi there. This is Corrine Woods. How is it going so far?"

She seems reluctant to give me much information. "Fine…"

"You're sitting at my desk while I'm working on a project." I offer as a subtle reminder.

"Oooookay. Did you need something?" She isn't putting together my name and my desk. This does not bode well for Jackson.

"Well, I guess you've been there a few hours. Do you have any questions?"

"Nooooo." She's obviously perplexed.

"Okay. Then may I speak to Mr. Graham?"

"Is he expecting your call?"

"I did tell him I would call when I landed, so yes."

"And your name again?"

Is this a joke?

I take a deep breath and try to control my frustration, but I can only imagine how upset Jackson's going to be when I get through to him. "Corrine Woods, executive assistant and project manager to Jackson Graham."

"I'll see if he's available for you." And she hangs up on me.

I count to ten and redial.

Four rings this time. "Hello? Jackson Graham's office."

"Hi. This is Corrine again. I think you disconnected me. I was waiting to speak with Mr. Graham."

"I didn't hang up on you."

You did, but it's not worth arguing. "May I speak with Mr. Graham?"

"What is this regarding?"

"He's expecting my call."

"He's in a meeting right now; he can't be expecting your call."

"Can you please let him know I called?"

"What is your name again?"

Oh, you've got to be kidding! "Corrine Woods."

"And your phone number?"

"Please tell him I'm at the Halona Moana. He has the number."

"I won't give him a message without a number."

I think I'm getting a headache. "You can tell Mr. Graham it's on the sticky note on the right corner of his computer monitor."

"Unless you give me a number, I won't give him a message."

I can hear the phone ringing, and I don't want to keep her from answering important calls.

I ramble off my cell phone number and disconnect.

She has me wound up. I can't even imagine what she's done to Jackson.

Me: I made it. Your new admin screened me out when I just called. She's tough. Call me when you're done with your meeting.

My phone rings moments later. Maybe she's not good with others but is good with him.

"Hey," I say brightly.

"I swear, I'm going to kill her."

Maybe not. "Call HR," I tell him. "They'll call the temp agency, and you can have her replaced tomorrow."

"Do you see why you're so important?"

"I'm sorry," I offer with a grin.

"Jesus, this woman is killing me. She must have sent through a dozen phone calls, and she screened *you* out?"

"I don't think she's right for you. Do you need me to call HR?"

"Can you?"

"I'll call now."

"Wait." I hear paper shuffling. "How was your trip?"

"I was tired, I guess. I started to work but then slept the entire way. Someone wore me out this weekend."

"I'm pretty proud of that, you know. How are the renovations coming?"

"I haven't looked yet. Leilani is making me breakfast, and then I'm meeting with Mr. Crier."

"Call me at the end of your day."

"I'll try, but first I'll call HR."

"Thank you."

I disconnect the call and dial HR. "Hey, Dawn. I just spoke with Jackson, and the woman covering my desk isn't going to make it. Can you call her agency and have them let her know she isn't a fit?"

"I'm not surprised. She was late, and a few people have complained about her."

"I'm sorry," I sympathize. Sometimes there's a reason people are temps.

"Apparently, Andy in development thinks it's my fault," Dawn adds.

"If it takes money, I'll approve fifty dollars an hour for someone spectacular," I tell her. "I'm guessing the agency pays them half, and maybe we'll get someone who can answer the phones and manage Mr. Graham's calendar."

"Thanks. I appreciate the increase. That may help us."

I hang up and head into the kitchen.

"Perfect timing," Leilani says. "Your breakfast is just now ready."

"You know, I dreamed of this all last week."

"Do you have any special requests while you're here?"

"Who do you cook for at night?" I ask.

"There's the staff that lives onsite, and I cook for Brian and his family."

"Are you making the same meal for all of them?" I want to

understand what she does before I make her do a bunch of unnecessary work on my behalf.

"I can, at least for the adults."

I look at her, puzzled.

"The twins are adorable, but they eat rice, chicken, french fries, and well, anything white."

I laugh. "I've heard about that. I don't want to be any trouble. I'll eat whatever you make the staff."

She nods. "Will you be assuming the majordomo role?"

"Probably not. I may manage the estate in terms of Mr. Graham's interests, but that just means I'll make sure there's enough money to do what needs to be done."

I take a bite of my eggs, and they're spectacular.

"Would you know of anyone interested in the job?" I ask her. I think she'd make a great majordomo. She's like a mother to most of the staff anyway.

Leilani shrugs.

I can read her body language. She's unsure about taking the risk. "Are you thinking you might be interested?"

She looks at me. "I think I can cook and be the majordomo. I might want an assistant when it comes to larger meals, but I don't think we need to spend the money. Mostly I cook three times a day for eight people. Occasionally there are more when you're here, but even Mr. Graham doesn't have a family, so it's him and a guest."

I like that she thinks about the cost of the estate. I could take over any bills, but that also means I would remain working for Jackson.

I heard what he said, but I'm still not sure he understands why it's a bad idea for us to live *and* work together. If I move in, after a few months, I could lose my job *and* my place to live. He's never had a relationship last longer than three months, and he didn't work or live with any of those women, so we'd be tempting fate by doing both.

After my tour with Jason, I'm happy with what they've done so far with the renovations, but also concerned that some things are not progressing as quickly as I'd like. I look at the time, and it's after seven in San Francisco, but I call Jackson on his phone.

"Hey," he answers. "How did it go today?"

"Not bad. I may move a little bit more money over. The designer has gone over budget because of some structural work that needed to be done. They didn't realize a wall was load-bearing."

"Whatever you need."

"I may have walked Leilani into a request today."

"What was it?"

I talk him through promoting her to majordomo, and he seems open to the idea.

"What do *you* think?" he asks when I've finished explaining.

"I'm not sure yet. I have three interviews, but if you're really not going to be here often, we need to conserve money. Promoting her would take at least seventy thousand dollars off the top line. Plus, I think Leilani's looking for some job security."

"I agree with you. Meet the other candidates and see if you feel the same after that. On another subject, I was wondering…when we saw Mia on Saturday, we joked about moving the poker game to the estate. What do you think? It would be roughly ten or twelve couples for a weekend, plus security and increased staff."

"You'd need to wait until the renovations are done, but we could probably make that work. Leilani would definitely need some help. Let me do some research, and I'll get back to you."

"I was thinking about sometime in May."

"I don't know much about organizing a poker tournament."

"I'll send you Jonathan Best's contact info, and he can talk you through it. Maybe find out if he, his dealers, and Gillian Reece, his manager of guest relations, can come to manage the game that night. Gillian would be great with bar recommendations and possibly food and entertainment."

"I can work on that. Did your afternoon get any better?"

He sighs. "Not in the slightest, and the temp left at four."

Ouch. That's not good. Jackson's just hitting his stride about four and usually needs help making and fielding phone calls.

"I spoke with HR, and she won't be back tomorrow," I assure him. "I increased the allowable cost, so maybe we can find someone more professional."

"God, I hope so. I can't take six weeks of this."

"Hopefully they have someone. If that agency doesn't, we'll call around. I can also put a push out to several of your friends and see who they know."

"But they won't be temporary."

I'm quiet a moment. "You mentioned that *if* I came back, I wouldn't be answering the phones anymore."

He takes a deep breath. "I know I did. You're right. I'm just reacting to having a bad day, and you aren't even here to come home to."

"Six weeks will fly by."

"I'll fly out before then."

That sounds good, but then I start wondering if it's wise. I honestly don't know what to do with this man—or myself where he's concerned.

I try to regroup. "How was your meeting with Dillon and Cheryl to go over the P&Ls?"

"He was surprisingly not upset. I was prepared to have to write a check and return their investment. Cheryl went back over the records, and it seems like Jeremy was writing the checks to himself and keeping them just under the point where I might notice. But it was over a million dollars in total."

"Holy crap. Can you chase Jeremy for it?"

"SHN's attorney is working with Cheryl, and we may prosecute."

"I know he didn't like me very much, so understand I

might be biased, but I think you should. It sends a message that you're generous, but those who take advantage will be held accountable."

"You're hardcore," he teases.

"Maybe. I always missed my mom, but her alcoholism would make her forget she had plans with me. I always want people to follow through on what they've promised or are supposed to do."

"You're a major stockholder in the company, so I will defer to you."

"I'm your assistant with an opinion," I remind him.

"An opinion I agree with," he counters.

"I need to run," I tell him. "Dinner is about to be served, and I get to meet Brian's family and the staff that lives on the property."

"Absolutely," he says. "Enjoy."

Chapter 26

Jackson

The office is quiet. Everyone else has gone. I pause to rub my hands over my face. Today completely sucked, and I can't even get it to end. I didn't get half as much done as I do when Corrine is here. She's the person in front of me, fending off the unnecessary, and the person behind me cheering me on. Right now, I feel abandoned, and it's all my fault.

One of the things that makes me a strong entrepreneur is that I go for what I want. Once I get it, I sometimes realize it's not the shiny object I thought it was, but maybe even better.

I pour myself a glass of bourbon from my office liquor stash, sit back in my chair, and look out over the East Bay. Corrine has been working for me for a little over a year. I remember when I hired her. She'd been working for a startup that went under. She was definitely hungry for challenging work, and she worked hard. At the time we were only a company of maybe a hundred people. She came in and created systems and structures where we had none. She was a godsend.

My mind turns to the women I've dated in that time period, which Corrine has dealt with. There've been several. I haven't slept with them all, but she's had to field calls and plans from all of them. And sometimes I see their names on the call sheets, but I don't return their calls. I start adding up the women, and I'm embarrassed.

Fuck. No wonder Corrine has trouble trusting me. She must think I'm a total manwhore. Especially since they're all Barbies and flotation devices, as she likes to tell me. She's right. And funny.

I look at my watch. I wonder what she's doing right now. It's after eleven here, but earlier there. Still, in case she's gone to bed already, I text her.

Me: Are you up?

Corrine: Yes. I just got settled in my room. Feel free to call.

I immediately dial her.

"Hey," she answers. Her voice sounds sultry, and it makes my dick hard.

"How was dinner?"

"I got to meet Brian's family and spend time with the staff. I like them all. Maybe I should take over the majordomo role?"

"Please, don't do that. I need you."

"You'd still have me, just in a different role. I'm teasing anyway. I'd get lonely here without my friends."

She's silent a moment, and I wait to hear if she says she's going to be lonely without me.

"How was the rest of your day?" she asks instead.

"Kind of still going," I sigh. "I did get a call from the

agency, and they're sending a woman in first thing tomorrow. They assure me I'll be impressed."

"I'll call when I wake up and see how she's doing."

I can't let it go. "Won't you miss me, too?"

"I don't know. I did ask for a casting of your dick. It's not the whole thing, but with some speed and maybe a set of ears, I might forget all about you."

Now I know she's teasing. "A set of ears?"

"Yes, they're like rabbit ears that nestle up against my clit and vibrate. It would make for a shattering orgasm." Her voice is low and really making me horny.

"But wouldn't you prefer the real thing? After all, the real thing comes with fingers, a mouth, and a live dick."

"I definitely like the sound of that."

"I miss you," I tell her truthfully.

"I haven't been gone twenty-four hours."

"I know, but going back to my apartment without you seems depressing."

"I'm sure there are plenty of people you can call to keep you company—and I don't mean naked company, people to hang out with."

"That's my problem. I only want to hang out with you naked."

"Brian has set up perimeter alarms and cameras and some other devices. The staff is concerned that the nocturnal life of the mongoose is going to drive him crazy, but he's going to try."

She's changed the subject, and that isn't lost on me.

"I met Brian's family," she continues. "His two little boys are adorable. I mean, just the cutest things. They're all trouble. They're mini versions of Brian, but I think they have their mother's sense of adventure, which gives Brian great anxiety. They were so much fun at dinner tonight. I've asked him to find a perimeter fence for the pool. I know it can obstruct the view to have a fence, but it's a safety issue. Plus, they're having problems with critters drowning in the pool."

"I defer to you for that. Can I change the subject?"

"Of course. You're the boss."

My heart stops. This again? I want to be more than Corrine's boss. I want to be her everything. But right now doesn't seem like the time to push.

I take a deep breath. "How's the view from the master suite?"

"It was stunning today. You're going to love it when you get here."

"Aren't you staying there?"

"No, that's your room. When you come, you can stay there. I'm staying in the same room I stayed in last time."

That's a knife through my heart. "Then what are you wearing?"

"I'm afraid it isn't very sexy. I'm wearing a pair of your boxer shorts and one of your MIT T-shirts."

That is a positive sign. "So, at least I'm close—in theory—to all my favorite parts."

She giggles, and my heart soars. "I suppose that would be true. I probably did that subconsciously." She chuckles. "What about you? What are you wearing?

"I'm sitting in my office with all the lights off except my desk lamp, watching the East Bay with my work clothes on. Ben is outside in your office—I think reading a book."

"You should go home unless you plan on sleeping on that crappy couch in your office."

"Hey! That couch cost a lot of money. It's not crappy."

"Sit down on it, and you'll see. It's like sitting on a concrete bench."

I walk over to the couch and sit down hard. I groan. "Oh my God. I think I hurt my tailbone. You're right. it's like sitting on a concrete bench."

"I always thought it was because you didn't want people to stick around long."

I chuckle. "That sounds like a reasonable excuse, but that's not why it's there—or at least that wasn't my intent." My voice softens. "I've had visions recently of bending you over the arm of this thing and fucking you."

"Mmmmm… That might be fun." She sighs. "Where else do you think about fucking me?"

"In the car, in the elevator, on the table at Jim's house, beside the flower stall at the farmers market… I think about licking your pussy at a restaurant—essentially everywhere I go with you. Do you ever think about fucking me?"

"Oh, only in the car, the elevator, in public, in private, and definitely in your office." She sighs again, and it turns me on. "I've never had the kind of sex I've had with you. And now I crave it, and it scares me," she says just above a whisper.

"I've never had this kind of sex with anyone else either. And I love that you crave it, but it shouldn't scare you. It should excite you."

"It's almost midnight there. You need to get home and let Ben get home, too. He'll have to be back with you very early tomorrow morning."

I'm disappointed that she's avoiding the conversation about her feelings with me, but I won't push—at least not right now.

"Ben has the next few days off, and I have a new guy named Quint covering me. I really wish you were here. Goodnight, my love."

"Goodnight."

My alarm clock sounds entirely too early. There was a time when I didn't have to wake to a clock. I was a machine. I slept five hours a night, I often worked eighteen-hour days, and I worked out every day. On occasion, I'd go to industry events, or I'd go on a date, but I hadn't had a serious girlfriend since grad school.

Now all of a sudden, a switch has been flipped. I care less

about long days at work, and I think one of my all-time favorite days was last Saturday. Corrine and I wandered the farmers market, had lunch with friends, and spent the rest of the day in bed, which led to spending a good part of Sunday in bed together. I want more of those kinds of weekends. I just need to convince her she wants that with me.

I trudge myself into work. Just after seven thirty, Quint knocks on my door.

"Sir, a Winifred Day is here as your temp," he says.

I nod and stand to go meet her. She is an older woman and seems formal, but maybe that's just how her name sounds to me.

When I walk out, she firmly shakes my hand. "Good morning, sir. I'm here to assist you with your day."

"Great. Corrine will check in with you shortly. She's on assignment at a piece of property I own in Hawaii."

"I see." She picks up a pad of paper and a pen. "Who are the people I can put through to you, and who should I take messages for without disturbing you?"

"You can put Corrine through whenever she calls, regardless of whether or not my door is closed."

She scribbles Corrine's name down and looks up at me.

"If I'm not on the phone or in a meeting, any of the executive staff can be put through. If they need to speak with me in person, and I'm not busy, they can interrupt, but also, my calendar is tight, so I need you to manage that."

She nods. "And I can find the names of the executives on the website?"

"I believe so."

"What about a wife, girlfriend, or lawyer?"

I don't want to get too excited, but she sounds incredibly efficient, and I like this. "If my mother calls, take a message. If the international IP attorney, Charlotte Ming, or our investor, Mason Sullivan, calls, you also can put them through."

"Anything else?"

"I'd like a double espresso with steamed milk from

Starbucks across the street." I start to look at the emails that are flooding in.

"Well, I think this is a good time to let you know I'm here for business reasons. I don't do personal errands outside of this office. If you need coffee for your appointments, I will make sure we get that to you, but I don't run to the coffee stores, dry cleaners, or pick kids up or anything like that."

I'm a bit taken aback, but I manage a nod. "Thank you, Winifred."

"Ms. Day, please."

I nod. "Can you print a copy of my calendar, and let's go through it?" *When will my Corrine be back?* "And while you do that, can you please send Quint in?"

"Yes, sir." She turns and leaves, and I just hope she's efficient in handling calls.

Quint walks in.

"Can you find me someone who will walk across the street and get us some coffee? I know we have any kind of coffee we want in our employee lounge, but I'd like a double espresso with steamed milk from Starbucks this morning."

"I'm happy to go get it," he says.

I'm relieved. "That would be fantastic. Here's a Starbucks card. Buy yourself whatever you want."

Ms. Day returns with my calendar, and we agree on when she needs to interrupt me, so I remain on time, and when we'll go through messages, so I don't miss anything.

Quint returns with our coffee, and I'm finally feeling efficient.

My phone rings shortly after nine, and it's Corrine.

"How was your night?" she asks.

"I missed you. I see you got through Ms. Day without issue."

"I talked to her for a few moments. She should be fine—very rigid, though, and that's going to challenge both of you."

"She refused to leave the building to do any personal errands, which include getting me coffee."

Corrine laughs so hard that I swear she snorts. "I'm sorry."

There's a knock at the door, and I'm perturbed when Ms. Day sticks her head in.

"There are two policemen from Las Vegas here to see you regarding Cecelia Lancaster's murder," she says. "May I send them in?"

"Corrine, I'm going to have to call you back. Do you remember the name of the criminal attorney we were referred to?"

"What's going on?" she asks, very alert.

I give her a quick rundown.

"Call Damien Lewis," she says. "He's Gabby's boyfriend. He's not a high-profile partner, but you shouldn't meet them without him there, and he'll jump for you. In fact, I'll call him and get him over to the office right away."

"Thanks." I look up, and Ms. Day is waiting for me to tell her where to put the police officers. "Please take them down to the twelfth-floor conference room. I'll meet them there."

I text Corrine and walk back and forth in front of the windows.

Me: Please give him my cell phone number and tell him to call when he arrives.

I hoped this day would never come. *Shit.* I knew the argument I got into that morning with Cecelia would come back to haunt me—we had our conversation in the dining room and very publicly. I blew my top in frustration, and she knew that. She wasn't mad at me. And never once did I threaten her.

Twenty minutes later, Damien arrives at my office. "Nice to meet you. I'm Damien Lewis."

This is Gabby's boyfriend? He's older than I thought he'd be. I expected him to be in his late twenties, but he's older by about a decade. He's well dressed, and I believe he works for one of the more prominent criminal defense firms in the city.

I can't sit. "Okay, the police have arrived to speak to me regarding Cecelia Lancaster's murder. She and I had an ugly disagreement before she died, and I was in Las Vegas when she went missing—but I had absolutely nothing to do with her disappearance, and I adored the woman."

He nods. "Let's just listen to what they have to say. Only answer the questions the officers ask. Don't give them any other information. For example, if one of the officers asks you if you have the time, you say *yes*. You don't tell him the time—you were only asked if you *had* the time. I will cut them off as soon as they veer into waters I'm uncomfortable with."

I nod. "Let's get this taken care of."

We take the elevator to the twelfth floor and join the officers in the conference room.

"Detectives, welcome to Soleil Energy. I'm Jackson Graham, and I understand you'd like to talk to me." I turn to Damien. "This is my attorney, Damien Lewis."

Damien steps forward and shakes their hands and hands them his card. "My client would have been happy to meet with you more promptly had you scheduled a time to speak to him."

They introduce themselves, but I don't hear what they say. The officers hand me cards that I slip into my pocket. They're agitated that I made them wait.

Ms. Day is standing inside the door, waiting to be dismissed. "Would you care for any more beverages?" she asks.

"No, thank you," they say in unison.

I shake my head at Ms. Day, and she closes the door behind her.

"We're working on the Cecelia Lancaster murder," the female detective says. "We understand your client had a disagreement with the deceased."

All eyes are on me. It seems we're jumping in at the deep end of the pool. "We did."

They wait for me to expand, but I don't.

"And what was it about?" the male detective asks.

"She was not a technology person, and I am, and we disagreed about technology," I reply.

"Wasn't it really more than that?" the female detective asks. "She fixed you up with a woman, and she was upset that you'd rejected her?" Her tone suggests she may have been jilted in a similar situation. *Why waste your time with someone who's clearly not your type?*

"No. Our disagreement was about technology," I say.

"But you did reject the friend she introduced you to?" she pushes.

"I did."

"And why was that?" she asks.

I'll be very direct, which I'm sure will be seen as offensive, but it's also the truth. "Christina Daniels was looking for a wealthy husband, and I was not looking for a leach of a wife."

"But that's not really how it went down, though, is it?" the male officer asks.

"That's how I saw it. Cecelia was disappointed, but she wasn't angry. I'm sure the woman was a good friend of hers, but she was the type to be interested only in my bottom line."

"You got Ms. Daniels pregnant, and she wanted you to make an honest woman of her." Disdain drips from the female officer's words.

My eyes must bulge. There is no fucking way I got her pregnant. "I didn't get her pregnant."

"Maybe she lied about being on the pill?" The male officer offers me a way out, but I know they probably have a noose on the other side of that offer. What they don't realize is that I have a trump card.

"We did not consummate our relationship." I've never been so satisfied with a statement, and Cecelia knew that was true. Thus, Christina is causing problems.

"Christina Daniels claims otherwise," the female officer says.

"Excuse me, but my client would submit to paternity

testing to prove any child Ms. Daniels is carrying isn't his. Is that all you have?" Damien interjects.

The officers look disappointed, but not surprised, and quickly move on. "Tell us about the disagreement over technology."

"They were developing a computer with a solar battery. My company, Soleil Energy, is a developer of alternative energy, and I believed they were given bad information. I tried to discuss it with her, but she believed I was wrong."

"Were you wrong?" the male officer asks.

"No," I answer.

"Christina Daniels claims to have lewd emails and texts from you," the female officer throws in.

They're trying to get me to say something I'll regret. Instead, I sit quietly, as I've been instructed. She didn't ask a question.

"Do you have a response?" she finally asks.

"Detective, you didn't ask a question," Damien reminds her.

"Did you send Ms. Daniels' lewd emails or text messages?"

I can hear the frustration in her voice. I hope this doesn't work against me being seen as a cooperative witness. I also know they must be under a tremendous amount of pressure to get this case solved. But this is amateur hour, and I have more faith in Jim's team finding the culprit than I do in Frick and Frack sitting in front of me.

"I can't be sure."

Her eyes grow wide. "Why not? Do you send lewd emails and text messages to all the women you date?"

"No. But I don't know her barometer for lewd."

I swear Damien is fighting a smirk. If I remember correctly, we exchanged two or three text messages after a phone call, all merely to confirm a time and location to meet.

"What's your barometer, Mr. Graham?" the female officer asks.

Damien interrupts. "It seems like you're fishing. Do you have any proof my client was involved with Cecelia Lancaster's murder? Because I can't see how Mrs. Lancaster would be so upset over a failed relationship for her friend."

The female officer shoots Damien a death stare. "Mr. Graham, were you in Ms. Lancaster's room?"

"Not that I can recall." If I've learned anything, it's never to say *definitely* because they already know the answer to the question.

"Then why was there a fingerprint of yours in her room?" She crosses her arms, sits back, and lets that sink in.

Damien stands. "I think we're done with this questioning."

I stand and am quite pleased with Damien, but a bit taken aback by their revelation. I was never in Cecelia's room.

"If you need to continue your questioning, please contact me at my office with a list of questions, and we'll make arrangements for you to meet with Mr. Graham. But until then, we're done," Damien stands to lead them out of the conference room.

We walk out, and I ask Quint, "Can you please see the detectives out?"

Damien follows me upstairs to my office, and we sit down. "Much of what they have is a bunch of crap. Why would you murder someone because she didn't like that you dumped her friend? If the fingerprint is all they have, they don't have very much."

"I was never in her room. They're lying about the fingerprint. But there isn't much where I'm concerned. We argued because a competitor of mine was trying to sell her computer batteries that have a very short life—three months max in the best of conditions. I tried to steer her elsewhere, but they were chirping in her ear. And Cecelia may have been mad at me over Christina, but I never slept with her, and I think maybe I had one email exchange with her. I'll go through my text and email messages and get you a copy of the call log. I'm confident she called a few times. I never returned her calls after our first drink date."

I move over to my computer and click a few buttons.

"Yes, one email, and it was just setting a time to meet for drinks, which my assistant arranged for us." I look up my email sent list, and there are messages to two other Christinas but nothing more.

Damien pushes his card across the desk to me. "Please send it to me. They like you because you're rich. I know I was a stand-in, but I'm happy to help you with this matter. I understand if you have regular counsel, though."

"Damien, I have plenty of lawyers, but they're all business lawyers. I don't typically have need for a criminal attorney. So for now, let's leave this as is. Send over a retainer agreement."

"You'll have that this afternoon," he says.

"As you know, Corrine is in Hawaii for a couple of weeks."

"Yes, Gabby and I are flying in on your jet this weekend, if it all works out."

"That's right. I'm considering joining you."

"That'd be great."

I nod. "I appreciate you coming in on short notice."

Damien extends his hand to me. "I'm sure you know this since you did so the first time, but please call me if they show up again. And I'll let you know if we hear from them."

He leaves with a nod, and I'm stuck ruminating about the fingerprint. I wasn't in Cecelia's room, so I don't know how it would be possible for my fingerprint to show up there. I've been to the Shangri-la in Las Vegas several times over the last year, like the dozen or so people we play poker with.

I'm considering a glass of bourbon when there's a knock at my door and Ms. Day enters.

"I finally got into your voice mail while you were in your meeting. You have a message from Mason Sullivan from yesterday at ten-oh-three. He'd like you to return the call."

I nod and jot it down.

"You received a call from your mother at eleven-oh-eight,

and again at two forty-seven."

"I'll call her later."

"You also had a call to confirm dinner tonight with a Valerie Knudsen."

I don't recall scheduling dinner with Valerie. Our last conversation was not pleasant after she set me up and was looking for a date.

"Please call her back and cancel dinner."

"May I say why?"

"She's not on the calendar…" I debate my options. I'm upset with her, and talking to her would only cause further problems. I take a deep breath. "Please let her know that I can't help her brother, and with Corrine out of the office, I'm overwhelmed right now. I'll call her soon."

Ms. Day looks over her glasses at me. "Are you going to call her back?"

"Probably not."

She cocks her head to the side. "If she doesn't hear from you, she'll call back and blame me for not passing messages on. How about I finish by telling her you're overwhelmed right now? If she presses to get on your calendar, I will tell her she needs to take it up with you. That way, you can be an adult and break up with this girlfriend."

"She was never my girlfriend. She wants to be, but I'm not interested."

"I'm old enough to be your mother, but you need to tell her that, not string her along."

"I know you're right; I just don't usually have a good reason why I don't want to date them, and I hate tears." I chastise myself silently as soon as I hear the words. Here I am telling everyone what a shit Bobby Sanders is for breaking up with Corrine on the news, and I'm trying to have my assistant get rid of a woman who doesn't hear that I don't want to see her.

"I understand. But 'it's not you, it's me' is a stupid platitude. Try being direct without being hurtful. 'You're beautiful and wonderful, and you will one day make someone very happy, but it needs to be with someone else and not me.'"

Ugh. That would definitely bring on the tears. I nod. I need to say it more diplomatically. "For now, please cancel the dinner, and she can call me to reschedule. She has my cell phone number."

I need to block her.

Ms. Day leaves, and I pick up the phone and call Mason.

"I'm sorry I didn't call you back yesterday. Corrine is dealing with the estate in Maui for a few weeks since the majordomo quit."

"Running off the staff already?"

"Sure does sound like it." I turn my chair and stare out at the gray, almost-spring day. We get spoiled when we have a beautiful day here and there this time of year. "What's going on?"

"I was curious if you'd heard anything more from Jeff Wong?"

I sit up straight in my chair. "I haven't. He left a message a while ago, but never got back to me after that. Have you? Is Hydro making a move?"

"Not that I'm aware of. It's going on four months since you applied for the patent, and I thought we'd have heard if we're being moved on to the next step by now."

"I'll have Corrine look into it."

"Are you around this weekend?"

"I was thinking about going out to the estate. What's going on?"

"Nothing really. Caroline and her friends are headed out of town. Dillon and I were putting together a few rounds of golf."

Not tempting enough to miss seeing Corrine. "Thanks, but I think I'll pass."

"I was serious about going somewhere else for our poker game. Do you think we could hole up at your place?"

"Corrine was going to find out if Jonathan Best could come out and manage it. But really, the biggest issue is that I won't know where we are with the renovations until next week."

"That works. Let me know. And let me know about the patent situation."

"Sure thing."

I call Corrine.

"Hey," she says in greeting. Her voice brings my blood pressure down a few notches. "What did the police want?"

I tell her how great Damien was. "Also, they say they found my fingerprint in Cecelia's room. I was never in her room."

"Is that all they have?" she asks.

I take a deep breath. Corrine and I are not on solid ground, but I feel like if I don't say something, I'll be sorry. "Two things actually. Jefferson Industries was trying to sell Cecelia a solar battery for the computers she was working on. She and I got in an argument about it at breakfast."

"That doesn't mean you'd kill her."

"That's what I say. But the police seem to think Cecelia was upset with me over a friend of hers she'd set me up with, because things didn't work out."

"Why would she care about that?"

"This woman is now saying I'm the father of her child."

"I see."

"Corrine, things aren't as solid between us as I'd like, but I promise you, it would be impossible for me to be the father of her child. She and I met once for drinks. That's it. Nothing more. I swear."

"I believe you. You have a history, and I'm sure this is bound to happen. Bobby had women who did the same thing to him."

I rub my hand over my face. "I'm not an ass like Bobby. I'm embarrassed to tell you how many women I've slept with, but I've always been careful. I promise."

"Did the police say anything else?"

"Those were their talking points. Damien was good. We got all we needed out of them, and he shut it down." Corrine's quiet a moment. "He's older than I thought he'd be," I add.

"Damien used to work for Gabby's dad. They met her sophomore year, and he was smitten. He came out with us from Texas. Well…he came out to San Francisco for Gabby. He's a good lawyer. I'm glad you liked him."

"Did Gabby decide you both were coming here or did you?"

"She did. She wanted me away from my dad."

"I'm glad she did—not just because she brought you, but because today would have been hard without Damien."

"Hopefully the police get this figured out soon. I can't believe you'd be a serious suspect. Nate must be so frustrated at this point."

"Speaking of Nate, any luck with Jonathan?"

"He's going to talk to Gillian and get back to me."

"Outstanding."

"I may have to do a bed count and check to make sure things are up to your friends' standards. Are you sure this is what you want?"

"I think so. We have the space if the renovations are done. Maybe in a month or so?"

"Okay. And, you know, if the police come by again, you should reach back out to Damien."

"Yes, I will. Damien's sending a retainer agreement. I'll also have you know that Ms. Day scolded me today."

"She did? About something other than doing personal errands?"

"Yes."

She chuckles. "What do I need to stop doing?"

"She wouldn't tell Valerie I would call her later if I didn't mean it. I'm too angry with her for doing what she did to talk to her right now."

She laughs. "I'm the person who breaks up with your girlfriends all the time."

I squeeze my eyes shut in frustration. "I tell them up front I'm not looking for a relationship. It's not my fault these women think they're the one who's going to change me. I don't like tears."

"I understand. But I know you're capable of restating your position. I've seen you eviscerate people at work."

"I've never been mean."

"Well, I don't know about that, but you're tough."

"Can I call you after hours tonight?"

"Of course, I'm here at your service."

I sigh. I can't ignore this any longer. "It bothers me when you say things like that. *My service* implies that you're only my employee and saying yes because I'm your boss. I hope you agree because you like me as more than a boss."

"I do like you more than I've liked any other boss," she teases.

"I thought if we talked later, you might be in the mood for some phone sex."

She giggles, and I feel a bit better. "Just try not to call during our dinner. It wouldn't be good for the twins to hear what you want to do to me."

"Twins?"

"Brian's sons?"

"Of course. I just didn't retain that information."

"Then they're my new boyfriends—we tag team."

"Not funny."

"Guess it depends. I thought it was quite funny, being that they're three years old."

"I'll talk to you later, and I expect you naked and ready to do all sorts of naughty things I tell you to do."

She giggles. "Talk to you then."

Chapter 27

Corrine

It's after two here, so it's the end of the day in San Francisco. I dial my phone and wait for Ms. Day to pick up. "How did it go today?" I ask her.

"Can you believe Mr. Graham got eighteen calls from various women all wanting to date him, and I don't think he's even met a one of them?"

"That's a good day. Crazy isn't it? Wait until you get a marriage proposal. I usually just let him know he got some calls and give him the call log at the end of the day."

"There's one who's a reporter for the *San Francisco Chronicle,* but I suspect she wants a date more than to interview him."

"I know who you're talking about. She's quite pushy." I look out and see Danny and Jimmy running circles around their dad as he checks the property, and it makes me smile.

"How was Mr. Graham after the police were at the office?"

"I won't gossip."

"I'm not looking for gossip. I'm asking about his mood. Do I need to clean anything up? Often when he's been gruff or difficult, I need to smooth things over for him."

"Oh, no. Mr. Graham talked to a few people and seemed fine."

"Okay. Will you be returning tomorrow?" I shut my eyes and will her to say she will.

"Yes, sure thing."

"Great. I suggest you print a copy of Mr. Graham's calendar, so you're ready when you walk in tomorrow morning. And before you leave, knock on his door and walk him through the phone calls he needs to return and see if he needs any phone numbers."

"Of course. Have a good night."

"You, too, Ms. Day. I'll check in on you in the morning."

I met with all the subcontractors today and offered a bonus if they get done within the next three weeks. They've been limping along, since that's the island way. The money is essentially what we'd pay them if they stretched out the work like they seemed to be doing. I also sat down with the designer, and we themed the rooms around the house so they would be easier to identify. She was resistant to some of my ideas, which is irritating at best. I'll figure out how to bring her around. I feel like I got something accomplished today.

I join the others in the dining room to find Leilani has made kalua pork for our dinner. With the first bite, I realize it is melt-in-your-mouth fantastic.

"This is outstanding!" I gush.

"It's nummy." Danny nods. He has rice stuck to his forehead and shredded kalua pork all over his fingers.

His twin brother, Jimmy, is too busy to stop eating and agree.

"What did you do today?" I ask Danny.

"We found some shells on the beach and went swimming

in the ocean with Mama."

"That sounds fun."

He takes a massive bite of his food, and it takes him a while to chew and eat it.

"What was your favorite part, Jimmy?"

"We raced in the yard. I'm the fastest." He nods, waiting for his brother to disagree.

The conversation around the table turns to things Danny, Jimmy, and Melanie can do around the island. It's fun with all of us here, enjoying our time together and getting to know one another.

Melanie helps with the dishes, and Brian takes Danny and Jimmy on patrol—which really means they explore the property on foot and in a golf cart. The boys love the time with their daddy, but mostly I think they enjoy the golf cart.

I offer to help in the kitchen, but I'm shooed away, so I head to my makeshift office in the library.

I settle in and work for a while longer, but my focus isn't what it should be, so I switch off my computer and begin the walk across the house to my bedroom. There's a book I started last night before I crashed that I wouldn't mind trying to read.

I put on a sexy negligee, and I begin reading a very saucy passage. It makes me think of Jackson. It's half past six, and I know he's still in the office. I decide to be a little cruel and naughty. I walk into the well-lit bathroom and let the strap of the dark blue silk baby-doll nightie fall off my shoulder. Through the material, you can see my pink nipple. I play with it a minute to make sure it's erect. Carefully I take a photo without my head. I look at it, and it's really sexy.

I then become inspired. I slather my lips in deep red lipstick, remove my breast from its covering, and snap a few pics of me licking my nipple. I hurt my neck doing it, but the pic itself is pretty sexy.

Using the full-length mirror, I do a few coquettish poses that show off the entire outfit, just without my face. I snap a few pictures at different angles, and the one of me just standing there is immediately deleted. Too much hip.

It takes some work, and I get a big headache as I take a picture of my ass split by the thong. I think he'll love it.

Climbing back in bed, I search through the pictures and pick a few, sending them off with a short message.

Me: Missing you.

As soon as I hit send, I become nervous. What if Jackson's with someone and they show up? I trust him today, but aren't sexy pictures what get women in trouble? You break up, and he posts the pictures as revenge porn. At least I cropped my head out of the photos.

Not even a minute passes, and my phone pings.

Jackson: This is what you do to me.

It's a short video of him stroking his cock. I shudder with excitement—was that a small orgasm? *Holy fuck.*

Me: I wish I was there to take care of that for you.

My phone rings.

"Really? What would you do?"

"So many options." I breathe into the phone. "Are you touching yourself?"

"Yes," he pants.

"Imagine me on my knees between your legs. I take your big, hard cock in my hand, and I suck your balls into my mouth and get them nice and wet. I caress them with my tongue, pulling them while I slowly stroke your hard cock."

"That feels so good."

"With my very wet tongue, I lick from the base of your cock to the tip from the underside. Licking and kissing. I lick the tip and taste your pre-cum. Mmmm, it tastes soooo good."

I touch myself. It isn't because what I'm doing to Jackson

turns me on—although it does. But what really turns me on are the pants and moans he makes while I describe what I want to do.

"I swallow your cock. It's so big that it's hard to take in my mouth."

"Relax your jaw, baby. I want to send it down your throat," he whispers into his phone.

My fingers dip into my wetness, and I play with my nipples, pulling and twisting. "I'm going up and down and sucking your cock."

"Are you playing with yourself?" he asks.

"I am. Can you hear how wet I am for you?"

"Are your fingers wet?"

"Yes," I pant.

"Taste it."

I put my fingers in my mouth and taste the musky moisture. I'm so amped. "I wish you were here and could lick my pussy."

Jackson groans. "I wish I was, too." I can hear the rustling of him stroking himself. Not too fast and not too slow.

"Are you thinking of me bent over the side of that couch in your office? Presenting my dripping pussy?"

He chuckles. "You know me too well."

"Fuck me hard," I pant, and my fingers strum my clit.

His breathing becomes ragged. "You're so tight."

"Oh, gawd. You're so big." I'm getting close. "What are your fantasies with me, Jackson?"

He's quiet, but I hear the slick sound of him sliding his hand up and down his rod.

"Do you want to spank me?"

"Yes," he moans.

"Do you want to withhold my pleasure?"

"Never." He groans hard into the phone and begins to breathe heavily. He's climaxed. "I want to dip your body in chocolate and caramel and lick it all off. I want you to become as addicted to my cock as I am to your pussy."

"Tell me more," I pant. I'm getting close, and I love hearing what Jackson wants to do.

"What do you like that I do?"

"I like it when you eat me out and finger-fuck me." I'm thinking of it now and envisioning him with me.

"How do you like to be fucked?" he rasps.

"I like you to fuck me hard from behind and pull my hair."

"Can I spank you?" he begs.

"Yes, please."

"I wish I was there to suck on your tits right now."

I imagine him licking and biting my nipples. My orgasm, which was slowly building, explodes. "Jaaaacksooooon," I moan.

I breathe hard into the phone. And I can hear him panting too.

"Imagine me riding your cock, and it's deep inside my slick channel. Feel my orgasm hit, and my body grabs your hard rod deep inside me like it's a vice."

"Coooorrrriiiiiiiine," he moans.

We're both silent, catching our breath and enjoying the moment.

"Thank you for that," I say softly.

"The pictures you sent are so beautiful. Thank you for sending them. I won't lie; I'll probably beat off to them later tonight."

I like that idea. "I appreciate the one you sent me, too. I might have to do the same."

"I wish I was there to show you in person."

"Me, too."

"I was thinking of joining Gabby and Damien this weekend. Would you mind?"

"Gabby and Damien can't come this weekend. They called during dinner and left a message. Gabby had a deadline moved up, and Damien wants to work his butt off on his new project, which is you. His bosses are impressed he has such a big-name client. Anyway, regardless, this is your house, and you're welcome to come whenever you want."

"What I'd like to do is come inside you."

"That usually takes a significant commitment."

"Like a ring?"

"No!" I respond. "Like a commitment to remaining monogamous. Like a commitment to not dating others. Stuff that really isn't your style."

He becomes quiet.

I know that's asking a lot. I realize it's something he's probably not capable of. Why did I have to respond that way? Why didn't I just tell him that would be great and not push an agenda? I know why. Because I can't have my heart broken again.

"I want that with you, Corrine. Without hesitation. I don't want to date anyone else. I told you before, you don't have a place right now, and I want you to move in with me. I've had blood work done, and I'm clean. I haven't been with anyone other than you in months."

"Really? No wonder women are climbing the walls to get to you. They want to take your second virginity."

He laughs hard and loud. "That's exactly it. Too late, you already did it, and I'm now broken for all other women."

"Let's not tell them so they can keep calling Ms. Day and driving her a little crazy."

"You're bad. They don't want me; they want my jet, company, cars, and bank accounts."

"Wait! You have a car that doesn't have a driver?"

"Oh, honey, it isn't just a car, it's a machine."

"You're a machine," I tease.

"I own a Bugatti La Voiture Noire—the only one in North America."

"If I didn't know better, I'd think you were compensating for a small penis."

"But you do know better."

"Yes, I do."

"If I come this weekend, do I need to bring a box of

condoms?"

"After Bobby broke up with me, I went to the doctor and had them check me for everything. I'm clean."

"You let him go bareback, and you were questioning me?"

"First, he didn't go bareback, but I still had myself checked, and of course I questioned you. How many calls did you get on your call sheet today from women looking for a date?"

"I don't know." He plays dumb.

I cross my arms and tap a proverbial cyber toe at him. "Count them on your call log. I'll wait."

"Ms. Day said there were eighteen," he says sheepishly.

"That's what she told me as well."

"I can't wait to see you this weekend." He tries to recover.

"Six hours on a plane is a long time just to get some action," I warn.

"I'd travel six hundred hours to see you. We can have a late-night dinner with your boyfriends when I arrive," he teases.

"Plus, you can do a perimeter check with Brian and the boys," I add. "Be prepared. The boys may want to understand your intentions. I heard them fighting over who was going to marry me. You've got some serious competition."

"I think I can make them understand," he warns.

"This is going to be so much fun."

"After I take you to places you've never been."

"Is that a threat or a promise?"

"Definitely a threat *and* a promise."

Chapter 28

Jackson

It's finally Friday, and I've been so excited to get on the plane and get to Maui. I want to lock Corrine in the master bedroom and never come out for three whole days. I think my cock has been at half-mast all week. I know the first thing I'm going to do is eat her beautiful pussy until she comes all over my tongue.

I left after lunch with the expectation that I'd make it midafternoon, and of course, I was later than I wanted to be. We're arriving at four thirty, and Brian is picking me up. We were flying into headwinds, so the flight took longer. I would pace if I could walk more than five steps in each direction.

Finally, we land.

I see the Range Rover pull up to the side of the plane, and my heart pounds when I see Corrine leaning up against the side of the car in a short dress, fuck-me heels, and sunglasses.

Her ankles are crossed. My cock is fully awake. I debate asking her up to the plane for a quick fuck, but I'd rather worship her.

I bound down the stairs. "There's my beautiful girl."

She opens her arms, and I gather her up and spin her around. "Damn, you look even more beautiful than you did last week."

I step in and kiss her, hard and aggressive. It takes us a moment to let go of one another, but I know if I don't, I'll take her right here, and the Range Rover doesn't have tinted windows or a partition. I do rub my hardness into her abdomen, and a slight pink crosses her chest.

She still blushes, and I love it. "Let's get you back to the estate," I tell her.

She turns, and Quint jumps into the vehicle and sits next to Brian.

"I spoke with Gillian Reece from the Shangri-la this morning," she says as we pull away. "She's going to supply us with two dealers, and she, Jonathan Best, and his girlfriend, Maggie, will be joining them. We went through the list, and between the players, Jim Adelson and his team, and us, that's over forty people."

"Over forty? Wow. How are we doing with rooms? I'm not willing to share ours."

"That's not really my thing," she assures me. "We have plenty of rooms."

"Even if Nate brings his family?" I ask.

"If Nate brings his girls, we may have to shuffle a few things around, but we'll make whatever he wants work," she says.

"When do you think everything will be done?"

"The designer assures me she'll have everything done a week before the last weekend I'm scheduled to be at the house." Corrine is confident and I'm glad she's taken over this project. "That's close to Memorial Day weekend. Do we dare try to schedule for then? Even if it takes a few extra days, we should be fine."

I shrug. "Why not."

I send off a group chat to all the players.

Me: Save the date. I'll be hosting poker at the Halona Moana Estate on Maui over Memorial Day weekend. Please plan on joining me with a date/partner/spouse. Buy-in remains $5 million. Be prepared to be mocked if you can't come.

I turn to Corrine. "It looks like we have a big party coming to the estate in a few weeks."

She smiles, but all the color drains from her face. I can feel her pulse increase.

"Don't worry. Remember those mad organizational skills? You're good. You may have to organize some day trips—maybe a flight or two to the Big Island to explore Kilauea and shopping trips into town or maybe Honolulu, and we can get them the name of tour boats for whale watching, fishing, and whatever else might be of interest."

She nods just as we pull onto the property. "Leilani has worked hard on dinner for everyone tonight," she warns.

I lean my head back in frustration. I'm going to have blue balls all night long. "I'm mad at myself for not getting out of the office sooner. Ms. Day is good with the phones, but less so with keeping me on schedule. She tells me she's not my mother."

Corrine laughs. "I don't think your mother kept you on schedule either."

I shake my head.

We enter the house, and everyone is waiting for us. Two little boys come running up to Corrine and grab her hands to show her a LEGO building they've made. They completely ignore me. I meet everyone, and Leilani greets me with a lei from the plumeria tree in the front.

"Mahalo," I tell her.

"You're learning." She smiles broadly.

We make our way into the dining room, where she has set a feast.

"This looks outstanding," I tell her.

We sit down, and the boys try to cockblock me by sitting on both sides of Corrine. The table erupts in laughter.

"I warned you. You have some competition," she says.

I look over at Brian, who's mortified, and his wife Melissa is laughing and trying to corral her children. When we finally get to sit down, I'm holding out Corrine's chair, but she starts to get up.

"What did you forget?" I ask in a low voice.

"My panties," she whispers in my ear.

I look at her, and she's smiling like the devil. She *is* the devil.

I can hardly concentrate.

"It looks like we're going to have over forty people come for Memorial Day weekend, and some may spill over into the following week," Corrine announces to the table. "What do we need to be ready for them?" She turns to Leilani first.

"I'll need the help of my two daughters all weekend," Leilani says. "They can stay at my apartment. The designer has replaced the beds in all the island rooms, so we should be good there. Donnie, how are the water heaters?"

"I think we need to talk about buying a few tankless water heaters," he says. "They don't require us to keep water in the tanks when they aren't in use."

I nod. "My company makes a good model. It was an acquisition we made for the electronic components. How many would you need to replace all of them?"

"I think six, but if you can point me to the website, I can look at capacity and then say for sure."

"What about the dorms?" Corrine asks. "We'll be putting probably six to eight guys out there. Do you need new beds and linens?"

Mr. Ono brightens. "That would be very much

appreciated."

The rest of the dinner has the team excited and working toward the common goal of getting ready for a big party.

After dinner, Corrine asks Leilani to join her and me in the library. I see her hand trembling.

I smile at her, and it seems to put her more at ease. "Dinner was outstanding."

"Thank you. You're easy to please."

"I don't know about that." She's quiet as she sits down and arranges her *muumuu*.

"Leilani, Corrine tells me you're interested in the majordomo role here at the estate."

She sits up straight. "Yes, sir. I've worked at the estate since I was eighteen. I know it well. I know what it takes to make this place shine, and the staff here respects me."

"Would you be upset if Corrine were to work with you from the mainland to help with bills and to coordinate with you on making some of the bigger decisions?"

She shakes her head and smiles. "Corrine is very easy to work with. She is cautious with your money and sometimes understands that things happen that require kicking someone in the *okole*."

"What's an *okole*?"

"It's ass in Hawaiian." Corrine giggles.

"She's pretty good at that back at my office, too. I have to admit, we're pretty lost without her." I smile at Corrine.

"I can see why. We're grateful you've lent Corrine to us."

"I'm right here, and not invisible last I checked," she says, and we all laugh.

"Well, I think it's settled then," I tell Leilani.

We make plans to discuss a few more details, and when Leilani leaves, I step in and kiss Corrine hard. My hands explore, and hot damn, the woman was telling me the truth. She's not wearing any panties. She starts to giggle mid-kiss.

"You're very naughty."

"Maybe I should be punished?"

"How many spankings does going out in public without your panties on deserve?"

"I'm sure you'll figure it out if you can catch me."

And before I know it, she's running out the room and racing through the house to the master bedroom. I'm not even sure where I'm going. I follow the sound of her giggles.

When I arrive at the master bedroom, she's lying provocatively across the bed in a black see-through satin robe and a killer pair of stilettos. My cock is instantly aching.

I stalk to the bed. "You're in trouble now."

"I guess you'll just have to show me."

I wake up hours before Corrine does. The staff has the morning off after a late night last night, so I wander to the kitchen to find Leilani making coffee. She looks at me sheepishly.

"I had to buy a new coffee maker after your last visit, Mr. Graham."

"Oh, sorry. I don't make my own coffee very often, and when I do, it tends to be single serve."

She smiles. "I trust you and Ms. Woods slept well?"

"I think so." I feel like I'm in trouble. "I want to marry her, but she's been hurt. I'm trying to take it slow."

Leilani nods. "She's an exceptional person. I think she is good for you, but it's important you don't crush her spirit."

Chapter 29

Corrine

What is this I'm feeling? Is it giddiness? Elation? Excitement?

Petrified is probably more like it.

I'm still not sure why I dropped the bomb about Jackson and me being exclusive. I'm supposed to be getting myself ready to be out of this. Once again, my heart has other ideas. Bobby and I had that conversation, but thankfully a little bird in the back of my head warned me to be careful, so I didn't do anything stupid. The last thing in the world I wanted was to be tied to him forever because I had his baby.

But Jackson doesn't look at every woman as she walks by. He's much more focused. I believe him when he tells me he wants monogamy, and I'm positive I'll get it, at least for now. That doesn't solve my issues at work, but I have to think we can figure those out. The question remains, how long will it take him to get bored with me? But my mom would have told me to "enjoy the ride." And I think that's what I'm going to do.

If someone were to take a picture of me this morning, they'd see a stupid grin on my face. I have a boyfriend!

I find my tankini bathing suit, put a cover on over it, and head downstairs. The modern-day uniform in Hawaii is a bathing suit, so I feel comfortable.

In the kitchen, I find Jackson with his coffee and his laptop open. He looks up at me. "Heading to the pool?"

I smile. "After I figure out your plan for the day."

He stands and walks over. With his finger on my chin and his other hand stroking my nipple, he kisses me, and I almost melt. I hear myself mewl.

"Maybe I should show you my appreciation for taking such good care of me last night?" I whisper.

His hands have just wandered to my bikini bottoms when we hear the squeal of Danny and Jimmy out at the pool, and we jump apart like two kids who just got busted making out.

"I see you have coffee. Would you like some breakfast?" I ask, smoothing my top. "Leilani showed me the secret recipe for her scrambled eggs."

"That's okay. I'm good right now. Brian and I are meeting shortly about the security around the estate, and I'm trying to go over some of the work from my development team so they can continue moving forward."

"No problem." I pour myself some coffee, and I see Brian and Melinda managing the boys outside. They have no fear of jumping in the deep end and swimming—a cross between a dog paddle and breaststroke. They're two fishes for sure.

I walk over to Jackson and kiss him on the head. He reaches up and caresses my ass. "I'll get out of your hair, but this afternoon I expect you to put sunscreen on me."

"I promise to lather you all over."

He winks at me, and I pick up my Kindle and head out to the pool deck.

"Corrine! Corrine!" The boys yell in unison.

"How's the water this morning?" I pull off my cover and dive in.

The boys and I splash around. After a few minutes, Brian gets out, disappears into the pool house, and then reappears dressed in shorts.

"Is Mr. Graham up?" he asks.

"Yes. He's in the kitchen working. He mentioned you were going to be meeting."

Melinda coaxes the boys out of the pool with the lure of pineapple and mango for breakfast. "Sometimes they're like herding cats," she says.

I nod. I know she's correct after spending a few days with them.

I get out of the pool, too, and enjoy the warmth of the sun as I sit under an umbrella and read the latest release from my favorite author. If only men in real life were half as awesome as they are in books.

I feel a trickle of cold water on the back of my legs, and I bolt up. Jackson is standing with a cup of pool water and the twins at his side, giggling.

"Hey!" I yell.

They all break out in hysterics.

"You were sleeping," Danny says.

"At least it was under the umbrella," Jackson tells him.

"Yeah." Jimmy nods. "You would've been a lobster otherwise."

"I think Corrine looks hot." Jackson looks at me with a devilish smile. "I think we should throw her into the pool."

I sit straight up. "Don't you dare!"

I jump up and dive in before he can throw me. The boys and Jackson quickly follow. Suddenly it's a real pool party with water guns and floaties, and the housemen are delivering frozen non-alcoholic drinks for everyone. The boys' parents appear and find seats around the pool.

"I never want to leave here," Danny says.

"Me neither," Jimmy agrees.

Melinda and Brian exchange smirks.

"You'd think going to preschool and driving their mother crazy was hard work," Melinda says. "The only peace I get is when they nap."

"Do you miss working?" I ask.

"I do miss adult conversation sometimes, but I'm grateful Jim pays Brian well enough that we can live conservatively in San Francisco and I don't have to work."

"I hear you. San Francisco's expensive."

I chat a few minutes more with Melinda and watch Jackson get out of the pool. He dries off and gives me a subtle signal, and I know he wants me to meet him in the house.

When I get out and dry off, I head for the master bedroom. As I approach, I hear the shower running, and I take off my wet suit and enter the bathroom. Jackson's reflection in the bathroom mirror takes my breath away. I love the curves in his hips and the happy trail line. I stand and watch him.

"You're welcome to join me."

"I'm enjoying the view."

"It's only for you."

I chuckle and step in behind him.

After an afternoon of lovemaking, I'm exhausted again. Jackson is taking me into town for dinner tonight, and our plan is to enjoy an evening out. It's not something we've done very often.

Brian and Ben drive us to a shopping area. Ben drops us and will meet back up with us shortly. As we wander in and out of the stores, it's fun to see Jackson's approach to shopping. If you like it, you buy it. I can't live that way. My expenses have decreased, and I'm not paying rent, so the girls will have to cover the cost of their closet, but that doesn't mean I have a ton of discretionary money. Jackson gave me a raise, which helps immensely, but I still haven't decided what I'm going to do after Hawaii. And even if I accept the stock options, today they're only a piece of paper. They have no value until we go to market.

Jackson's whole life is discretionary money. We wander in and out of stores, and he picks things up and offers to buy them for me. A woman I've never met leans over and says, "Honey, if the man wants to spend money on you, you have to let him."

I force a smile. "Thanks, I'm sure you're right."

Jackson steers me into a high-end, Hawaiian-themed jewelry store. It's filled with designs of plumeria flowers, turtles, waves, and palm trees. My heart's beating fast. I've never been given jewelry before and never been shopping for jewelry with a man—let alone one I was sleeping with. Thankfully, there doesn't seem to be any engagement displays.

Jackson stops at a table of plumeria jewelry. Immediately the saleswoman approaches. "Can I show you anything?"

Jackson looks at me. "What do you think?"

I shrug noncommittally.

"I'd like to see this one in the white gold." He's pointing to a choker that's a stunning cascade of plumeria.

She gets it out and starts reciting the figures—eighteen inches long and thirty-nine twenty-four-karat-gold plumeria flowers. She hands it to Jackson, and he looks it over.

"Would you like to try it on?" he asks.

It's beautiful. Who wouldn't like it? I turn around and hold my hair up while he clasps it.

"It comes with matching earrings, a bracelet, and a cocktail ring," the saleswoman jabbers on.

I turn around and look at him and touch the necklace. "I love it."

"I know you don't want me to buy too much for you, but may I please buy this necklace? It will be a great memory of our early trips to Maui."

I debate. The delicate necklace encircles my neck and really does say Hawaii, but once she quotes the price, I almost faint—it's over five thousand dollars.

Jackson leans in, and I can smell his cologne. "I can afford it. Please…"

I nod. I may hate myself later for giving in, but it is a beautiful piece, and no matter what, I'll always have it to remember our time together.

She packages up the necklace, and after Jackson pays for his purchase, we walk toward a seafood restaurant on the water.

"Now, you have a permanent lei." Jackson laughs at his own joke.

"Is that what this is?" *Permanent* is a scary word.

"Or maybe you can get laid while only wearing the lei."

Now he really is pulling out his twelve-year-old humor. It's my fault. I started it to get a rise out of him.

"Uh-huh." But I do like the idea of wearing the necklace and nothing else.

"Are you wearing panties tonight?" Jackson asks in a low voice.

"I am. I guess I'm being a good girl." I give him my best pouty face and pop my shoulders back, so my breasts are prominent.

His eyes become hooded, and I know what he's in the mood for.

He steps in and kisses me.

I nibble at his lower lip. "You need food after your crazy day."

He nods. "I wish I wasn't leaving you tomorrow."

"I have a lot to accomplish over the next few weeks if we're going to be prepared for almost fifty people to come to the house."

We walk hand in hand into the restaurant, and I turn to see Ben and Brian staying close. I'd forgotten they were with us.

At the restaurant, we're shown to our water-facing booth. The ambiance is what I would envision for the dining room of a cruise ship—very elegant with a hint of nautical decor. Once they take our drink orders, Jackson sits back and puts his arm around me.

"I'm happy to be here with you."

Snuggling close. "I'm glad you're here, too."

"I wish the police were closer to finding out who's been bothering you."

I nod. I'd say the stalker is doing more than bothering me. She's displaced me.

"I spoke briefly to Jim about this during the week," he continues. "They feel confident it isn't Collette. Jim's team has worked with Bobby's manager, and they've identified six possible candidates—women who have stepped over the line of normalcy when it comes to Bobby—and they're working on eliminating them from the pool of suspects."

His hand moves to my leg, and he's rubbing his thumb across my thigh. I can't look at him, or I might break out in tears.

"Regardless of where they are in their investigation, we believe that after the party over Memorial Day Weekend, if we still don't have a definitive answer, we want you to come back to my apartment, with Brian and Jim's team close by to protect and watch over you. We'll make sure you keep far away from Bobby, and you'll be safe."

I see the outline of several large yachts in the harbor. I wish I could be teleported away from here and this woman who has taken my freedom away for a man who doesn't even like me, let alone love me.

What Jackson has proposed isn't what I want. I want to be far away from this psycho, which means I need to be far away from Bobby. So unless he's going to be traded to the Houston Oilers or the Dallas Cowboys, I still don't have a way to live comfortably in San Francisco.

I'm never going to fall for a well-known man again. I want

to have a normal life far away from the professional sports world—and the billionaire tech world Jackson lives in, for that matter. I guess I've gone from one mess right into another.

Instead of telling him how I feel and starting a fight at dinner, I talk about the Memorial Day Weekend party.

"My goal this week is to make sure the renovation remains on schedule, work with the designer to get things finished, and begin ordering what we'll need to accommodate so many guests."

Our dinners arrive, and we continue talking about the party and planning activities. It's going to be a lot of work over the next month or so as I oversee the renovations, but the end result is going to be a blast.

Chapter 30

Jackson

Dinner was excellent, and I love spending time with Corrine. Every time I think I have her figured out, she throws another curveball. I just wish she felt confident enough to understand that I'm not going anywhere. A part of me feels like she has one foot in and one foot out of this relationship. I need to figure out how to make her more comfortable and more secure in us.

When we return to the house, Brian asks to show me something. Corrine is dead on her feet, so I send her on up to bed and promise to join her as soon as I can.

"What do you have?"

"Well, when I got here, the first thing I did was put up motion sensors around the property, motion-activated floodlights, and camera by the house. Mostly what sets them off is the local wildlife—the feral chickens being the worst during the day and mongoose at night. We put in an invisible fence that tends to run most of them off the property. Anyway, when these devices are activated, they send a video alert to my phone. If it's a person, it tends to be hikers who've gotten turned around wandering the national park on the east side of the property. We drive up in the golf cart and shoo them off."

"What happened tonight?" I press.

"We had someone cross the invisible fence and trespass about forty feet from the house on the western side." Brian points to a spot at the neighbors' property by the garage.

"When my team investigated, they didn't see anyone. We believe the floodlights alarmed them, and they left, but we feel it's an odd place for a breach."

"Do we know if the neighbors are home?"

"No. I'll look into it during the daylight tomorrow."

"Keep me posted."

"I will, sir."

"As you talk to Jim about Memorial Day weekend and all the high-profile guests that will be coming, let me know if you have any recommendations for security. And that really goes for any time. I want the staff and your family to be absolutely safe. I know the crime rate is pretty decent, but we do have a target on our backs, given the size of the estate."

"I may have some suggestions. Give me some time to put together a firm plan."

I nod. My number-one priority is Corrine and her safety.

By the time I make it back to the master bedroom, Corrine is lying diagonally in the bed. I chuckle to myself. I hope she can make room for me. Carefully, I squeeze myself in with her.

She sits up in bed, and the sheets fall to her waist, exposing her bare breasts. "Sorry, I fell asleep." She then rolls over and falls right back to sleep.

"Sleep, my love. We have tomorrow before I have to leave," I say softly as I stroke her hair.

It's been a long day for me, too. I spoon in behind her, my cock fitting against the slit of her ass. I slip my arms around her and pull her in close. Despite everything on my mind, I quickly fall into a deep slumber.

Morning comes very quickly. Corrine stretches like a cat in the sun. My body clock had me up before four yesterday, but today, I slept in. I never sleep in.

"Hey," she says as her hand wanders.

"Hey, yourself. How did you sleep?"

"I actually sleep better with you. I have ever since the first night you stayed with me when I had my nightmare."

"I never sleep in, and yet with you, I do. Must mean the same thing."

She strokes my cock. "I'm going to miss you when you're gone."

"I'll be back as soon as I can. I do have the plane—it's more a matter of when I can leave on Fridays."

Her eyes grow wide and twinkly. "Do you plan on coming next weekend?"

"I don't know." I want to, but how hard would it be to be gone two weekends in a row? "If I don't, I'll come the following weekend. Maybe every other weekend is best?"

"I'm happy with whatever you can make happen." She rolls on top of me and expertly maneuvers herself so I'm inside her.

She's wearing her necklace and nothing else, and she's stunning.

She sets a slow pace, and I enjoy her breasts.

Moaning her appreciation, she strokes my chest and her channel tightens on my cock. We have a leisurely morning, and I make sure she reaches her pinnacle twice before my own climax.

When we're both out of breath and lying in each other's arms, I can't help myself. "So, you got laid while wearing your lei."

"Has anyone ever told you that you were funny?" she snarks.

"All the time," I say with a grin.

"Are they on your payroll?" She looks at me skeptically and grins like a Cheshire cat.

A little while later, I put the *San Francisco Chronicle* down and take a life-altering sip of much-needed caffeine. We're still lying in bed and enjoying a slow morning. But Corrine has begun fidgeting. I look at her.

"I hate to ask, but when do you think you'll be heading out tonight?"

"I spoke with the flight crew yesterday, and I think we're going to leave about eleven. It's six hours back, and I can go right into the office after we land."

"That will make a short night for you. Are you sure?"

"Are you trying to get rid of me earlier?" I raise an eyebrow.

"Yes, I have another boyfriend I want to see tonight." She says this so deadpan that I feel the testosterone build, and I have a desire to fight this guy. Then I see her smile wide. "No! I just want to prepare myself. I'll miss you."

"Good, because I want to spend the day with you. Anything in particular you'd like to do?" I ask, hoping it includes her naked breasts.

"We can wander up into the park and enjoy a nice, casual walk. We can pack a picnic and enjoy nature?"

I play with her nipple as I lie next to her. "This is pretty natural."

"We do this very well." She smiles, and my heart soars.

"But I think we should get out and enjoy the day."

"That's fine, but I want a breakfast scramble first, and I definitely need some more coffee."

"I saw the guys hooking up your espresso machine yesterday. We should be able to make that work, although I hope you know how."

"It's the same one I have at home. I'll show you."

She gets out of bed and begins to walk away. "I'll race you downstairs."

She slips into a pair of shorts and a T-shirt, and she's out the door before I can get out of bed.

I dress, and as I round the corner to the kitchen a few minutes later, I hear Leilani and Corrine talking.

"There were six chickens with their necks broken this morning," Leilani tells her.

"Six? Are you sure?"

"One of them was our best egg producer. She had large eggs." Leilani is audibly upset. She begins to cry. "Why would anyone hurt the chickens?"

I walk in, and Leilani is whimpering on Corrine's shoulder.

"Leilani, I heard the end of the conversation. Would another animal do that?"

She straightens. "We used to get wild pigs, but we hunted those off the property. If it was another animal, they would have eaten the chickens. This is different. Poor things. They're just loud when you go near them. They work like dogs, really."

I pull a cup from the shelf and prepare a double espresso. "I think we need to talk about this with Brian. Let me call him." I pull my cellphone from my pocket and step out of the kitchen.

Brian answers on the first ring.

"Can you please come to the kitchen? Leilani is upset. It seems someone has broken the necks of several of her chickens."

"I'm on my way."

I look out the back window to the pool house and see Brian walking out the door toward us.

"Leilani, can you point us to where you found the chickens this morning?"

She nods and wipes her nose with a napkin. "They're next to the garage on the west side."

Brian and I look at each other. That's the same spot we discussed last night. We leave Leilani in Corrine's capable hands and walk over to the garage. It's not hard to miss the dead chickens.

"Do you see any footprints?" I ask.

Brian shakes his head. "No." He pushes the oleander bushes back, and we see an area that could be where someone hid, but we can't be sure.

"What do you think?"

He looks out over the neighbors' property. We can only see the sloping of a driveway and can't be sure anyone is home. He pushes through the dense plants, and the branches crackle and some pop. "I don't know if they came through. They'd have to be pretty small."

"You don't think it could've been the boys playing hide and seek that left that spot in the bushes?"

He shakes his head. "They're never out of our sight. We're too nervous with the pool and the cliffs."

"Makes sense." The boys wouldn't hurt the chickens, but it needed to be asked.

Brian studies the area and takes a lot of pictures. "I'm going to send these off to Jim and get his opinion."

I nod. After Brian's done, we walk along the side of the house, circling to the front door. When we get inside, he sends the photos to Jim, and we go to the library to call him.

"Jim Adelson."

"Jim, it's Jackson and Brian."

"I'm just going through the pictures. Tell me what I'm looking at."

Brian walks him through the photos as I listen. He's efficient and clear in his description.

"What do you think, Jackson?" Jim asks.

"It does seem strange that this is the same spot where we had the trespassing. But the cameras didn't catch anything."

"I agree," Brian says.

Brian and Jackson talk about the cameras and the invisible fence. They determine they may have a short in the fence. "I'll work with the grounds crew to look at where it could be."

Brian heads out, and I continue talking to Jim. "We sent Corrine here to be safe. If she's in more danger here than she is back in San Francisco, I'll move her back."

"Killing the chickens and leaving their carcasses behind is disturbing. Let's see where the guys land after we research a little more. Then we'll figure out if we need to do something else with Corrine."

"I don't want to alarm her."

"Agreed."

We disconnect the call, and I sit back in my chair. I'm almost ready to cancel my flight home tonight when Corrine walks in.

"What did you learn?" she asks.

"Not much. Last night we had someone trespass, but the floodlights went on, and we figured the culprit was scared away. It showed us that the system was working."

"But now?"

"The dead chickens are a concern. Brian and his team will look into finding the dead spot in the fence and shore that up. I'm contemplating remaining here."

She sits down in my lap. "You know I'd love it if you stayed, but I think given that we have Brian and the small team here, we're fine. You have to work back in San Francisco. You need to get the solar film out to customers before Hydro does."

This woman is completely amazing. She won't show me any fear, and she's focused on the company's bottom line.

"I know, but I don't want to leave you vulnerable."

"I'll be fine. I'll move back to the downstairs bedroom so I'm not so far away from everyone else."

"Should we have Brian and his family move into the main house?" I ask.

"No, I think that would be counterproductive. Brian has a great set up in the pool house, and we'd upset the boys' routines."

"Then do you think Brian needs help?" I ask the question more for myself than Corrine.

"That's something only he can answer, but I have to believe we're a little paranoid because of everything that happened in San Francisco."

"Okay, I guess you're right." I kiss her softly. "I'm hungry. Is Leilani able to make the scramble?"

"She's just waiting for you. You also need to show her how to use that fancy machine you got."

We walk back into the kitchen. Leilani's eyes are still puffy and red-rimmed, but she's in a happy mood. "I'm sorry, Mr. Graham. I'm not usually quite so emotional about the chickens on the estate."

"That's okay. I heard you say one was your best egg producer."

"She was, yes. But we still have several others. We won't go hungry."

She places a steaming bowl of rice and eggs with all the fixings in front of me.

"You know," I tell her. "I came back just for this breakfast."

She beams. "Ms. Woods knows the recipe for when you're both back in San Francisco."

"I could never make it as good as you do," Corrine says with her mouth full.

"It doesn't take much talent. If you can scramble an egg, you can certainly build the marinade, cut the green onions, and dice up the SPAM. If you can't, we'll start some cooking lessons."

"I'd be up for that. I'd like to learn to make your kalua pork, too."

"I can't be giving all my secrets away. You may not come back to visit."

"We'll be back. The weather is too nice not to come," I assure her.

"I'll have a picnic lunch ready for you in about an hour."

"Sounds perfect. Thank you."

After breakfast, Corrine and I move to the lanai to drink more coffee and prepare for our afternoon together.

Chapter 31

Corrine

Jackson left as planned after a late dinner. As I close the door behind him, I touch my neck, looking for my necklace and talisman, but it isn't there. I took it off when I showered up in the master bathroom. I need to go get it. Right now, I'm just feeling too lazy.

I settle in to read my book. After a little while, my cell phone pings.

Jackson: Be sure to text me when you wake up. Sweet dreams, my love. Miss you already.

I miss him, too. And I'm feeling overwhelmed. I've moved back to the downstairs bedroom, and I feel safer here. An hour or so later, I turn off the light, but I struggle to sleep alone. I've always been a bad sleeper, but I do sleep well with him. I watch the clock hit two, and then it's three. I try reading again, but nothing catches my interest. I keep thinking about where Jackson is in the air, and now he should be close to landing.

I take my tablet out and pull up Netflix, searching for something to listen to while I fall asleep. I settle on *Dawson's Creek* from the late '90s. I've seen it before, but I'm hoping I can listen and fall asleep.

My mind is still active. It just bounces from one subject to another.

Bobby and Collette.

What a move back to Houston would look like.

Leaving Gabby behind.

Jackson my boss.

Jackson my lover.

I keep returning to the trespasser. They walked on the property despite all the preventative measures, and Brian and Jackson were here. In the back of my mind, I worry that they'll be back, and Jackson won't be here to protect me. I know the trespasser didn't know Jackson was here, but there was a lot of activity over the weekend, and it didn't stop them.

Eventually, I fall asleep, but I wake before six.

Me: Good morning. How are you feeling?

Jackson: Missing you. I just got into the office.

Me: Enjoy your day. Talk to you later.

I make my way to the kichen, and Leilani is offering eggs, but I think the scramble is too much. "Can I have some fruit—maybe a few slices of pineapple and whatever you have? With toast and coffee?"

"Of course. How does tuna poke sound for lunch today?"

"Yummy." Tuna poke is one of my favorites, and I'm sure Leilani's is absolutely fantastic.

"Any requests for dinner?" She busies herself around the

kitchen, chopping pineapple and mango. When she offers me fresh coconut, I nod enthusiastically.

I haven't had anything she's made that hasn't been outstanding.

"Something healthy?" I offer. I'm going to gain forty pounds at this rate.

"I'll come up with something. Are you okay with fish twice a day?"

"Without a doubt."

"The guys went fishing, and I have a dozen mahi-mahi filets we can throw on the grill tonight."

"Sounds fantastic." My mouth is already watering.

"I'll need to roast the chickens, but I can't bring myself to do it yet."

Mo, one of the groundskeepers, is inside getting coffee and listens to her. "You hated Gigi."

"Who is Gigi?" I ask.

"She was the egg-laying hen," Leilani explains. "She was mean as a wild boar on a hunt, but that didn't mean I wanted her dead."

She begins to weep again. I reach for her hand. "I'm really sorry."

"I swear, I don't know why I'm so upset. Mo's right. She was a mean bird, but I always rationalized that I wouldn't be happy if someone was taking all my hard work either."

After I've eaten my pineapple, coconut, and a few slices of mango, I take my toast and coffee into the library.

I check in with Ms. Day. She's managing. She wouldn't be a great fit to replace me permanently, but for now, she's taking care of the phones and Jackson's schedule okay.

Before I know it, Leilani brings my tuna poke lunch in. I feel bad I'm not eating with the rest of the staff, but I'll lose the team in California in a few hours, and the team back east is already gone for the day.

I call Jackson just after 7:00 p.m. his time. He sounds beat. "How did it go today?"

"Good enough. I've been reminded I'm getting old."

I laugh. "We're going to have to put you out to pasture at thirty-two?"

He laughs. "I like that you always make me laugh and call me on my shit."

"Isn't that in my job description?"

"The line 'Duties as assigned' fits perfectly."

"How much longer are you sticking around at the office?" I ask.

"I have two more things to accomplish, but I may try to get them done later. I didn't sleep well on the plane."

"I didn't sleep well last night without you either."

"I hope that means that you're considering moving into my apartment when you return."

"I don't know yet. It's tempting, but it's also scary."

"I promise to put the whips and chains away," he teases.

"Damn it, I was hoping they were there to stay."

"You're such a tease."

"When have I ever told you no?" I ask.

He doesn't respond, and I realize he's thinking about the first time we came back from Hawaii, and I moved home.

"I mean sexually," I add.

"You're going to give me a hard-on," he warns.

"I'm sure I can give you a better reason to have a hard-on."

"I'm going to go home and rub one off while I look at the naughty pics you sent me. Then I'm going to get some sleep and be back in the office by five."

"Wow, you're ambitious."

He chuckles.

"Have a good night," I say in my sultry voice.

Chapter 32

Corrine

I've searched everywhere for the necklace. Turns out it wasn't in the bathroom like I thought. Where the hell did I put it? I took it off to shower, and then I moved from the master bedroom downstairs, and I've checked both places. No one really ventures down to my room, so I'm positive I tucked it somewhere safe. But I can't find it, and I'm mad at myself for not being able to remember where I put the damn thing.

My cell phone rings, distracting me from my frustration. The number's blocked, and usually, I don't answer blocked calls because they're just trying to sell me something. But for some reason, this time I do.

"Hello?" I say with disdain.

"Corrine, this is Nate Lancaster."

Oh crap. Backpedal quick. "Hey, Nate. Thanks for getting back to me."

"No problem. I'm a little slow these days." He sounds depressed, and I don't blame him.

"I'm really sorry about Cecelia." I take a deep breath, not sure if he wants condolences, but I decide it's the right thing, and I need to manage my own grief. "I worked with her on the Lancaster Foundation. She was a visionary and an inspirational woman. I loved working with her and miss her terribly."

He doesn't respond, and I'm sure I've caused him pain. Finally, I hear his voice again. "Thank you. I can't tell you how much I needed to hear that today. I miss Cecelia so much."

"I can only imagine."

"Anyway," he says. "How can I help you?"

"I was calling because Jackson was approached by Mason to host the next poker event," I explain. "I think it's just an excuse to make Jackson spend a bunch of the money he won last time, but also let everyone see what he won, since I have a feeling he was gloating."

Nate laughs out loud. "You know Jackson far too well. He was gloating. I think it's a great idea and thankfully it's not in Vegas. I love the Shangri-la, but I can't go there right now."

"Well, the Halona Moana may be the perfect place then." I walk him through the players who seem interested, the guest list, and the plans for the weekend, which people may extend through the week, if they're able.

We then discuss the plan for rooms and my backups if I need them.

Nate laughs. "I like the way you think."

"We thought having dealers from the Shangri-la would be wise. They're more experienced, plus they're aware this isn't a game that needs to get out to the tabloids. I've spoken with Gillian, and she's willing to help us manage the game and the guests."

"Great." He talks about a few other minor details and gives me some additional player ideas if we need them. "When are you thinking—date wise?" he asks.

"The estate is undergoing renovations, and I've ordered some new beds and linens so everyone will be comfortable. We think everything should be done in the next month, but we're pushing for Memorial Day weekend to be safe and also give people a better reason to fly so far. We thought we might put you and the girls up in the second master suite. And I have a place for your nanny, if you want to bring her."

"Actually, your timing is perfect. That weekend my sister-in-law is taking the girls on a weekend trip, so it would be just me. Is that okay?"

"Of course. I thought I would send you the invite for approval. And I'm happy to run menus by you and timelines, if you'd like. I don't want you to feel like I'm overtaking your party."

Nate releases a big sigh. "No, this is perfect. Cecelia took care of a lot of this with Gillian, so I'm glad you're willing to take it on. Just do me a favor and make sure Jackson has some Mitchner's. I've become rather fond of that for our games at the Shangri-la. If you can't find it easily, reach out to Jonathan Best, and he'll tell you where to find it."

"No problem. I think I have your email address." I recite it to Nate. "You should see an invite soon."

"Yes, that's my email. I'll see you in a few weeks."

"Thanks, Nate."

I hang up and quickly put together what I think the invitation should say. Then I send it off to Nate.

He sends it back with some redlines. Despite the fact that we've already determined where people are staying, Nate's added that the better rooms will go to those who respond quickly. I add my name and contact information, reminding everyone that I'm on Hawaii time, and then it's ready to go.

I've been sitting all morning, and I wander into the kitchen looking for a drink and a snack or maybe lunch.

I'm not a foot outside the library when my phone rings.

"Hello?" I answer.

"This is Caroline Arnault. Do you remember meeting me

at Cecelia Lancaster's service?"

Of course I do. She could call anyone, and after saying her name, they'd know who she is. "Yes, I remember you. How are you?"

"I'm great. Mason just forwarded me the invite. We're looking forward to coming. Do you need any help with the planning?"

An idea hits me. Caroline knows these guests' expectations better than I do. "Actually, if you could be a bit of a sounding board for me on occasion, that would be so valuable. Nate has left the menus, entertainment, and whatnot for me. Would you mind helping me look over my notes to make sure I haven't forgotten anything?"

Leilani appears with a sandwich and a drink for me. I look at the time, and it's already past two thirty. Where did my day go? I mouth *thank you* to her, and she leaves me to my call.

"Food and entertainment? Perfect. Count me in. I'm a great sounding board, and I'm also very good at getting people to help, so let me know if you need me to wrangle some extra hands for you."

That takes a massive weight off my shoulders. "Thank you."

I no more than disconnect the call, and my phone rings again. I bounce from call to call for the rest of the afternoon, and by five, I've heard from everyone except Jackson. I decide to call to tease him a bit.

"Hey, beautiful," he says in his sexy, deep voice that makes my lower body clench with eagerness, despite the distance.

"Hey, you. I've talked to all your friends and gotten their preferences for alcohol, as well as a few Keto, lactose-free, and vegetarian requests."

"I got a call from Landon asking if you were single," he counters.

I laugh. "And what did you tell him?"

"To keep his fucking hands to himself."

"I never pegged you as a jealous guy."

He lowers his voice. "Trust me, you're mine, and I don't share."

I'm a little stunned by his alpha-maleness. I don't really know what to say to that, so I shift subjects. "Any word from Hydro or Jeff Wong?"

"Funny you should ask. My understanding is that Jeff Wong was apprehended coming into San Francisco through customs with samples of his solar film this morning. Apparently, ICE doesn't take well to corporate theft, and he was arrested for importing stolen goods."

"You're kidding. How did customs know he was coming?"

"Wellllll, a little bird may have told them."

I can tell Jackson is incredibly happy, and he deserves to be. "That's fantastic news. I'm so happy for you."

"This is a big deal. Jeff Wong's not a US Citizen and was here on a permanent resident card. That has been revoked, and he won't be able to return."

I'm stunned. "Jeff Wong's been banned from coming to the US?"

"Yep. The government views him as trafficking in stolen goods."

"This is really amazing news." My stomach does a few turns. "But how do we prevent Hydro from just giving the plans to someone else and selling them to our customers?"

"Certainly, there's a strong chance they'll try, but when I hang up with you, I'm leaving for New York. I'm doing all the morning shows tomorrow, and there will be writeups in the *New York Times, Technology Today, Silicon Valley Business Journal,* and the *San Francisco Chronicle.* We know the news went out over the wires, so it will be picked up worldwide. There will be people who buy fraudulent materials, but they'll know what they're paying for."

"Holy crap, Jackson! That's amazing. And, not to mention, talk about some incredible publicity. I'm so excited for you."

"The only thing that would make it better is if you were

here, too."

"Your phones are going to blow up with women asking you out for the rest of the week—or even longer. You'd better warn Ms. Day."

"I'm scared of her. I don't want to talk to her if I can avoid it. She does not give me an inch."

I laugh. I wasn't assertive enough in the beginning to do that. "Something I should have done myself."

"You were perfect with the way you handle me—both at work and in private."

I know where he's going, but I shouldn't go there. "I don't want to keep you." I turn and look out over the setting sun. "I'm really happy though."

"You know what that means," he says. "Your stock options are worth some serious money at this point."

"All thanks to you."

We hang up, and a smile engulfs my face. With Jeff Wong out of our hair, life is almost perfect. Now to get this Bobby fanatic out of our life, and all will be good.

Chapter 33

Jackson

This has been one crazy week. I started Monday by flying in from Maui. Wednesday morning, I landed in New York and spent the day doing talk shows and news interviews. Our public relations firm has pulled one hundred and twenty-six different press clippings, which expanded coverage to include other companies who have had similar things happen to them and a discussion of what trade-secret theft by foreign entities does to the world economy. Everyone knows about Soleil Energy and our solar window film. We couldn't have asked for this level of publicity if we tried and paid for it.

And Corrine was right. My phone blew up, and Ms. Day quit. She couldn't take the phones ringing nonstop with *the silly women,* as she called them. I know if Corrine were here, she would have managed it just fine. I now have *the twins* answering my phones. I don't really think they're twins, but they're odd. They dress alike and look a little alike, and they work together. Whatever. They both sit at Corrine's desk and answer the phones and don't get too caught up in all the craziness.

Mason and Caroline have insisted that I join them for drinks at The Big 4 Restaurant in the Huntington Hotel this evening.

I'm actually on time for a change, even though Corrine isn't here to manage me. Still, Caroline and Mason have beat me there.

They stand to greet me, and I give Caroline a hug and kiss on the cheek. "Thanks for the invite out tonight. It's a nice reason to leave the office at a reasonable hour."

"After the week you've had, I would bet that's hard," Mason says.

I shake my head. "The phones are ringing off the hook. I'm stunned at the number of women who call and ask me to marry them or father their children."

"How is Corrine dealing with it?" Caroline asks.

"Thankfully, she's in Maui planning the poker tournament."

Caroline puts her head back and laughs. "You're in the big leagues now. The microscope you live under will be on high-res at this point."

I *tsk* and shake my head, willing her statement to not be accurate.

"It was like that for my twin brother, Trey, when we were growing up. When he met Sara, they had to go up to Stinson Beach and hide just to get time together without a zoom lens."

She would know, but I still don't appreciate her perspective. "The only good thing is the value of Soleil Energy has shot through the roof."

Mason leans in across the table. "I'm not supposed to say this, but if I were you, I'd hold on to being a private company as long as you can."

A sigh of relief runs through me. "Thanks. All this interest has the sales pretty high right now, and we're hoping we won't need the infusion of cash, plus all the chaos going public would bring. I can buy out your options, if you'd like."

"Right now, don't worry about it. Let's get through the launch and see a few quarters of profit before we make any decisions. We're fine with that. You'll only be the second company in our history of more than five thousand extremely successful investments where we sell the shares back to the company because they don't go public. I like the feel of this."

"You look dead on your feet," Caroline says. "You headed to see Corrine this weekend?" She peers at me over her martini glass.

I shake my head. "I'm going to try next weekend, if I can."

"I like her a lot," she says.

"I do, too. I'm not sure Corrine's in as deep as I am, but I'm working on her."

We talk for a short while longer before I give up and go home. I'm so tired, I'm grateful I'm not driving. I can hardly keep my eyes open. I text Corrine before I lose access to all rational thought.

Me: Good night, sweetheart. Counting the days until I see you again.

I wake up to my phone ringing. It takes a few seconds for my brain synapses to connect and remind me it's Saturday, and I'm not late for work.

"Hello?"

"Sorry to wake you, Mr. Graham."

It's Brian. I sit up in bed, and I'm alert. "Is everything okay?"

"We had some campers show up on the northeast side last night, and again there was a break in the invisible fence. The cameras aren't seeing anything."

"How is that possible? We have infrared and motion, and nothing is showing up on the cameras? Do you think it's an electrical short?"

"Honestly, I don't," Brian says with a sigh. "It's not the same spot as last time, but I can't figure out why the camera isn't seeing anything."

"Is Corrine alright?"

"Yes, I have one of the guys outside her room, and we have sentries wandering the property."

I blanch at the thought of them armed—and misfiring and shooting someone. These aren't Jim's guys who are former military and FBI; these are local Hawaiians. Don't get me wrong, they're scary dudes if you run into them in a dark parking lot, but they can't match Jim's team where training is concerned.

"What do you suggest?" I ask him.

"Jim and I are talking about it a little later. He'll probably follow up with you with our recommendations."

I don't like that they don't know very much right now. I lie back in bed and put my hand on my forehead to fend off the headache I can feel coming on. "Keep me posted. Is Corrine awake?"

"I'm not sure. It's still early here."

"Thank you for keeping me posted."

I walk to the kitchen naked and make myself a single serving of coffee. My dick has its morning wood, and it only gets stronger as I think about her. I know I can't push her or make her do anything she doesn't want to do, but until we can confirm that whoever is bothering her is out of the way, she's not going to make any commitments.

I take my first sip, and the headache dulls.

I've only felt this passionate about Soleil Energy before—I knew what I wanted, and I was going to get it. But with Corrine, I know if I push too hard, I'll push her away. Still, my future is with her.

I take a shower, and then I text her.

Me: Good morning. I'm just getting up. Call when you're awake.

For the last four days, Corrine has been in my dreams *every* night. I'm sure it's because we speak before I go to bed, and then I can't get her off my mind. Last night she was wearing white lingerie, including thigh-high stockings and crotchless panties. I woke up sporting the biggest wood—like I was thirteen again.

I'm still unhappy that we can't figure out why we're having a nightly breach in the lines at the Halona Moana. It's irritating at best. I've spoken to Jim about it twice in the last couple days, and even he's confused. We have the best security system available, and his team is working with the manufacturer to figure what's going on. I'm trying not to talk about it with Corrine so I don't stress her.

On top of all of that, the last three days I've been dealing with production issues. We've stuttered Hydro's entrance into the market, and our sales are through the roof. We're having problems keeping up with the demand.

There seems to be a small reprieve from the phone calls here in the office today. I would love to hear Corrine's voice. It's too early to call her, or I would, and maybe we could have some dirty phone sex. I'm flying back tomorrow, and I can't wait. I talk to Corrine every morning when she wakes and again after work. We seem to have a delicate balance of professional and naughty. But phone sex is not enough. I need to see and feel her. Sometimes I think I feel her slipping away, and it worries me.

This weekend my plan is to have lots of sex, spend as much time with her as I can, and help her with the poker tournament arrangements.

My cellphone rings, and it's the house on Maui. It's just after 5:30 a.m. there. For a second, I'm excited, thinking it's probably Corrine, but then I realize she always calls from her cell phone.

"Jackson Graham."

"Mr. Graham, this is Brian."

These are never good calls.

"We had an issue this morning," he says.

"What happened?"

"Actually, it was the boys who pointed it out to me. It seems someone was flying a drone over the estate this morning. It was a quiet one, so it wouldn't have alerted us, but this morning the boys saw it outside the pool house at eye level. It even got so low as to look inside one of the windows in the pool house and in one of the estate windows—Corrine's room."

My radar moves to high alert. "Are Melinda and the boys okay?"

"Yes. Melinda was a bit shaken, but she's fine. The boys thought it was cool, so what does that say about three year olds?"

"Have you alerted Corrine?"

"Yes, but she was in the library preparing for an early call with a vendor, so she wasn't walking around the house or anything. But it concerns us that they seemed to know which room was hers."

"I agree. What do we do?"

"The police are on their way. Legally I can't shoot it down without violating FAA regulations. But Jim is flying out some radar-jamming devices that should arrive this evening. We'll deploy these jammers, which will make the drones drop to the ground once they reach the area."

I know Brian is a great guy, but I'm worried about Corrine. I'm responsible for my own schedule these days, and I was going to come in tomorrow, but I have meetings I think I can take over the phone or through video chat. "Brian, I'm going to fly in tonight. I'll connect with Jim about bringing the jamming devices with me."

"I'll coordinate with the flight crew to be at the airport to pick you up."

"Thanks. See you this evening. I suspect I'll be in before dinner."

I call Jim, we agree on our plan, and I alert the flight crew and still leave myself time to run home and pack my bag before heading into the airport.

Ben arrives in my office as I'm finishing up.

"Has Jim called you?" I ask.

"Yes, sir. He's sending someone over so I can run home and pack my go bag, and then I'll join you for the weekend."

"Great. I've alerted the flight crew, and we'll leave the office at three."

"I understand. Would you like me to walk across to Starbucks?"

"You've read my mind, Ben."

I bounce from call to call all morning. Shortly after nine, Corrine calls in.

"Good morning. How was your night?" I ask.

"I understand you've heard," she says.

"I have. I'm flying in tonight."

"That's fantastic. I'm excited to see you, but I do hope it's not because of the drone."

It is entirely because of the drone, but I'm not going to make a big deal of it. "Not completely, I also miss you. I hate this distance between us. Have you given any further thought to moving in?" Because that's all I think about when I'm not at work.

"No. I'm more focused on getting everything done on time for Memorial Day. I'll let Amber, the designer, know you'll be in tonight, and hopefully you can figure out where we're going with the décor in the island rooms."

"Remind me which are the island rooms?"

"The Big Island is the second master, and the other seven rooms are all on the other side of the house."

"Right. Why does she want to meet me?"

"She has design questions."

"You know I don't care about that."

"I do, but I've made some changes, and she wants to talk to you specifically about them."

I groan internally. Amber has worked with Corrine since the beginning. Why she needs me involved is beyond my comprehension.

"Whatever you need. I'm here to support you. Say, do you think we can have dinner out on the cliffs tonight? I think I'll land by seven, and we can eat when I arrive."

"Wherever you'd like."

We talk for a while longer, and I hang up. I'm leaving in six hours and should be with Corrine within ten. Today's going to be a great day.

Ben is my saving grace. Even though he becomes an overpaid errand runner, I'm grateful he doesn't mind. He gets our coffee and orders our lunch. When Corrine returns, I'll hire her an assistant to answer the phones and run errands.

I alert Ben that I'm ready to go, and it isn't even three. He's surprised, but I follow him out to the car, and we're on the plane and airborne before three thirty.

I'm so excited that I can't work or do much other than will the jet to go faster. When we finally land, I'm thrilled to see Corrine waiting in my favorite dress. I wonder if she has panties on.

I walk down the eight steps to meet her, and I bring her into my arms. It just feels right. I kiss her deeply. "God, I've missed you," I breathe when we break.

"I've missed you, too."

I hand Brian the box of jammers, we climb into the back of the car, and I'm ready to pounce. Corrine, on the other hand, is all business.

"Amber will be by tonight after dinner," she tells me.

"It can't wait until tomorrow?"

"No, we need to make some decisions, and things get shipped from the mainland, so we need to order quickly, and I don't want any delay."

I nod, a little disappointed.

"Brian will grab you when you're done to go over the schematics for the drone jammers."

"Do I at least get to sleep with you?"

She flashes me a smile, gathers the hemline of her dress, and winks. "I'd be disappointed if you didn't."

That makes me feel better, but I'd prefer these meetings happen tomorrow morning.

A little while later, we're settled in for dinner on the cliffs. I love it here. Corrine's face is lit by tiki torches, and Leilani delivers our excellent dinner. I don't think I could ever give this place up. I hope Viviana understands.

As we're finishing up, one of the housemen approaches. "Mr. Graham, a Miss Amber Chin is here for you."

I look over at Corrine. "Why am I meeting with her?"

"She asked."

"Are you joining us?"

"Nope. I have a call with Caroline Arnault to go over the menu for Memorial Day weekend to make sure she thinks I've got everything covered."

"Why do I feel like I'm being set up?"

She stands and kisses me. "Just remember, I trust you."

"What does that mean?"

She's walking away and smiles. "You'll see."

I follow her, and she greets Amber, who is not friendly to her at all. I walk in behind her, and she lights up and gushes all over me. She's a small woman, and she's wearing a dress that seems more appropriate for a nightclub.

"Mr. Graham, welcome to Hawaii." She rushes up to me, teetering on her high-heeled sandals. "May I call you Jack?"

No one calls me Jack. They only do that if they don't know me. "Mr. Graham is fine."

I sit down on the couch, still not sure what she needs. She's between me and enjoying some time with Corrine.

"What's the problem?" I ask.

Amber shimmys up close to me. "Shall we have a drink?" she says with bedroom eyes.

"No, thanks. Why am I here?"

She seems to think this is some kind of date or something.

"Well, I've been having some problems with Corrine. I didn't want to call her out on this, but she's not very helpful. I've presented her with beautiful designs, and she's rejected them. She wants pillows from Bullseye."

"Amber."

She looks at me and is positioning herself so I can take a peek down her dress. I'm so not interested.

"Corrine is in charge," I continue. "She knows what she wants. If she wants you to fill the rooms with rubber balls, you do as she says. I promise you, if you piss her off, she'll fire you, and she has my blessing to do so."

Amber's face twists in confusion. This is evidently not what she expected from me. "But—"

I stand to get away from her heavy perfume.

"Whatever Corrine wants, she gets. Ultimately, this is her house. Anything else?"

She adjusts her stilettos and stands. "Thank you, Mr. Graham. I'll order them tomorrow."

"Thank you, Amber," I say as I leave without looking at her.

I find Corrine in the library, and I listen to her phone conversation.

"—so too many appetizers and more low-brow?" She giggles.

She turns to me and grins. She glances at her watch and raises her eyebrows.

I sit down and wait for her to finish her call.

"Alright, I have Gillian's order for food, and we should be all set. Thanks so much for your help. This is the first time I've organized a party for my boss."

I watch as Corrine nods and turns crimson. I'm guessing Caroline is playing matchmaker. She has quite the reputation for that.

"He flew in tonight. I have him booked with activities all weekend. Alright, I'll talk to you next week. Thanks again."

She hangs up and turns to me. "I guess Amber didn't get her way."

"She didn't want to order from Bullseye?"

"Well, that was part of it. Every time Amber came to meet with me, she was hoping you were going to be here. She questioned every decision I made, wanting to make sure it was something you'd want. That girl has it bad for you."

"Well, I think I made it clear that this was your house, and you were in charge."

"It's not my house," Corrine says indignantly.

"When can I show you my appreciation for all you do for me?" I ask.

"After you meet with Brian."

I sigh in frustration. "Meet me in the master, and I expect you naked."

She salutes me. "Anything else, sir?" She pops her tits, and lust rushes through me.

"Yes. Come here."

I sit down on the couch.

"Straddle my lap."

She lifts her dress, and I can't quite determine if she is wearing panties, but she does as she's told.

"Kiss me."

She leans down, and we stare into each other's eyes. She kisses me, softly at first but it soon becomes deeper. I reach beneath her dress and grab the globes of her ass, massaging them. She's wearing a thong that I'm going to enjoy removing later with my teeth.

When we stop, her eyes are hooded with desire.

"I'll try not to be too long," I tell her.

She nods.

Chapter 34

Corrine

The last three weeks have been a blur. Being so far away from San Francisco has been challenging, both professionally and personally. Not being in Soleil's offices has been difficult, but we've worked our way through. I miss Gabby the most. I talk to her some days during her lunch break, and I'm excited she and Damien have finally found the time to come visit.

I watch as the plane touches down, and I can't believe it's been almost five weeks since I've seen Gabby. While the flight crew does their thing, the cabin door opens and extends the stairs. I can see Gabby in one of the plane windows, waving frantically at me.

I grin and wave back with the same enthusiasm. Once Gabby's allowed, she bursts out the door and is down the steps. She squeezes me in a ferocious hug. "I'm never flying commercial again!" she announces.

When she lets me go, I step into Damien's arms and hug him.

I reach for the leis I brought. "Welcome to Hawaii." I place a lei on each of their necks.

"These smell amazing," Gabby says.

She takes Damien's hand, and he winks at her.

"I thought we'd go back to the house this morning," I tell them as we begin walking. "Leilani makes an incredible breakfast. We'll set you up on the cliffs over the ocean, and you can enjoy an amazing egg scramble over white rice with some Kona coffee."

Gabby nods. "I'm starved. To my body clock, it's past lunch, and I'm ready to gnaw off Damien's left arm."

He looks at her, his eyes wide.

She shrugs. "Well, you're right-handed."

Damien laughs. "Well then, eat away."

I cover my ears. "I don't want any sexual innuendos. Seeing you two that one time when we were in college scarred me for life."

"Awww, my sex-kitten roommate was scarred. We hadn't seen each other in a while, and it's amazing we made it to the apartment at all. We didn't know you were hiding in your bedroom."

"It was finals week, and I had one more test to go," I protest.

"I also seem to remember seeing some guy's furry white ass that one time our senior year," Gabby reminds me.

"Okay, you two, if you're so hungry, let's get to the house," I say, ending the conversation. "I also want to give you your agenda for the rest of the day."

"We have an agenda that doesn't require us by the pool and on the beach frolicking in our bikinis?" Gabby asks.

"Yes. But I know it's your first time here, so I've given you the morning to check out the estate and your bedrooms."

"See, Damien? She wants me to finally take your virginity. I told you she'd push for that."

Damien shakes his head, appearing to think hard about this. "I've been saving myself for marriage, so I don't know."

I cover my ears and laugh until I'm snorting. It's ugly. "Stop it, both of you."

When we've all recovered, I give them some additional details. "I've scheduled you a tour of the island by helicopter this afternoon. Brian will drive you to the heliport, and I'll meet up with you for dinner downtown. After dinner, Brian will whisk—"

"Jackson won the house in a poker tournament, right?" Gabby asks.

I nod. "Technically Jackson paid a dollar for it, and he's put some money into the place for renovations." Just then, we drive up to the gate and roll in.

Gabby grabs my arm. "Holy shit, where is the hou—"

We've crested the hill, and the view opens to the majestic house that is all Hawaiian, with full-length windows open to allow the ocean breeze through the house.

"That's not a house, that's a compound," Gabby says with awe.

I guess that's one way to look at it. "We'll have almost fifty people here in three weeks for Memorial Day weekend," I tell them. "It'll be crazy."

Gabby turns to Damien. "Honey, go invent something and become a billionaire. I want to live next door."

We laugh. A houseman comes out to greet us, and we follow him into the house. He disappears down the hall toward the room Gabby and Damien will be staying in, and I show them around the living area and where I'll be working, if they need me.

"I thought you might want to change into some shorts," I tell them at the end of the tour. "Let me show you your room."

I lead them out of the library and down the hall. "I only wanted to show you all this because I helped with the decor. The decorator did not appreciate my taste. I think she thought it was too low-brow for Jackson. And, she thought she could hit on Jackson, and he'd take her up on it."

"Oh no, she didn't," Gabby says.

I chuckle. "Jackson went so far as to tell the designer my wishes were to be followed, or I could fire her because it was my house."

"Are you kidding me?" Gabby asks.

I shake my head.

They follow me down the glass hallway. "I'm guessing you and Jackson don't walk around here naked?" Gabby teases.

I laugh. "Watch this." I flip a light switch, and suddenly the glass becomes opaque.

"Woah," Damien says.

"I know! Isn't it amazing?"

Gabby turns to Damien. "If she actually gets this house, we're moving in. She'll never know we're here."

We stop in front of their room. "This is the Big Island suite. You just need to remember the name. That way, if you need help or someone asks you where you're staying, the staff will know what you mean."

"Aren't you clever?" Gabby winks at me as she enters. "It's beautiful." She looks around the brightly colored room. "I love it."

"Just so you know, everything came from Bullseye."

"Don't they have the most amazing stuff? And it's so affordable."

"I figured these rooms didn't need ten-thousand-dollar décor. We were fine with five hundred dollars in décor, and that's probably stretching what it cost."

"That decorator must be pissed at you."

"Probably, but I paid all her bills on time, so she better be careful. She has lots of competition on this island, and I could very easily make sure it got out that she presented us with Bullseye décor and charged her designer fees. That would take her reputation down a few notches."

"I think you're part evil," Damien says with pride.

"I'll leave you to change. Breakfast will be ready when you come out," I tell them. "The view is stunning. I think you'll love it."

"The view is better than this room?" Gabby shakes her head as if it's impossible.

I nod. "Every room has a beautiful view."

I walk back to my office and sort through most of my morning email before they come looking for me. I show them to the kitchen to meet Leilani.

She greets them warmly. "Help yourself to whatever you find. If you want something made, just let me know, and I'm happy to whip it up for you."

"My own chef?" Turning to Damien, Gabby says, "If Jackson dumps her and comes to me, you're toast for this house alone."

"I'm not worried. Jackson would spend one hour with you and send you back to me."

"What?" she feigns indignance.

"He'd know you were only after his money, and my measly partnership at the law firm will have to suffice."

"Wait? You were named partner?" I ask. This is big news, and I'm so excited for him.

He nods with an all-tooth grin. "I did. I owe it to you for tipping the scales when you referred Jackson to me."

I jump into his arms. "That's fantastic." Turning to Gabby, I say, "Your dad must be disappointed since that means you won't be moving back to Dallas."

"Totally."

We walk out to the pool deck, and I point out various points of interest until Leilani appears with their breakfast.

Gabby's eyes go wide. "Holy crap. This is stunning. And you're living here? Why would you ever want to leave?"

"Enjoy your breakfast," I tell them. "Leilani will serve a light lunch for us at one by the pool."

"You're amazing." Gabby hugs me and whispers in my

ear, "I love you."

"I love you, too," I whisper back.

I leave them to their morning and head back to work through the bills for the estate, a laundry service for table linens, and dish rentals for fifty people over the poker tournament weekend—so much to do, and I'm running out of time.

A little while later there's a knock at the open door to the library. "Hey, we met Brian's boys. Aren't they cute?" Gabby walks in.

"I agree. I keep trying to get Brian and Melinda to take an evening without them and go out for dinner. The boys could hang with me, but Melinda is sure Brian would be fired because the boys are a handful."

"I believe it. One of them crawled right into Damien's lap and ate part of his breakfast."

I chuckle. "Do we need to get Damien another breakfast? Leilani won't mind."

She shakes her head and plops down on the couch in my office. "I miss you so much in San Francisco."

"I miss you, too."

"Why do I get the feeling you won't be moving back?"

I shrug. "I haven't decided. Jackson wants us to be committed, but I think being with him will still be really hard. Not only is he intense, but he's incredibly handsome."

"And, that's a bad thing?"

I nod. "Women are always throwing themselves at him. Literally. Wait staff give him their phone numbers, women call the office daily asking for time on his calendar, and I understand that the marriage proposals are averaging about one every three or four days. They go up whenever he's profiled in the media."

"Do you think that would go away if he was married or put it out that he was seeing someone?"

I shrug. "It's really more than that. I adore Jackson, but I don't want this world. I want a nice little house, a few kids, and a husband who adores me and comes home to me every night."

"Why can't that be Jackson?"

"I'm not sure deep down he wants that. He thinks he does, but Jackson's married to his work, and in the back of my mind, I keep thinking he's only attentive because he's worried about losing me as his assistant. We can't find anyone to take over, and it's hard for him."

"Isn't the sex amazing, though?"

I blush. "Probably the best I'll ever have, but...I'm not sure I can take Jackson walking away from me when he's no longer interested. That's always been my concern. I just keep talking myself into ignoring it for a while."

"Why would you think he'd ever do that? What has he said that makes you think that would happen?"

I take a deep breath. "I can't put my finger on it. He's a lot like my dad. I just see what my dad did to my mother...the constant stream of women in his life. And, like my dad, when Jackson is hot about a project or a woman, he has tunnel vision. But once he's done, they're gone—never to be talked about or seen again. I can't." I struggle to hold back the tears. "I can't set myself up for that. Please don't say anything. I'm going to tell him when he comes for Memorial Day weekend."

Gabby brings me into her arms. "He's not your dad."

"I know that, but I just can't sort through all this. He did give me twenty percent of Soleil Energy. I'll have money for the rest of my life."

Her eyes grow large as she looks at me. "He did what?"

"Jackson gave me five percent from the employee allocation and fifteen of his personal allocation, and he gave the shares to me outright. No vesting."

"Holy shit. This solar film is all over the news and the internet. They're calling it a real game-changer. Not that I don't think you deserve it, but what was his reason for giving you such a high percentage?"

"My job title gave me five percent. And he gave me fifteen

of his because I keep him on task, helped write the patent application with the IP attorney, and was the one who caught our CFO stealing."

"You don't have to live in a closet ever again."

"It was a big closet—I could put a twin bed inside," I remind her. "A little bit of money goes a long way in Texas. I can buy a nice house and find a nice guy and start a family. I think I'll set it up so the Lancaster Foundation gets the lion share of the money."

"When is the plan to go public?"

"There isn't one. Jackson's hoping to keep the company private for as long as possible, so I'll get twenty percent of the net profit."

"That man is in love with you. Has he told you that?"

I shake my head. "He's made noises, but I think he *thinks* he is in love with me. It's probably short-lived."

Gabby sighs loudly. "You deserve to be loved—even by a drop-dead gorgeous billionaire. Don't walk away so easily."

"We'll see." I look at the clock on the wall. "We need to have some lunch by the pool, if you're interested. Otherwise, Brian should be looking for you to get you to the heliport in a little over an hour. Jackson and I did this tour when we came on our first visit. It's stunning to see places you can't get to by car or by foot. You'll love it."

She kisses me on the forehead. "I'll just grab something from Leilani in the kitchen. See you tonight at dinner."

I nod. "I'm buying."

"Of course you are. You just told me you were a millionaire." She winks at me and waves as she goes in search of Damien and Brian.

I text Jackson as I watch her go.

Me: Gabby and Damien made it okay. They're off for the helicopter ride.

I take a deep breath and think for a moment about what

Gabby said. Maybe I'm not giving Jackson the chance he deserves. I return to my phone and add how I really feel, which I don't usually offer until he's offered it first.

Me: I wish you were here.

My phone rings, and it's him. "You wish I was there?" he asks.

"I do," I say in a low voice.

"That makes me very happy. I should make sure Gabby and Damien come more often."

"She's ready to move in."

He laughs. "You've done such a great job with the renovations that I think most of the players are going to be looking for me to lose the estate once they visit."

"That will be tough if you lose it."

"I'm not even considering it." He's silent a moment. "Not only did I just barely win it, but we have good memories there that I want to preserve."

"I agree, but I'm partial, given all the work I've done here."

He changes the subject. "Dinner tonight with Gabby and Damien?"

"That's the plan. I can call you after, if you'd like."

"Whatever," he says.

"Alright. Talk to you later."

His seeming lack of interest feeds right into my fears about him, but I force myself to set it aside. We're thousands of miles apart. Who knows what else he has going on… Right?

Rather than focus on it, I turn my attention to my latest project until Brian lets me know he's ready to leave for dinner.

"Crap. I need to change, but I'll be right there." I run upstairs and go crashing through my closet, looking for my cute come-hither sandals.

Shit! Where did I put them?

I look under the bed, in the other bedroom, and both bathrooms, but I can't find them, so I grab another pair of cute-enough sandals and run out the door.

"We'll only be a few minutes late," I say, looking at Brian.

He nods.

When we arrive, Brian drops me, then goes to park the car before he joins me in the restaurant.

I sit down at the table, a bit frazzled. "Sorry I'm late. Couldn't find my sandals."

"Hawaiian life doesn't require shoes," Gabby says with a laugh.

I nod. "Mostly that's true. How was your helicopter tour today? What did you think?"

"Oh my God!" Gabby begins.

For the rest of the evening, I'm regaled with stories of what they saw and discovered.

As we're served dessert, Damien becomes very serious. "I've asked everyone but you," he tells me. "You know I love this beautiful woman very much and have since I met her when she was twenty."

"At least it was legal," I snark, and we all laugh.

He grins and grasps her hand, and I see a stunning new ring on her finger.

"Holy crap!"

I start to get very excited, but Damien interrupts. "Would you mind if I married your best friend? I promise never to come between you and love you like the sister-in-law you pretty much are."

I jump up from the table and run around to hug them. "I'm so excited for both of you. It's about time."

Damien looks at me. "You haven't answered the question."

"Of course the answer is yes! Any guy who'd follow two girls across the country, leaving a good job where he was on track for partnership, and start over, and who showers my best friend with gifts, love, and support gets my vote. "

We spend the rest of the night doing some wedding planning.

"Do you think Jackson would mind if we had it at the

estate?" Gabby asks.

"I can ask him. I'm not sure what his plans are for it. There's always the possibility that he'll lose it the same way it was won."

Gabby's face falls.

"He assures me he's not going to, though." I'm so happy for them. I knew this was coming; I just didn't know when. "I will ask him when I talk to him tonight."

We finally return to the estate, and I send them off to bed, grateful I'm on the other side of the house.

I call Jackson, and the phone goes to voice mail, so I leave a message. "Sorry I missed you. Gabby and Damien are engaged. They're hoping you'll allow them to marry here on the cliffs. Call me tomorrow. Miss you."

When I wake the next morning, there's a text from Jackson.

Jackson: Sorry I missed you last night. I fell asleep. Congratulations to Gabby and Damien, and of course they can marry at the Halona Moana. I'm off to the factory in Ohio shortly. We'll talk soon.

I'm happy I've heard from him, but I'm disappointed he can't talk. I wonder what's going on that he needs to go to Ohio.

I manage to enjoy the rest of the weekend with Gabby and Damien. We have plenty of pool time and find a beautiful sandy beach. The temperatures are in the mid-70s, so the locals think we're crazy, but we don't mind. For early-May, it's warm to us.

As Gabby and Damien board the plane to leave late Sunday night, I talk to Matt, the pilot, for a moment.

"How was Ohio?" I ask him.

He looks at me funny. "I was here all weekend and haven't been to Ohio in ages."

My heart stops. *Where did Jackson go if he wasn't in Ohio?*

I feel like an idiot. I shouldn't have listened to Gabby. I've watched him distance himself these last few weeks. I'm yesterday's news. He's moving on without me.

I can't stop myself.

Me: Gabby and Damien just left. How did you get to Ohio?

Jackson: Checking up on me?

I'm not going to answer. I just put the phone away and head into the kitchen.

"What's wrong?" Leilani asks.

I paint a smile on my face. "I'm fine. Just missing my friends. Their visit reminded me of how much they mean to me."

Leilani looks at me. "And selfishly, I want you to move here for a while."

"You're so sweet."

She hands me a mug of hot cocoa, and I thank her before heading up to my room.

Twenty minutes later, there's a knock at my door. I open it to find Brian standing there.

"Is everything alright?" I ask.

"Mr. Graham couldn't reach you, so he wanted me to check on you."

I'm completely horrified. "I'm sorry, Brian. I left my phone down in the library. I'll go get it and call Mr. Graham."

"No problem." He turns and walks down the hall with me.

"Please apologize to Melinda. I'm sure she's not very happy that he dragged you out of bed."

"I'm still working. The invisible fence went off again."

"Why do you think that keeps happening?"

"We're remaining vigilant, but we think it's a critter."

I nod. When we reach the library, I pull the phone out of the drawer I stuffed it in. Twelve missed calls. I look at the text messages.

Jackson: Just kidding. You can check up on me all you want.

Jackson: I'm at the Marriott in Blue Ash, Ohio. Call the switchboard or information. I'm in my room.

Jackson: I keep trying you. I'm sorry. I was only teasing.

Jackson: I flew with Mason Sullivan on his jet. Please talk to me.

Jackson: I'm sending Brian to you if you don't respond.

I take a deep breath and dial his number. I'm ready to get yelled at for not responding to him.

"I'm sorry," he says in greeting.

"I left the phone in the library and went to bed. You didn't have to get Brian up to come to check on me."

"Well, I was only teasing, and then it occurred to me that you'd talked to the flight crew and couldn't figure out how I got to Ohio."

"I'm sorry you couldn't reach me. I just figured you were unhappy I was asking."

"I wasn't unhappy; I just wasn't funny."

"Usually you're funny."

"I do try, but I missed the mark."

"Why did you go to Ohio?"

He spends the next half hour telling me about a manufacturing problem. "Your stock options may dip in value."

"I don't care about that. You can have your fifteen percent back, and I'm fine with my five percent."

I hear him take a deep breath. "I want you to have everything of mine."

"I know you think you do, but in six months or even a year, you'll change your mind."

He doesn't respond.

"Thanks for bringing Gabby and Damien out," I say after a moment. "We really had a great time together."

"What did they think of the Big Island suite?"

"They liked it."

"Jim just pulled up in a car with Mason. Can I call you later?"

"I'm here at your disposal."

"Miss you, I can't wait—" And the line goes dead.

It's six o'clock in the morning in Ohio, and his workday is just starting. I'm determined to get some sleep before I check in with this week's temp.

Chapter 35

Jackson

We're in the home stretch. Corrine has worked the last month and a half from Maui, and I'm ready to see her every day—not just every other weekend. I'm not leaving Hawaii without her. She's done a fantastic job organizing the poker tournament, and I know it will be crazy for her while everyone is here, so I've flown in with San Francisco sourdough bread, her favorite chocolates, and a dozen roses. I'd give her more jewelry if I didn't think it would send her packing.

Right now, she's meeting with an event person to bring in hula dancers for the luau we're planning for the first night, so Brian picked me up on his own. I watch the scenery as he drives me away from the airport, and I'm surprised by what I see. Usually Corrine has my attention, and I'm not watching the landscape.

I've made dinner reservations in town at a quiet restaurant

Leilani recommended, and I'm more than ready to enjoy some time with Corrine. I'm tired of not being in the same city and not happy we still don't have answers about who's been harassing her.

When we arrive at the house, I see her outside with a man I don't recognize and one of the groundskeepers.

"Hello!" I call as I walk over.

"Hey, look who's here," Corrine says with a big grin.

I put my arm around her, pull her in close, and kiss her temple.

"We were worried we'd need a tent for the luau, but we may not. Either way we'll watch the weather, and if we do, it'll go here." She motions to where we're standing. "And behind us is where they'll dance. The hope is to get most of the guests up and doing the hula."

I chuckle. "That may take a few mai tais."

"I've got you covered," Corrine says with a wink and a smile.

I'm introduced to Marty, the man standing with them, who's the dance company salesperson. We talk for a few more minutes, but once he heads out and the groundskeeper goes back to his job, I finally have Corrine to myself—and in person. "You look absolutely stunning this evening."

She kisses me, and my cock is alert. "I've missed you."

"I'm going to show you how much I missed you later tonight, but Leilani made some dinner reservations for us."

"I'm ready to go whenever you are." Corrine curtsies, and it only makes me want to take her up to our room and have my way with her. I can't believe I'm this way around her. I've never wanted or needed someone like I do her.

"Let me drop my bag and change into a Hawaiian shirt so I can blend in."

"I'll be in the library waiting for you."

"You could come with me, you know." I wiggle my eyebrows.

She laughs, and I love that sound. "But if I do, we'll never get to dinner."

She's right. And if we don't go to dinner, we won't get home. "I'll be right back."

When I walk down to the library a few minutes later, the house smells like freshly baked bread. Corrine and I detour to the kitchen. Everyone is eating homemade pizza.

"Leilani is working on our idea for a pizza bar," Corrine explains. "We have a large grill and a pizza oven we can do this with."

I nod. "How did it go?"

"It was a little slow." Leilani points to the table where some people are finished, and others still waiting. "I need to see what I can come up with."

"I was just telling Leilani that I think we can rent some propane pizza ovens," one of the housemen says.

"That would be great." Corrine turns to me. "Don't you think your guests will be in a hurry to eat so they can get started?"

I nod. "Most likely, but if we start dinner early—most of them will be on Pacific Time—we should be fine to start the game by seven. Plus, we'll always have *pupus* and booze."

Corrine is inspecting the latest pizza to emerge from the oven. "Looks fantastic. Did you like the crust recipe you made?" she asks Leilani.

"Definitely. This was a great idea."

"It's sooo good," Danny says.

"Totally," Jimmy adds.

"They're turning into surfer dudes," I warn Brian.

"Tell me about it. It's the kids they play with at the park." Melinda laughs.

"Don't ever change, boys." I wink at them, and they give me the hang loose sign.

The whole table cracks up.

Twenty minutes later, Corrine and I are seated at a small, quiet restaurant in a booth facing the beach. The waves lap quietly at the shore.

"This is the life," Corrine says.

She's clearly more relaxed than she was at the estate. "You're doing a fantastic job getting ready for the party."

"I'm just trying to stay within budget. If it rains, the tent will blow it out."

"Don't worry about it." I pull her in and kiss her on the temple. "The number is purely arbitrary. Whatever it takes."

"Nate asked for Mitchner bourbon, and I ordered a case of the twenty-five-year. I mentioned it to Gillian, but she thought he was probably interested in the gold something. I need to track that down."

"No, you don't. I can't imagine Nate will be unhappy with twenty-five-year-old bourbon. You're fine."

"Landon wants a vegetarian meal."

"What? He's full of shit. We went out for burgers last week." I dig my phone out of my pocket.

Me: You're eating vegetarian now?"

Landon: Only organic vegetarian.

Me: You're full of shit. My cook is going crazy trying to accommodate you. It's okay if you are, but if you're doing that to yank Corrine's chain, she has a nasty bite. I'd beware.

Corrine's phone pings.

Landon: I was just kidding about being vegetarian. Please don't go out of your way for me. I'll eat whatever you have.

We laugh.

Corrine: Pig shit for you then. Leilani will put rat poison in your meals as payback.

Landon: I will bring her something special from the mainland.

Landon: Something for both of you.

Corrine: Groveling works well.

Our meal arrives, and we talk about the state of the company and my admin worries, politics, and issues with the final stage of the renovations at the estate.

"Do you think Leilani is going to do well as majordomo?" I ask.

"The staff loves her. She struggles with the bills, but I can set those up on automatic pay, no problem."

When we've finished, they deliver a chocolate soufflé for dessert. Corrine's moans of appreciation make me want to spread it all over her body and lick it off all night long. But first I need to gauge where we are.

"I hear you when you tell me you're worried I'm going to end this after a few months," I tell her, taking her hand. "But I need you to know that's not going to happen. I miss waking up with you and spending the days working by your side and the nights… Tell me you're considering moving in when we return."

She sighs. "I was thinking I could move into Gabby's place since she's moving in with Damien."

My heart drops. "You don't want to move in with me?"

"I don't think that's a good idea."

"Why not?" I implore.

She plays with her napkin, and I know she has something to say, but she's reluctant to tell me. "I just don't think it's a good idea."

I lean in and kiss her temple. "Corrine, if this distance between us has done anything, it's given me a lot of clarity. I'm hopelessly in love with you. I have been since long before we started dating, and I didn't even realize it. I will wait for you as long as you need me to."

She smiles. But she doesn't return my declaration.

"At least we'll still work together, right?" I ask.

She looks away and takes a deep breath. "Not when this is over. I need to find another job. I can't work for you any longer. You knew this when you moved me here, and that hasn't changed."

"Why not?" I demand louder than I mean to.

"Have you looked at your call sheets over the last few weeks?"

"I look at them every day." I'm confused about what that has to do with anything.

"They're filled with the women you've slept with, who want to sleep with you, and those that would do *anything* to sleep with you. I can't answer those calls anymore."

"I've already told you, I'll hire you an assistant who answers the calls."

"I still can't work for you. I need some separation, something that's my own. You can keep the stock options if you want them."

My head hurts. "I want to make this work."

"If we're going to make *us* work, we'll have to do it while I'm working for someone else."

"You don't think men look at you and want to bed you?"

She snorts as if she has horns and warts all over her face. She truly has no idea how stunning she is. "No, I don't."

My voice drops. "Let me assure you, a lot of married *and* unmarried men would give their left testicle to have one small taste of what I've had."

"That's gross."

I can tell she also dismisses it as not accurate, but it's a cold fact, and the idea that she doesn't know it is the four-hundred-thousandth reason I love her.

"But true."

"If you have any feelings for me at all, you'll listen to what I'm saying."

"I'm listening. I just don't like what I'm hearing." I try to control my frustration. I'm mad that I'm not getting my way. I always get my way. Why is she so difficult?

"I'm sorry. It's not going to change."

This is exactly the opposite of what I want to hear. I have to take a moment to breathe. "Can we go for a walk when we get back tonight?"

"Of course. I'm here at your disposal."

"I don't want you to do it because I'm your boss, or that we have Earth-shattering sex. I want you to spend time with me because you like me, and you have feelings for me."

I see tears pool in her eyes. "I do have feelings for you."

"Then please tell me what's going on."

"You know how broken Nate is over Cecelia's death?"

"Of course. He's incomplete without her."

"He's lost and heartbroken. That's how I'll be when you decide you're going to move on."

"Why would I move on? I don't understand."

She smiles. "I'd love to go for a walk with you when we get back."

This conversation isn't over, but I'm obviously missing something. It's times like this that I wish I had a sister or someone who could translate women to me. I just don't understand.

Corrine and I sit quietly for a while. *How can I make her comfortable coming back to work with me?* I'm lost without her. I need her almost as much as I need oxygen.

I pay the bill, and we walk back to Brian and our waiting car.

"Could we run through all the things I need to do before everyone arrives in two weeks?" Corrine asks.

I nod, and we spend the drive back to the estate talking

about what needs to get done and how I can help her. The cloud of her leaving weighs heavy on me—and now we're not even talking about it.

Brian pulls into the driveway, and we get out before he parks the car for the night in the garage. Walking hand in hand, we wander out toward the cliffs. As we enter the back patio, Corrine stops short, and her hands go to her mouth.

The mesh fence around the pool has been cut and shredded. Brian rounds the corner from the garage and immediately makes a phone call. Security comes running in.

I'm pissed. "What the hell am I paying you all for if this person keeps coming on the property and doing damage?"

There's so much commotion that Leilani comes out of her apartment. She sees what's going on and pulls Corrine into the house. I can hear the sirens wail as Brian takes pictures and directs one of his team members to pull the video of the last three hours.

This night can't get any worse.

Chapter 36

Corrine

Seeing the fence shredded scared the crap out of me.

It wasn't the fence itself that alarmed me, although if the twins were to come tearing out of the pool house, it could be dangerous. What scares me is that it happened just feet from the pool house and Leilani's apartment *with* the security cameras and invisible fences. I feel violated and vulnerable, not only for myself but for everyone living on the property.

Why does this keep happening with me around? It's been quiet in San Francisco, and I know there are no updates on the harassment situation.

We're sitting inside when Brian comes in to report that the camera feed indicates the intruder is a petite female, all in black. I meet with the detective assigned to the case. We have over sixty cameras throughout the property, but I guess it makes sense that they'd miss actually seeing someone enter the property if they didn't trip the alarms.

Jackson rubs my back as they finish interviewing us. "Let's go upstairs."

I'm grateful for the break from all the activity. When we walk into the master bedroom, it's lit with candles, and I can see a beautiful display of roses and my favorite chocolates.

I turn to Jackson and wrap my arms around him. "There couldn't be a better ending to this night."

"I was hoping it would be an open salvo to a weekend in bed, doing all sorts of naughty things to one another."

I lean in and kiss him, our tongues doing an aggressive dance. He dropped the L-word at dinner, and I was shocked. We've known each other a year, but we've not really been dating for very long—if that's even what you call going out when we're in the same town and having incredible sex and delightfully naughty phone calls.

I stand before him naked, and I try to get down on my knees. I may not be able to tell him I love him, but I can show him.

He reaches for me. "This is about you, tonight and always."

Jackson hadn't planned to stay the week, but after the vandalism, he was determined to oversee things personally until security gets it sorted out. Secretly, I'm grateful. I felt safe with Brian on property, but I've felt safer these past few days with Jackson in my bed.

When Jackson left for a meeting in Honolulu with the governor early this morning, he made it clear he wanted the security team to figure out where the break in the sensors is—and do it yesterday. They've been working on it for a week with little progress, and his patience is incredibly thin. Fortunately, the week since the pool incident the night he arrived has been quiet—no alarms going off or any strange things like the drone. I think it's good news, but Brian is urging us to all remain vigilant because we still don't know who is behind this, and we don't want to let our guard down. They could come back when we least expect it.

This line of thinking is sadly familiar to me. My stress is at an all-time high, and I'm not managing it well. I've snapped at Jackson and even Leilani. She doubled down, brushed off my behavior, and made kalua pork, which made me feel worse. We just have a week or so until the poker tournament, and I'm trying to keep it together.

It's been a day, but my second-to-last meeting before dinner is with her.

"We have fifty-two people coming in a little over a week," I tell Leilani, looking over my list of action items. "I think we've got as much as we can under control."

"Just know that the *Menehunes* are destined to cause problems," she replies.

"What is a *Menehune*?" I ask.

"They're mythological people who live in the forest. Hawaiians think of them as the ones who designed the beautiful waterfalls and rock formations, but they're also troublemakers. They like to cause problems. We just expect it." Leilani shrugs.

"Do you think they're the ones behind the cut pool fence?"

"You never know."

My cell phone pings.

Jackson: I'm on the ground. Meet me in the library, and I expect you naked.

Me: That will make my meeting difficult, and honestly embarrassing to the caterers.

Jackson: Get Leilani to cover for you and meet me there.

I take a deep breath. "Leilani, can you cover the meeting with the caterer? Mr. Graham has landed and apparently wants to meet with me."

She smiles. "No problem. In fact, I know you're stressed. We've gone through the menus, and we're there. Let me take care of the food and entertainment for the party. I want you to enjoy your guests. You've done a lot."

"Thank you, Leilani. You've done such a great job preparing for the party. I'm going to miss you. I wanted to let you know, I'm leaving Soleil Energy. I'm no longer going to work for Mr. Graham." I have to start saying it out loud if I have any hope of making it real.

I see her eyes cloud with worry.

"All the bills are set up to be automatically paid. When you need extra funds for something, go to Mr. Graham the same way you've come to me. He'll have another assistant shortly, and I know you'll work great with her—or maybe this time it'll be him." I wink at her. "You're a strong majordomo, and you don't need my help."

She dabs her eyes. "I hope you find your happiness."

"Thank you. But you're not rid of me yet."

As I leave the kitchen, I hear Jackson arrive, and I follow the scent he's left in his wake. I find him waiting for me in the library.

"I asked you to *meet* me in the library," he says.

He's upset about something. I haven't seen this Jackson Graham in several months. I look him in the eyes. "I apologize. I was transitioning my meeting with the caterer to Leilani. We've agreed that she'll be taking care of all the food and entertainment for the party."

He shuts the door behind me and locks it. In two steps, he fogs the windows with a flip of a switch.

He's been upset about things going sideways with the production of the solar film in the factory in Ohio, and I know he's nervous that the sales are so high we aren't producing fast enough. And, I think he's also beginning to realize I'm serious about not coming back to work in the office or moving in with him.

I open my mouth to speak.

"No talking."

I nod and wait for him.

"I asked you to be naked in this room when I arrived."

He's staring at my breasts. I reach to the back of my dress and unzip it. The fabric falls from my chest, exposing my aroused nipples. Under his watchful eyes, I wiggle my hips a little and the dress lands at my feet. I'm standing only in my thong, and his eyes are hooded with desire.

"Put your hands on the couch arm and spread your legs."

I do as I'm told, and I feel him reach up and fondle my breast. Lust rushes through me. He plays with the nipple, pinching and pulling it. "I'm unhappy that you won't move into my apartment."

He pinches the nipple hard. I gasp, and shiver with excitement.

"You like that, don't you?"

I nod.

He pulls my panties aside and slides his fingers into my slit. "You're wet for me." His thumb brushes over my clit, and I go from zero to sixty in a microsecond. "I'm going to fuck you. You can tell me to stop when you've had enough."

He continues to rub at my clit, and I hear his belt buckle clink and the sound of the zipper just before his pants hit the ground. Then he grabs my hips with both hands, and I know I'll be bruised tomorrow. In one movement, he's buried deep inside me, and it takes a minute to adjust to his size. He ruts into me like a wild animal, spanking me and pulling my hair to bite at my neck.

The rocking has my nipples rubbing against the rough fabric of the couch, and every sensation is matched by Jackson's fury. I climax quickly. And he keeps going harder and faster.

"You...can't...leave...me..." He pumps into me.

"I…can't…live…with…out…you."

My second orgasm is close. I reach down and strum my clit. Jackson groans his own pinnacle but keeps rutting. The head of his cock rubs me just right, and my orgasm hits me like a wave and keeps crashing, harder and harder, again and again.

When I can't stand it any longer, he slips out and lies with me on the couch as we catch our breath.

"Was that an angry fuck?" I ask.

"Yes. I got myself all worked up on the flight back because you're leaving me."

I think about what he's saying. "I'm not leaving you. I'm just not moving in with you. It doesn't mean we won't spend every night together."

"But you won't work for me anymore."

"Tell your lawyers you're fucking your assistant and see what they say."

My head rests on his chest, and his heartbeat is steady and strong.

"That's not enough," he says. "And you promised you'd find someone to replace your before you left."

"You're right. I did promise that, but then you sent me here for six weeks."

"You act like it's my fault you have a crazy stalker. That blame belongs to your ex, *Bobby Sanders*."

I sit up. I know Jackson's angry because he's not getting his way, but he's also not respecting my choices. "I'm sorry this upsets you so much."

"It does upset me." He sits up and runs his hands through his hair. "I'm not a cheater. I have women fall all over me, and I've never even looked at them twice since we became involved. I'm happy to announce that you've stolen my heart, and I'm only yours, but I can't make these women stop calling me. I don't even see why that matters. Ignore them. They're nothing to me."

He's right, and I know that, but I'm not very good at

explaining why I need to protect my heart. "I know. Please understand, my mother depended on my father for everything. What do I do if I'm working for you *and* living with you and you decide to move on? I'll be left with nothing. I'd be broken and homeless, like my mother was."

"You won't be left with nothing; you have stock options. And anyway, that's not what's going to happen with us. I need you."

It's the broken part he doesn't understand. I need to change the subject, because right now we're never going to agree. "Leilani is making a nice dinner. Are you hungry?"

"You're done talking about this?"

I choose my words carefully. "I think we're at an impasse and continuing to talk about it will only make matters worse."

"Damn it, Corrine. You can't change the subject or ignore it. We need to figure this out."

This is it. Unless I bend to Jackson's will, he's going to break this off. I knew this was coming, so I might as well rip off the Band-Aid. "There's nothing to figure out." I stand up and put my dress back on. "You want me working for you, listening to the women who want to fuck you, and then living in your home so you can fuck me at night when it's convenient for you. I hear you."

"I've told you we'll hire someone else to answer the phones."

"Have you heard anything I said? Do you think you'll make demands to fuck me in your office in San Francisco like you've done this afternoon?"

"Maybe."

"And what will you do when a former lover calls and asks you to meet her? Go running, leaving me home alone in your apartment with no place to call my own?"

"I won't do that again. I've learned my lesson. Plus, you'll always have this house. You'll never be homeless again."

What. The. Fuck? "You're not listening to me. Yours is not the only perspective that matters in this relationship—if it's actually going to be a relationship. I'm going to sleep downstairs tonight. I need to think about this." I whip around. "Alone."

"You walk out on this conversation and we're done."

I look at him, and I see the pain in his face. But I shrug. "Better now than after I am living under your roof."

Chapter 37

Corrine

The sun has fallen below the horizon. I've missed dinner, but I'm not hungry. I keep replaying our conversation earlier. I hear the bathroom door slide open, but I ignore him. Our relationship can't be his way or the highway. Jackson can't always be in control.

"I knew he'd dump you eventually," says a female voice I don't recognize.

I roll over in bed, and although it takes me a minute to place her, I realize I'm looking into the eyes of Valerie, or Jennifer—or whatever she calls herself. She's dressed in all black, her hair slicked back into a high ponytail, and she stares at me, but her eyes don't seem focused.

"What are you doing here?" I look around the room in a panic. There is nothing I can see beyond a pillow to defend myself. I don't even have my cell phone. I left it in the library.

Crap.

"You fucked up my life. I warned you." Venom drips from her voice.

I'm confused. But then it hits me. She's the one who's been harassing me. *It never had anything to do with Bobby Sanders.*

"What do you want?" I ask her.

"If you were out of the picture, he'd be with me."

This woman is delusional. I sit up and look to the door, hoping and praying he's going to come in.

"He's not coming for you," she growls.

"He'll have caught you on video trespassing." I try to reason with her, hoping she'll say what she needs to and go away.

"They're so dense. They open the gates all the time for delivery drivers and cars. Then they open up all the doors and windows, and I walk right in. This house is so big. You know I slept right in the next room for days, and you never even knew."

My pulse quickens, and I pull the covers up as a wall between us.

"I've been watching you for months. I know all about you."

I'm saying a silent prayer, begging Jackson to come look for me. *Where is he?*

"What did I ever do to you?"

"You had a perfectly reasonable man, and then you had to go after what was rightfully mine."

"What do you mean? I didn't go after anyone."

She begins to pace. "I called, and you didn't ever give my fiancé my messages. You didn't think I was good enough for him."

Fiancé? "That's not true. I always give Mr. Graham all of his messages. I can prove it to you. I keep a phone log, and he makes the decision whether to call people back."

"You're lying!" she yells. "Then your little boyfriend breaks up with you. You can't even keep that man, so instead, you decide to go after what's mine."

She continues to pace, and I'm struggling to follow.

"I wanted to stake my territory with him, so you knew what I meant to him. We went to the bar where you like to hang out with your little friend. He sees you all upset, and he goes to you." She's stopped pacing and points her finger at me. "You knew he'd come running, and that's exactly what he did. You cast a spell with your vagina, and he dropped me right then."

"I have no idea what you're talking about. Mr. Graham bought Gabby and me a drink. I work for him." I'm trying to remember our conversation that night, or even determine which night she means, but I can't.

She goes back to pacing and is pulling on the sleeve of her coverup. "Right. I saw how you smiled at my man when he came running up to you. I'd had it. I wasn't going to let you steal him away. I was going to make him realize what a whore you are, so he'd come back to me."

"You sent the box with Bobby Sanders' jersey?"

"You bet your ass. I didn't want you shitting all over my relationship—you could shit all over your own."

I need to think rationally, because she's not being reasonable.

She pulls a gun from her waistband and points it at me. Immediately I think of all the things I didn't tell Jackson—like how much I love him. I should have worked harder to help him understand why I'm scared to go all-in with him. I close my eyes and wait for her to fire.

"You two were all over the newspapers. *I* should have gone with my love to Cecelia Lancaster's funeral—not you!"

She's crazy. I have to defuse her anger. "He doesn't love me," I sob.

"No! Because he loves me."

I say another silent prayer for a rescuer.

"Come on, we're leaving." She waves the gun at me and pulls the covers back. "Get out of the bed. You. Are. Coming.

With. Me."

I know that if I go with her, I'm in trouble. But if I don't, I'm also in trouble. Because I'm slow to figure out my plan, she slaps me with the gun. After that I can't tell if I'm standing or sitting, and it takes me a minute to figure out what's going on over the ringing in my ears.

I begin to stand, but I trip. Valerie's holding my arm so tightly I'm sure she's going to break it, and I can't see out of my left eye because of the blood from where she hit me.

She guides me through the empty house, and I'm shocked and worried about how well she knows her way. She walks me through the garage and out the side door. I know the cameras don't typically pick her up because she's walking out the door and not in. I stumble and fall to the ground outside the door, and I look up at the camera, so I know it sees me.

She almost rips my arm out of the socket as she pulls me into the bushes. I feel the mud between my toes. "Where are you taking me?"

"Not to worry. Once my love realizes I'm ready to carry his children and take care of him, maybe I'll release you into the ocean, and you can swim back to the mainland."

The hair on the back of my neck is standing on end. I need to send a signal of some sort. I know Jackson and Brian will come looking for me. We've cleared the oleander between the two estates, and we're in front of the next-door neighbors' garage. I fall again on the driveway, and with a bloody finger, I paint an arrow toward the neighbors' front door. Between my muddy footprints and the arrow, I hope they'll know where to look for me.

Valerie grabs me by the hair and pulls me back to my feet. "Don't you fucking dare even think about it. If you want your precious Jackson to live, you will do what I say without this nonsense."

She pulls me by the hair into the house next door and down a set of stairs. Valerie continues to rant, and when she hits me again, everything goes black.

Chapter 38

I reach for the bottle of bourbon and pour myself four fingers—a quadruple. I'd prefer ice, but that would require walking to the kitchen, and right now, I just want to feel numb. How does that woman make me so angry and so happy at the same time? I just wish she could see that my love is real, and I don't have eyes for anyone else. I'll do whatever it takes to make this work, if only I can get her to see it my way.

I take a deep pull on the glass just as the library door opens with a bang and slams against the wall.

I jump and spill my drink. "Fuck!"

"Sorry," Brian says. "The alarm on the side of the house just went off. Where's Corrine?"

I sit up straight. "We had a fight. She hasn't wanted anything to do with me since this afternoon. I assume she's gone to bed."

Brian looks like he's ready to tell me off, but instead, he goes running. I start to follow him, and I can hear him yelling her name repeatedly. He runs to the room where I think she is, but she doesn't appear.

"Corrine!" he yells again. He looks down at the floor, and his speed increases.

It suddenly dawns on me—she should be responding to Brian. If it was me calling, I'd guess she was ignoring me, but she wouldn't do that to Brian.

I hear him on a radio. "Check the feed. Corrine is missing, and she's bleeding."

"Bleeding? Missing? What do you mean?" My slight buzz from the bourbon is gone.

"She isn't upstairs, and I can't find her downstairs." He points to brown spots on the dark wood floors.

Brian's radio pops. "Brian, you're going to want to see this."

I follow him to the security office, and they have Corrine on the screen. She has a dark streak on her face.

Brian turns to me. "You may not want to see this."

"What the fuck!" An arm comes out of the bushes and pulls her in.

"How did this motherfucker get on my property?" I rage.

It's four seconds max, and we replay it and replay it. Brian runs out the door, grabbing a pair of night-vision goggles. He suddenly appears on the screen, but we can't tell where he came from. We watch him and someone else go diving into the bush.

I can't watch this any longer. I grab another pair of goggles and follow him out the door.

Fitting through the bushes is tight. The oleanders are large with thick stalks, but they're also dense. Brian spots a footprint. But the trail just stops, and he thinks maybe they got into a car. We look inside the neighbors' glass front door, and the house is black.

Corrine is nowhere to be seen.

I scream in frustration. "No!"

Less than fifteen minutes later, the police come racing up the driveway with lights flashing, but no sirens. An officer gets out of the car. "What's going on?"

Brian explains who we are and the situation.

"Why weren't you with your girlfriend?" one of the officers asks.

"We had a disagreement."

"Did you hit her?" the other officer asks.

The idea of striking Corrine in anger makes my blood run cold. But I did spank her during sex, and it was angry sex. *Fuck*!

"Absolutely not," I tell them.

My heart races. I begin to make a deal with Corrine in my mind. Whatever she wants—I just need her back.

You can rent Gabby's old apartment, just come back to me.

Take whatever job you want, as long as you stay with me.

I need you.

I can't live without you.

The tears hit, and I'm beside myself.

Please come back to me, Corrine.

I'll give you all the time you need, just please come back to me.

I'm numb. I've never been scared for anyone like I am for Corrine right now. Has her stalker come all the way from the mainland?

The police are hesitant to do anything. But they manage to get everyone who lives on the property together and interview the staff.

"What is the relationship between Corrine and Jackson?"

"Is he abusive to her?"

"Would he hurt her?"

"Has she ever run away before?"

I'm furious that they're focusing on me. We have proof in the feed that she was grabbed, but they don't think it's compelling enough. It could be a friend of hers.

We explain the footprints, and they knock on the front door of the house next door.

That's it. Nothing else.

Leilani gives me a comforting hug. "Corrine loves you. She's going to be fine."

I nod. I want to believe Leilani's right and it isn't an empty platitude.

Time is clicking by, and the police are not in any hurry.

Don't they understand? Corrine is missing, and we don't know where she is or who took her. They've watched the video, and yet they're acting like she ran away because of our argument.

As the minutes tick by, Leilani passes out coffee and snacks. "I don't know what to do," she says.

"This is perfect." I give her my best smile. I can see she's as worried as I am.

Eventually, the police leave. They've accomplished nothing and tell us if Corrine doesn't appear in forty-eight hours, they'll see what else they can do.

Forty-eight hours? I saw the cut above her eye. She's in danger, and I don't have forty-eight hours of patience.

Chapter 39

Jackson

Early Saturday morning, Brian announces Jim's arrival on the property. We've been standing, pacing, and milling around for hours while teams scoured the estate and found nothing. The sun is at the horizon, trying to bring in a new day, but I need it to stay where it is so we have more time to find Corrine. I need her to be safe and in my arms.

"Jim flew in?" I ask as Brian passes.

He nods. "I called him as soon as you alerted me, and he left late last night for the airport."

How can it already have been more than eight hours since this ordeal began? We've gotten nowhere.

The SUV comes racing up the driveway, and Jim and Kate jump out before it even comes to a complete stop.

"What do you know?" Jim demands.

"Nothing," I tell him. "We had an argument, and the

police think Corrine just ran away."

"That's not like her," Kate says.

"I know. Corrine had been hit with something, and her eye was a swollen, bloody mess, but they think I hit her." Turning to Jim, I ask, "Have you seen the video?"

He nods. "I saw the blood, and the hand that pulls her through the bushes."

"What do we do?"

"Give me a minute," he says.

Jim talks to Brian and the security team. As they work out a plan, Kate goes over to spend time with Melinda and the boys—trying to keep them occupied and not interested in the investigation.

A little while later, Leilani makes her pineapple pancakes for everyone. They're an immediate hit. I'd love them, too, if I wasn't worried about Corrine.

While Jim is eating his pancakes, he asks Leilani about the house next door.

"Have you ever met the people who own the house?"

She nods. "They've owned it for a while. They don't come very often—maybe once a year or so. They live in Japan. He's an executive for an automaker."

"How do you get a hold of them if you need to?"

"We don't. They have a landscaping service that keeps up with the yard, and once a month, a cleaning crew comes in, but it may not even be that often."

"Do you know the landscaping company? They may know how to reach them."

She thinks for a moment. "I think it's Grass, Flowers, and Fauna, but I could be wrong."

He nods. "It's worth a try."

Jim gives one of his team members a look, and he disappears down the hall.

I reach for the carafe of coffee, but Leilani stops me. "I know you're tired, Mr. Graham. Corrine would want you well rested when she returns. Maybe you should go for a nap."

I couldn't sleep if I tried, but I must look dead on my feet since everyone is shooing me away.

Jim walks with me to the master bedroom.

"I need her back," I tell him, though I know I'm babbling. "I want to tell her she can rent her friend's apartment, and if it's that important that she doesn't come back to Soleil Energy, I'll make it work. I get it, but just come back."

"We're going to get this figured out," he assures me. "Get some rest."

We walk into my room, and Jim looks around before he leaves me. I lie down on the bed and stare at the ceiling.

Who could have taken her? I search my mind for someone who could be behind this. I wonder again if Bobby Sanders' girlfriend would fly all the way here. That seems awfully extreme.

I huff in frustration. *Damn it!*

She's hurt, and she needs help. Why does no one see that? Corrine didn't leave me. She told me she wants to be with me. She just doesn't want to work or live with me. And anyway, that wasn't *her* arm that pulled her into the bushes.

How could she have just disappeared? The gate to the house next door requires an opener. Could someone from their gardening or housekeeping service have taken her?

My heart races. I've never felt so helpless.

I close my eyes.

Even skipping the physical, Corrine is perfect, but she doesn't see it.

I think back to how funny she is. She had me going from the very beginning with that story about selling bull sperm, and there was no looking back after that. She's fucking hilarious.

I've never seen anyone as focused as she is. Despite dating a professional football player, she was in the office day in and day out, and her professional life never faltered.

She's fearless. When that fire alarm went off, she got the panicked applicant down the stairs and didn't think twice about making sure they both got out of the building.

Then there's her absolute lack of interest in my bank accounts. She's always treated both the company and my personal money with the utmost respect—not like so many who think I'm an open checkbook.

I need her not just in my bed, but in my life—no matter what. And I'll take it at whatever speed she wants to go. *Just be okay. Please come back to me.*

Chapter 40

Corrine

Slowly, the world comes into focus. My arms are zip-tied behind me and connected to some sort of pillar. I have a ball-gag in my mouth that's secured behind my head. I'm lying on a cold marble floor, and it's freezing, and there isn't a sliver of light coming from anywhere. It comes back to me in pieces… Valerie brought me into the neighbors' house and hit me.

I yell, but I don't think anyone can hear me. The room is sealed tight. I fight back tears and breathe deeply, in through my nose, to calm myself.

I pull on the restraints, trying with all my might to break them, but they only cut into my wrists. The pole I'm wrapped around is smooth metal and adds to the coldness.

I'm in an awkward position, and I try to adjust, but it only puts pressure on the restraints. My foot is tucked under my leg, and it tingles from lack of blood flow.

I can feel myself hyperventilating. *Hold it together!*

I think of all the good things I've done to help myself. I made sure I looked into the camera, and I'm sure they saw her pull me into the bushes. I made sure I made muddy footprints toward the house. I drew an arrow pointing at the front door. I know Jackson will find me.

My head is killing me, and my eye is almost swollen shut. I can't believe she hit me.

God, I'm thirsty. What I wouldn't give for a gallon of water.

Where is Jackson? What about Brian? Or Ben? Or the rest of the team?

Jackson. I've been so stubborn, holding on to my heart and worrying he'll be like all the other men in my life who've stomped on it. I need him, and he needs me. I can keep Gabby's apartment if I'm really that nervous, but he's done everything he can to make me feel comfortable. He's recognized my professional work, and despite my baggage, he loves me.

He told me he loves me. I love him too, but I never told him. I didn't want to believe him. I didn't want to give him my heart, but the truth is, he already has it. I can feel hot tears on my cheeks. I need him.

I close my eyes, and after a moment, I imagine I hear a voice.

"Corrine?"

I open my eyes, and it's my mother. "Mommy?"

"You're going to be fine, baby."

"I miss you so much."

"I miss you, too. I think Jackson is a fine man."

"He's good for me."

"Don't let my relationship with your dad hold you back, sweetheart. We both love you so much and want the best for you, and I think Jackson is perfect for you."

"Mommy, I'm so sorry about everything."

"There's nothing to be sorry for, but you need to be strong

right now. They're going to figure out where you are. Don't go to sleep. They're close and going to be here before too long. Jackson is so worried about you. Be strong, sweetheart. I love you."

She disappears, and I close my eyes again. While I know she was only a figment of my imagination, I also know she's right. Jackson will find me; I just need to stay awake.

Chapter 41

Jackson

Though I believed it was impossible, I fall asleep at some point. My body is exhausted. Then I feel the bed dip, and I half-open my eyes. It's Corrine. I start to drift off again, but my eyes shoot open. Something deep within me sounds an alarm.

"Corrine?"

"Yes, baby. I'm right here."

That's not Corrine.

It's Valerie. *Holy fuck.* I rub my eyes and realize she's wearing Corrine's lei necklace and her blue bikini. "Wha—What are you doing here?"

"I'm sorry about our fight. I love you, sweetheart, and I'll do anything you ask."

She's not making any sense. *What the fuck?*

Valerie's hand goes to my cock, and she starts to play with

it. It isn't responding. I'm repulsed by her.

"Where's Corrine?" I ask.

"I'm right here." She shakes her head as she takes her top off. Her large, augmented breasts are in my face.

I get out of bed. "Corrine, where is my friend Valerie?"

"She's not here." She crawls across the bed toward me like she's stalking her prey.

"I can see that." I look around the room frantically and locate my phone on the nightstand. I never take my eyes off her, but I slowly inch toward the nightstand, pick up my cell phone, and slide it into my pocket.

"Come make me happy," she purrs. "Please do that magic with your tongue."

My stomach sours. We were together once, and it was anything but magic.

"Corrine, I need to use the bathroom. Why don't you get ready for me while I'm gone."

"Oh, baby, I'll be here waiting for you."

I slip into the bathroom and text Brian.

Me: 911 help. I'm in the master.

I push send just as she slides the door open. I casually tuck the phone into my pocket.

"Come on, you stud. Mama needs to feel your big, fat cock inside her."

I'm physically sickened. Valerie's wearing Corrine's things and not acting sane. Somehow, I need to find out where she's put Corrine.

"Do you know where Corrine is?" I ask her again.

She shakes her tits like a stripper. "I'm right here, baby."

I take a deep breath. "Do you know where my friend is?"

She puts her hand inside the bottom of the bathing suit. Then she shows me her wet fingers. "I'm already wet and waiting."

"How about my admin? She was here earlier, and she's

working on a big party I'm hosting. I just need to run a few details by her."

"She's gone. I'll be taking over."

My heart sinks.

There's a commotion, and Brian comes charging in with Jim and the others behind him.

With wild eyes, Valerie turns to me. "How could you? I love you."

I grab a T-shirt and throw it over her naked torso. "Where is Corrine?"

"I'm Corrine," she keeps repeating.

I hear sirens approaching in the distance. I'm ready to throttle Valerie for information, but Brian and his team pull her away from me. We step out into the hall.

I pace back and forth. "I've asked her all different ways where Corrine could be, but she keeps calling *herself* Corrine."

"What's her name?"

"Valerie Knudsen. She works at Organic Energy, and I met her at a trade show. She's the woman who's been harassing Corrine."

"Valerie Knudsen?" Jim looks at me, confused.

I nod.

Jim pushes a few buttons on his phone and shows me the screen. "This is Valerie Knudsen."

I lean against the wall. The woman in the picture looks nothing like the woman I know as Valerie Knudsen.

"Who is she then?" I pound on the bedroom door. "Where is my Corrine?"

Inside, "Valerie" screams profanity at everyone around her. "He's my fiancé. How dare you touch me?"

Brian steps back inside. "Ma'am, do you know where Corrine Woods is?"

"*I'm* Corrine Woods," she roars.

I follow Jim back into the bedroom.

"Jackson, baby, tell these people who I am," she pleads.

"I don't know who you are. You told me your name was

Valerie Knudsen, but it isn't. Who are you, and what did you do with Corrine Woods?"

Her breaths are coming in short, staccato bursts. The police officers have handcuffed her. She squints at me, and I see an evil smirk, but she doesn't say anything.

I'm crazy with worry and concern. I want to grab Valerie by her hair extensions and shake her until she tells me where the fuck Corrine is. She didn't ask for this shit.

The police lead her away. "We'll put her in an interview room and see if we can get her to talk."

"I have a feeling she's not going to say very much," Jim says as they go.

I look at Jim. "How were we so off the mark on who was terrorizing Corrine?"

"I'm sorry. We talked to the real Valerie Knudsen. You did meet her at the same conference and actually spoke to her. She checked out. We just had no sense until now that your Valerie wasn't the real Valerie."

"Corrine always called her Jennifer, and I don't know why. I wonder if her actual name is Jennifer? Fuck! What are we going to do?"

Brian comes in. "The police are taking her to Kahului. I'm going to follow. I have Gabe back at Clear Security looking through the state and federal databases for a match on her fingerprints."

I nod.

Jim gets on his radio with the team who are sitting at the camera feeds. I follow him outside, and they alert us when they see us on the camera. We can see an impression in the mud where Corrine dropped to her knees and looked up at the cameras. Jim points to the garage. We try the door, but it's locked.

As we walk around the house, he gets updates from his team as they look at different angles and watch us. We step inside the estate and walk out of the garage. With a gloved hand, Jim opens the garage door. "Can you see me?"

"No, sir."

"What about now?"

"No." Jim is in the bushes before the camera picks him up on the feed. "I see you now."

"Shit! This is a big blind spot we didn't catch." He radios his team to be sure they pull fingerprints off the door handle from the door. We push through the bushes into my neighbors' property and wander around the garage area. I know we looked here last night and didn't see anything. "You guys think maybe she drove her somewhere?"

"The footprints stopped about halfway across the driveway, but we can't be sure. We looked in the house, but everything was dark, and the gate at the road is locked."

Jim picks up his phone. "Gabe, did we get the name of the owners from the gardening service?"

He listens a few moments, and as I look inside, suddenly I'm convinced Corrine is in there. I know it as surely as I know anything.

I try the door, but nothing. It's locked, though I can see the panel for the alarm is green, which means the house alarm isn't set. I notice a rock garden across the driveway. I pick up a rock as big as my hand and throw it as hard as I can at the window. It beams itself right at me. I duck seconds before it nails me in the face.

Jim turns and looks at me. "Gabe, call them and call me back." He disconnects from his call. "What are you doing?"

"The house alarm is not armed—I can see the panel with a green light. I thought I'd break the window."

Jim pulls a slim, zippered case from his back pocket. "Gabe is calling the owners in Japan to tell them we're breaking in because we fear Corrine is being held hostage."

Jim positions himself in front of the lock and manipulates his picks until the door pops open. He motions me to stand back.

"Hello?" Jim yells into the house.

Three more from the Halona Moana security team follow

us in. The house is silent, and my stomach is in knots. I was really hoping to hear Corrine call for help. We walk through the main level. The house is a good size, but between the five of us, we cover it quickly. Stairs lead down to the basement. We follow them and immediately fan out once we get downstairs. This house goes down the cliffs, so the view looks over the ocean.

We move from room to room. Nothing. There is a gated barrier, and I look through and see a door in the back. I have no idea what I'm looking at. There's a lock on the gate. There are rows and rows of empty shelves for wine bottles.

I turn to Jim. "Why would they lock this gate if there isn't even one bottle of wine?"

He looks over. "Good question." He pulls out his tools and quickly picks the lock. We walk into the dark room with empty shelves, but I don't see anything.

"Where is she?" I yell.

We hear a thumping, but I can't quite tell if it's someone upstairs. It's very faint.

We hear thumping again. "Where is that coming from?"

Jim looks at each shelf carefully. Suddenly he pulls on a section of shelving, and a door behind the racks opens.

Immediately I see Corrine's foot. "There she is!"

We rush in, and I see her tear-stained face. She's bound and gagged.

"I'm here, baby." I cradle her in my arms.

Jim cuts her free and removes the ball-gag. "Are you okay?"

Corrine nods and begins to sob. "I'm so glad you found me."

Chapter 42

Jim cuts my wrists free of the zip-ties, and it feels so good to be able to move again. Stretching my fingers to get the circulation running through them, I look at my wrists. There are cuts and bruises from my pulling on the bindings, trying to break them. My fingers are freezing, but I feel better.

"Are you okay, Corrine?" Jackson looks me over and inspects my injuries. I know I must be a complete mess.

"Yes," I whimper. "I couldn't scream loud enough to be heard, so I kept kicking the shelves behind me. Thank God it worked."

There's a flurry around me, and Jackson lifts me into his arms and carries me up the stairs.

"I can walk," I tell him, but he's not listening.

Jackson sets me down on the stairs outside the door. The staff comes running and surrounds me.

"Did she hurt you?" I hear someone ask.

I touch my face to feel how swollen it is. I must look absolutely awful. "It was that woman who told me her name was Jennifer," I tell Jackson. "And you always called her Valerie."

"I know," he chokes out. "She was arrested but wasn't telling us where you were."

"Thank God you figured it out," Leilani says.

Jackson puts his arms around me. "It was my fault. I'm so sorry."

"How is it your fault?" Jim asks.

"I brought that woman into our lives."

"I don't think you brought her in; I think she snuck in. Her fingerprints came back as Jennifer Carlson. She's been diagnosed with histrionic personality disorder, or HPD, which is characterized by a pattern of excessive attention-seeking behaviors. In her case, she stole identities and became other people to get close to the targets of her obsession."

"That's why she called herself Jennifer when I met her," I say.

The crowd around me begins to disburse when the police arrive, and I explain what happened. I'm exhausted, and I just want a hot bath and some sleep. The paramedics look me over, give me a few stitches above my eye, and determine I'm fine. They take a thousand pictures of my bumps and bruises.

When the police begin to ask the same questions for the third time, Jackson holds up his hand. "Okay, guys, Corrine needs to get some rest. You know enough to hold Jennifer. If you need anything else, we'll make arrangements to come into the station."

Standing is not easy. After spending nearly twenty-one hours in the same position, my muscles are in total revolt—stiff, sore, and screaming at me. Jackson tries to pick me up. "No," I tell him. "I want to walk. I need to stretch my muscles."

Slowly I make my way into the house. The twins come

crashing into me.

"Corrine, Corrine, we thought you were dead."

You gotta love the honesty of children.

Melinda cringes and quickly admonishes them.

I lean down and say, "I'm too tough to die."

"Good. What happened to your face? It looks scary. Are you a monster?"

I raise my arms up high. "And I like to eat little boys."

They laugh and run away.

Melinda turns to go after them, but before she leaves, she pulls me into an embrace. "We were so worried about you. We're glad you're okay."

Leilani is standing nearby with two of the groundskeepers. She steps in and gives me a huge hug, so tight I can hardly breathe. "Thank you for coming back to us," she whispers. "We were all worried about you, but Jackson worried the most."

"Thanks, Leilani."

She pulls back but won't let go. "Are you hungry?"

"No. The paramedics gave me what is probably a thousand-dollar Motrin, and now I just want to take a warm bath and go lie down."

"Tomorrow morning, I'm going to make you my pineapple pancakes and an egg scramble."

The groundskeepers both touch my arms as they leave. "We're glad you're back safely."

Jackson walks with me as we climb the stairs to the master bedroom. "I'll start your bath. I think I saw bath shit somewhere."

I giggle. "Bath shit? What are you talking about?"

He shrugs. "You know, the shit you pour in the bath to make you feel better."

"Oh." I do my best to smile at him, but it makes the split over my eye hurt. "There's a lemon and lavender bath bomb under my sink."

"What the fuck is a *bath bomb*?"

I roll my one eye. "Just put it in the water and stand back." I have to play with him a little bit.

While he starts the tub, I sit carefully on the bed. My tailbone is super sore, and my limbs don't want to move fluidly. I can't even pull my shirt over my head.

I get caught, and Jackson walks out to help me undress. Usually he'd make a few jokes about what he's going to do to me, but right now he's in caregiver mode.

He helps me into the tub. The temperature is perfect. I lean back on a towel he's bundled up for my head to rest on. I love this tub. It's enormous, and I sit deep enough that when I lie back, my feet don't touch the end, and the water comes to my chin. Just what I need to repay my muscles for all they endured.

I shut my eyes. "Ahh."

"Fuck. I forgot the bath bomb."

I kick my feet in the water. "Just drop it in down by my feet."

He picks it up. "It stinks."

I open my good eye. "Go ahead, put it in the water."

He looks at me skeptically.

"Please?"

He drops it in and steps way back, worried he's going to get wet. The bath bomb fizzes and releases its scent. "What the hell?"

I watch him lean over the tub, inspecting the roar of the bubbles, and I can't help but smile. I love this man. He's the yin to my yang, and the cherry on the ice cream sundae.

He doesn't say much and lets me relax. Eventually he disappears out into the bedroom, but I know he's close by. When the water turns tepid, I pull the plug and stand, which was harder to do than I would have imagined.

After all my grunting and groaning, Jackson comes flying into the bathroom to help. "You could have called me; I would have helped."

"I know. I just didn't think it would be that hard."

He helps me to the bedroom and dresses me in his MIT T-shirt and a pair of cotton boxers. "I thought this might be more comfortable than a sexy negligee, and easier to get on and off."

I glance at the clock, and it's after nine. Exhaustion weighs on me like lead. I can't stand or keep my eyes open. Jackson helps me crawl into bed and turns the lights off. Then he gets into bed behind me.

He spoons me close, and I whisper, "Please don't ever let me go."

I feel him kiss the back of my head. "Good night, my love."

Chapter 43

Corrine

I slept most of Sunday, and by Monday, the first guests have begun to arrive for the poker tournament. People are staggering their arrivals all week, and despite all that's happened, I'm excited to have everyone at the estate. I don't want anything to derail this event we've spent weeks putting together.

We spend the next few days doing final preparations, though Leilani doesn't let me do much. She keeps insisting I take the time I need to recover. It'll be embarrassing to have to explain to everyone why I look so bad during the tournament weekend, but thankfully, Leilani has given me an old Hawaiian remedy. It's warm and wrapped in a banana leaf when she brings it to me—twice a day like clockwork. It doesn't smell the greatest, but it has brought the swelling down.

Even that can't do much about the wound and stitches, but I temper the green bruises with makeup. As the end of the week approaches, I'm looking better.

By Friday afternoon, everyone has arrived. I've been relieved of all duties. Leilani and Gillian have the weekend under control, and I'm just supposed to play hostess and enjoy myself. And that's my plan.

As our guests wander from the pool deck to the living room, drinking mai tais and enjoying soft Don Ho music piped in over the speakers, we take in the sunset. A professional photographer takes pictures, and there are Hawaiian arts and crafts, which everyone seems to get into. Jackson makes me a puka shell anklet and makes a big deal about putting it on.

"Get a room," someone yells, and the crowd laughs.

The gamblers congregate and talk. "Have any of you talked to the police officers from Las Vegas?" Nate asks.

There are nods all around, and it looks like everyone has.

"I got into an argument with Cecelia that morning, so I guess I'm high on the list of suspects," Jackson says.

"Me, too." Landon says. "I guess there was one of my fingerprints in her room, but I was never in the room, so I'm not sure how it got there."

"Mine, too," Mia says. "I hadn't been in her suite, so I'm at a loss on how it got there."

"They said that to me, too," Mason adds. "Though Caroline and I were in there that weekend, so it made sense."

"I think I'm the number-one suspect," Nate says.

Everyone looks at him, confused.

"How can that be?" Caroline asks.

"I was her husband." He shrugs. "They said she'd talked to a divorce lawyer."

"There is no way that's true," Caroline says. "She glowed when she talked about you just hours before she went missing."

"It sounds like they were fishing," Jim says. "My team is

working on this. We've looked at all of you, and there's nothing there. We're looking at what she was doing the last few weeks, and there are some pretty big holes we can't account for."

"I'm not comfortable with them lying to all of you," Walker Clifton says. He's the US attorney for Northern California. "Jim, maybe someone from my team should talk to you about what you have, and we can work together. I adored Cecelia, and I want an answer."

"I would be eternally grateful if you got involved," Nate says.

Drinks are passed, and as we prepare for dinner, musicians and dancers appear and perform dances from various Hawaiian and Polynesian islands. One of the male entertainers climbs a coconut tree and showers us with flower petals, blowing a conch shell to announce our luau dinner.

As we take our seats at long rows of picnic tables, the estate staff and their families join us. We're treated to a fantastic opening where Leilani works with the entertainers to show off her kalua pork cooking in the underground oven. Everyone is stunned to see how she does this the traditional way.

"I was hoping she made it in a crockpot," I lament, and everyone laughs.

Our emcee for the night leads us through a traditional Hawaiian prayer, followed by a full luau meal of kalua pork, lomi salmon, and various other dishes. When they place the poi on the table, Leilani says, "This is first-rate paste, Mr. Graham. Try it; you'll like it."

The table laughs.

After dinner, there is a traditional Hawaiian revue. I lean back in Jackson's arms, and he holds me tight. He kisses the side of my head and whispers, "I love you."

Everyone eventually dances, and it's after midnight when the party finally breaks up. Everyone agrees that the poker games will start on the lanai at one o'clock tomorrow afternoon.

Housekeepers will spend the remainder of the night cleaning, and tomorrow morning Leilani tells us there will be a breakfast buffet beginning at seven.

The next afternoon, the poker games have been set up on the lanai, overlooking the pool deck and the ocean. They'll start with two tables of six players.

Gillian announces the rules. "Ladies and gentlemen, it's great to see you all again. We're playing Texas Hold'em. The buy-in is five million, and all bids start at fifty grand. As a reminder, day one allows only poker chip bets. We have two tables today and will go until we have six players left for a game tomorrow. We have cocktail servers here to fetch you drinks and snacks. Dinner break is at seven. We'll agree to bio breaks every hour for ten minutes. No smoking at the table. Any questions?"

"Yes, this question is for Jackson. When are you putting the Halona Moana Estate up for bid?" Landon asks.

"I can't bet what's not mine. I sold it to Corrine Woods, and last I checked, she's not playing."

I stop and stare at Jackson. He did what? I know he must be joking because there's no way he "sold" me a twenty-five-million-dollar estate.

Jackson looks at me with a crooked smile and shrugs.

He must be kidding, right? I decide to let it go for now.

I can't watch him play. I know it's his money, but it makes me nervous watching him throw around millions of dollars, even though he almost always wins.

So instead I wander around, talking to the other wives and girlfriends, and eventually we all find a shaded spot by the pool and relax.

During a bio break, Jackson comes over. "You should

wander around in a bikini this evening. It'll drive Landon crazy." Jackson grins like he's the king of the world, and to many—and my heart—he is.

"No way. That would be embarrassing," I murmur. "And what is this about me owning the estate? You didn't sell it to me."

He shrugs. "What's mine is yours. Plus, if you decide you can't live with me any longer, you'll always have a place to go. I want you to understand that I mean that. You always have options. Wish me luck." He stands and shoves the last bite of pizza in his mouth.

I'm stunned by his statement. Every time I think he isn't listening, he's not only heard me, but he's found a way to address my concern. I look at him with a stupid grin.

"I can't wait to get you alone tonight," he whispers.

"Don't lose on my account. Take Landon for all he has." I wink at him, and he grins.

"I'll do anything you ask."

By the end of the night, Jackson, Mia Couture, and Landon Walsh are the last three standing at their table. And Walker Clifton, Mason Sullivan, and Nate Lancaster are the final three at the other one.

Gillian stands. "Well, it looks like we're done for the night, and it's still early."

I look at my watch, and it's just after eleven.

"I'm going to bed," Jackson announces, and he reaches for my hand.

"Tomorrow morning, breakfast will be out by nine," I tell everyone. "Some of you have signed up for helicopter tours of the island. For those of you not playing in the afternoon, there's a plane heading over to the Big Island to explore Kilauea. There are options for whale watching and fishing if you're not interested in shopping in town, or you can just hang out by the pool. Lots of activities."

People nod and head off to different parts of the estate.

When Jackson and I finally retire for the night, we're both

exhausted. We walk quietly to the room. I've been rehearsing what I want to say to him, and that must show on my face.

"What's wrong?" Jackson asks once the door is closed behind us.

I smile at him and sit on the bed. "I've been wanting to tell you—my mother came to me while I was kidnapped."

He looks at me, puzzled since he knows my mother has passed.

"I know it sounds crazy, but she talked to me. She reminded me how great you are. Thank you."

Jackson hasn't touched me since the incident, and I'm still a bit bruised, but in this moment, I need him.

"She came to me in a vision," I continue. "She wanted to be sure I didn't fall asleep, and she assured me you were looking for me."

"I was frantic looking for you," Jackson says.

I stand on my tiptoes and kiss him softly. "I've been needlessly worrying that you'd see my flaws and would look for someone else. I thought you'd be like my dad and leave me, like he did my mother. I was missing all the signals you were giving to show me that you were listening. You gave me your stock options, a raise, and you've told everyone this is my house."

"I know I'm stubborn, but I have been listening." Jackson tucks a wayward wisp of hair behind my ear. "No one will ever compare to you. They never have and never will. You're smart, hysterically funny, perfect in every way," Jackson reaches for my hand. "And you're positively beautiful."

While the game continued after dinner, I came back to our room and dressed for Jackson—not for anyone else. I know he'd wanted me to wear something to distract Landon, but I wanted to dress for him. I put my hair in an updo to show off my neck, I applied makeup to highlight my big eyes and full lips, and I added a silver choker, diamond bracelet, and a few sparkly clips in my hair. I felt like a princess.

Standing before Jackson, I slip out of my dress, vulnerable

in just a lacy thong.

His eyes become hooded as he watches me.

"I want you to know that I love you. I've loved you since the day I interviewed with you. I can't imagine my life without you."

Jackson steps forward and kisses me softly. "You've made me so happy." His hands reach for my breast, and he suckles the nipple. "Can I make love to you?"

I nod. "Please."

Reaching for my hand, he leads me to the bed and sits on the edge. "You've made me the happiest man on Earth."

He kisses my stomach, hooks his thumbs into my thong, and pushes it down. "You're the most beautiful woman in the world."

One second he's staring at me with those intense blue eyes, and the next he's pulling my body against his. His hands slide down to my ass, squeezing and pulling as his mouth descends onto mine.

I can't get enough of his mouth. It is intoxicating. The way his tongue pushes in and owns me just makes me stupid and lights something on fire deep within me.

I can't control the sounds coming out of me.

With his hands on my ass, Jackson lifts me off the ground. I wrap my legs around his waist and feel his hardness pressing against me. He kisses with abandon, as if we've never kissed before. It makes my toes curl and my pussy clench.

"God, woman. What you do to me," he mutters. He lowers me to the bed, sliding his hands off my ass. They roam all over my legs, which are still locked around his waist. I'm fucking his mouth, kissing his neck, sucking and biting at him between little panting moans.

He lays me back, and the sensation of his mouth on my body is electric. I squirm and moan, my hands grasping at the sheets, desperate for something to hold on to as shocks of sensation flow through me.

It feels so fucking good the way he sucks as much of my breast into his mouth as he possibly can. I gasp as he pulls his mouth off of my nipple, sucking so hard that his lips leave my flesh with a little pop. I look down to meet his gaze, and the devious smirk on his lips steals my breath and makes it hard to think.

"Mmmm, fuck, my love," Jackson says, his voice low and husky. "You've made me so happy."

I sigh and close my eyes, enjoying the sensation of Jackson sucking and kissing his way down the inside of my leg, his tongue dipping and sliding across that sensitive, ticklish spot just behind my knee. He slides a wet trail up the inside of my thigh, stopping to suck and bite and taste all that smooth skin.

Jackson seals his mouth over my pussy, his tongue lapping at the slick juices that drip from me.

"Right there," I gasp. "Don't stop."

A growl reverberates against my skin as my bliss overtakes me. "You're so fucking sweet."

I'm reduced to nothing but a writhing, squirming, moaning puddle of need.

When my vision returns, Jackson's as hard as a lead pipe. One look at that big cock, hard and seeping, and I want it. Every damn inch of it. I need it buried deep and forcing me open.

He strokes himself a little before lifting his cock up and pushing his hips forward, sliding down to my entrance, nudging the fat head of his dick into my slick channel.

As my walls stretch around the sheer girth of Jackson's cock, I moan my pleasure. He pushes in and out, slowly and deliberately. "I want to do this with you for the rest of my life," he grunts.

I can feel my climax climbing again, and together we reach our pinnacle. Afterward, as we try to catch our breath, we lie next to each other.

"I'm serious," he says. "I'm not perfect, and I will absolutely get things wrong. But I love you. We can go with whatever pace you need—keep Gabby's apartment, or work somewhere else, just promise me you'll be with me."

I roll over and hold him tight. "I will be with you forever."

His kiss is soft and luscious. I can already feel his hardness returning.

He rolls over and picks up his pants off the floor. He goes rummaging in the pocket and pulls out a stunning, emerald-cut diamond ring.

Getting down on one knee, he asks, "Corrine, will you marry me?"

The answer seems obvious. I nod. "Yes."

Kissing me deeply, he rolls me onto my back. "You've made me so happy. Can we do it tomorrow?"

"No!" I giggle. "I want Gabby and your mom there."

"I just want to lock it down before you change your mind."

I stroke him. "Trust me, I'm locked."

"Should we call your dad and tell him?"

"Maybe after we're married. I don't want him to spoil our day."

We enjoy each other throughout the night, even though I should be sleeping, and I'm exhausted and spent by the time I get any rest.

In the morning, we're late for breakfast, but it seems so is everyone else.

Most of the guests are relaxing and sitting around the pool, enjoying the morning. There are six players left for the big day, and it's usually a long session. Those that aren't playing have excursions around Maui, quick trips over to see the volcano on the Big Island, or downtime by the pool.

Gradually everyone finishes breakfast and disperses for the day, but I'm sticking close to help, if needed.

When four o'clock comes around, the game begins again. I

stand next to Caroline as we watch our men battle.

"I told Mason he couldn't bet any property," she says.

"I can't believe Jackson won this place. I would be devastated if he lost it."

"He won't." Caroline turns to me with a big smile. "I couldn't help but notice your left hand is a little heavier than it was yesterday."

My stomach churns with excitement. "Yes, Jackson asked me last night. I'm overwhelmed and excited."

"Trust me, you're perfect for him."

Nate is the next to lose, and he comes over and sits with me to watch. "You really did a fantastic job this weekend."

"Thank you. I had fun. I hope everyone else did too."

"I understand you're not interested in working for Jackson any longer," he says after a moment.

"I figured since we're getting married, I should find something else."

"Congratulations." Nate smiles, and I know he means it. "I have a proposal for you. I know you're familiar with the Lancaster Foundation, and I really want that work to continue. I've been looking for an executive director. Would you be interested?"

I'm sure my mouth drops open in shock. "I…I think I would love to do that. I suppose I should talk to Jackson about it."

"I understand. Cecelia traveled with me and managed it fine from the road, so I think you could live anywhere. You've met most of our contributors, and I'd be looking for more contributions and ways to spend them. Let me know, and we can talk about it when you return to San Francisco."

I nod. "Absolutely." Suddenly, what has seemed impossible to manage for so long is all falling into place. A sense of peace washes over me, and I'm so grateful for everything I have.

As the sun sets, people come and go, watching the game. After over five hours of play, there are still four players.

Landon is high in the chip count and goes all-in. Mason debates. He keeps looking at Landon and trying to figure out if he has something good or is bluffing. Finally, he pushes his chips in. Mia doesn't hesitate and puts the ranch in Montana in the pot, along with her remaining chips: all-in. Jackson looks at me and smiles as he pushes all of his chips into the middle. I know he has a good hand.

The last card turns. Mason has nothing. Mia has three aces. Jackson has a royal flush, minus the ace from Mia's hand, so he's out, and Landon has three kings and two eights. A full house takes the pot. The crowd erupts.

Landon just took Mia's ranch and won the game. Nate and Jackson high five, and he shoots me a dazzling smile.

"Next time, Landon Walsh, the game is at the ranch in Montana," Nate says.

Sleight of Hand

Tech Billionaires book 3

A Preview

by:
Ainsley St Claire

Chapter 1

"Look at that man who just walked in the door, Tinsley. Holy guacamole, he's sex on a stick and hot, hot, hot."

I turn to look at my best friend, Chrissy Matthews, and follow her line of sight. The man she's looking at *is* a sight to behold: dark, messy hair with dark, brooding eyes, and his body... I fan myself. His T-shirt is stretched over his arms and chest and his jeans are showing off…well, his massive package.

I lean over to Chrissy. "How much you want to bet he stuffed a sock in his pants?"

She looks him over. "No way is he that big."

He looks over at us and smiles. When he makes eye contact with me, I smile back.

It seems to encourage him, and he makes his way over to us. "Hello, ladies."

"Hi," Chrissy offers.

"What are we celebrating?"

I look over at Chrissy and give her a careful shake so hopefully, she understands to not go there.

"We're celebrating a Tuesday night," she says.

"I like that. May I celebrate with you?"

He looks at me, and how can I refuse?

I have to say, Chrissy and I look fantastic tonight. Not club-ready, but I have on a dark blue strapless sundress that is fitted in the bodice, and a pair of peep-toe stilettos. Chrissy is in a pair of jeans and a wrap sweater that shows a tremendous amount of cleavage.

He pulls up a stool between the two of us.

Chrissy picks up her almost-empty glass of wine and takes a big swig. "My name is Madeline, and this is Amanda."

I chuckle that she uses our fake bar names. She's out to tease this poor guy. I almost feel sorry for him. Maybe.

"Nice to meet you both. My name is Peter Landon." He leans toward my ear and whispers, "It's not a sock. Care to feel for yourself?"

I'm shocked that he heard me in a crowded bar on a busy weeknight. "Thanks," I manage. "But I don't typically feel men up until I've had at least a few drinks."

I'm out with my best friend, celebrating the sale of the company I started to a larger startup, which officially happens tomorrow morning. I sold to Disruptive Technologies in the hopes that together we can do something truly amazing.

He motions to the bartender. "Can we get a sloe comfortable screw, a sex on the beach, and a blowjob, please?"

Chrissy and I exchange looks. We may have met our match.

He takes out a black American Express card and hands it to the bartender. "Please open a tab for these beautiful women."

I roll my eyes. "Laying it on a little thick, don't you think?"

"Trust me, nothing is little, and you did say it would take a few drinks for you to verify that I don't stuff my pants with socks."

I shake my head and smile. My panties have officially melted. He puts his arm around me, and his hand rests on my back. I feel the electric charge shoot right down to my core. The only thing that's been keeping me company lately is Bob—my battery-operated boyfriend, and while Peter's forwardness should have me throwing what's left of my drink in his face, instead it has me turned on.

"So what do you both do for work?" he asks.

This is where Chrissy shines. Watching her spin a web of deceit is really quite fun. "I teach fourth grade at St. Anthony Catholic School, and Amanda is a nurse."

"So, it's either hot for teacher or naughty nurse?"

Damn, he's good. That's our joke. I might actually like this guy.

Chrissy swears that men don't like smart women, so we downplay our smarts. She has an MBA from Harvard and runs marketing for a major bank, and I went to Stanford and have a degree in electrical engineering and software development.

"Which is your preference?" I ask.

He gives me a salacious grin. "They all sound good to me."

The bartender places our drinks in front of us. Chrissy reaches for the shot glass and puts it down on the bar in front of her. Peter and I watch as she leans over and picks up the glass with her mouth, downing the shot in one gulp. When she puts the glass back on the bar, she wets her lips and makes a moaning noise as she licks the whipped cream away. Her little act has caught the attention of several here in the bar.

"Thanks for the drink," she says.

"I'm happy to order you another round." He smiles at her while his arm remains wrapped around me.

She shakes her head.

Peter turns to me. "Which do you prefer? Sex on the beach or a sloe comfortable screw?"

I reach for the sloe comfortable screw and raise the glass to him. "To an evening of fun."

His eyes lock with mine. "I'll drink to that."

"Well, I need to go. I have a date with a beautiful blond pussy with an amazing tongue." Chrissy picks up her bag and winks at Peter. She's talking about her cat, but he doesn't need to know that. "Thanks for the blowjob."

"Any time, Maddy." He reaches for her hand and kisses her knuckles.

Chrissy turns and gives me a quick hug. "I want a text later tonight to verify if it's one sock or two." She steps back and stares at his package. "I'm guessing two."

I pick up the sloe comfortable screw and take a deep pull. I need to cool off.

"So, tell me more about you." Peter's whisper in my ear makes my nipples pebble.

Damn, this man is becoming my kryptonite.

I shrug. "There's not much to tell. I work at the hospital as a surgical nurse. What about you? What gets a man a black American Express card?"

He signals the bartender and points to our drinks, asking for a second round. "I suppose…" He doesn't look at me. "…a solid idea that someone is foolish enough to buy."

I'm not interested in his money, so I won't push. I can relate, given that my partially formed idea will be bought tomorrow for ten million dollars. But I'm not telling him that. He thinks I'm a naughty nurse.

"You must be very thirsty to be ordering another round so quickly."

He leans in, and I can smell his pine scent. I like it. "I'm ready to show you that I don't stuff my pants with socks, and I, too, have a wicked tongue."

With over a million people living in less than seven square miles, I have two choices: I can go home to Bob—again, or I can take this fine specimen of a man up on his offer. If he doesn't have a sock in his pants, he may be more than I can take.

"Then what are we waiting for?" I ask.

"There's a hotel just across the street."

"I was thinking the coatroom," I suggest. I don't want to spend the night with him. I just want a quick and thorough fuck.

He nuzzles my neck. "I like the way you're thinking."

The bar has a coatroom that's heavily used during colder seasons, but given that the May weather is perfect tonight, there's nothing going on. It's a large closet, with a bench and a mirror. It might be fun, and a bit adventurous.

I grab Peter by the hand and lead him to the closet, and the door isn't shut behind me before his lips are on mine. His tongue is aggressive as it probes my mouth.

I'm dizzy with desire. I can't be sure, but I think this man just kissed my lips off.

I step back and try to regain some composure. "I want to see your cock."

"I promise you will, but first, it's all about you." Turning me around to face the mirror and bending me over the bench, he pushes my skirt up and looks at me as he caresses my ass. Then he bends down and licks the insides of my thighs, which are glistening wet already.

Yanking my panties down, he spreads my legs apart. I can see him behind me in the mirror. He's watching me, too, as he puts his fingers deep into my pussy, sliding them in, nice and easy. It feels good. I begin to breathe heavy, small moans escaping my mouth.

"You're so tight. Do you like that?"

I nod, enjoying his thumb strumming my clit while his fingers rub my g-spot.

He smacks my right ass cheek, and it stings. He's made me want this, and I'm powerless to stop my body from responding.

He's fucking me with his hands, and he pushes my hair off my neck, caressing the hollow of my throat with one thumb as he bangs me from behind. I press myself into his hand, my legs open, and my hands holding the bench and wall to keep me steady.

His tongue is everywhere, inside me, on my clit, licking my thighs. He winds his hand around in my hair and pulls. He arches my back deeply and then puts his fingers inside me again, not just banging, but more like he's feeling me from the inside. My orgasm hits quickly, and my legs quiver.

"That's it, sweetheart."

He licks up my cum as it leaks down my legs. "It's sweet nectar." He holds my head in one hand and puts the fingers of his other hand into my mouth so I can taste myself.

I comply and suck his fingers.

"You're so sexy," he rasps.

I want to see if he's genuinely as big as I think he is. I get down in front of him on my knees. I reach up and unbutton his jeans, looking at him the whole time.

There's no sock; he's just big. I free the hard rod from his pants—the purple head glistening with pre-cum and the veins bulging. I've only seen cocks this big in adult toy stores. I didn't think they came like this in real life.

"Now that you know I don't stuff my pants with socks, what are you going to do with me?" he asks.

As he threads his fingers in my hair, I lick the tip, and I hear his sharp intake of air. I'm not sure how much of this I'll be able to swallow, but I really want to find out. I wrap one hand around the base of his cock and guide him in. He walks toward me, filling my mouth, and I slide back to keep from gagging, until he has me shoved up against the wall.

He pulls out and yanks me back to my feet. He spins me around and throws me back over the bench again, bent forward at a ninety-degree angle with my legs apart.

He pulls out his wallet, and I watch as he sheaths his cock.

I shiver with excitement.

He rubs the shaft through my slit and pushes inside. Little explosions happen across my vision as I reach another climax.

The feeling, oh God, it's more orgasmic than I've ever felt before.

Forget Bob. This is what a real orgasm feels like.

I see stars, and I'm squirting, coming. He's pounding me, and it's all happening at once. I've never been so overwhelmed with pleasure. It feels like honey dripping down my thighs. I can't stop myself, and I let out a long, screaming groan, my eyes squeezing shut as fireworks explode.

An hour later, I stumble out of the coatroom on a multi-orgasmic high. We didn't exchange numbers or anything. It was just hot sex. Damn, that man was amazing. This is going to be a good week. Tomorrow I get a big fat check and a bunch of stock options. Life is perfect.

I text Chrissy.

Me: No sock. I may have to replace Bob, though.

Chrissy: Did you exchange contact info?

Me: Nope. If it's meant to be, I'll see him again. But I'm not counting on it.

"Welcome, Ms. Prat." The receptionist greets me as I walk in. "Would you like a cup of tea this morning?"

It's pretty bad when the receptionist knows my name *and* my drink order. "That would be wonderful. Thank you."

"Mr. Arnold will meet you in the large conference room shortly." She opens her arm to the all-glass room beyond reception with a stunning view of the bay and Berkeley on the other side.

I can't sit down. I'm both nervous and excited. I've met with Claire Walsh several times, and we've hashed out our deal. I wish I could take the obscene amount of money they're paying me and go sit on a beach for a few months and decompress, but unfortunately, part of the contract requires that I remain with the company for the next five years for the first ten percent of the shares, and another five years for the next ten percent.

My phone rings, and it's my mother. "Hi, Mom."

"I just wanted to wish you luck today. Are you nervous?"

My mom is a high-powered attorney and partner in her law firm in Denver. I owe her everything. My dad left us when I was a baby, and it was always just the two of us. She's the reason I've worked so hard to do so well.

"A little nervous, but I now have a regular paycheck, and you can finally drop me from your health insurance."

She chortles, and I know she's smiling. I was coming off of her insurance in a few months on my twenty-sixth birthday anyway. "We'll have to find some warm sand to celebrate on."

"Sounds good to me."

"Sweetheart, congratulations on a tremendous accomplishment. I'm very proud of you."

My mom has never been one to shower me with compliments, so I'm more than thrilled that she called. "I'll talk to you later tonight."

I walk over to stand at the windows. I'm watching the barges make their way behind Treasure Island and underneath the Bay Bridge, headed for port, when I hear my lawyer enter the conference room behind me.

"Good morning, Tinsley. How are you today? Did you go out and celebrate last night?"

He has no idea. "I did. Thank you. I still can't believe the deal we got."

He nods. "Don't be fooled. *They're* getting a deal with your idea. Today you'll sign off on all the contracts and get a nice check."

I nod. I take a big breath of air as I watch Claire arrive with her lawyers.

Two more men fall in behind them, and as we make our way through the introductions, I freeze.

"Tinsley, this is my brother, Landon, head of development, and our chief investor, Mason Sullivan, with SHN."

He recognizes me at the same moment I realize it's Peter from last night.

Holy fucking shit.

"So nice to meet you, *Tinsley.* Claire has told me so much about you." He smiles, and my knees almost buckle.

I've committed the next ten years to working for the one man I never thought I'd see again.

Also by Ainsley St Claire

The Venture Capitalist Series

Forbidden Love (Venture Capitalist Book 1) **Available on Amazon**
(Emerson and Dillon's story) He's an eligible billionaire. She's off limits. Is a relationship worth the risk?

Promise (Venture Capitalist Book 2) **Available on Amazon**
(Sara and Trey's story) She's reclaiming her past. He's a billionaire dodging the spotlight. Can a romance of high achievers succeed in a world hungry for scandal?

Desire (Venture Capitalist Book 3) **Available on Amazon**
(Cameron and Hadlee's story) She used to be in the 1%. He's a self-made billionaire. Will one hot night fuel love's startup?

Temptation (Venture Capitalist Book 4) **Available on Amazon**
(Greer and Andy's story) She helps her clients become millionaires and billionaires. He transforms grapes into wine. Can they find more than love at the bottom of a glass?

Obsession (Venture Capitalist Book 5) **Available on Amazon**
(Cynthia and Todd's story) With hitmen hot on their heels, can Cynthia and Todd keep their love alive before the mob bankrupts their future?

Flawless (Venture Capitalist Book 6) **Available on Amazon**
(Constance and Parker's story) A woman with a secret. A tech wizard on the trail of hackers. A tycoon's dying revelation threatens everything.

Longing (Venture Capitalist Book 7) **Available on Amazon**

(Bella and Christopher's story) She's a biotech researcher in race with time for a cure. If she pauses to have a life, will she lose the race? He needs a deal to keep his job. Can they find a path to love?

Enchanted (Venture Capitalist Book 8) **Available on Amazon**
(Quinn and William's story) Women don't hold his interest past a week, until she accidentally leaves me a voice mail so hot it melts his phone. I need a fake fiancée for one week. What can a week hurt?

Fascination (Venture Capitalist Book 9) **Available on Amazon**
(CeCe and Mason's story) It started when my boyfriend was caught in public with a girls lips on his you know what. People think my life is easy - they couldn't be more wrong. As my life falls apart, can we make the transition from friends to more?

Clear Security Holiday Heartbreakers

Gifted **Available on Amazon**
(Kate and Jim's story) Forty kids are not going have a Christmas and I don't know how to fix it. I send out a call for help and my prince appears and that's when the wheels really fall off this wagon. Can he help me or am I doomed to fail all these deserving kids?

Tech Billionaires

House of Cards (Tech Billionaires Book 1) **Available on Amazon**
(Maggie & Jonnie) Would you agree to a marriage to avoid going to jail? Maggie is the heiress to the Reinhardt Department Store fortune. Her father died and the board of the company expect Alex to run the company but they've never had a nonfamily member run the company. The board

has a simple solution—she needs to put the family first and marry Alex. Forget the fact that she isn't his type and she loves someone else.

Royally Flushed (Tech Billionaires Book 2) **Available on Amazon**
(Corrine & Jackson) Staying with him will be dangerous…They call him Billionaire, Environmentalist, and Playboy. I call him Boss. I try to keep it professional, I want to resist him, but the pull is too strong. A bomb threat, a ransacked apartment, mysterious warnings, all telling me to leave him alone. Yes, staying will be dangerous, but leaving him will destroy me.

Sleight of Hand (Tech Billionaires Book 3) **Available on Amazon**
The night was magical, the morning after wasn't. I was celebrating selling my company when I noticed him enter the bar. Landon knew just what to say and one thing led to another. It was supposed to be a onetime thing, but reality slapped me in the face the next morning. He arrived to sign the purchase papers, and now I was committed to work for him for an entire decade. When I can't make my code work, his patience runs thin. Someone is sabotaging us, and if we can't figure it out, I'll have no company, no money, and no future.

Coming Soon

Running Hot (Tech Billionaires Book 4) **Available for Preorder On Amazon**
He must marry. She's the only one he wants he can't have. Can he convince her in time? Becoming Governor is the next step toward my destiny. But, my history will be a problem. The voters always favor a family man. I've done Marcella favors for years and now it's time to collect. She'll make the perfect Governor's wife. It's all for show, and she knows that. With this union, she'll be able to write her own ticket. Danger lurks around every corner, and I may be the only one who can protect her.

All In Tech (Billionaires Book 5)
February 2021

Follow Ainsley

Don't miss out on New Releases, Exclusive Giveaways and much more!

www.ainsleystclaire.com

Join Ainsley's **newsletter**
And get a FREE copy of GIFTED!
https://dl.bookfunnel.com/zi378x4ybx

Follow me on **Bookbub**
https://www.bookbub.com/profile/ainsley-st-claire

Like Ainsley St Claire on **Facebook**
https://www.facebook.com/ainsleystclaire/

Follow me on **Instagram**
https://www.instagram.com/authorhainsleystclaire/

Follow Ainsley St Claire on **Twitter**
@AinsleyStClaire

Follow Ainsley St Claire on **Goodreads**
https://www.goodreads.com/author/show/16752271.Ainsley_St_Claire

Visit Ainsley's website for her current booklist

I love to hear from you directly, too. Please feel free to email me at **ainsley@ainsleystclaire.com** or check out my website **www.ainsleystclaire.com** for updates.

Made in the USA
Columbia, SC
30 January 2021

32051766R00211